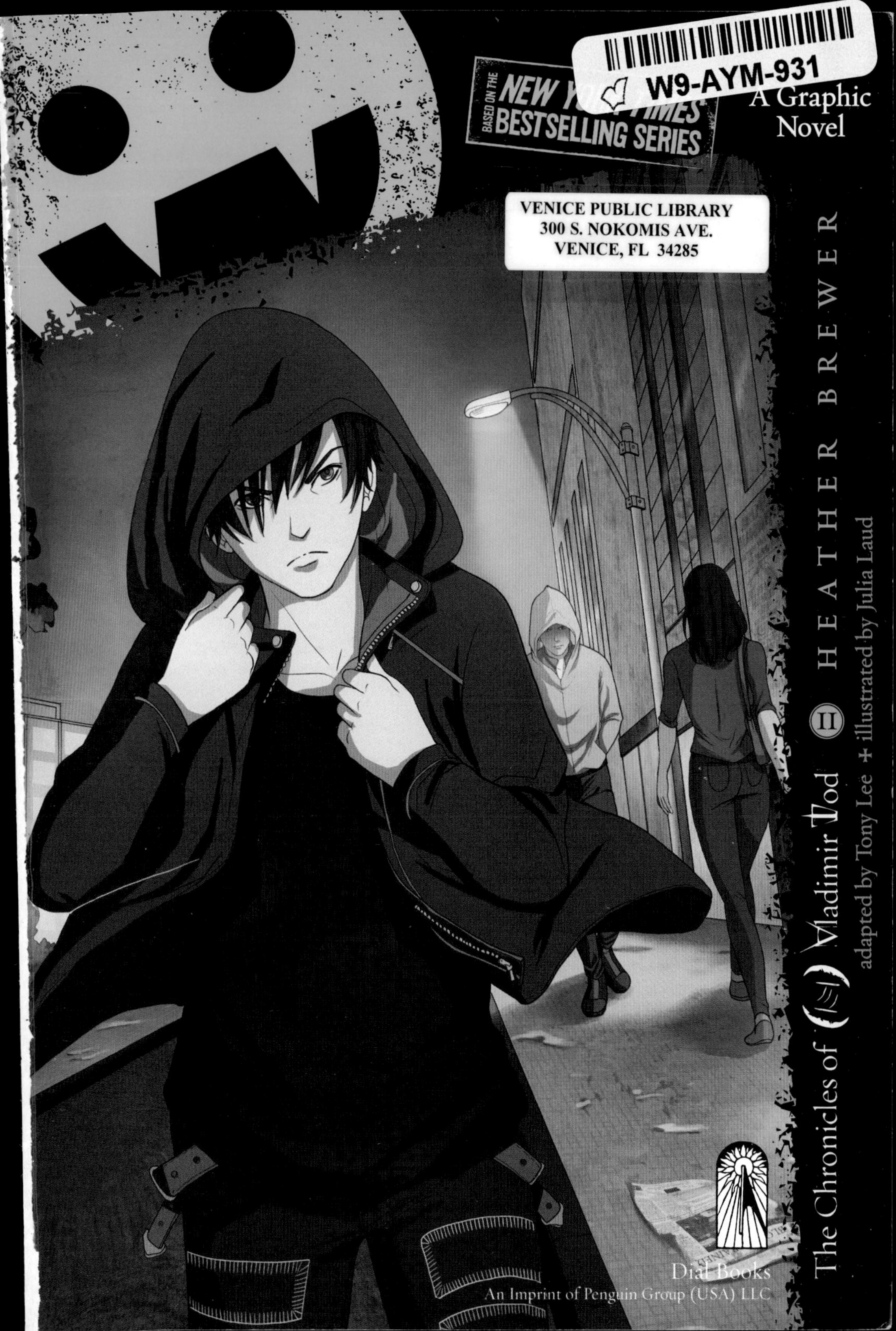
BASED ON THE NEW YORK TIMES BESTSELLING SERIES
A Graphic Novel
The Chronicles of Vladimir Tod II
HEATHER BREWER
adapted by Tony Lee + illustrated by Julia Laud
Dial Books
An Imprint of Penguin Group (USA) LLC

DIAL BOOKS
An imprint of Penguin Group (USA) LLC

PUBLISHED BY THE PENGUIN GROUP
Penguin Group (USA) LLC, 375 Hudson Street, New York, New York 10014, USA

USA | Canada | UK | Ireland | Australia | New Zealand | India | South Africa | China

penguin.com
A Penguin Random House Company

Text copyright © 2014 by Heather Brewer. Illustrations copyright © 2014 by Penguin Group (USA) LLC.

Library of Congress Cataloging-in-Publication Data is available.

Penciled by Julia Laud
Inked by Julia Laud & Angie Nathalia
Colored by Caravan Studio
Cover design by Ching N. Chan and lettering by Ching N. Chan and Natasha Sanders

Printed in the USA

ISBN 978-0-8037-3812-6

1 3 5 7 9 10 8 6 4 2

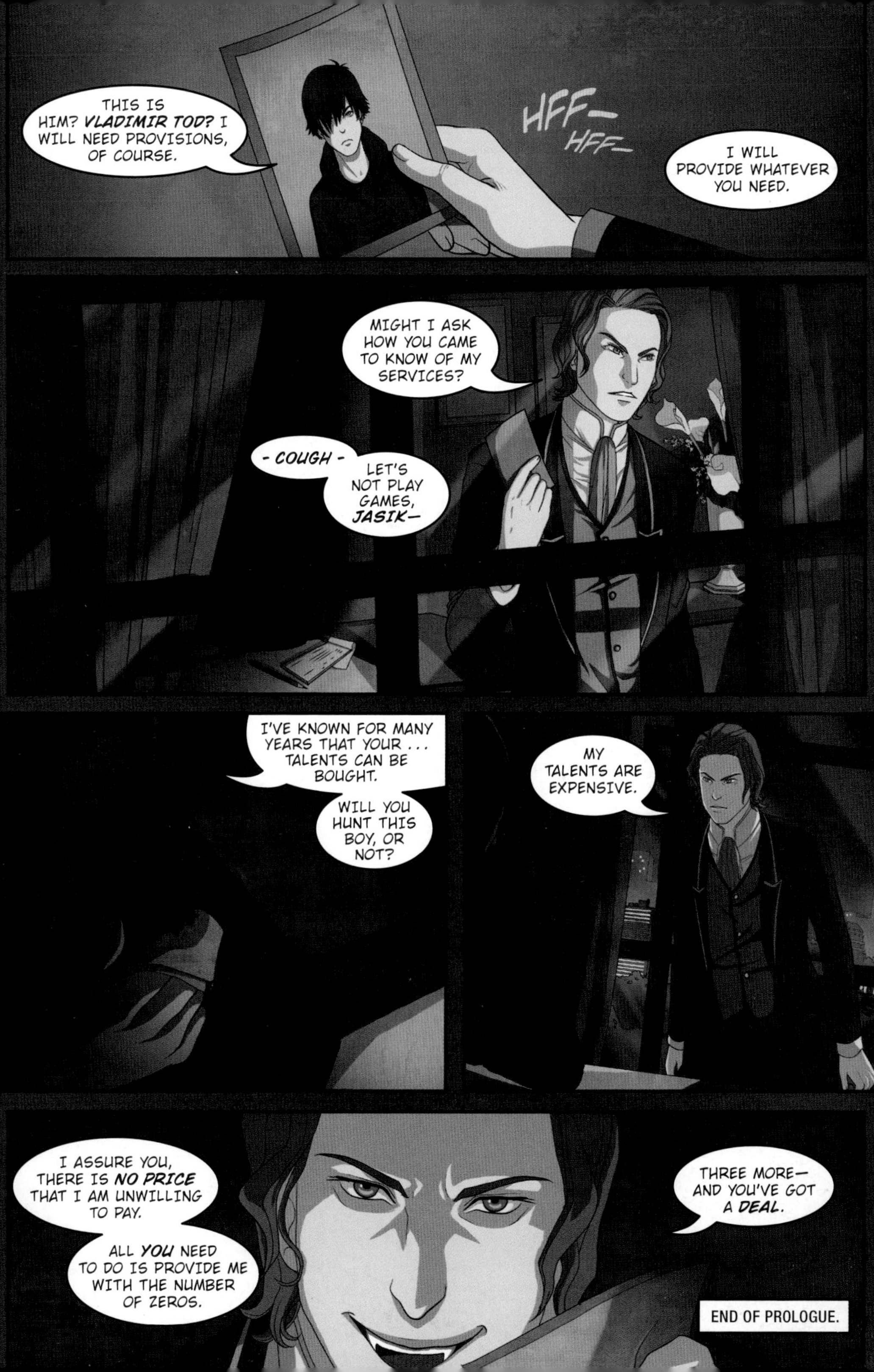
THIS IS HIM? VLADIMIR TOD? I WILL NEED PROVISIONS, OF COURSE.
HFF— HFF—
I WILL PROVIDE WHATEVER YOU NEED.
MIGHT I ASK HOW YOU CAME TO KNOW OF MY SERVICES?
- COUGH -
LET'S NOT PLAY GAMES, JASIK—
I'VE KNOWN FOR MANY YEARS THAT YOUR . . . TALENTS CAN BE BOUGHT.
WILL YOU HUNT THIS BOY, OR NOT?
MY TALENTS ARE EXPENSIVE.
I ASSURE YOU, THERE IS NO PRICE THAT I AM UNWILLING TO PAY.
ALL YOU NEED TO DO IS PROVIDE ME WITH THE NUMBER OF ZEROS.
THREE MORE— AND YOU'VE GOT A DEAL.
END OF PROLOGUE.

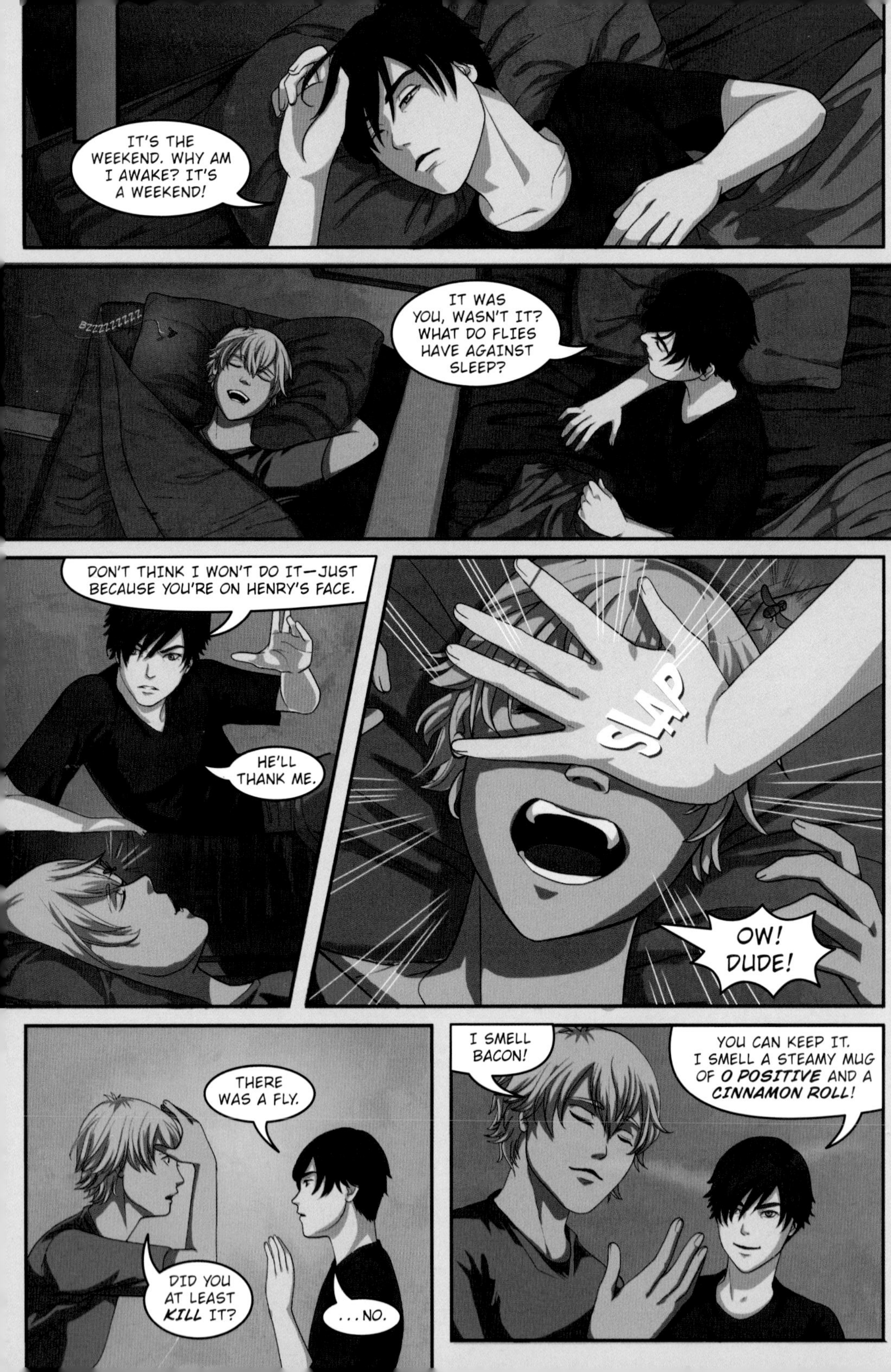
IT'S THE WEEKEND. WHY AM I AWAKE? IT'S A WEEKEND!
BZZZZZZZZZ
IT WAS YOU, WASN'T IT? WHAT DO FLIES HAVE AGAINST SLEEP?
DON'T THINK I WON'T DO IT—JUST BECAUSE YOU'RE ON HENRY'S FACE.
HE'LL THANK ME.
SLAP
OW! DUDE!
THERE WAS A FLY.
DID YOU AT LEAST *KILL* IT?
. . . NO.
I SMELL BACON!
YOU CAN KEEP IT. I SMELL A STEAMY MUG OF *O POSITIVE* AND A *CINNAMON ROLL*!

AH! FOOD!

AH! FOOD!

I TAKE IT THAT MEANS YOU BOYS ARE HUNGRY?

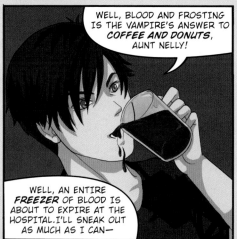

WELL, BLOOD AND FROSTING IS THE VAMPIRE'S ANSWER TO *COFFEE AND DONUTS*, AUNT NELLY!

WELL, AN ENTIRE *FREEZER* OF BLOOD IS ABOUT TO EXPIRE AT THE HOSPITAL. I'LL SNEAK OUT AS MUCH AS I CAN—

—*VLAD!* YOU'VE GOT BLOOD ALL OVER YOUR SHIRT!

CONTRARY TO POPULAR BELIEF, LAUNDRY *DOESN'T* TOP MY LIST OF FAVORITE THINGS TO DO!

SORRY—I WAS REALLY HUNGRY!

SO DID YOU GET YOUR *SCHEDULE* YET? I GOT MRS. BELL FOR ENGLISH, FIRST PERIOD.

LOOKS LIKE YOU'RE NOT ALONE. I'VE GOT HER, TOO.

AND FROM WHAT MY MOM SAID YESTERDAY, SO DOES JOSS.

WHEN'S YOUR COUSIN MOVING TO BATHORY?

SUNDAY. OH, AND JUST SO YOU KNOW, DON'T COUNT ON *SEEING* ME MUCH THAT DAY.

MY MOM'S ON SOME *FAMILY TOGETHERNESS* KICK.

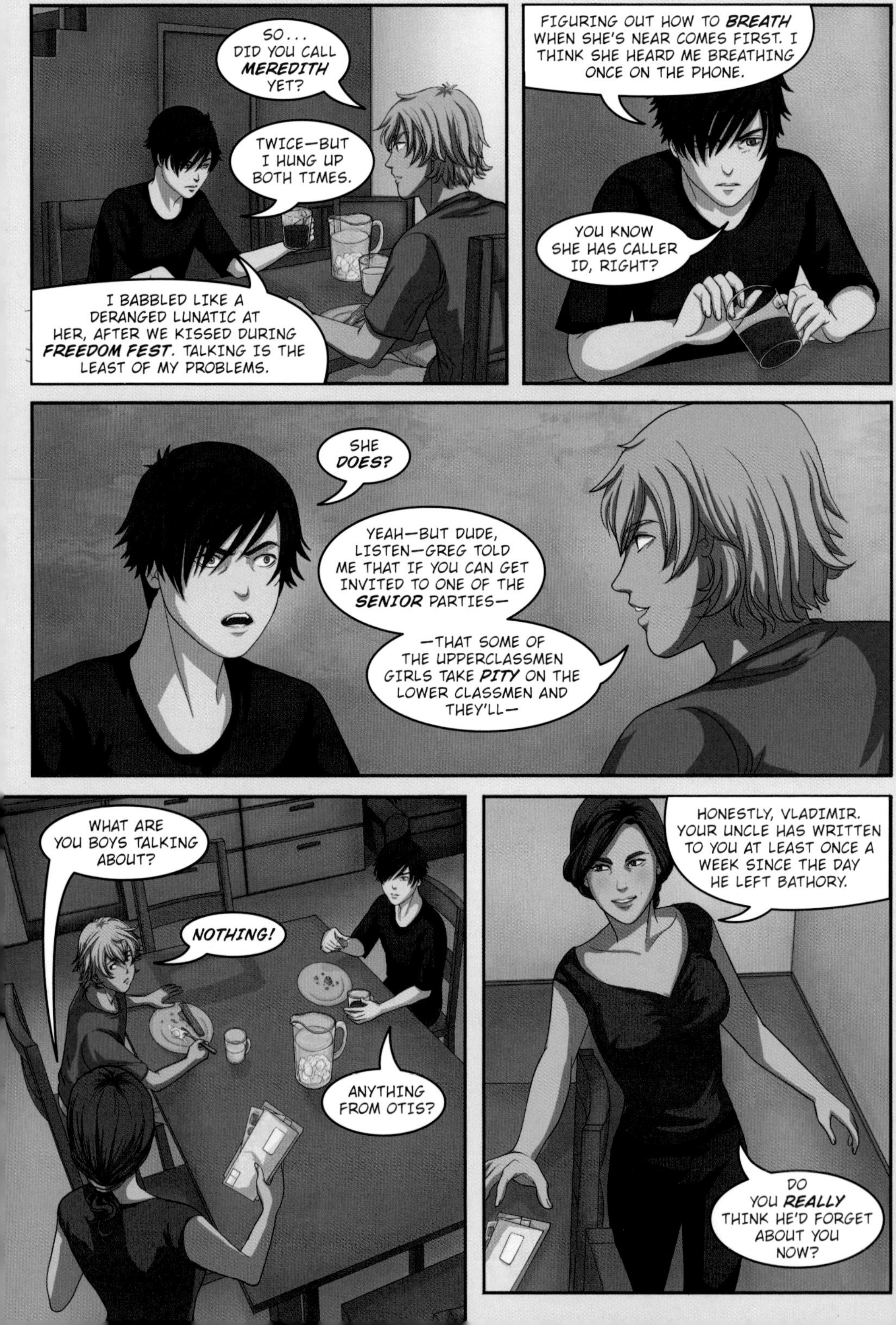
SO . . . DID YOU CALL **MEREDITH** YET?
TWICE—BUT I HUNG UP BOTH TIMES.
I BABBLED LIKE A DERANGED LUNATIC AT HER, AFTER WE KISSED DURING **FREEDOM FEST**. TALKING IS THE LEAST OF MY PROBLEMS.
FIGURING OUT HOW TO **BREATH** WHEN SHE'S NEAR COMES FIRST. I THINK SHE HEARD ME BREATHING ONCE ON THE PHONE.
YOU KNOW SHE HAS CALLER ID, RIGHT?
SHE **DOES?**
YEAH—BUT DUDE, LISTEN—GREG TOLD ME THAT IF YOU CAN GET INVITED TO ONE OF THE **SENIOR** PARTIES—
—THAT SOME OF THE UPPERCLASSMEN GIRLS TAKE **PITY** ON THE LOWER CLASSMEN AND THEY'LL—
WHAT ARE YOU BOYS TALKING ABOUT?
NOTHING!
ANYTHING FROM OTIS?
HONESTLY, VLADIMIR. YOUR UNCLE HAS WRITTEN TO YOU AT LEAST ONCE A WEEK SINCE THE DAY HE LEFT BATHORY.
DO YOU **REALLY** THINK HE'D FORGET ABOUT YOU NOW?

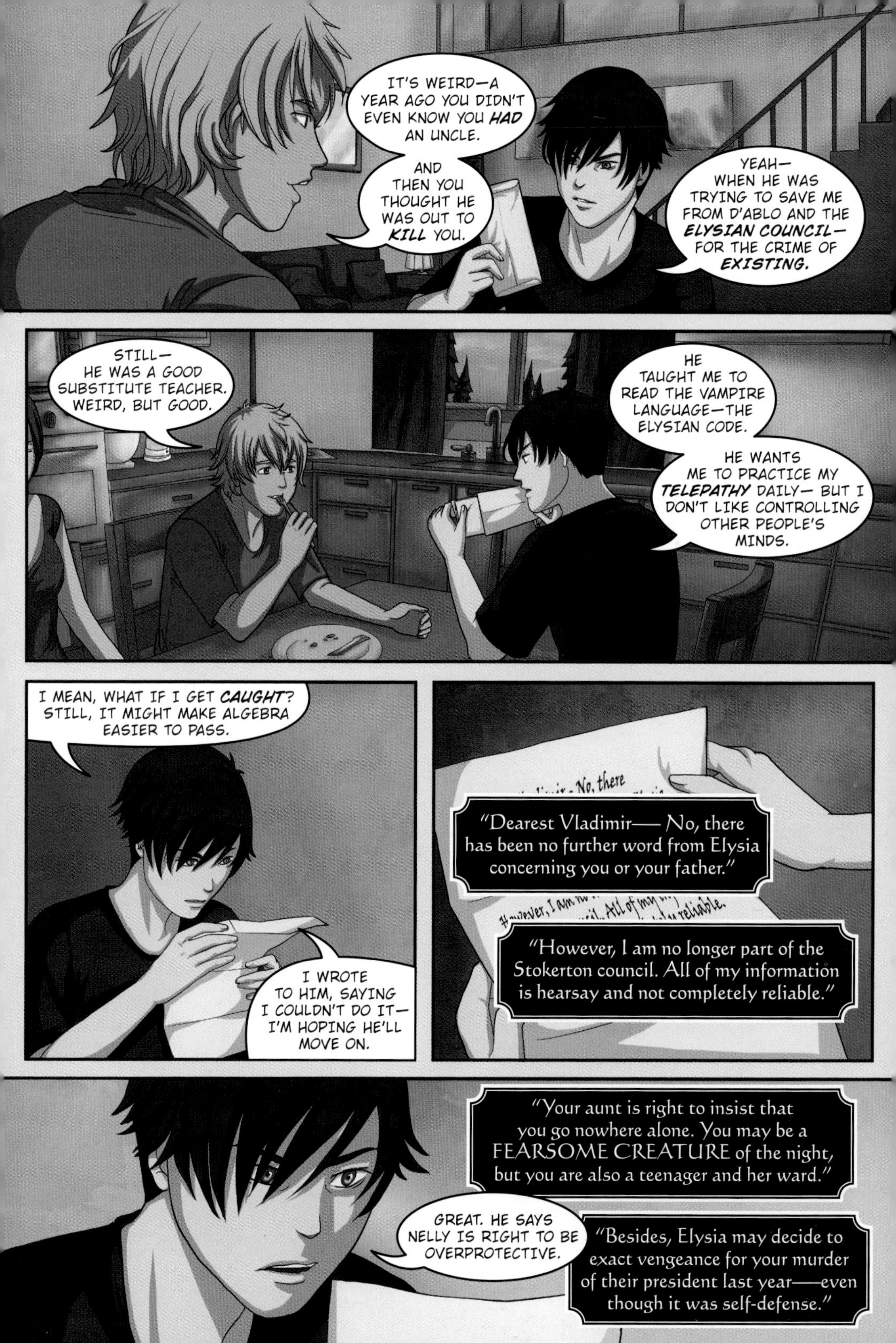
IT'S WEIRD—A YEAR AGO YOU DIDN'T EVEN KNOW YOU *HAD* AN UNCLE.
AND THEN YOU THOUGHT HE WAS OUT TO *KILL* YOU.
YEAH— WHEN HE WAS TRYING TO SAVE ME FROM D'ABLO AND THE *ELYSIAN COUNCIL*— FOR THE CRIME OF *EXISTING.*
STILL— HE WAS A GOOD SUBSTITUTE TEACHER. WEIRD, BUT GOOD.
HE TAUGHT ME TO READ THE VAMPIRE LANGUAGE—THE ELYSIAN CODE.
HE WANTS ME TO PRACTICE MY *TELEPATHY* DAILY— BUT I DON'T LIKE CONTROLLING OTHER PEOPLE'S MINDS.
I MEAN, WHAT IF I GET *CAUGHT*? STILL, IT MIGHT MAKE ALGEBRA EASIER TO PASS.
I WROTE TO HIM, SAYING I COULDN'T DO IT— I'M HOPING HE'LL MOVE ON.
"Dearest Vladimir—— No, there has been no further word from Elysia concerning you or your father."
"However, I am no longer part of the Stokerton council. All of my information is hearsay and not completely reliable."
"Your aunt is right to insist that you go nowhere alone. You may be a FEARSOME CREATURE of the night, but you are also a teenager and her ward."
GREAT. HE SAYS NELLY IS RIGHT TO BE OVERPROTECTIVE.
"Besides, Elysia may decide to exact vengeance for your murder of their president last year——even though it was self-defense."

WHAT ELSE?

WELL, A VAMPIRE'S ABILITY TO CHARM A WOMAN WITH A GAZE IS *RIDICULOUS*, APPARENTLY.

OTIS SUGGESTS I *ASK* MEREDITH IF SHE LIKES ME, RATHER THAN CONTINUE BREATHING INTO A PHONE.

HE SAYS THAT MY MOTHER'S HUMAN DNA MAKES IT DIFFICULT TO KNOW WHAT VAMPIRIC SKILLS I *HAVE*—SO I HAVE TO KEEP PRACTICING. I HAVE TO PRACTICE *MIND CONTROL* MORE—AND STOP USING TELEPATHY FOR BETTER GRADES.

HE WAS A TEACHER—THEY'RE *ALL* PSYCHIC. HE'LL KNOW IF YOU DO.

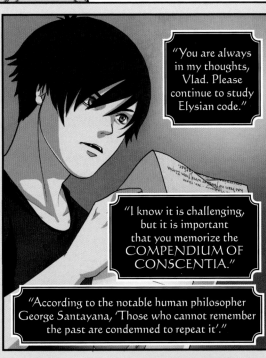

"You are always in my thoughts, Vlad. Please continue to study Elysian code."

"I know it is challenging, but it is important that you memorize the COMPENDIUM OF CONSCENTIA."

"According to the notable human philosopher George Santayana, 'Those who cannot remember the past are condemned to repeat it'."

Next week I will be in London – the address where I can be reached is enclosed. I will write as often as I am able to.

Please give my warm regards to Nelly.

Yours in Eternity,

Otis

"YOURS IN ETERNITY."

MY *DAD* USED TO END EVERYTHING WITH THAT. EVERY BOOK, EVERY BIRTHDAY CARD.

Next week I will be in London – the address where I can be reached is enclosed.

Please give regards to Nelly.

Yours in Eternity,

Otis

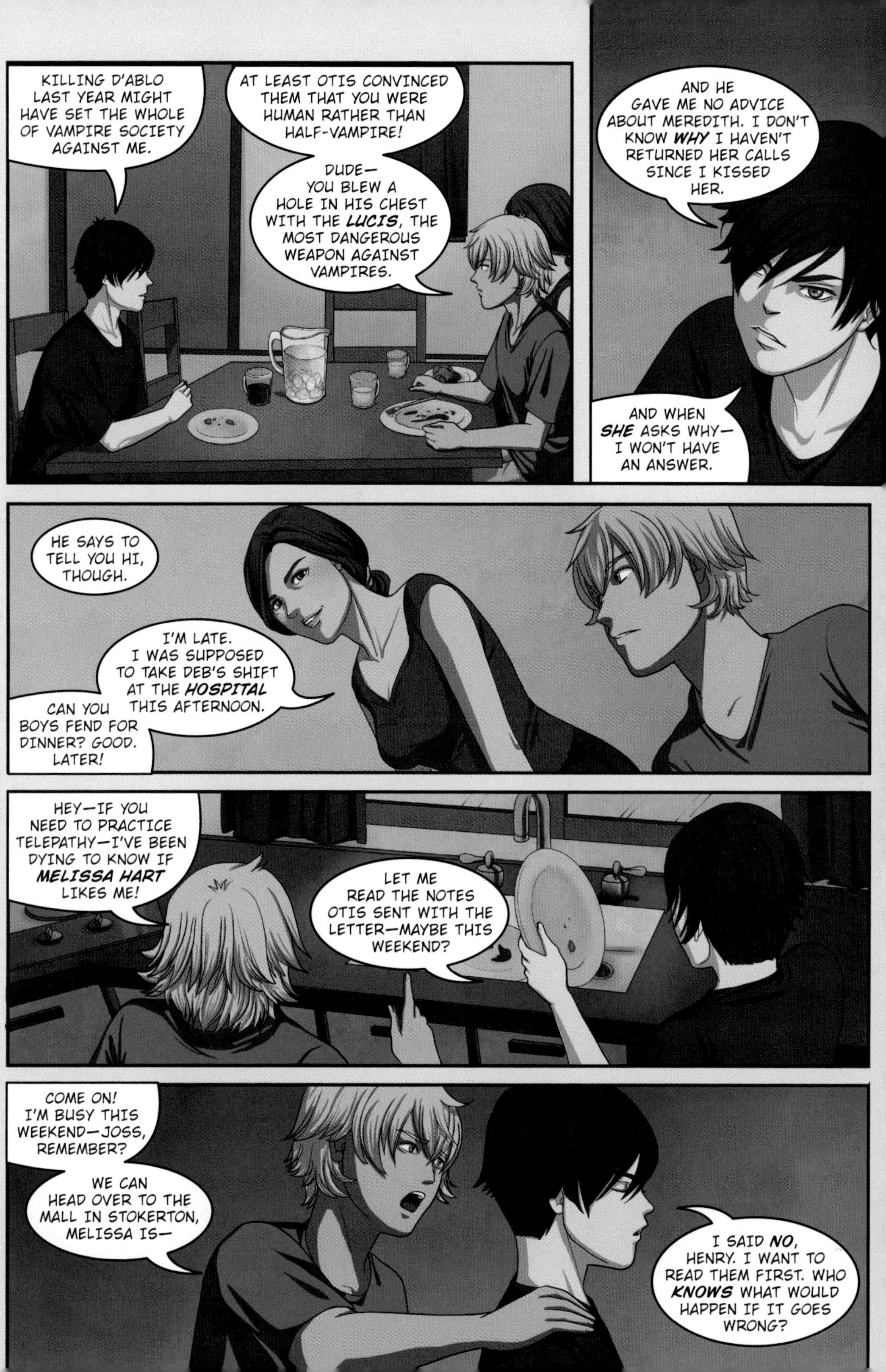
KILLING D'ABLO LAST YEAR MIGHT HAVE SET THE WHOLE OF VAMPIRE SOCIETY AGAINST ME.
AT LEAST OTIS CONVINCED THEM THAT YOU WERE HUMAN RATHER THAN HALF-VAMPIRE!
DUDE— YOU BLEW A HOLE IN HIS CHEST WITH THE LUCIS, THE MOST DANGEROUS WEAPON AGAINST VAMPIRES.
AND HE GAVE ME NO ADVICE ABOUT MEREDITH. I DON'T KNOW WHY I HAVEN'T RETURNED HER CALLS SINCE I KISSED HER.
AND WHEN SHE ASKS WHY— I WON'T HAVE AN ANSWER.
HE SAYS TO TELL YOU HI, THOUGH.
I'M LATE. I WAS SUPPOSED TO TAKE DEB'S SHIFT AT THE HOSPITAL THIS AFTERNOON.
CAN YOU BOYS FEND FOR DINNER? GOOD. LATER!
HEY—IF YOU NEED TO PRACTICE TELEPATHY—I'VE BEEN DYING TO KNOW IF MELISSA HART LIKES ME!
LET ME READ THE NOTES OTIS SENT WITH THE LETTER—MAYBE THIS WEEKEND?
COME ON! I'M BUSY THIS WEEKEND—JOSS, REMEMBER?
WE CAN HEAD OVER TO THE MALL IN STOKERTON, MELISSA IS—
I SAID NO, HENRY. I WANT TO READ THEM FIRST. WHO KNOWS WHAT WOULD HAPPEN IF IT GOES WRONG?

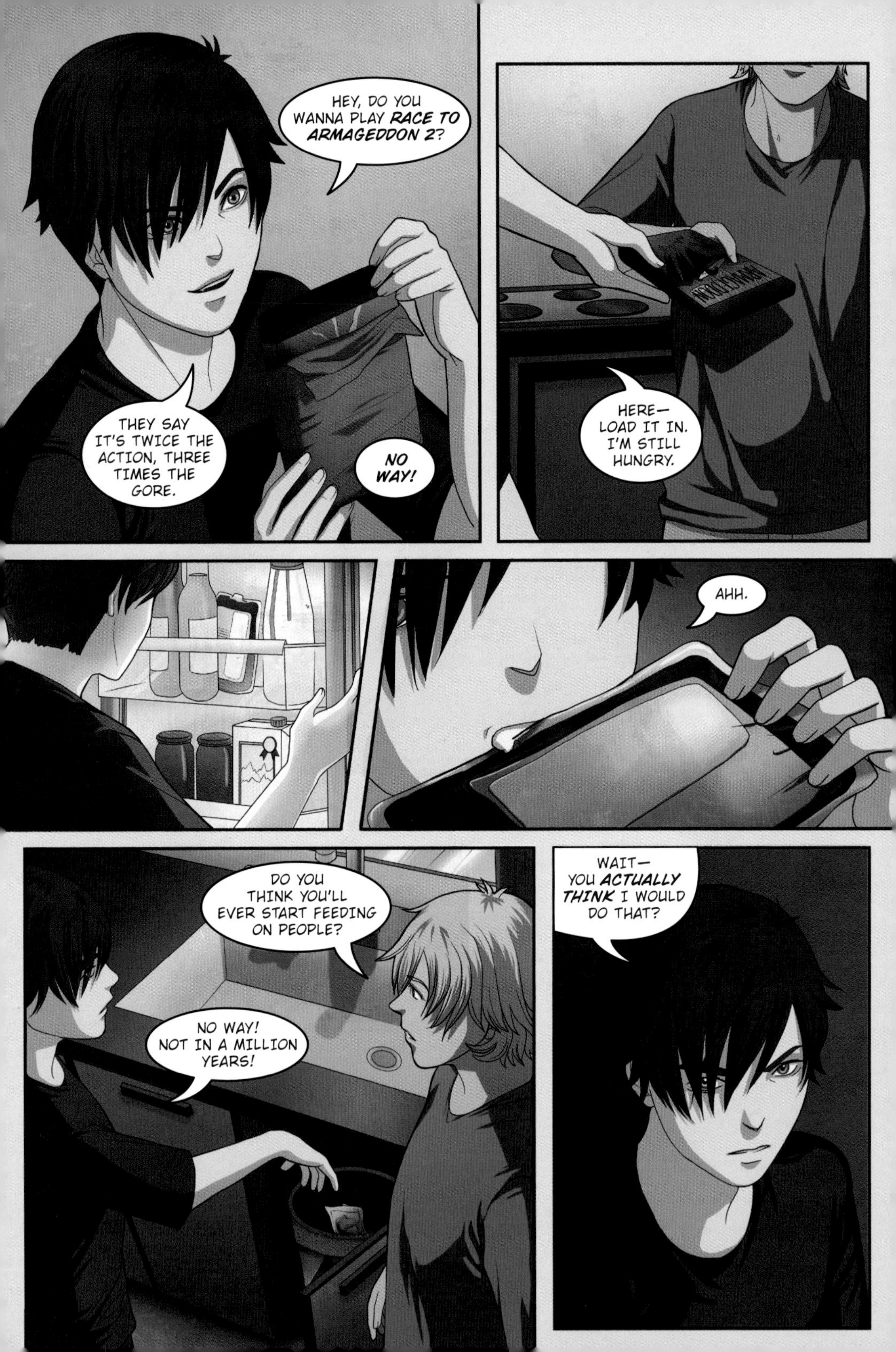
HEY, DO YOU WANNA PLAY *RACE TO ARMAGEDDON 2*?
THEY SAY IT'S TWICE THE ACTION, THREE TIMES THE GORE.
NO WAY!
HERE—LOAD IT IN. I'M STILL HUNGRY.
AHH.
DO YOU THINK YOU'LL EVER START FEEDING ON PEOPLE?
NO WAY! NOT IN A MILLION YEARS!
WAIT—YOU *ACTUALLY THINK* I WOULD DO THAT?

WELL, YOU DID BITE ME WHEN WE WERE *EIGHT*. MADE ME YOUR *DRUDGE*, WHATEVER THAT MEANS.

DUDE— *WE WERE EIGHT!* BESIDES, YOU *TOLD ME* TO!

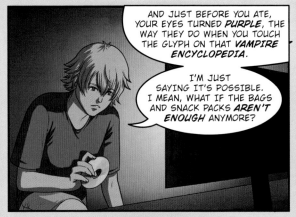

AND JUST BEFORE YOU ATE, YOUR EYES TURNED *PURPLE*, THE WAY THEY DO WHEN YOU TOUCH THE GLYPH ON THAT *VAMPIRE ENCYCLOPEDIA*.

I'M JUST SAYING IT'S POSSIBLE. I MEAN, WHAT IF THE BAGS AND SNACK PACKS *AREN'T ENOUGH* ANYMORE?

IF THEY WERE GOOD ENOUGH FOR MY *DAD* TO LIVE ON, THEY'RE GOOD ENOUGH FOR ME.

BESIDES, THE DAY I START FEEDING ON PEOPLE— IS THE DAY I START BEATING YOU AT VIDEO GAMES.

SO YOU'RE SAYING IT'LL NEVER HAPPEN?

IN YOUR DREAMS!

LOOK OUT— THE ALIEN KING HAS *SIX HEADS!* THAT'S NEW!

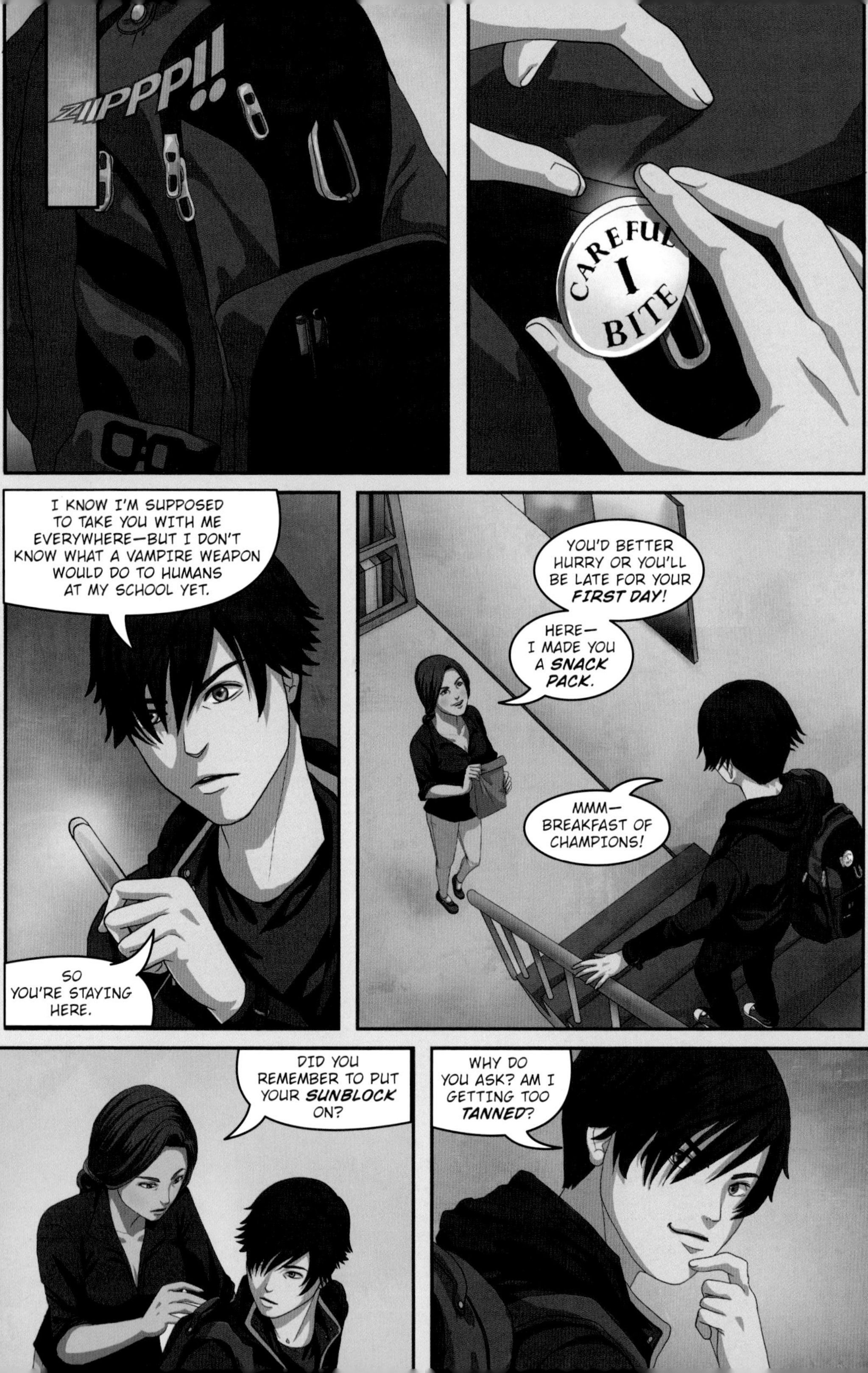
ZIIPPP!!
CAREFUL I BITE
I KNOW I'M SUPPOSED TO TAKE YOU WITH ME EVERYWHERE—BUT I DON'T KNOW WHAT A VAMPIRE WEAPON WOULD DO TO HUMANS AT MY SCHOOL YET.
SO YOU'RE STAYING HERE.
YOU'D BETTER HURRY OR YOU'LL BE LATE FOR YOUR FIRST DAY!
HERE— I MADE YOU A SNACK PACK.
MMM— BREAKFAST OF CHAMPIONS!
DID YOU REMEMBER TO PUT YOUR SUNBLOCK ON?
WHY DO YOU ASK? AM I GETTING TOO TANNED?

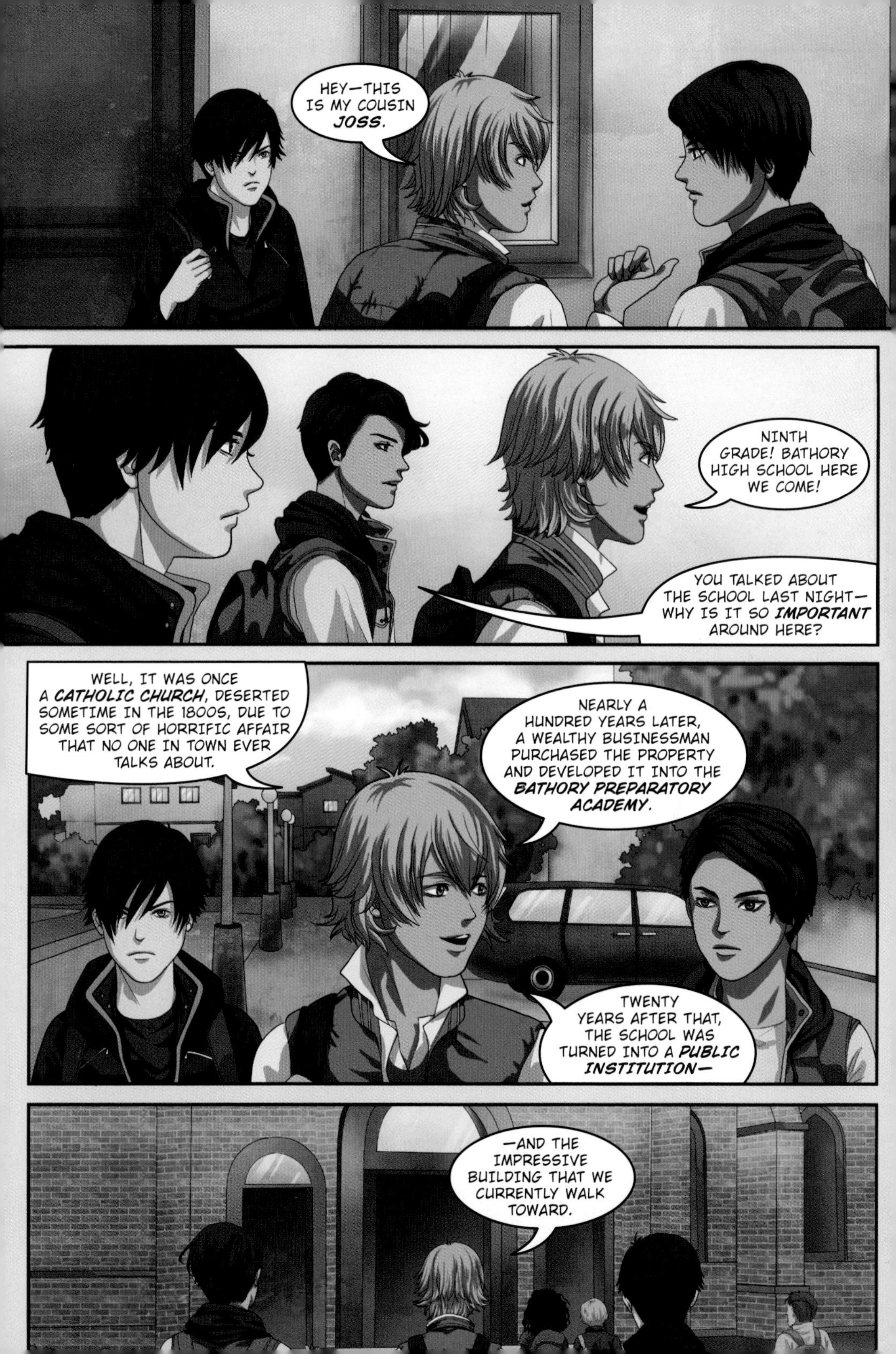
HEY—THIS IS MY COUSIN ***JOSS***.
NINTH GRADE! BATHORY HIGH SCHOOL HERE WE COME!
YOU TALKED ABOUT THE SCHOOL LAST NIGHT—WHY IS IT SO ***IMPORTANT*** AROUND HERE?
WELL, IT WAS ONCE A ***CATHOLIC CHURCH***, DESERTED SOMETIME IN THE 1800S, DUE TO SOME SORT OF HORRIFIC AFFAIR THAT NO ONE IN TOWN EVER TALKS ABOUT.
NEARLY A HUNDRED YEARS LATER, A WEALTHY BUSINESSMAN PURCHASED THE PROPERTY AND DEVELOPED IT INTO THE ***BATHORY PREPARATORY ACADEMY***.
TWENTY YEARS AFTER THAT, THE SCHOOL WAS TURNED INTO A ***PUBLIC INSTITUTION***—
—AND THE IMPRESSIVE BUILDING THAT WE CURRENTLY WALK TOWARD.

HENRY!

BE RIGHT BACK, GUYS.

HENRY SAYS YOU MOVED IN FROM *CALI*.

HE TELLS ME YOU *SUCK* AT VIDEO GAMES.

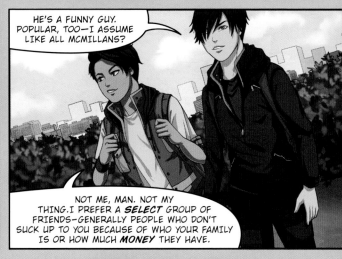

HE'S A FUNNY GUY. POPULAR, TOO—I ASSUME LIKE ALL MCMILLANS?

NOT ME, MAN. NOT MY THING. I PREFER A *SELECT* GROUP OF FRIENDS—GENERALLY PEOPLE WHO DON'T SUCK UP TO YOU BECAUSE OF WHO YOUR FAMILY IS OR HOW MUCH *MONEY* THEY HAVE.

WELL . . . SEE YA, I GUESS.

YEAH, SEE YA.

WELCOME TO YOUR FIRST DAY OF *HIGH SCHOOL*, GOTH BOY.

SLAM!

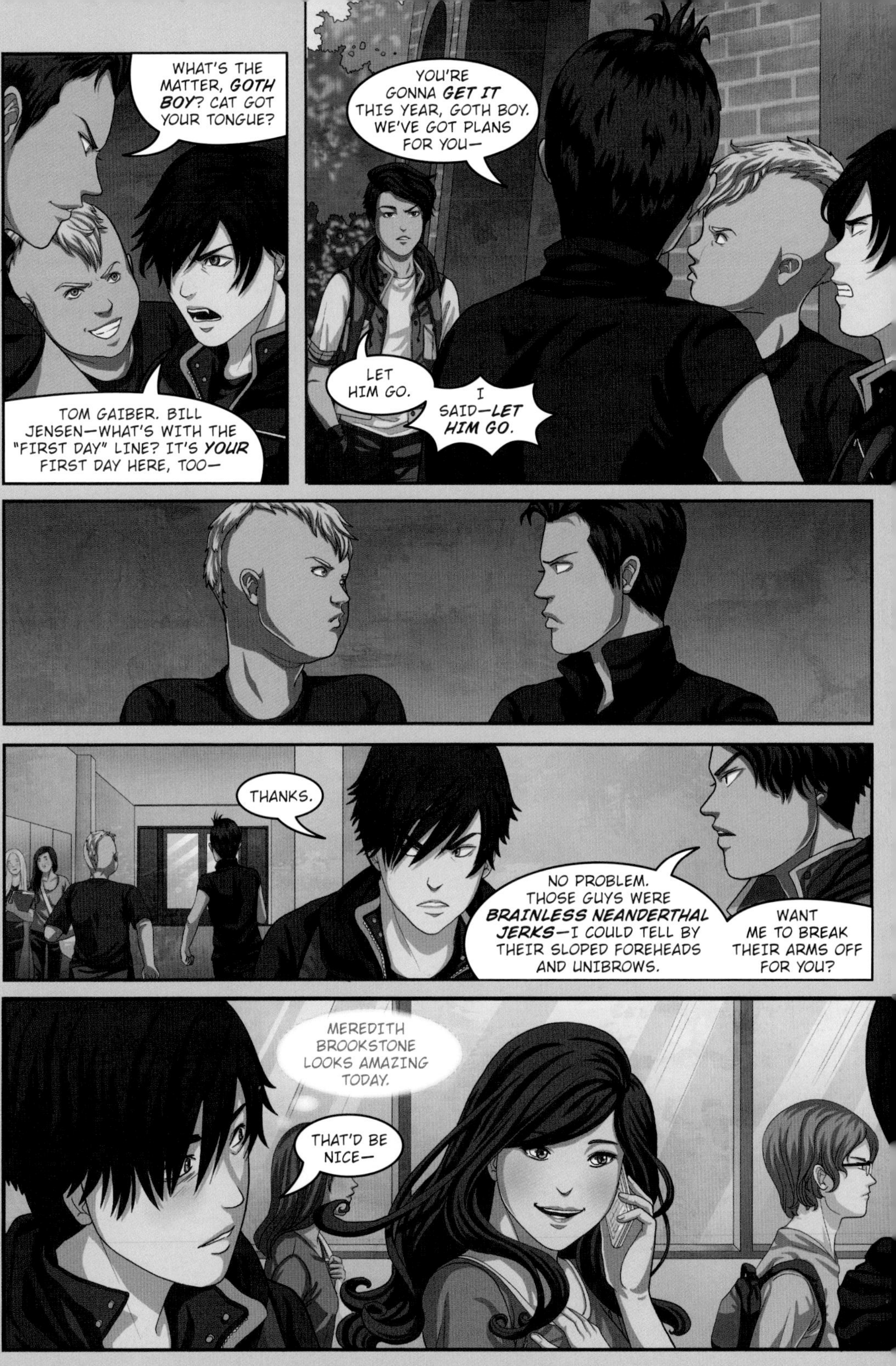
WHAT'S THE MATTER, GOTH BOY? CAT GOT YOUR TONGUE?
TOM GAIBER. BILL JENSEN—WHAT'S WITH THE "FIRST DAY" LINE? IT'S YOUR FIRST DAY HERE, TOO—
YOU'RE GONNA GET IT THIS YEAR, GOTH BOY. WE'VE GOT PLANS FOR YOU—
LET HIM GO.
I SAID—LET HIM GO.
THANKS.
NO PROBLEM. THOSE GUYS WERE BRAINLESS NEANDERTHAL JERKS—I COULD TELL BY THEIR SLOPED FOREHEADS AND UNIBROWS.
WANT ME TO BREAK THEIR ARMS OFF FOR YOU?
MEREDITH BROOKSTONE LOOKS AMAZING TODAY.
THAT'D BE NICE—

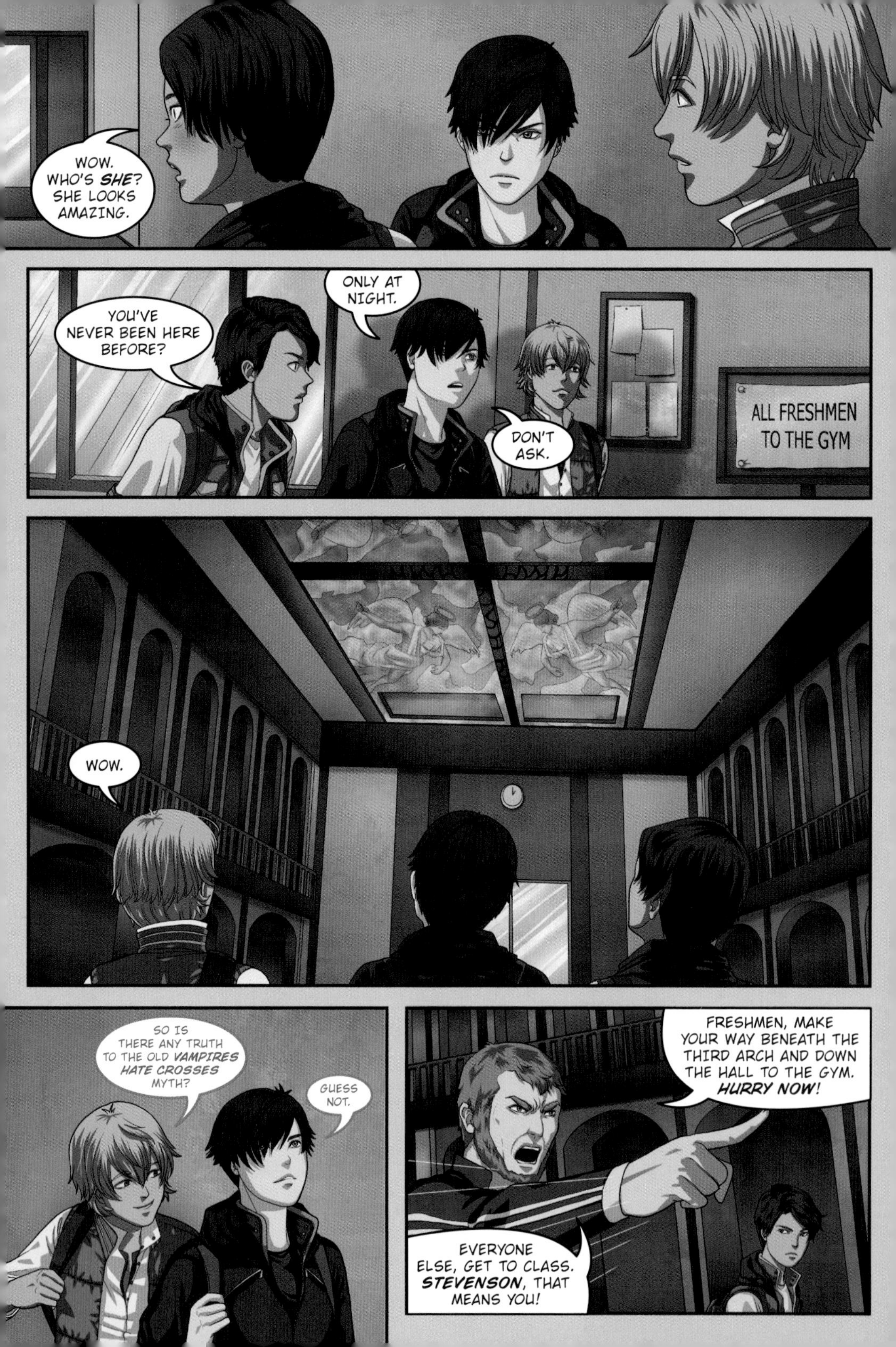
WOW. WHO'S *SHE*? SHE LOOKS AMAZING.
YOU'VE NEVER BEEN HERE BEFORE?
ONLY AT NIGHT.
DON'T ASK.
ALL FRESHMEN TO THE GYM
WOW.
SO IS THERE ANY TRUTH TO THE OLD *VAMPIRES HATE CROSSES* MYTH?
GUESS NOT.
FRESHMEN, MAKE YOUR WAY BENEATH THE THIRD ARCH AND DOWN THE HALL TO THE GYM. ***HURRY NOW***!
EVERYONE ELSE, GET TO CLASS. ***STEVENSON***, THAT MEANS YOU!

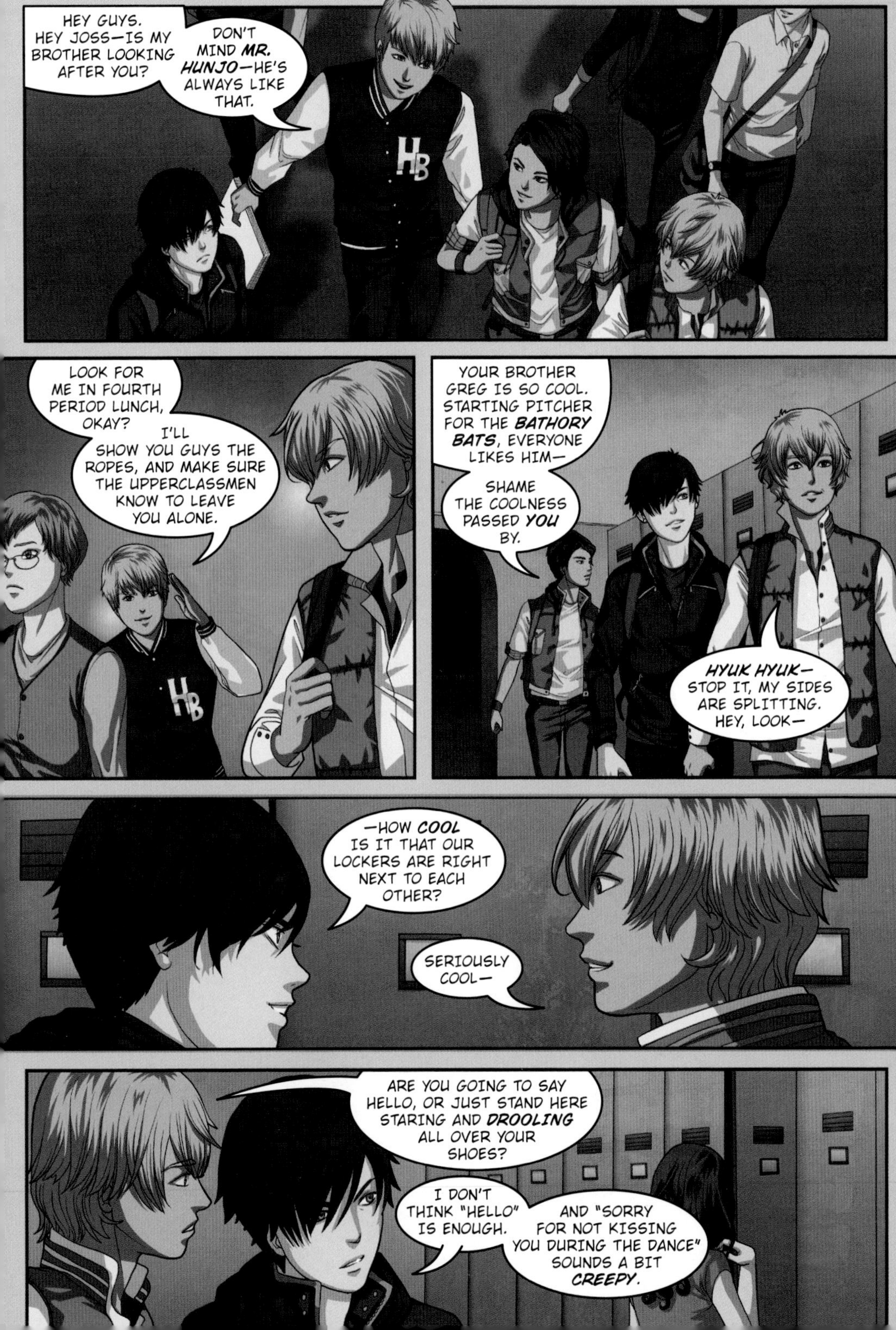
HEY GUYS. HEY JOSS—IS MY BROTHER LOOKING AFTER YOU?
DON'T MIND MR. HUNJO—HE'S ALWAYS LIKE THAT.
LOOK FOR ME IN FOURTH PERIOD LUNCH, OKAY?
I'LL SHOW YOU GUYS THE ROPES, AND MAKE SURE THE UPPERCLASSMEN KNOW TO LEAVE YOU ALONE.
YOUR BROTHER GREG IS SO COOL. STARTING PITCHER FOR THE BATHORY BATS, EVERYONE LIKES HIM—
SHAME THE COOLNESS PASSED YOU BY.
HYUK HYUK—STOP IT, MY SIDES ARE SPLITTING. HEY, LOOK—
—HOW COOL IS IT THAT OUR LOCKERS ARE RIGHT NEXT TO EACH OTHER?
SERIOUSLY COOL—
ARE YOU GOING TO SAY HELLO, OR JUST STAND HERE STARING AND DROOLING ALL OVER YOUR SHOES?
I DON'T THINK "HELLO" IS ENOUGH.
AND "SORRY FOR NOT KISSING YOU DURING THE DANCE" SOUNDS A BIT CREEPY.

HI, VLAD.

HI, MEREDITH. SO YOU ... UM ... HAVE CLASS?

OF COURSE YOU HAVE CLASS. I HAVE ENGLISH ...

UM ... WE SHARE IT ... BUT YOU PROBABLY KNOW ...

SHUT UP SHUT UP *STOP TALKING NOW.*

COME ON, MEREDITH— WE'LL BE LATE FOR CLASS.

HI, MELISSA ...

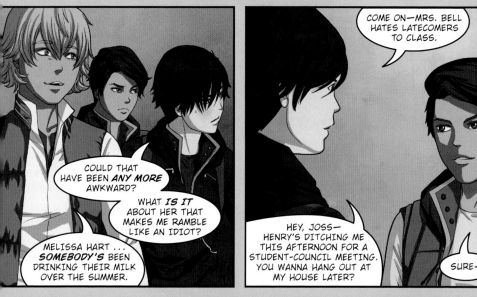

COULD THAT HAVE BEEN *ANY MORE* AWKWARD?

WHAT *IS IT* ABOUT HER THAT MAKES ME RAMBLE LIKE AN IDIOT?

MELISSA HART ... *SOMEBODY'S* BEEN DRINKING THEIR MILK OVER THE SUMMER.

COME ON—MRS. BELL HATES LATECOMERS TO CLASS.

HEY, JOSS— HENRY'S DITCHING ME THIS AFTERNOON FOR A STUDENT-COUNCIL MEETING. YOU WANNA HANG OUT AT MY HOUSE LATER?

SURE—

—ANYTHING TO AVOID AUNT MATILDA'S *QUILTING* CLUB.

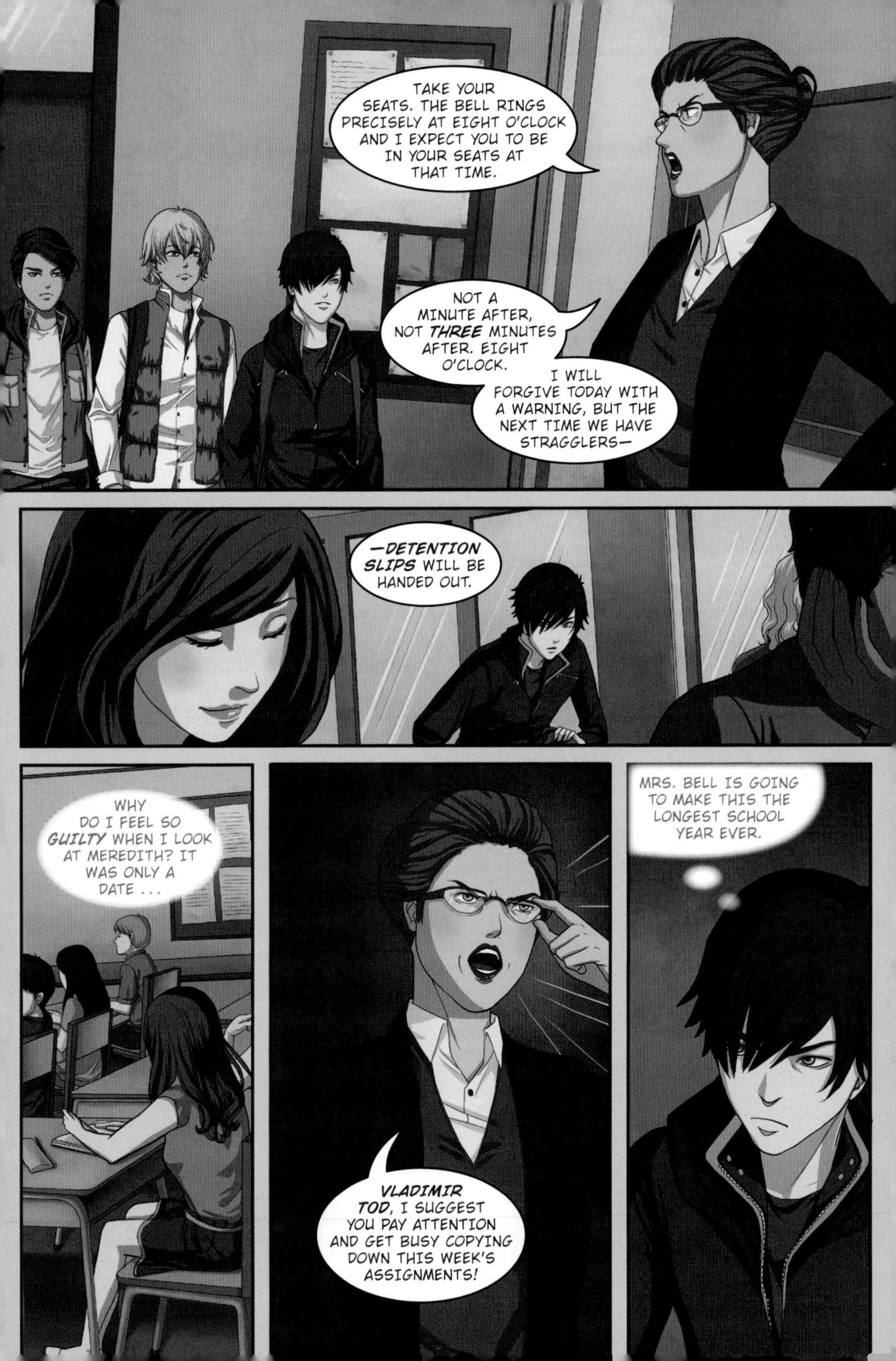
TAKE YOUR SEATS. THE BELL RINGS PRECISELY AT EIGHT O'CLOCK AND I EXPECT YOU TO BE IN YOUR SEATS AT THAT TIME.
NOT A MINUTE AFTER, NOT *THREE* MINUTES AFTER. EIGHT O'CLOCK.
I WILL FORGIVE TODAY WITH A WARNING, BUT THE NEXT TIME WE HAVE STRAGGLERS—
—*DETENTION SLIPS* WILL BE HANDED OUT.
WHY DO I FEEL SO *GUILTY* WHEN I LOOK AT MEREDITH? IT WAS ONLY A DATE . . .
VLADIMIR TOD, I SUGGEST YOU PAY ATTENTION AND GET BUSY COPYING DOWN THIS WEEK'S ASSIGNMENTS!
MRS. BELL IS GOING TO MAKE THIS THE LONGEST SCHOOL YEAR EVER.

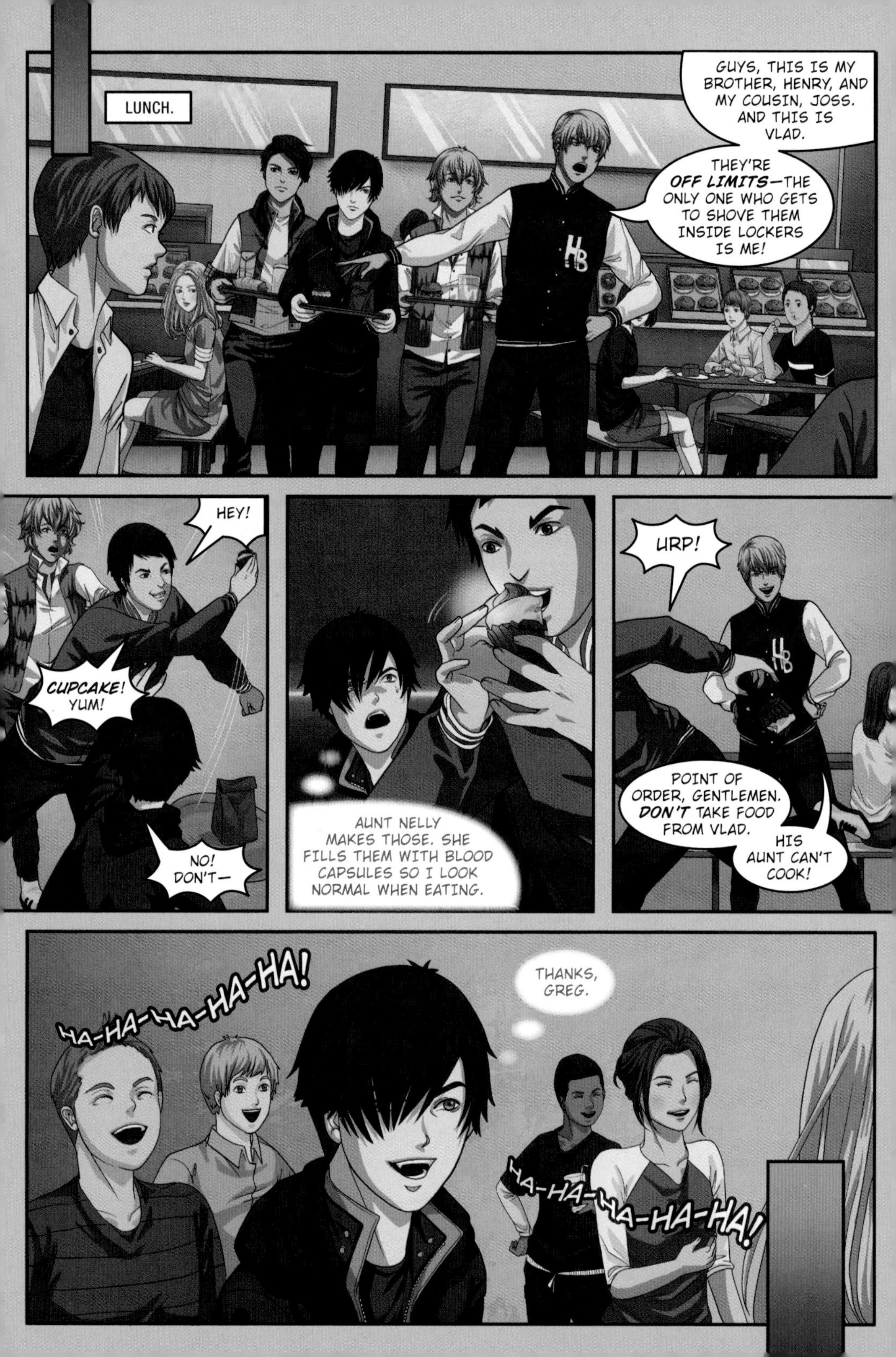
LUNCH.
GUYS, THIS IS MY BROTHER, HENRY, AND MY COUSIN, JOSS. AND THIS IS VLAD.
THEY'RE *OFF LIMITS*—THE ONLY ONE WHO GETS TO SHOVE THEM INSIDE LOCKERS IS ME!
HEY!
CUPCAKE! YUM!
NO! DON'T—
AUNT NELLY MAKES THOSE. SHE FILLS THEM WITH BLOOD CAPSULES SO I LOOK NORMAL WHEN EATING.
URP!
POINT OF ORDER, GENTLEMEN. *DON'T* TAKE FOOD FROM VLAD.
HIS AUNT CAN'T COOK!
HA-HA-HA-HA-HA-HA!
THANKS, GREG.
HA-HA-HA-HA-HA-HA!

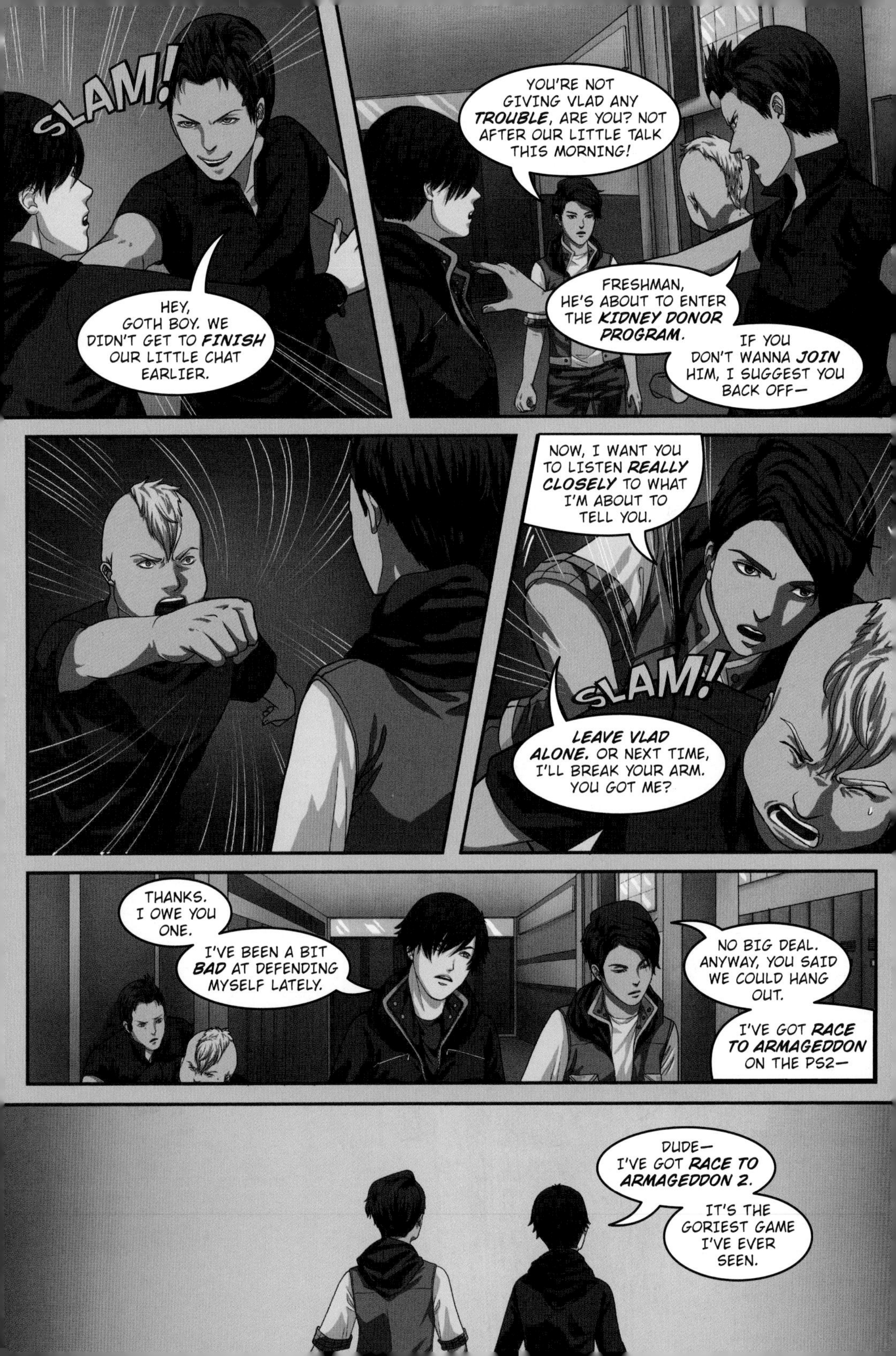
SLAM!
HEY, GOTH BOY. WE DIDN'T GET TO FINISH OUR LITTLE CHAT EARLIER.
YOU'RE NOT GIVING VLAD ANY TROUBLE, ARE YOU? NOT AFTER OUR LITTLE TALK THIS MORNING!
FRESHMAN, HE'S ABOUT TO ENTER THE KIDNEY DONOR PROGRAM.
IF YOU DON'T WANNA JOIN HIM, I SUGGEST YOU BACK OFF—
NOW, I WANT YOU TO LISTEN REALLY CLOSELY TO WHAT I'M ABOUT TO TELL YOU.
SLAM!
LEAVE VLAD ALONE. OR NEXT TIME, I'LL BREAK YOUR ARM. YOU GOT ME?
THANKS. I OWE YOU ONE.
I'VE BEEN A BIT BAD AT DEFENDING MYSELF LATELY.
NO BIG DEAL. ANYWAY, YOU SAID WE COULD HANG OUT.
I'VE GOT RACE TO ARMAGEDDON ON THE PS2—
DUDE— I'VE GOT RACE TO ARMAGEDDON 2.
IT'S THE GORIEST GAME I'VE EVER SEEN.

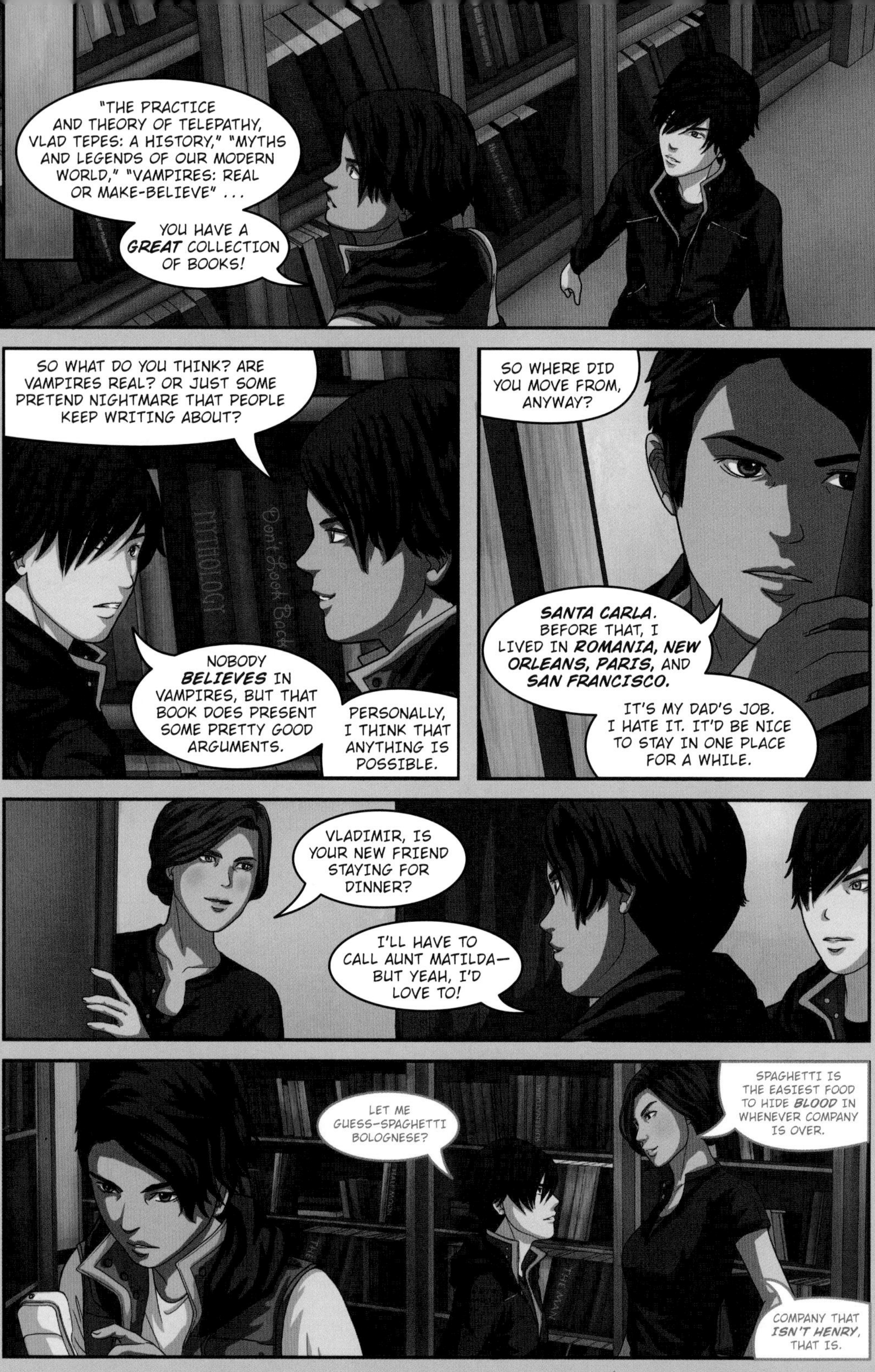
"THE PRACTICE AND THEORY OF TELEPATHY, VLAD TEPES: A HISTORY," "MYTHS AND LEGENDS OF OUR MODERN WORLD," "VAMPIRES: REAL OR MAKE-BELIEVE" . . .
YOU HAVE A GREAT COLLECTION OF BOOKS!
SO WHAT DO YOU THINK? ARE VAMPIRES REAL? OR JUST SOME PRETEND NIGHTMARE THAT PEOPLE KEEP WRITING ABOUT?
MYTHOLOGY
Don't Look Back
NOBODY BELIEVES IN VAMPIRES, BUT THAT BOOK DOES PRESENT SOME PRETTY GOOD ARGUMENTS.
PERSONALLY, I THINK THAT ANYTHING IS POSSIBLE.
SO WHERE DID YOU MOVE FROM, ANYWAY?
SANTA CARLA. BEFORE THAT, I LIVED IN ROMANIA, NEW ORLEANS, PARIS, AND SAN FRANCISCO.
IT'S MY DAD'S JOB. I HATE IT. IT'D BE NICE TO STAY IN ONE PLACE FOR A WHILE.
VLADIMIR, IS YOUR NEW FRIEND STAYING FOR DINNER?
I'LL HAVE TO CALL AUNT MATILDA—BUT YEAH, I'D LOVE TO!
LET ME GUESS—SPAGHETTI BOLOGNESE?
SPAGHETTI IS THE EASIEST FOOD TO HIDE BLOOD IN WHENEVER COMPANY IS OVER.
COMPANY THAT ISN'T HENRY, THAT IS.

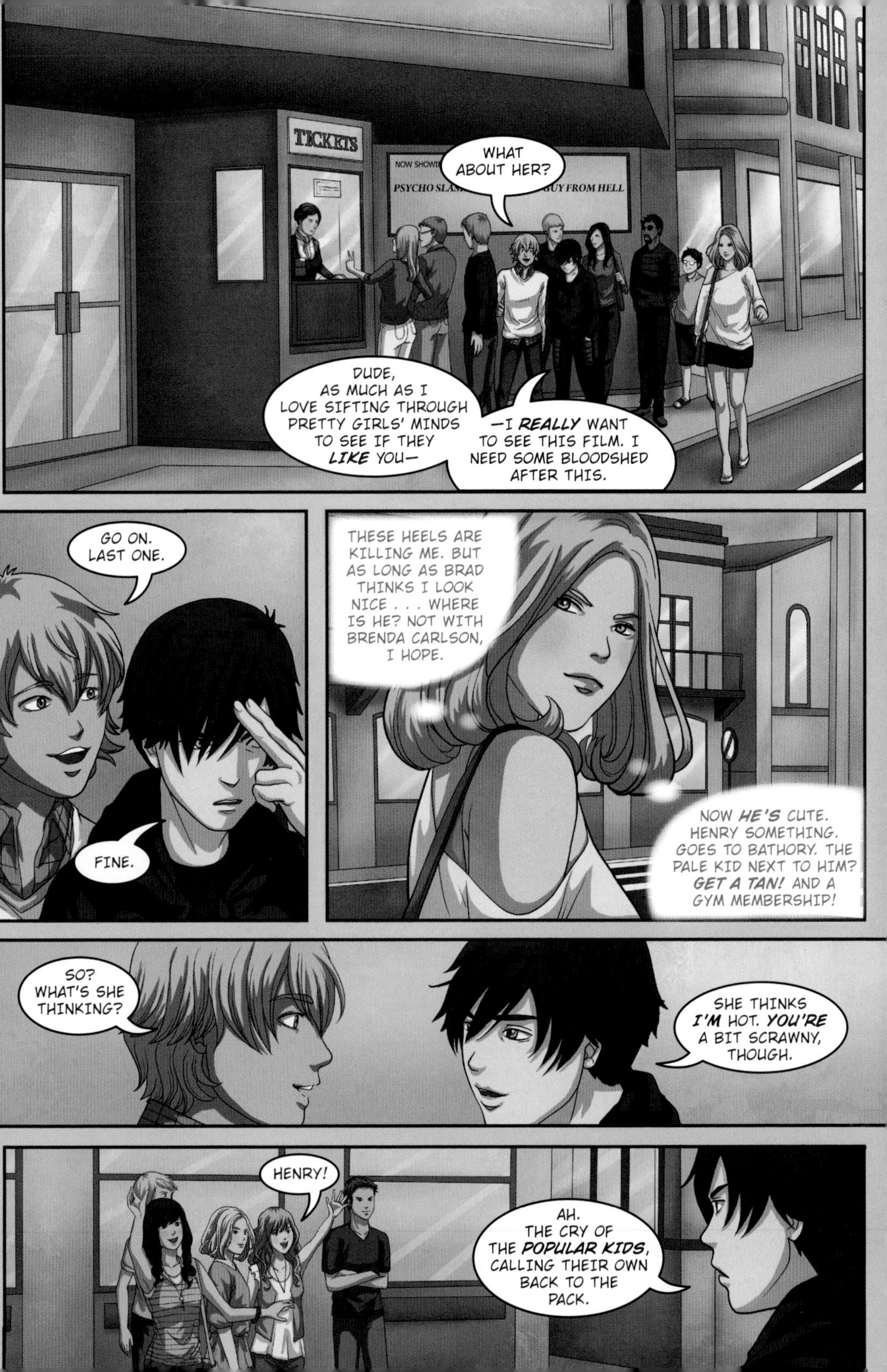
TICKETS
GUY FROM HELL
WHAT ABOUT HER?
DUDE, AS MUCH AS I LOVE SIFTING THROUGH PRETTY GIRLS' MINDS TO SEE IF THEY LIKE YOU—
—I REALLY WANT TO SEE THIS FILM. I NEED SOME BLOODSHED AFTER THIS.
GO ON. LAST ONE.
FINE.
THESE HEELS ARE KILLING ME. BUT AS LONG AS BRAD THINKS I LOOK NICE . . . WHERE IS HE? NOT WITH BRENDA CARLSON, I HOPE.
NOW HE'S CUTE. HENRY SOMETHING. GOES TO BATHORY. THE PALE KID NEXT TO HIM? GET A TAN! AND A GYM MEMBERSHIP!
SO? WHAT'S SHE THINKING?
SHE THINKS I'M HOT. YOU'RE A BIT SCRAWNY, THOUGH.
HENRY!
AH. THE CRY OF THE POPULAR KIDS, CALLING THEIR OWN BACK TO THE PACK.

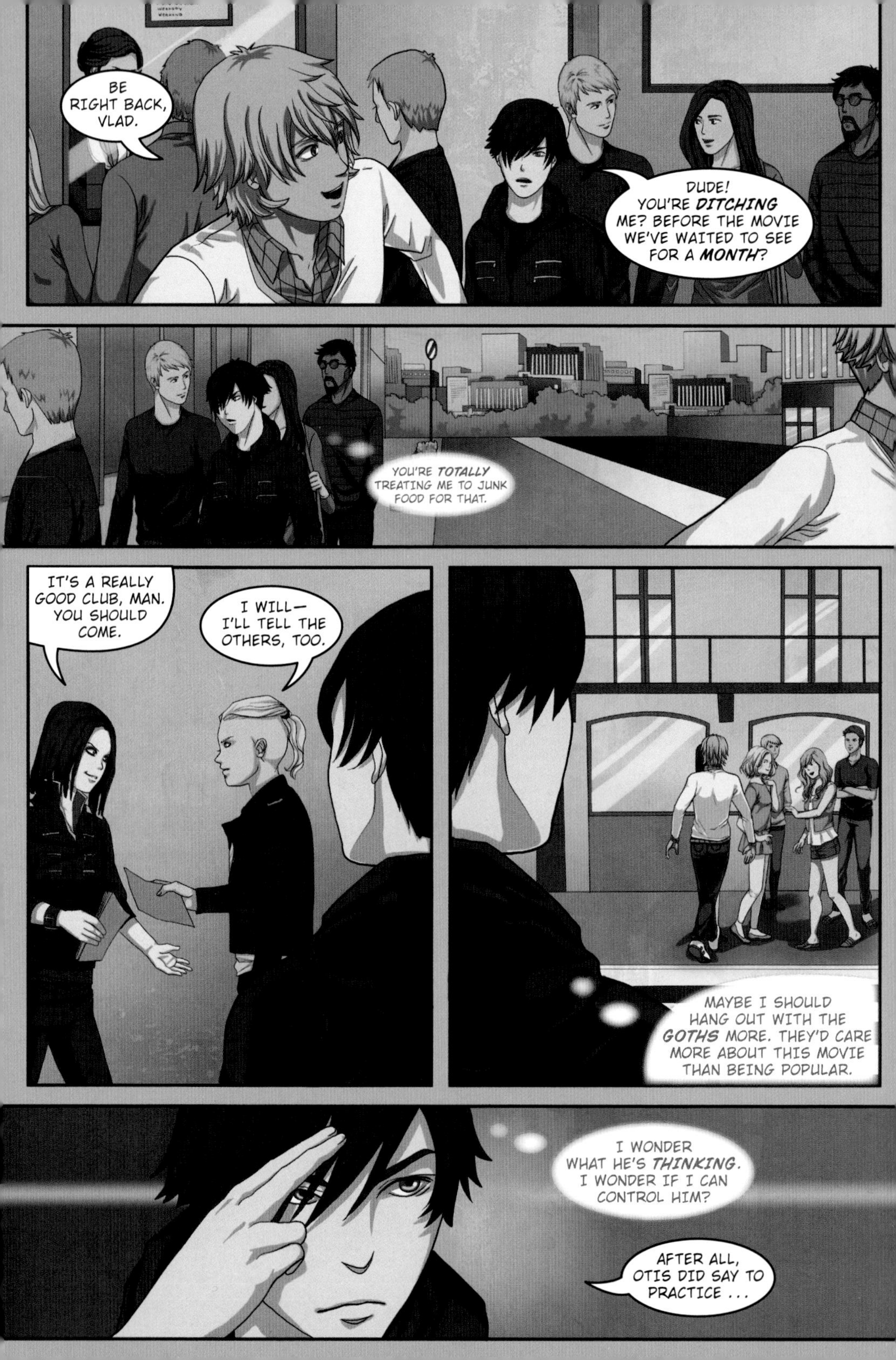

BE RIGHT BACK, VLAD.
DUDE! YOU'RE DITCHING ME? BEFORE THE MOVIE WE'VE WAITED TO SEE FOR A MONTH?
YOU'RE TOTALLY TREATING ME TO JUNK FOOD FOR THAT.
IT'S A REALLY GOOD CLUB, MAN. YOU SHOULD COME.
I WILL— I'LL TELL THE OTHERS, TOO.
MAYBE I SHOULD HANG OUT WITH THE GOTHS MORE. THEY'D CARE MORE ABOUT THIS MOVIE THAN BEING POPULAR.
I WONDER WHAT HE'S THINKING. I WONDER IF I CAN CONTROL HIM?
AFTER ALL, OTIS DID SAY TO PRACTICE . . .

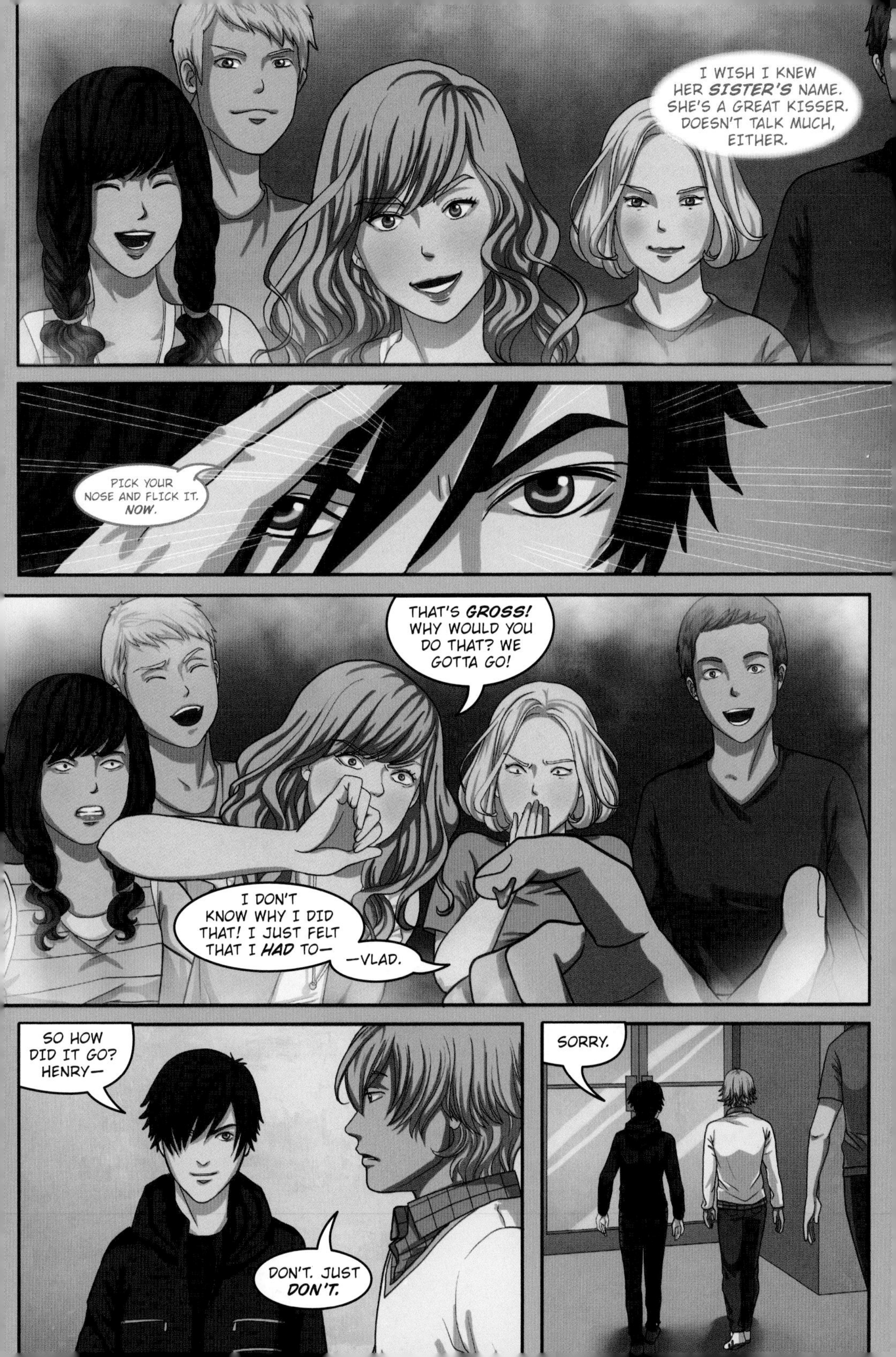
I WISH I KNEW HER SISTER'S NAME. SHE'S A GREAT KISSER. DOESN'T TALK MUCH, EITHER.
PICK YOUR NOSE AND FLICK IT. NOW.
THAT'S GROSS! WHY WOULD YOU DO THAT? WE GOTTA GO!
I DON'T KNOW WHY I DID THAT! I JUST FELT THAT I HAD TO—
—VLAD.
SO HOW DID IT GO? HENRY—
DON'T. JUST DON'T.
SORRY.

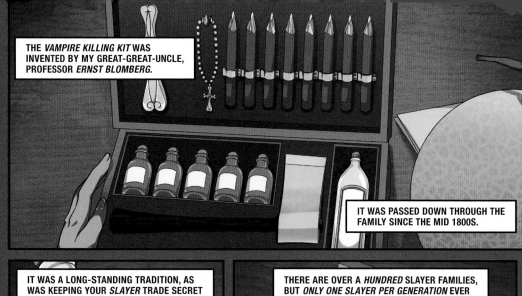

THE *VAMPIRE KILLING KIT* WAS INVENTED BY MY GREAT-GREAT-UNCLE, PROFESSOR *ERNST BLOMBERG.*

IT WAS PASSED DOWN THROUGH THE FAMILY SINCE THE MID 1800S.

IT WAS A LONG-STANDING TRADITION, AS WAS KEEPING YOUR *SLAYER* TRADE SECRET FROM EVERYONE IN THE FAMILY.

WELL, OTHER THAN THOSE WHO HAD SLAIN *BEFORE* YOU——AND THOSE WHO WOULD SLAY *AFTER* YOU.

THERE ARE OVER A *HUNDRED* SLAYER FAMILIES, BUT *ONLY ONE SLAYER PER GENERATION* EVER JOINS THE *SLAYER SOCIETY.*

AND ONLY A SLAYER CAN RECOGNIZE THE TRAITS OF THE *NEXT* SLAYER IN HIS FAMILY LINE. I DIDN'T WANT TO JOIN——UNTIL CECILE DIED.

I HAD THOUGHT HER SCREAMS WERE A *NIGHTMARE.* BUT WHEN I REACHED HER ROOM TO WAKE HER——

——I SAW THE *VAMPIRE* OVER HER BODY, DRINKING HUNGRILY.

AT HER FUNERAL, I BECAME A SLAYER. AND EVERY KILL I MAKE IS FOR YOU, CECILE.

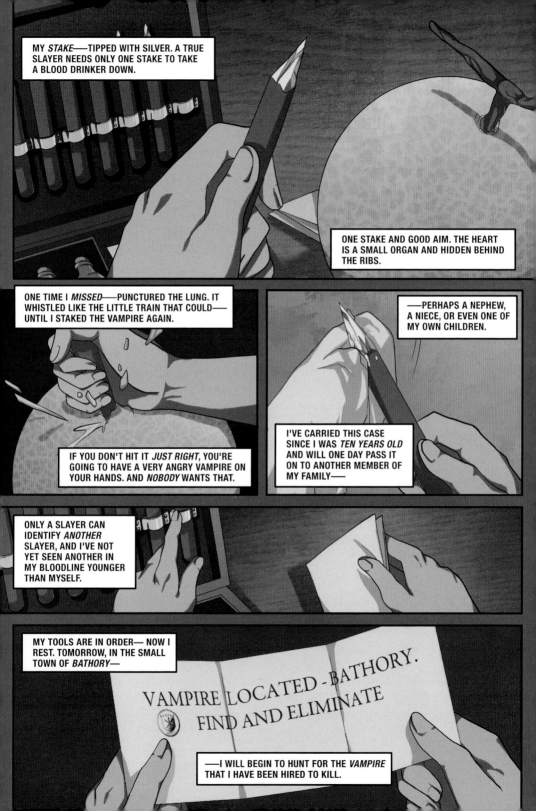

MY *STAKE*——TIPPED WITH SILVER. A TRUE SLAYER NEEDS ONLY ONE STAKE TO TAKE A BLOOD DRINKER DOWN.

ONE STAKE AND GOOD AIM. THE HEART IS A SMALL ORGAN AND HIDDEN BEHIND THE RIBS.

ONE TIME I *MISSED*——PUNCTURED THE LUNG. IT WHISTLED LIKE THE LITTLE TRAIN THAT COULD—— UNTIL I STAKED THE VAMPIRE AGAIN.

——PERHAPS A NEPHEW, A NIECE, OR EVEN ONE OF MY OWN CHILDREN.

IF YOU DON'T HIT IT *JUST RIGHT*, YOU'RE GOING TO HAVE A VERY ANGRY VAMPIRE ON YOUR HANDS. AND *NOBODY* WANTS THAT.

I'VE CARRIED THIS CASE SINCE I WAS *TEN YEARS OLD* AND WILL ONE DAY PASS IT ON TO ANOTHER MEMBER OF MY FAMILY——

ONLY A SLAYER CAN IDENTIFY *ANOTHER* SLAYER, AND I'VE NOT YET SEEN ANOTHER IN MY BLOODLINE YOUNGER THAN MYSELF.

MY TOOLS ARE IN ORDER— NOW I REST. TOMORROW, IN THE SMALL TOWN OF *BATHORY*—

VAMPIRE LOCATED - BATHORY. FIND AND ELIMINATE

——I WILL BEGIN TO HUNT FOR THE *VAMPIRE* THAT I HAVE BEEN HIRED TO KILL.

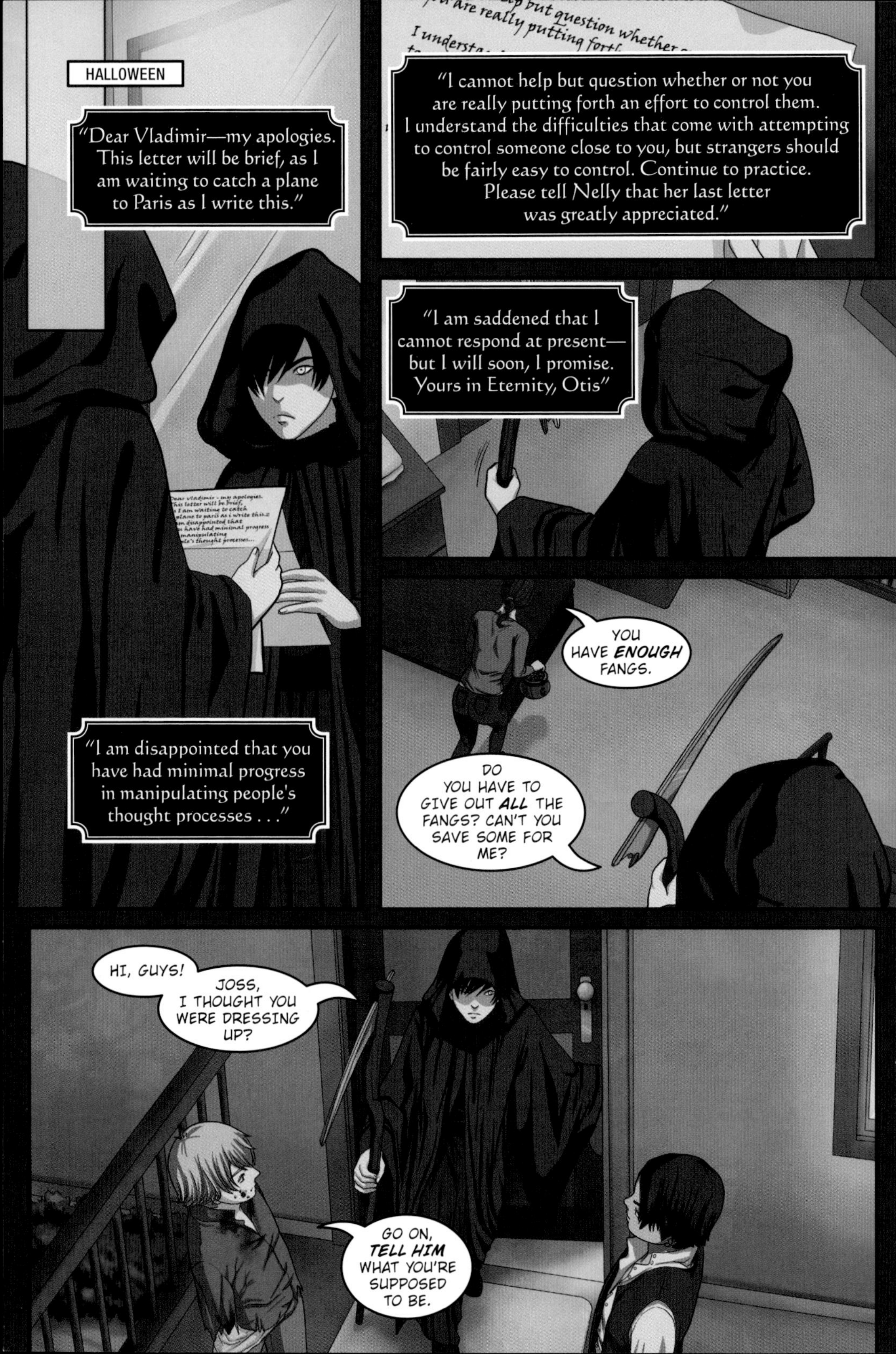
HALLOWEEN
"Dear Vladimir—my apologies. This letter will be brief, as I am waiting to catch a plane to Paris as I write this."
"I cannot help but question whether or not you are really putting forth an effort to control them. I understand the difficulties that come with attempting to control someone close to you, but strangers should be fairly easy to control. Continue to practice. Please tell Nelly that her last letter was greatly appreciated."
"I am saddened that I cannot respond at present—but I will soon, I promise. Yours in Eternity, Otis"
"I am disappointed that you have had minimal progress in manipulating people's thought processes . . ."
YOU HAVE ENOUGH FANGS.
DO YOU HAVE TO GIVE OUT ALL THE FANGS? CAN'T YOU SAVE SOME FOR ME?
HI, GUYS!
JOSS, I THOUGHT YOU WERE DRESSING UP?
GO ON, TELL HIM WHAT YOU'RE SUPPOSED TO BE.

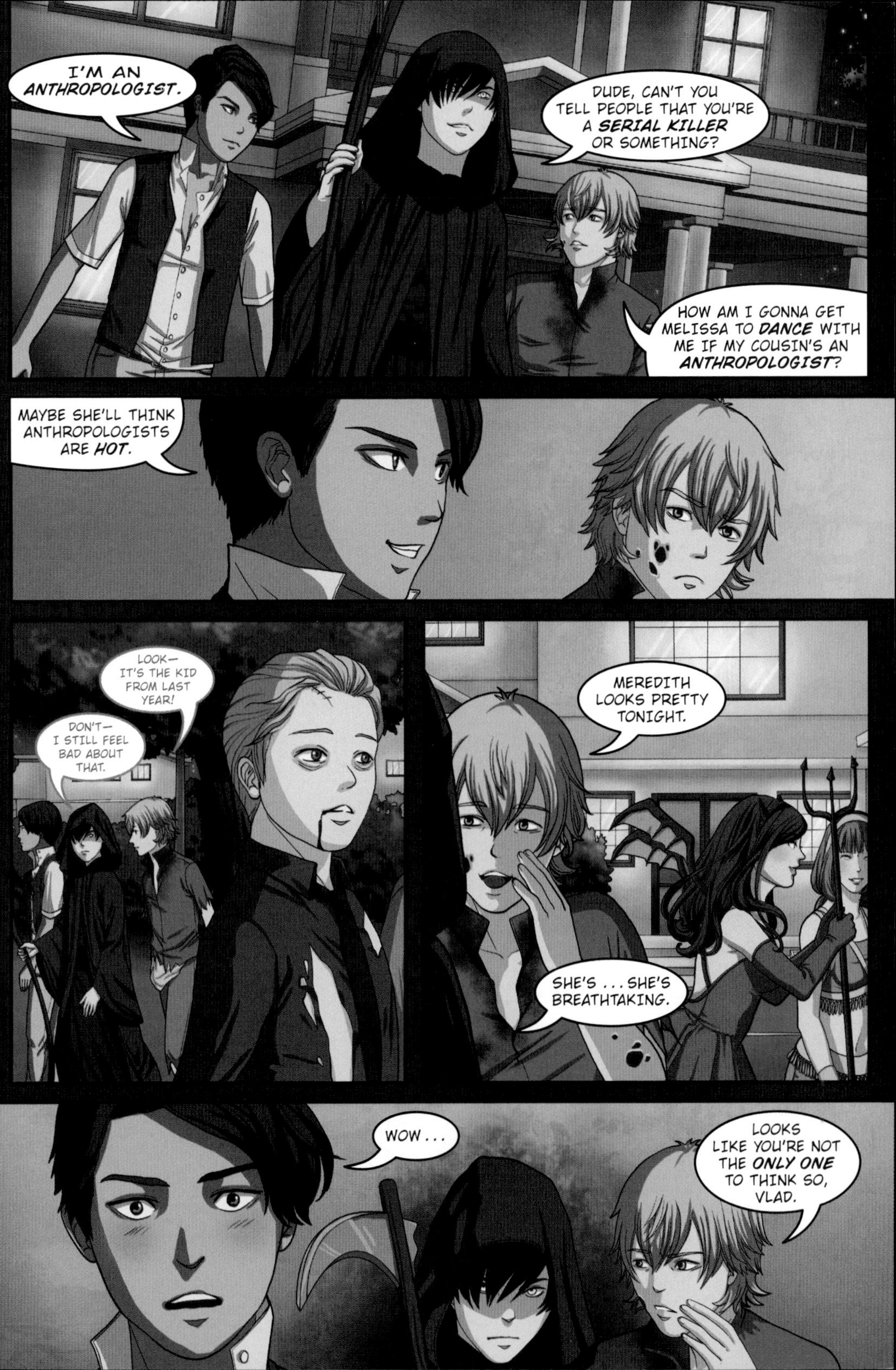
I'M AN ANTHROPOLOGIST.
DUDE, CAN'T YOU TELL PEOPLE THAT YOU'RE A SERIAL KILLER OR SOMETHING?
HOW AM I GONNA GET MELISSA TO DANCE WITH ME IF MY COUSIN'S AN ANTHROPOLOGIST?
MAYBE SHE'LL THINK ANTHROPOLOGISTS ARE HOT.
LOOK— IT'S THE KID FROM LAST YEAR!
DON'T— I STILL FEEL BAD ABOUT THAT.
MEREDITH LOOKS PRETTY TONIGHT.
SHE'S . . . SHE'S BREATHTAKING.
WOW . . .
LOOKS LIKE YOU'RE NOT THE ONLY ONE TO THINK SO, VLAD.

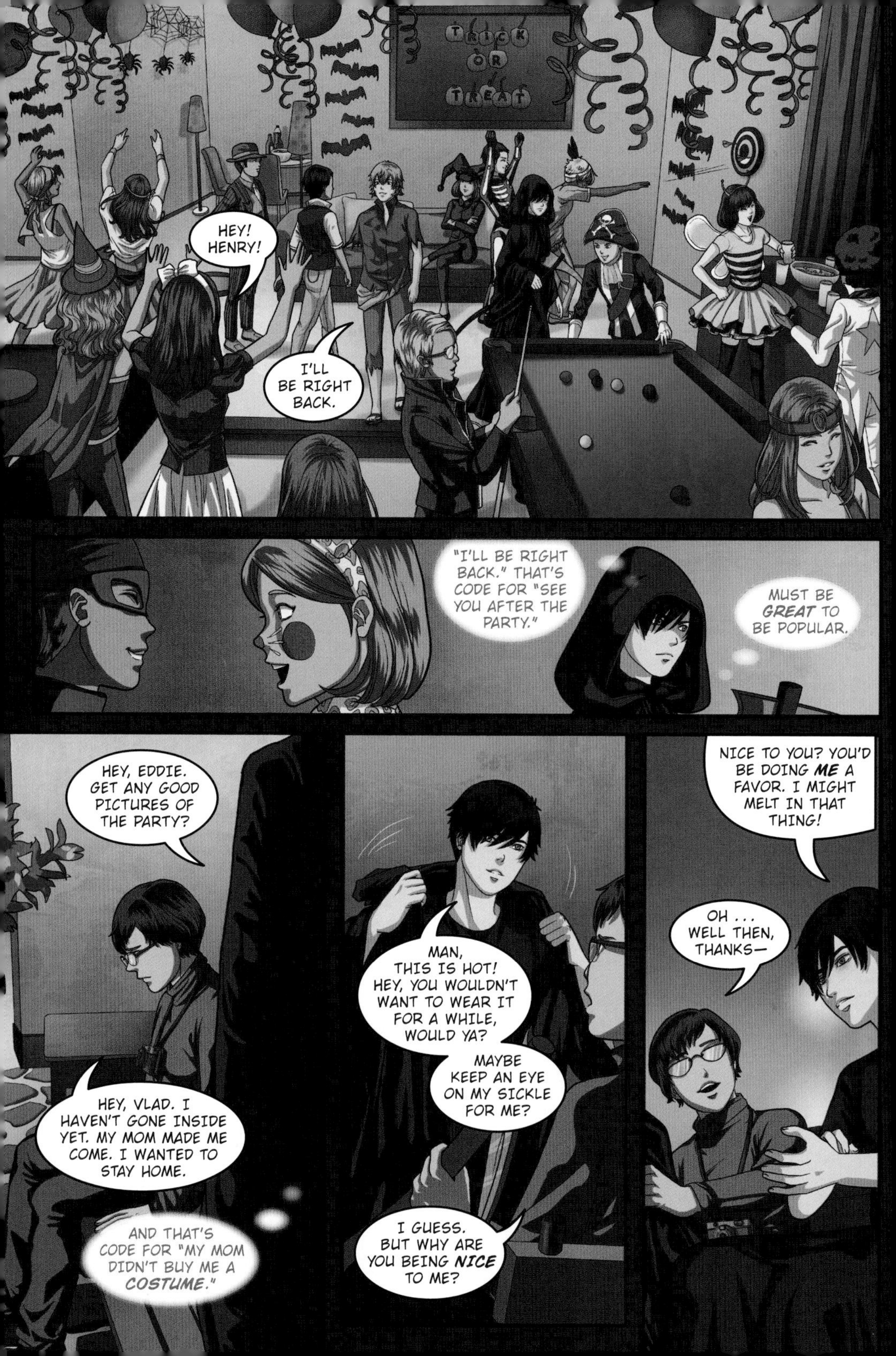
TRICK OR TREAT
HEY! HENRY!
I'LL BE RIGHT BACK.
"I'LL BE RIGHT BACK." THAT'S CODE FOR "SEE YOU AFTER THE PARTY."
MUST BE *GREAT* TO BE POPULAR.
HEY, EDDIE. GET ANY GOOD PICTURES OF THE PARTY?
HEY, VLAD. I HAVEN'T GONE INSIDE YET. MY MOM MADE ME COME. I WANTED TO STAY HOME.
AND THAT'S CODE FOR "MY MOM DIDN'T BUY ME A *COSTUME*."
MAN, THIS IS HOT! HEY, YOU WOULDN'T WANT TO WEAR IT FOR A WHILE, WOULD YA?
MAYBE KEEP AN EYE ON MY SICKLE FOR ME?
I GUESS. BUT WHY ARE YOU BEING *NICE* TO ME?
NICE TO YOU? YOU'D BE DOING *ME* A FAVOR. I MIGHT MELT IN THAT THING!
OH . . . WELL THEN, THANKS—

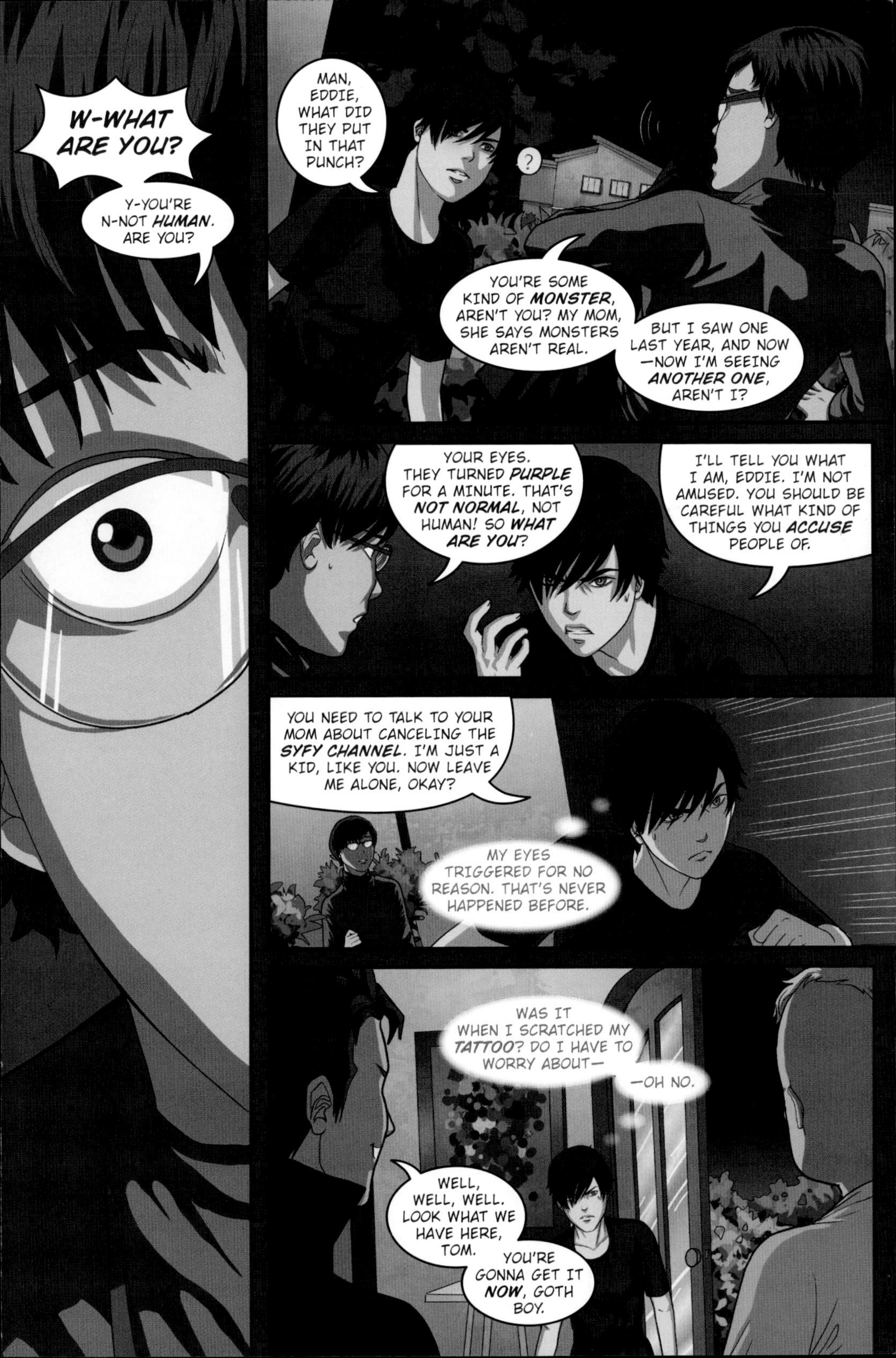
W-WHAT ARE YOU?
Y-YOU'RE N-NOT HUMAN. ARE YOU?
MAN, EDDIE, WHAT DID THEY PUT IN THAT PUNCH?
?
YOU'RE SOME KIND OF MONSTER, AREN'T YOU? MY MOM, SHE SAYS MONSTERS AREN'T REAL.
BUT I SAW ONE LAST YEAR, AND NOW —NOW I'M SEEING ANOTHER ONE, AREN'T I?
YOUR EYES. THEY TURNED PURPLE FOR A MINUTE. THAT'S NOT NORMAL, NOT HUMAN! SO WHAT ARE YOU?
I'LL TELL YOU WHAT I AM, EDDIE. I'M NOT AMUSED. YOU SHOULD BE CAREFUL WHAT KIND OF THINGS YOU ACCUSE PEOPLE OF.
YOU NEED TO TALK TO YOUR MOM ABOUT CANCELING THE SYFY CHANNEL. I'M JUST A KID, LIKE YOU. NOW LEAVE ME ALONE, OKAY?
MY EYES TRIGGERED FOR NO REASON. THAT'S NEVER HAPPENED BEFORE.
WAS IT WHEN I SCRATCHED MY TATTOO? DO I HAVE TO WORRY ABOUT—
—OH NO.
WELL, WELL, WELL. LOOK WHAT WE HAVE HERE, TOM.
YOU'RE GONNA GET IT NOW, GOTH BOY.

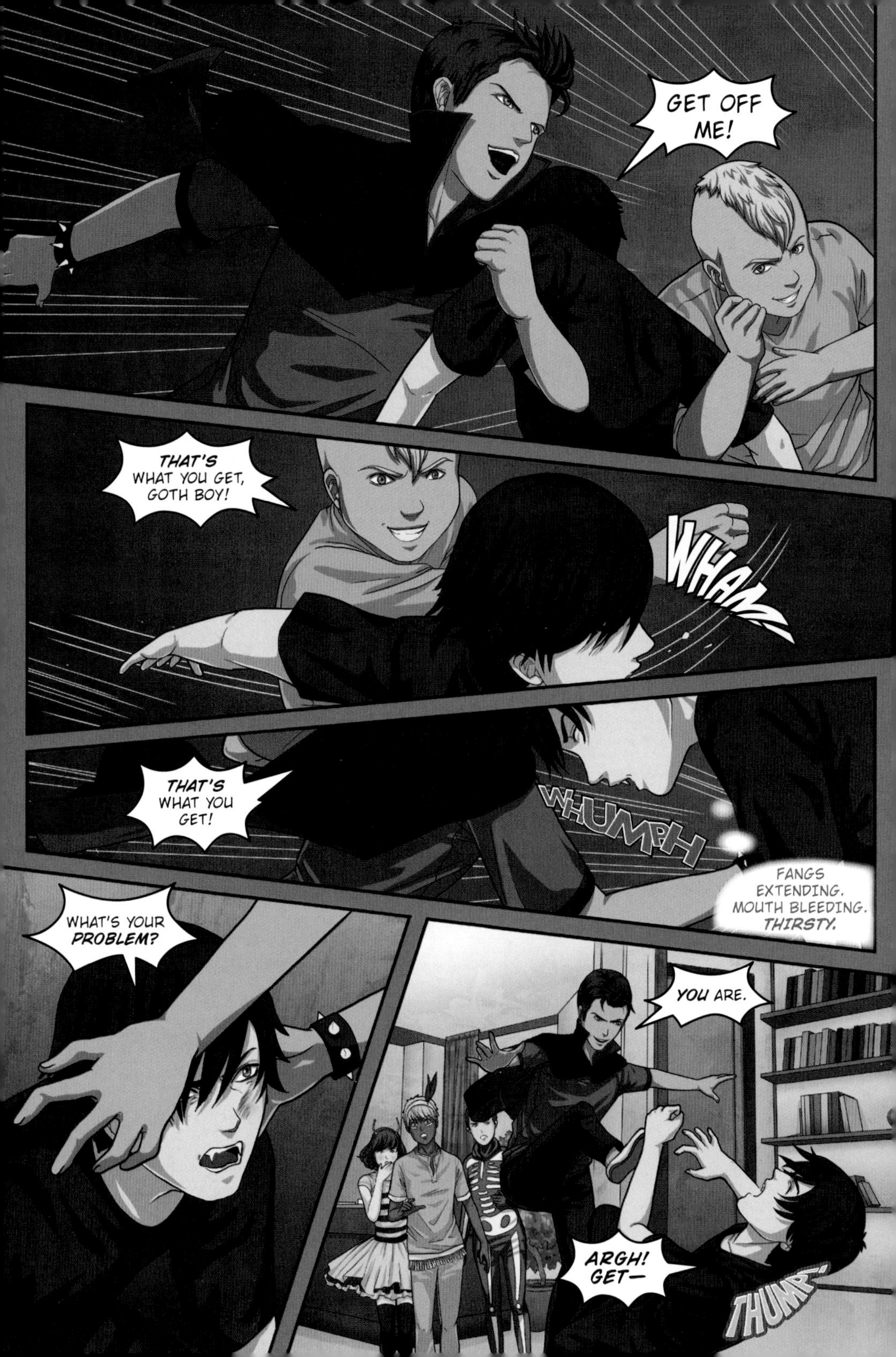
GET OFF ME!
THAT'S WHAT YOU GET, GOTH BOY!
WHAM
THAT'S WHAT YOU GET!
WHUMPH
FANGS EXTENDING. MOUTH BLEEDING. *THIRSTY.*
WHAT'S YOUR *PROBLEM?*
YOU ARE.
ARGH! GET—
THUMP

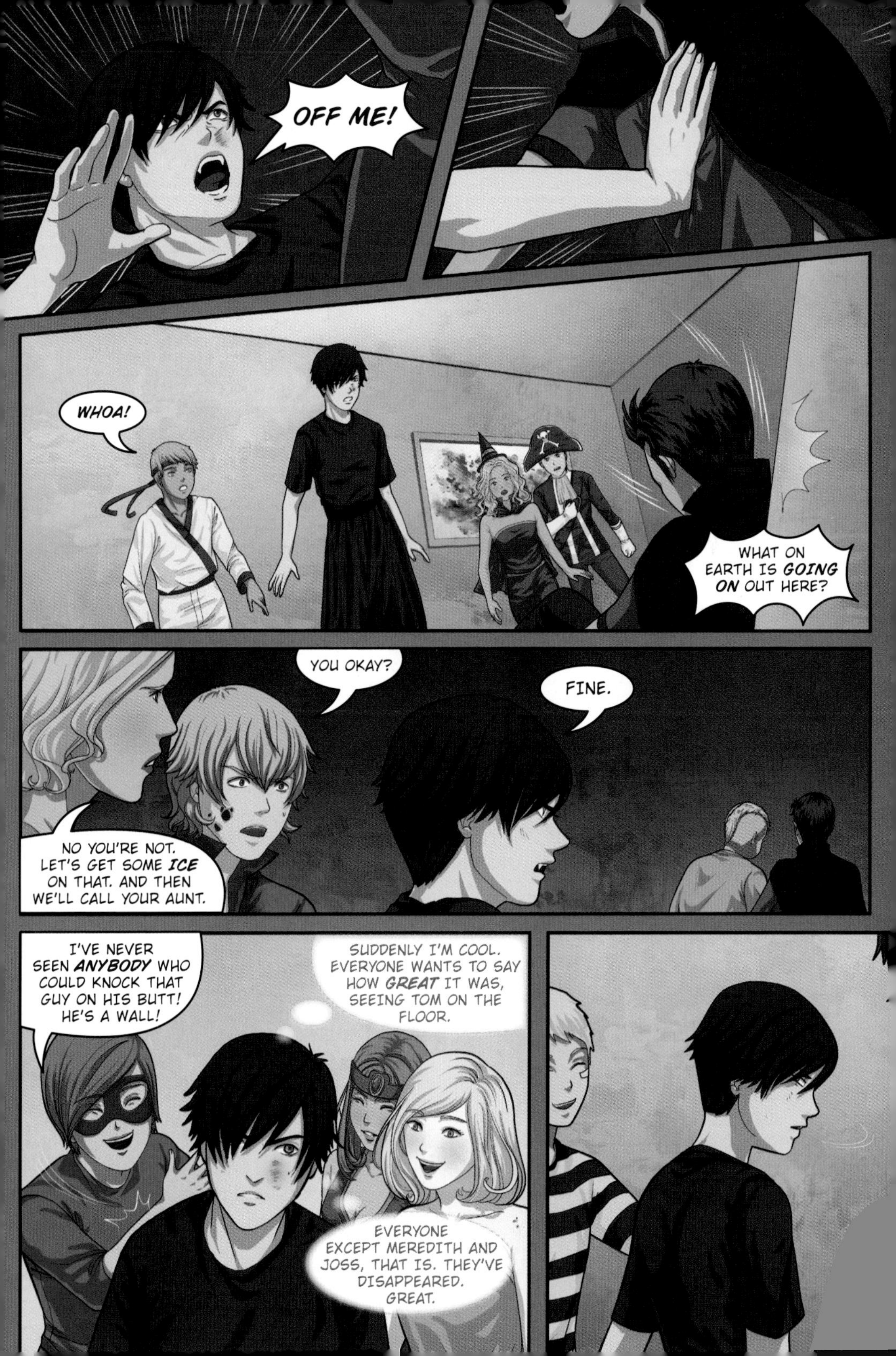
OFF ME!
WHOA!
WHAT ON EARTH IS GOING ON OUT HERE?
YOU OKAY?
FINE.
NO YOU'RE NOT. LET'S GET SOME ICE ON THAT. AND THEN WE'LL CALL YOUR AUNT.
I'VE NEVER SEEN ANYBODY WHO COULD KNOCK THAT GUY ON HIS BUTT! HE'S A WALL!
SUDDENLY I'M COOL. EVERYONE WANTS TO SAY HOW GREAT IT WAS, SEEING TOM ON THE FLOOR.
EVERYONE EXCEPT MEREDITH AND JOSS, THAT IS. THEY'VE DISAPPEARED. GREAT.

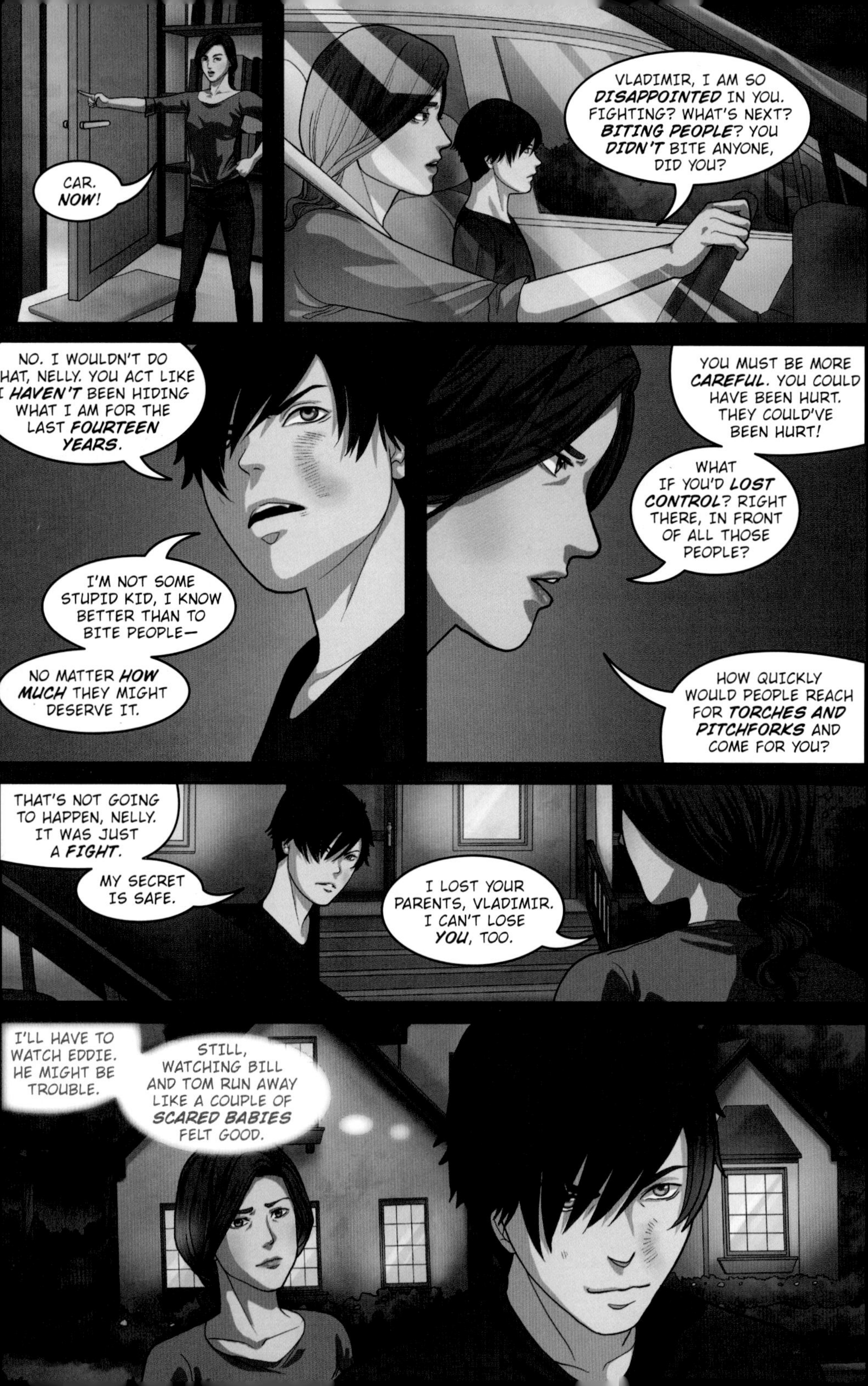
CAR. NOW!
VLADIMIR, I AM SO DISAPPOINTED IN YOU. FIGHTING? WHAT'S NEXT? BITING PEOPLE? YOU DIDN'T BITE ANYONE, DID YOU?
NO. I WOULDN'T DO THAT, NELLY. YOU ACT LIKE I HAVEN'T BEEN HIDING WHAT I AM FOR THE LAST FOURTEEN YEARS.
I'M NOT SOME STUPID KID, I KNOW BETTER THAN TO BITE PEOPLE—
NO MATTER HOW MUCH THEY MIGHT DESERVE IT.
YOU MUST BE MORE CAREFUL. YOU COULD HAVE BEEN HURT. THEY COULD'VE BEEN HURT!
WHAT IF YOU'D LOST CONTROL? RIGHT THERE, IN FRONT OF ALL THOSE PEOPLE?
HOW QUICKLY WOULD PEOPLE REACH FOR TORCHES AND PITCHFORKS AND COME FOR YOU?
THAT'S NOT GOING TO HAPPEN, NELLY. IT WAS JUST A FIGHT.
MY SECRET IS SAFE.
I LOST YOUR PARENTS, VLADIMIR. I CAN'T LOSE YOU, TOO.
I'LL HAVE TO WATCH EDDIE. HE MIGHT BE TROUBLE.
STILL, WATCHING BILL AND TOM RUN AWAY LIKE A COUPLE OF SCARED BABIES FELT GOOD.

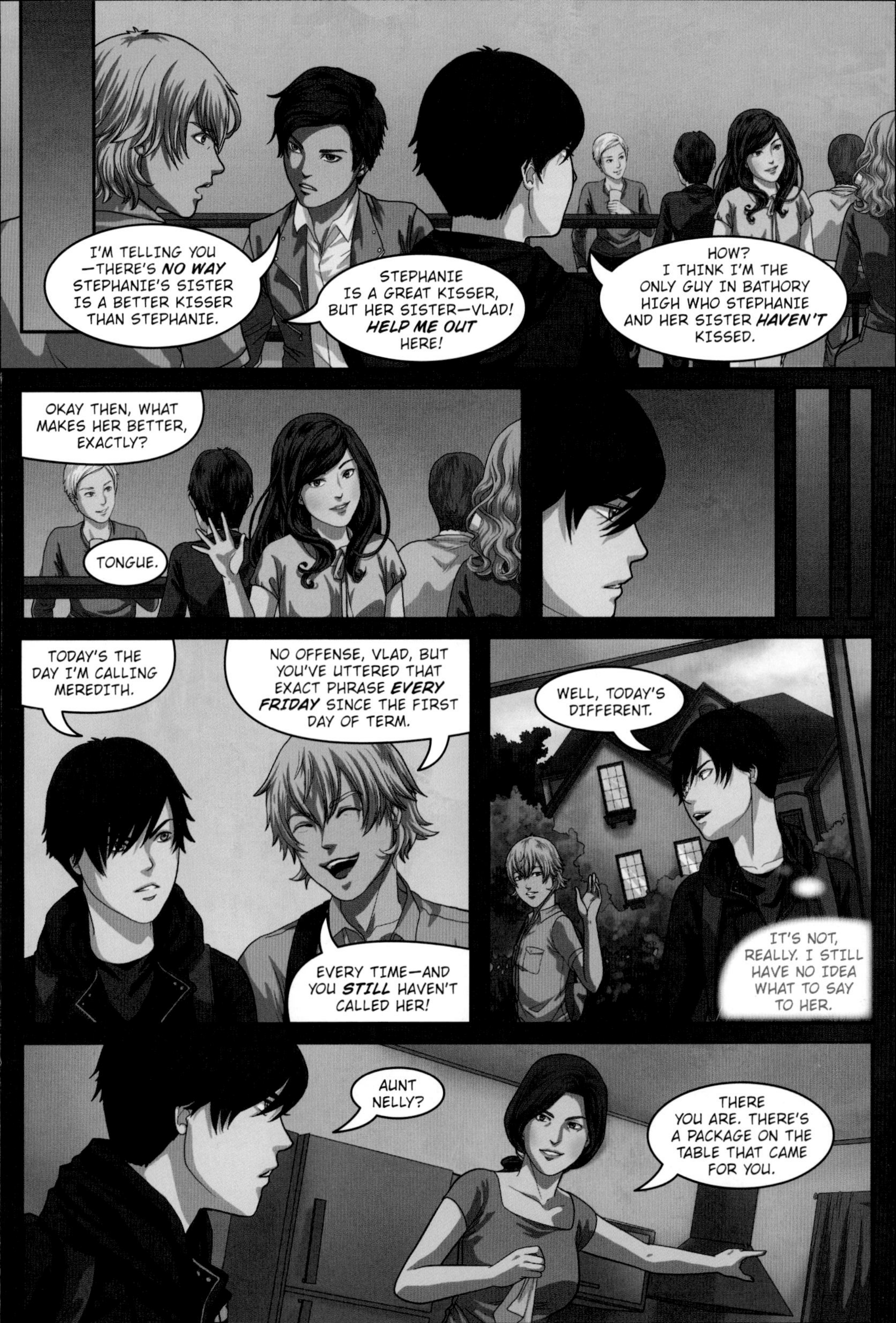
I'M TELLING YOU —THERE'S NO WAY STEPHANIE'S SISTER IS A BETTER KISSER THAN STEPHANIE.
STEPHANIE IS A GREAT KISSER, BUT HER SISTER—VLAD! HELP ME OUT HERE!
HOW? I THINK I'M THE ONLY GUY IN BATHORY HIGH WHO STEPHANIE AND HER SISTER HAVEN'T KISSED.
OKAY THEN, WHAT MAKES HER BETTER, EXACTLY?
TONGUE.
TODAY'S THE DAY I'M CALLING MEREDITH.
NO OFFENSE, VLAD, BUT YOU'VE UTTERED THAT EXACT PHRASE EVERY FRIDAY SINCE THE FIRST DAY OF TERM.
EVERY TIME—AND YOU STILL HAVEN'T CALLED HER!
WELL, TODAY'S DIFFERENT.
IT'S NOT, REALLY. I STILL HAVE NO IDEA WHAT TO SAY TO HER.
AUNT NELLY?
THERE YOU ARE. THERE'S A PACKAGE ON THE TABLE THAT CAME FOR YOU.

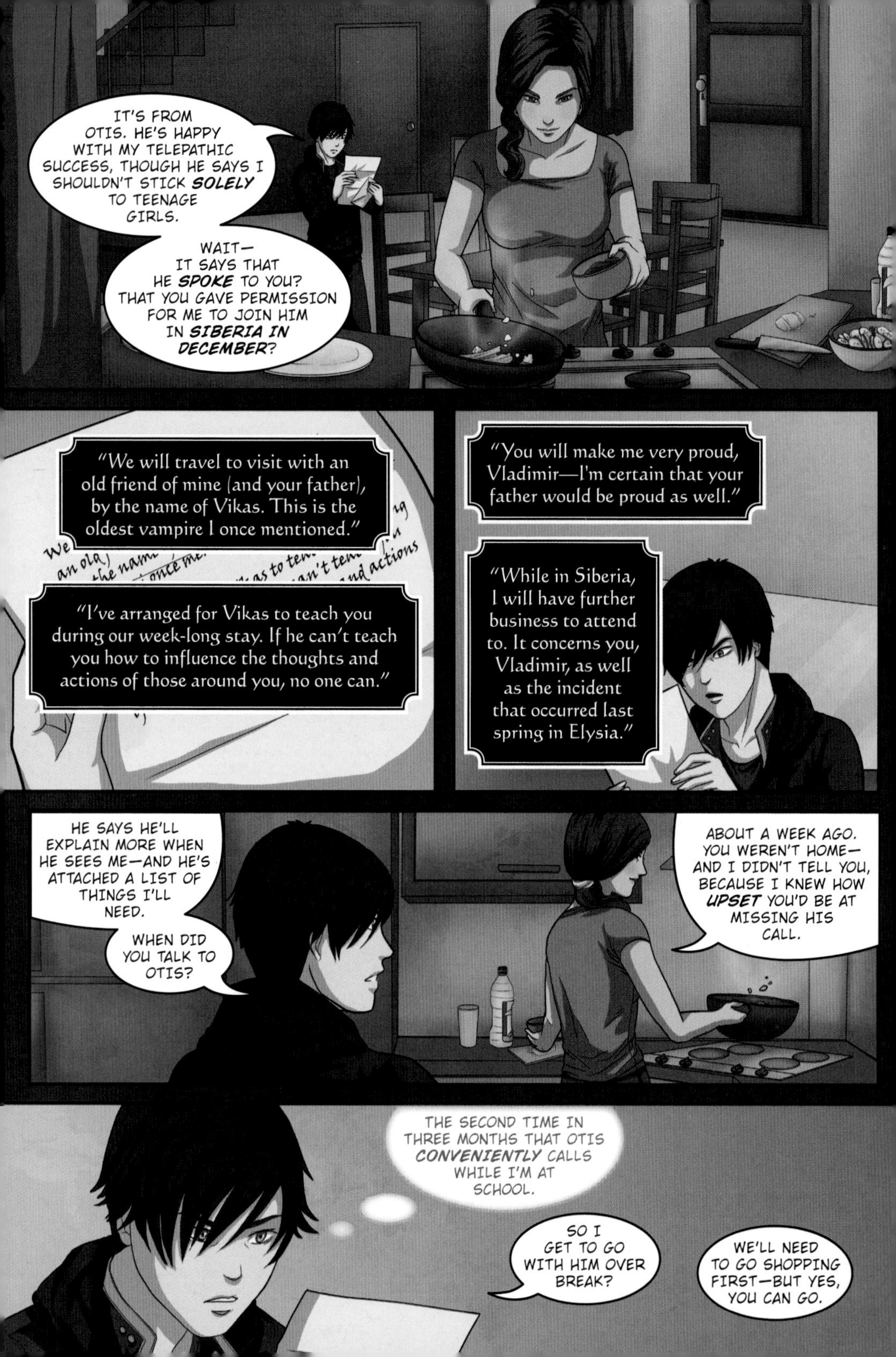
IT'S FROM OTIS. HE'S HAPPY WITH MY TELEPATHIC SUCCESS, THOUGH HE SAYS I SHOULDN'T STICK SOLELY TO TEENAGE GIRLS.
WAIT— IT SAYS THAT HE SPOKE TO YOU? THAT YOU GAVE PERMISSION FOR ME TO JOIN HIM IN SIBERIA IN DECEMBER?
"We will travel to visit with an old friend of mine (and your father), by the name of Vikas. This is the oldest vampire I once mentioned."
"I've arranged for Vikas to teach you during our week-long stay. If he can't teach you how to influence the thoughts and actions of those around you, no one can."
"You will make me very proud, Vladimir—I'm certain that your father would be proud as well."
"While in Siberia, I will have further business to attend to. It concerns you, Vladimir, as well as the incident that occurred last spring in Elysia."
HE SAYS HE'LL EXPLAIN MORE WHEN HE SEES ME—AND HE'S ATTACHED A LIST OF THINGS I'LL NEED.
WHEN DID YOU TALK TO OTIS?
ABOUT A WEEK AGO. YOU WEREN'T HOME—AND I DIDN'T TELL YOU, BECAUSE I KNEW HOW UPSET YOU'D BE AT MISSING HIS CALL.
THE SECOND TIME IN THREE MONTHS THAT OTIS CONVENIENTLY CALLS WHILE I'M AT SCHOOL.
SO I GET TO GO WITH HIM OVER BREAK?
WE'LL NEED TO GO SHOPPING FIRST—BUT YES, YOU CAN GO.

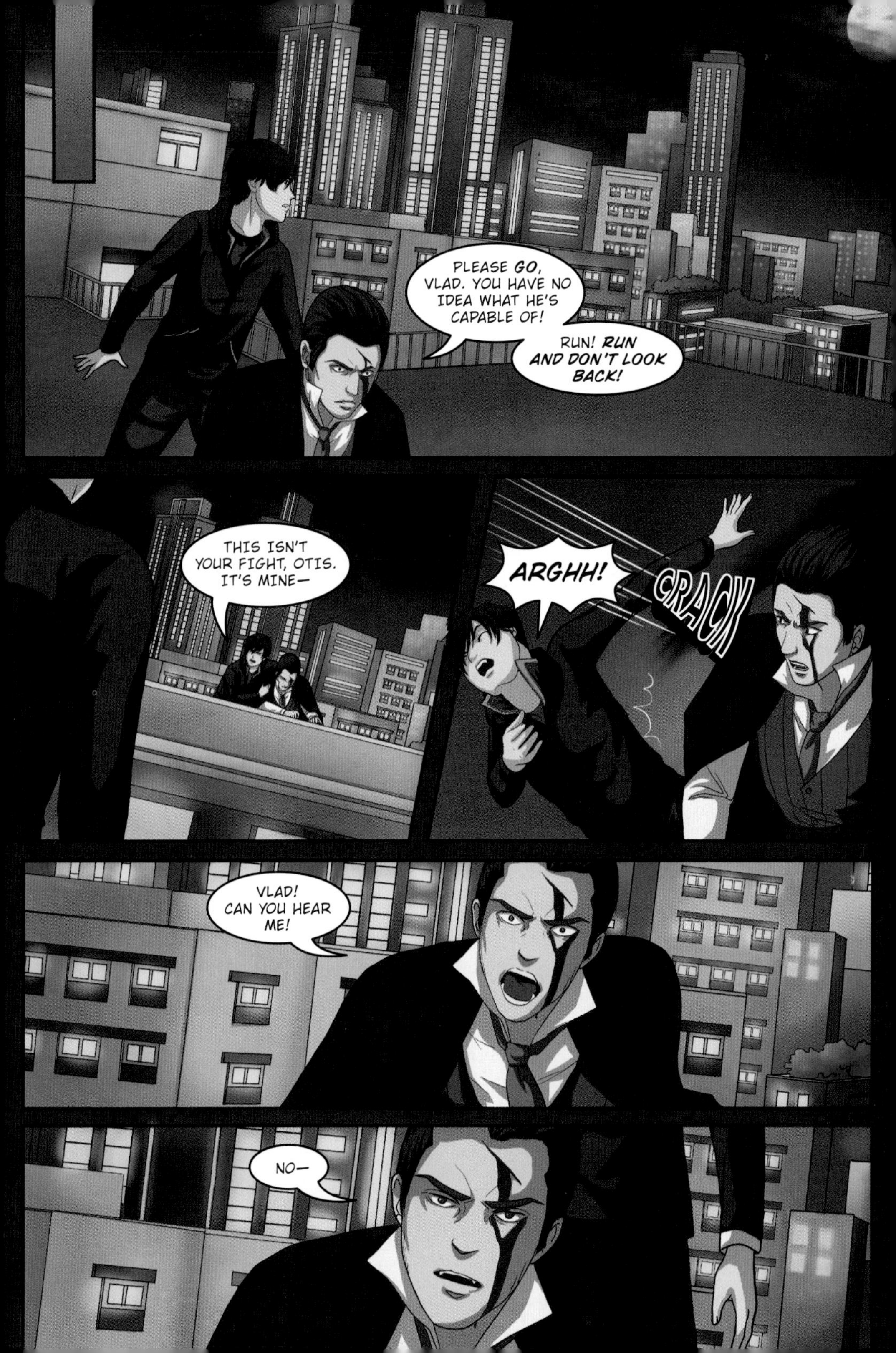
PLEASE GO, VLAD. YOU HAVE NO IDEA WHAT HE'S CAPABLE OF!
RUN! RUN AND DON'T LOOK BACK!
THIS ISN'T YOUR FIGHT, OTIS. IT'S MINE—
ARGHH!
CRACK
VLAD! CAN YOU HEAR ME!
NO—

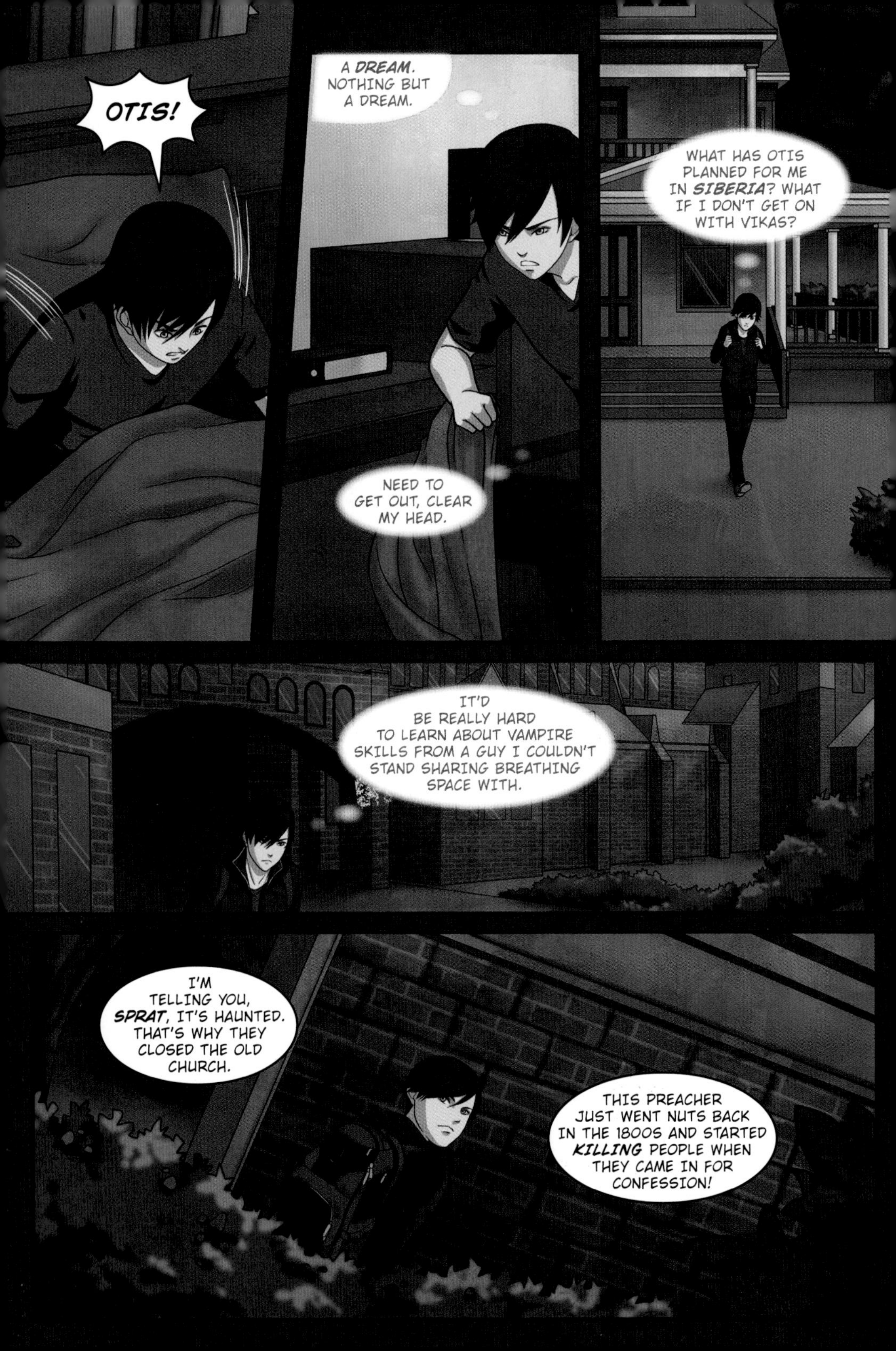
OTIS!
A DREAM. NOTHING BUT A DREAM.
NEED TO GET OUT, CLEAR MY HEAD.
WHAT HAS OTIS PLANNED FOR ME IN SIBERIA? WHAT IF I DON'T GET ON WITH VIKAS?
IT'D BE REALLY HARD TO LEARN ABOUT VAMPIRE SKILLS FROM A GUY I COULDN'T STAND SHARING BREATHING SPACE WITH.
I'M TELLING YOU, SPRAT, IT'S HAUNTED. THAT'S WHY THEY CLOSED THE OLD CHURCH.
THIS PREACHER JUST WENT NUTS BACK IN THE 1800S AND STARTED KILLING PEOPLE WHEN THEY CAME IN FOR CONFESSION!

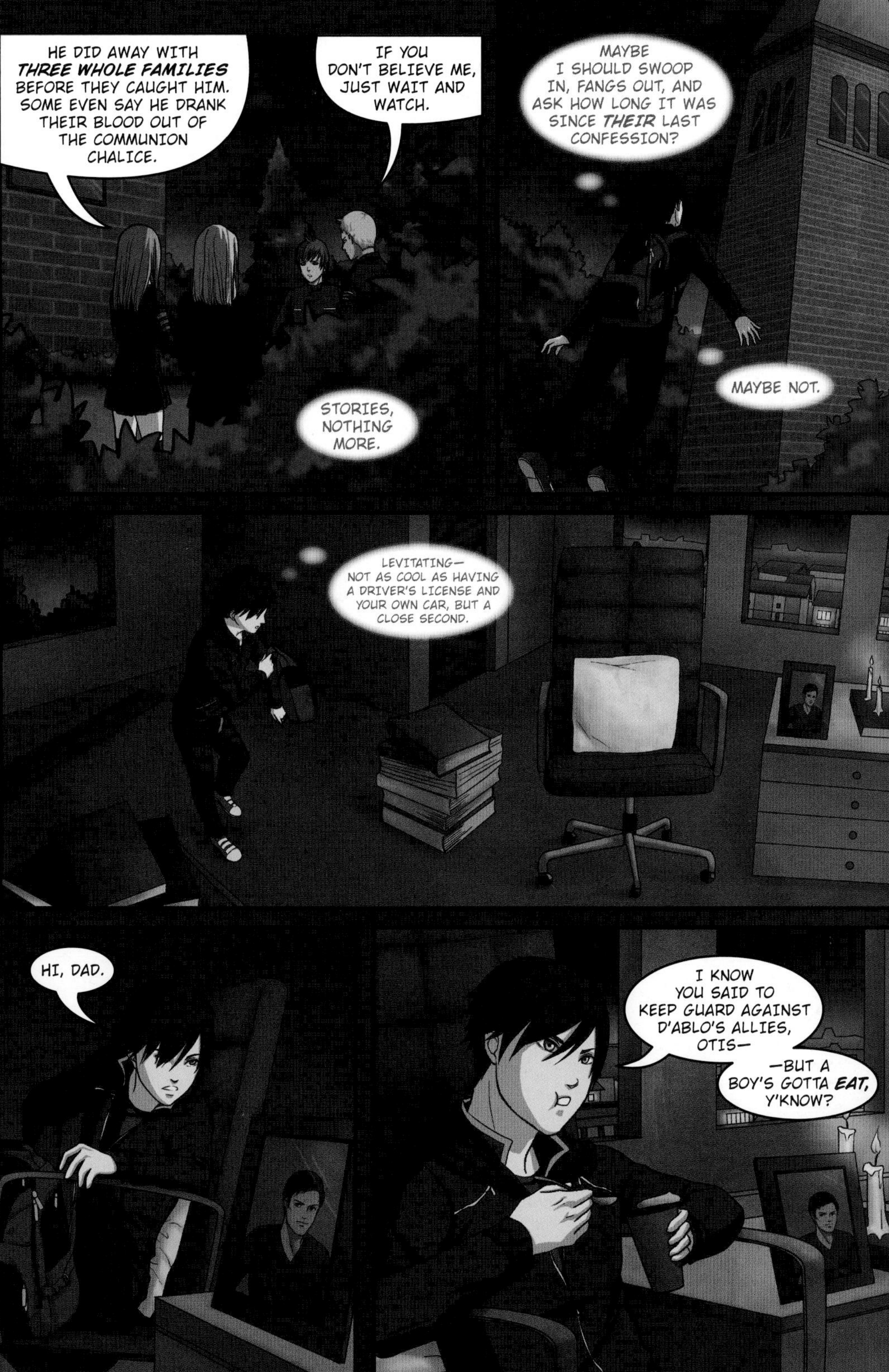
HE DID AWAY WITH THREE WHOLE FAMILIES BEFORE THEY CAUGHT HIM. SOME EVEN SAY HE DRANK THEIR BLOOD OUT OF THE COMMUNION CHALICE.
IF YOU DON'T BELIEVE ME, JUST WAIT AND WATCH.
STORIES, NOTHING MORE.
MAYBE I SHOULD SWOOP IN, FANGS OUT, AND ASK HOW LONG IT WAS SINCE THEIR LAST CONFESSION?
MAYBE NOT.
LEVITATING— NOT AS COOL AS HAVING A DRIVER'S LICENSE AND YOUR OWN CAR, BUT A CLOSE SECOND.
HI, DAD.
I KNOW YOU SAID TO KEEP GUARD AGAINST D'ABLO'S ALLIES, OTIS—
—BUT A BOY'S GOTTA EAT, Y'KNOW?

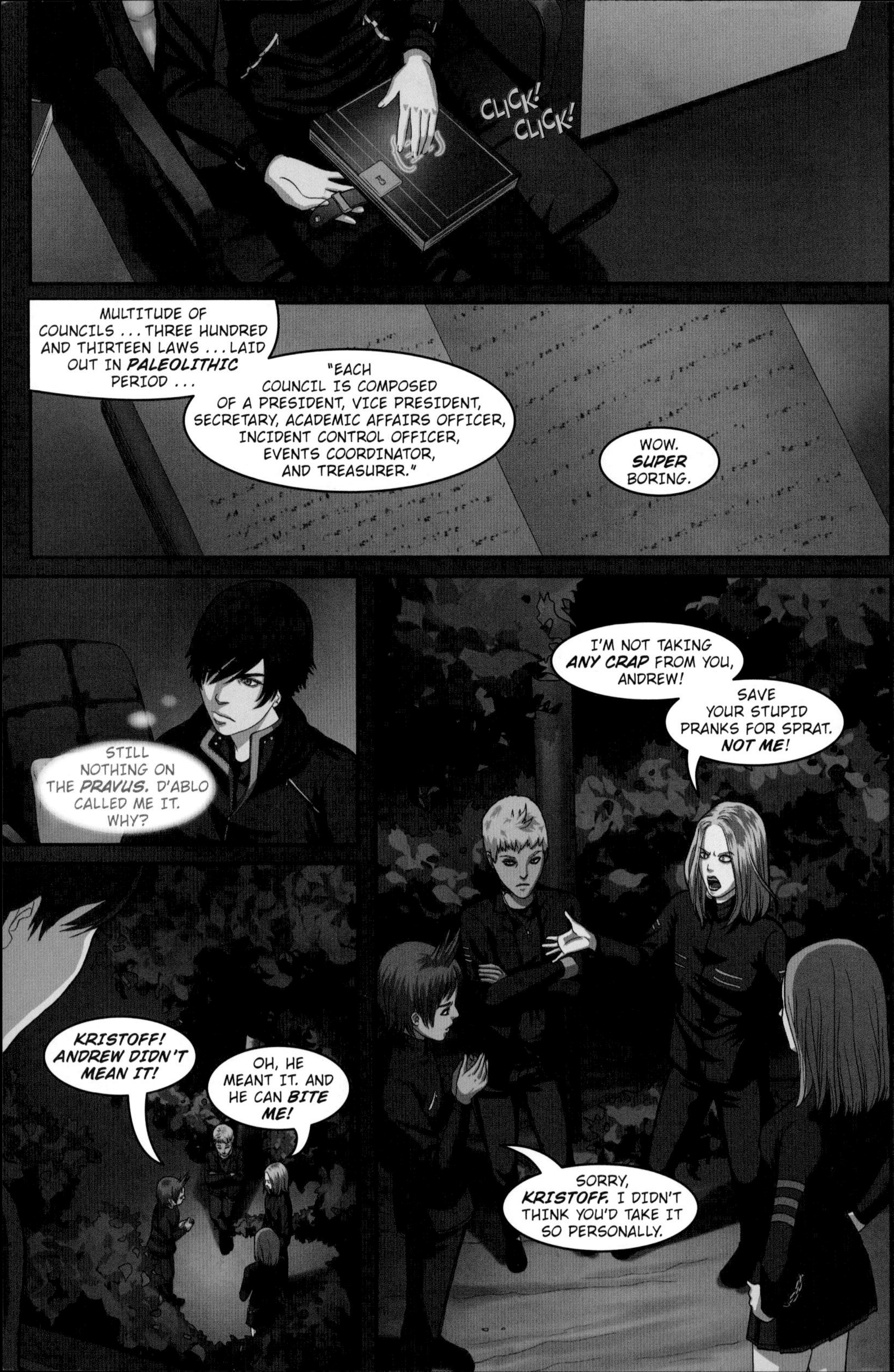

CLICK!
CLICK!
MULTITUDE OF COUNCILS . . . THREE HUNDRED AND THIRTEEN LAWS . . . LAID OUT IN PALEOLITHIC PERIOD . . .
"EACH COUNCIL IS COMPOSED OF A PRESIDENT, VICE PRESIDENT, SECRETARY, ACADEMIC AFFAIRS OFFICER, INCIDENT CONTROL OFFICER, EVENTS COORDINATOR, AND TREASURER."
WOW. SUPER BORING.
STILL NOTHING ON THE PRAVUS. D'ABLO CALLED ME IT. WHY?
I'M NOT TAKING ANY CRAP FROM YOU, ANDREW!
SAVE YOUR STUPID PRANKS FOR SPRAT. NOT ME!
KRISTOFF! ANDREW DIDN'T MEAN IT!
OH, HE MEANT IT. AND HE CAN BITE ME!
SORRY, KRISTOFF. I DIDN'T THINK YOU'D TAKE IT SO PERSONALLY.

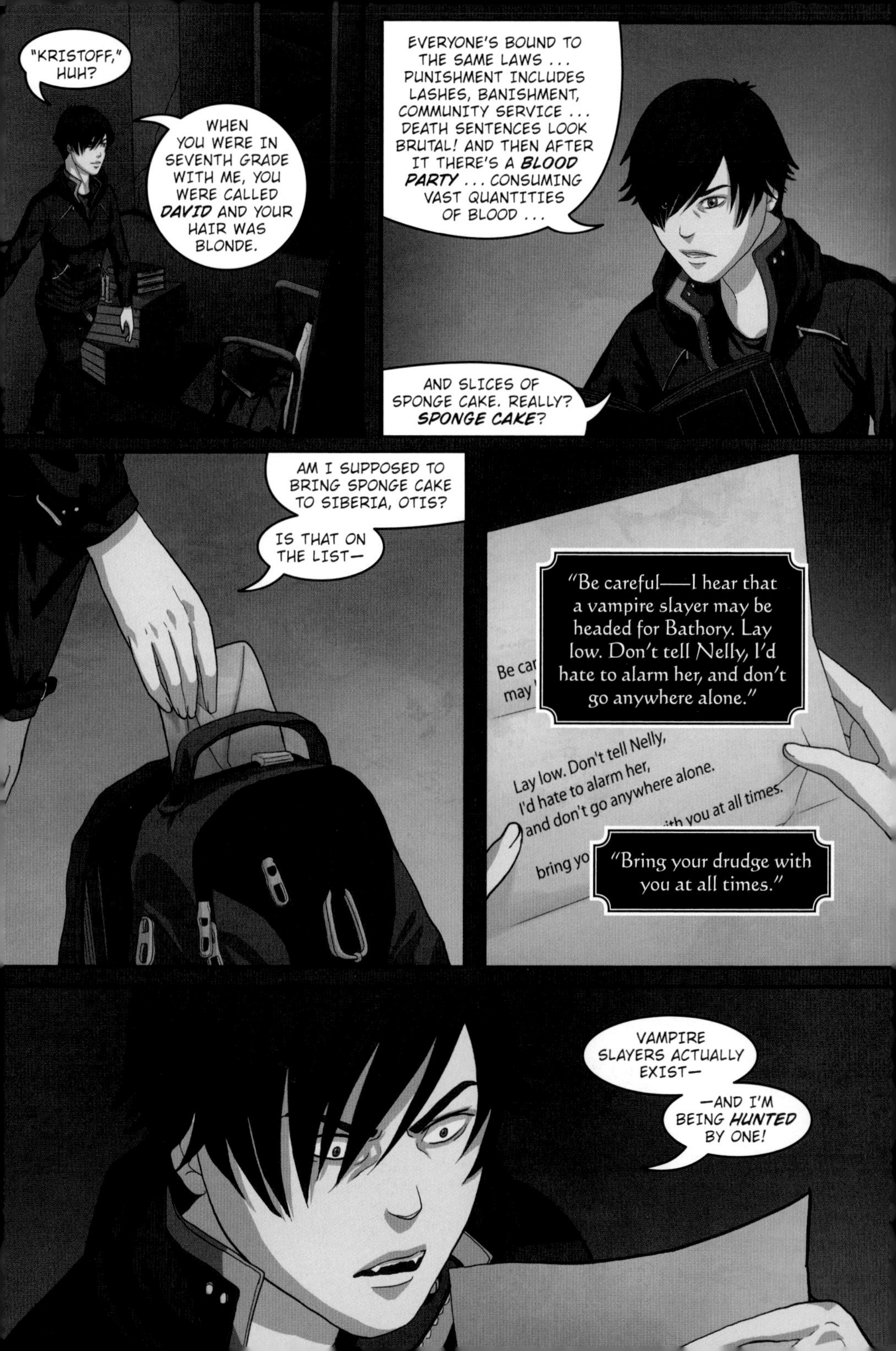
"KRISTOFF," HUH?
WHEN YOU WERE IN SEVENTH GRADE WITH ME, YOU WERE CALLED *DAVID* AND YOUR HAIR WAS BLONDE.
EVERYONE'S BOUND TO THE SAME LAWS . . . PUNISHMENT INCLUDES LASHES, BANISHMENT, COMMUNITY SERVICE . . . DEATH SENTENCES LOOK BRUTAL! AND THEN AFTER IT THERE'S A *BLOOD PARTY* . . . CONSUMING VAST QUANTITIES OF BLOOD . . .
AND SLICES OF SPONGE CAKE. REALLY? *SPONGE CAKE*?
AM I SUPPOSED TO BRING SPONGE CAKE TO SIBERIA, OTIS?
IS THAT ON THE LIST—
"Be careful—I hear that a vampire slayer may be headed for Bathory. Lay low. Don't tell Nelly, I'd hate to alarm her, and don't go anywhere alone."
Lay low. Don't tell Nelly,
I'd hate to alarm her,
and don't go anywhere alone.
"Bring your drudge with you at all times."
VAMPIRE SLAYERS ACTUALLY EXIST—
—AND I'M BEING *HUNTED* BY ONE!

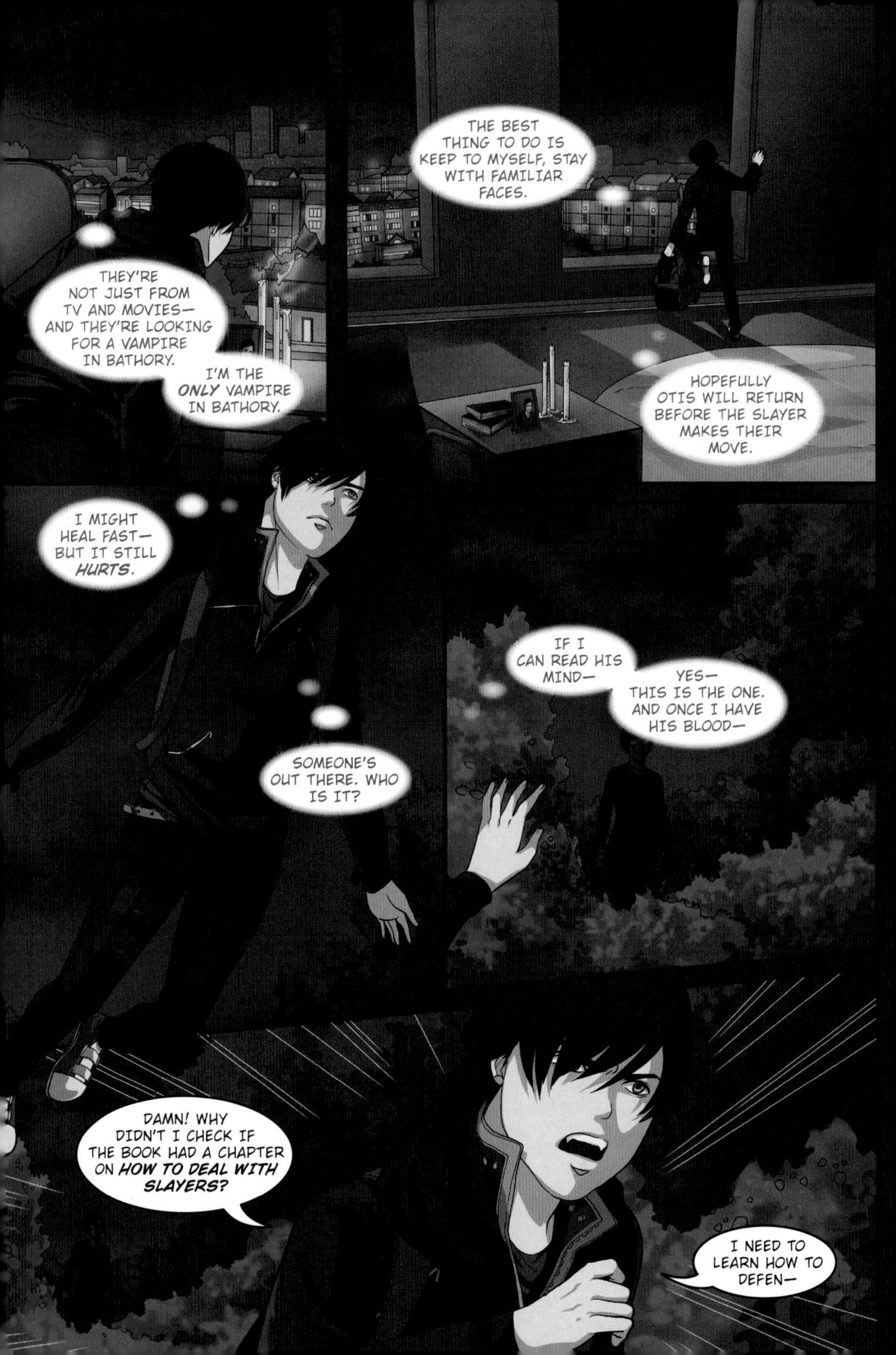
THEY'RE NOT JUST FROM TV AND MOVIES— AND THEY'RE LOOKING FOR A VAMPIRE IN BATHORY.
I'M THE *ONLY* VAMPIRE IN BATHORY.
THE BEST THING TO DO IS KEEP TO MYSELF, STAY WITH FAMILIAR FACES.
HOPEFULLY OTIS WILL RETURN BEFORE THE SLAYER MAKES THEIR MOVE.
I MIGHT HEAL FAST— BUT IT STILL *HURTS*.
SOMEONE'S OUT THERE. WHO IS IT?
IF I CAN READ HIS MIND—
YES— THIS IS THE ONE. AND ONCE I HAVE HIS BLOOD—
DAMN! WHY DIDN'T I CHECK IF THE BOOK HAD A CHAPTER ON *HOW TO DEAL WITH SLAYERS?*
I NEED TO LEARN HOW TO DEFEN—

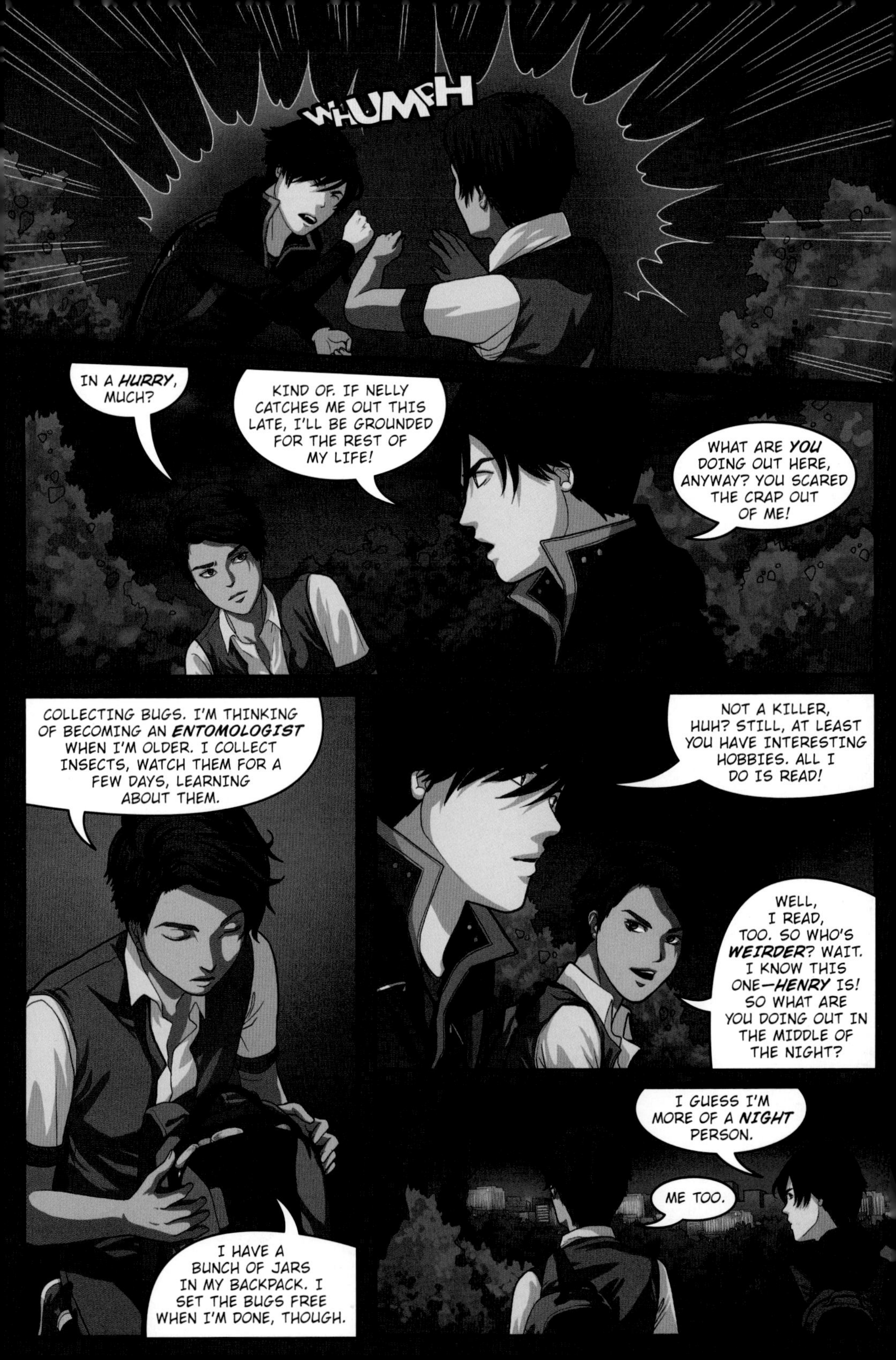
WHUMPH
IN A HURRY, MUCH?
KIND OF. IF NELLY CATCHES ME OUT THIS LATE, I'LL BE GROUNDED FOR THE REST OF MY LIFE!
WHAT ARE YOU DOING OUT HERE, ANYWAY? YOU SCARED THE CRAP OUT OF ME!
COLLECTING BUGS. I'M THINKING OF BECOMING AN ENTOMOLOGIST WHEN I'M OLDER. I COLLECT INSECTS, WATCH THEM FOR A FEW DAYS, LEARNING ABOUT THEM.
I HAVE A BUNCH OF JARS IN MY BACKPACK. I SET THE BUGS FREE WHEN I'M DONE, THOUGH.
NOT A KILLER, HUH? STILL, AT LEAST YOU HAVE INTERESTING HOBBIES. ALL I DO IS READ!
WELL, I READ, TOO. SO WHO'S WEIRDER? WAIT. I KNOW THIS ONE—HENRY IS! SO WHAT ARE YOU DOING OUT IN THE MIDDLE OF THE NIGHT?
I GUESS I'M MORE OF A NIGHT PERSON.
ME TOO.

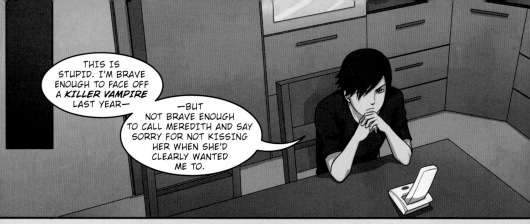

THIS IS STUPID. I'M BRAVE ENOUGH TO FACE OFF A *KILLER VAMPIRE* LAST YEAR—

—BUT NOT BRAVE ENOUGH TO CALL MEREDITH AND SAY SORRY FOR NOT KISSING HER WHEN SHE'D CLEARLY WANTED ME TO.

MAYBE SHE'S NOT HOME. MAYBE SHE'S ALREADY LEFT FOR SCHOOL—

-click- HELLO?

RINNNG

HI, MEREDITH, THIS IS VLAD—I JUST WANTED TO CALL AND . . .

. . . AND . . .

I WANTED TO ASK YOU IF YOU HAD A DATE TO THE *SNOW BALL* YET.

VLAD, ARE YOU ASKING ME OUT?

IT'S JUST THAT— WELL, I ALREADY **HAVE** A DATE TO THE SNOW BALL.

YOU KNOW, WHEN YOU DIDN'T CALL AFTER THE **FREEDOM FEST** DANCE, I WASN'T SURE YOU WERE STILL INTERESTED IN GOING OUT WITH ME. SO, I ASKED SOMEONE ELSE.

ME? GO TO A SEMIFORMAL DANCE? THAT'S JUST NUTS. NO, I WAS JUST ASKING FOR . . . A *FRIEND!*

I HAVE WAY TOO MUCH STUFF TO DO! ANYWAY, I GUESS I'LL SEE YA AROUND.

YEAH . . . SEE YA.

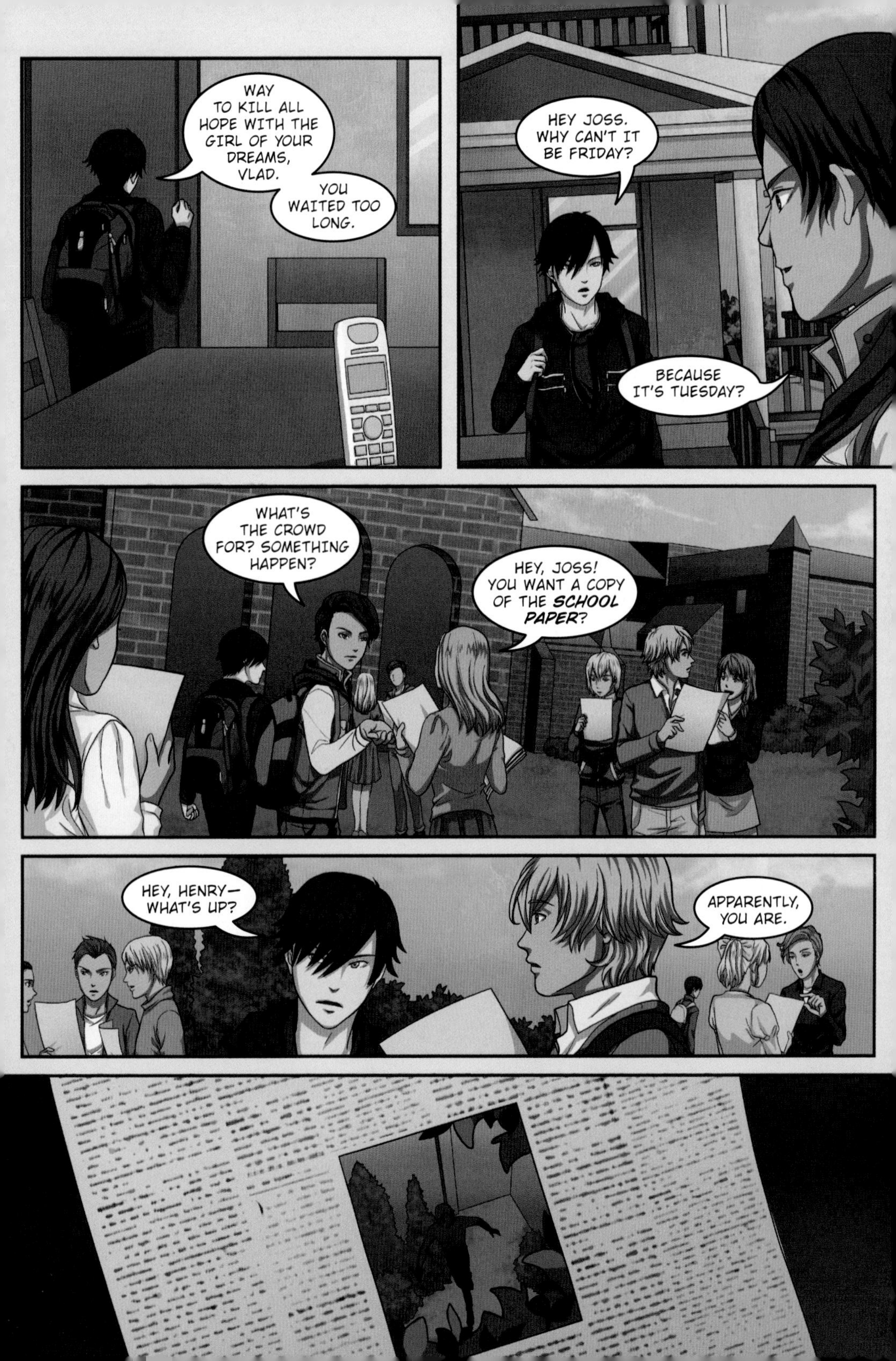
WAY TO KILL ALL HOPE WITH THE GIRL OF YOUR DREAMS, VLAD.
YOU WAITED TOO LONG.
HEY JOSS. WHY CAN'T IT BE FRIDAY?
BECAUSE IT'S TUESDAY?
WHAT'S THE CROWD FOR? SOMETHING HAPPEN?
HEY, JOSS! YOU WANT A COPY OF THE SCHOOL PAPER?
HEY, HENRY— WHAT'S UP?
APPARENTLY, YOU ARE.

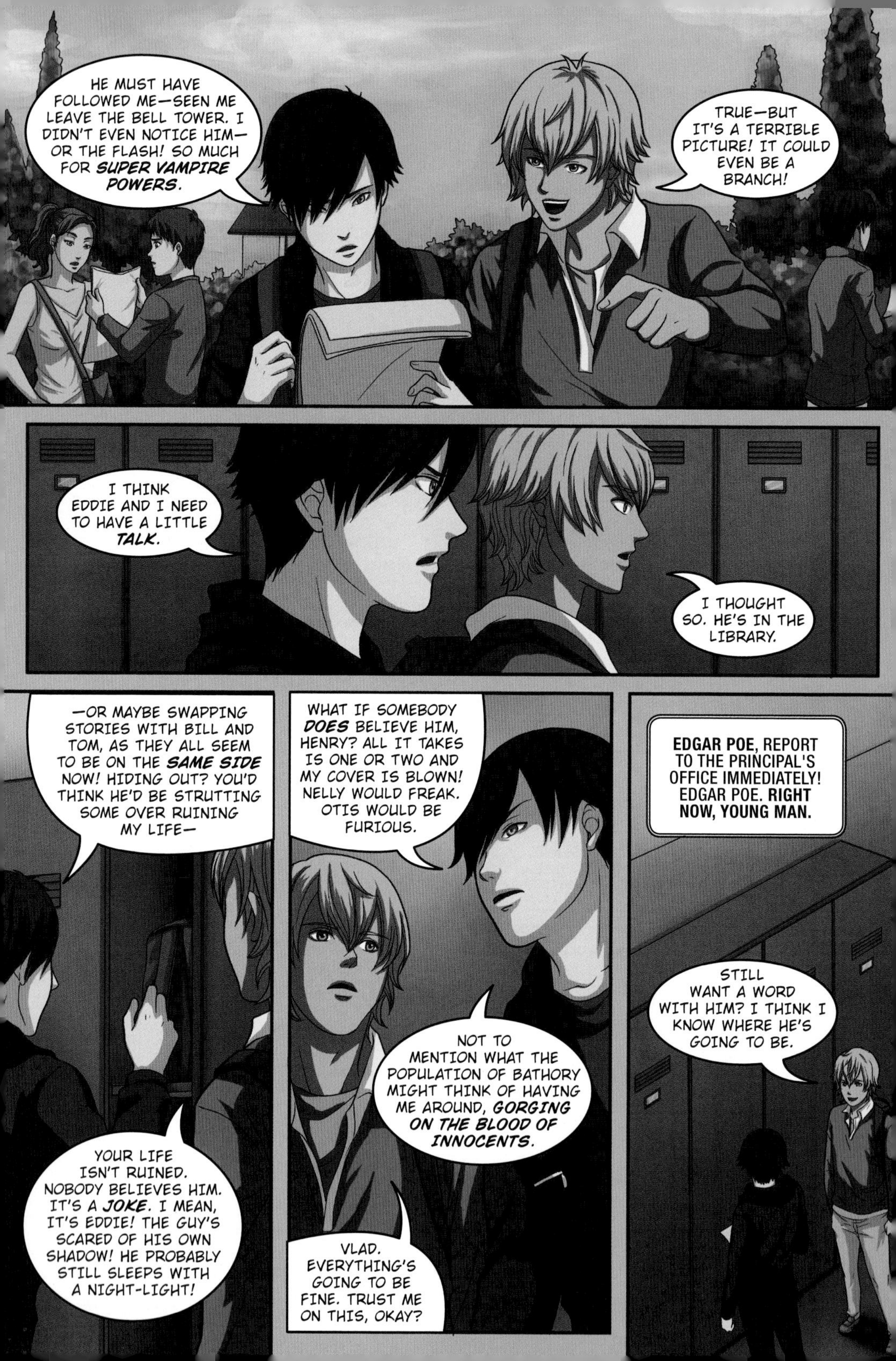
HE MUST HAVE FOLLOWED ME—SEEN ME LEAVE THE BELL TOWER. I DIDN'T EVEN NOTICE HIM—OR THE FLASH! SO MUCH FOR *SUPER VAMPIRE POWERS*.
TRUE—BUT IT'S A TERRIBLE PICTURE! IT COULD EVEN BE A BRANCH!
I THINK EDDIE AND I NEED TO HAVE A LITTLE *TALK*.
I THOUGHT SO. HE'S IN THE LIBRARY.
—OR MAYBE SWAPPING STORIES WITH BILL AND TOM, AS THEY ALL SEEM TO BE ON THE *SAME SIDE* NOW! HIDING OUT? YOU'D THINK HE'D BE STRUTTING SOME OVER RUINING MY LIFE—
YOUR LIFE ISN'T RUINED. NOBODY BELIEVES HIM. IT'S A *JOKE*. I MEAN, IT'S EDDIE! THE GUY'S SCARED OF HIS OWN SHADOW! HE PROBABLY STILL SLEEPS WITH A NIGHT-LIGHT!
WHAT IF SOMEBODY *DOES* BELIEVE HIM, HENRY? ALL IT TAKES IS ONE OR TWO AND MY COVER IS BLOWN! NELLY WOULD FREAK. OTIS WOULD BE FURIOUS.
NOT TO MENTION WHAT THE POPULATION OF BATHORY MIGHT THINK OF HAVING ME AROUND, *GORGING ON THE BLOOD OF INNOCENTS*.
VLAD. EVERYTHING'S GOING TO BE FINE. TRUST ME ON THIS, OKAY?
EDGAR POE, REPORT TO THE PRINCIPAL'S OFFICE IMMEDIATELY! EDGAR POE. **RIGHT NOW, YOUNG MAN.**
STILL WANT A WORD WITH HIM? I THINK I KNOW WHERE HE'S GOING TO BE.

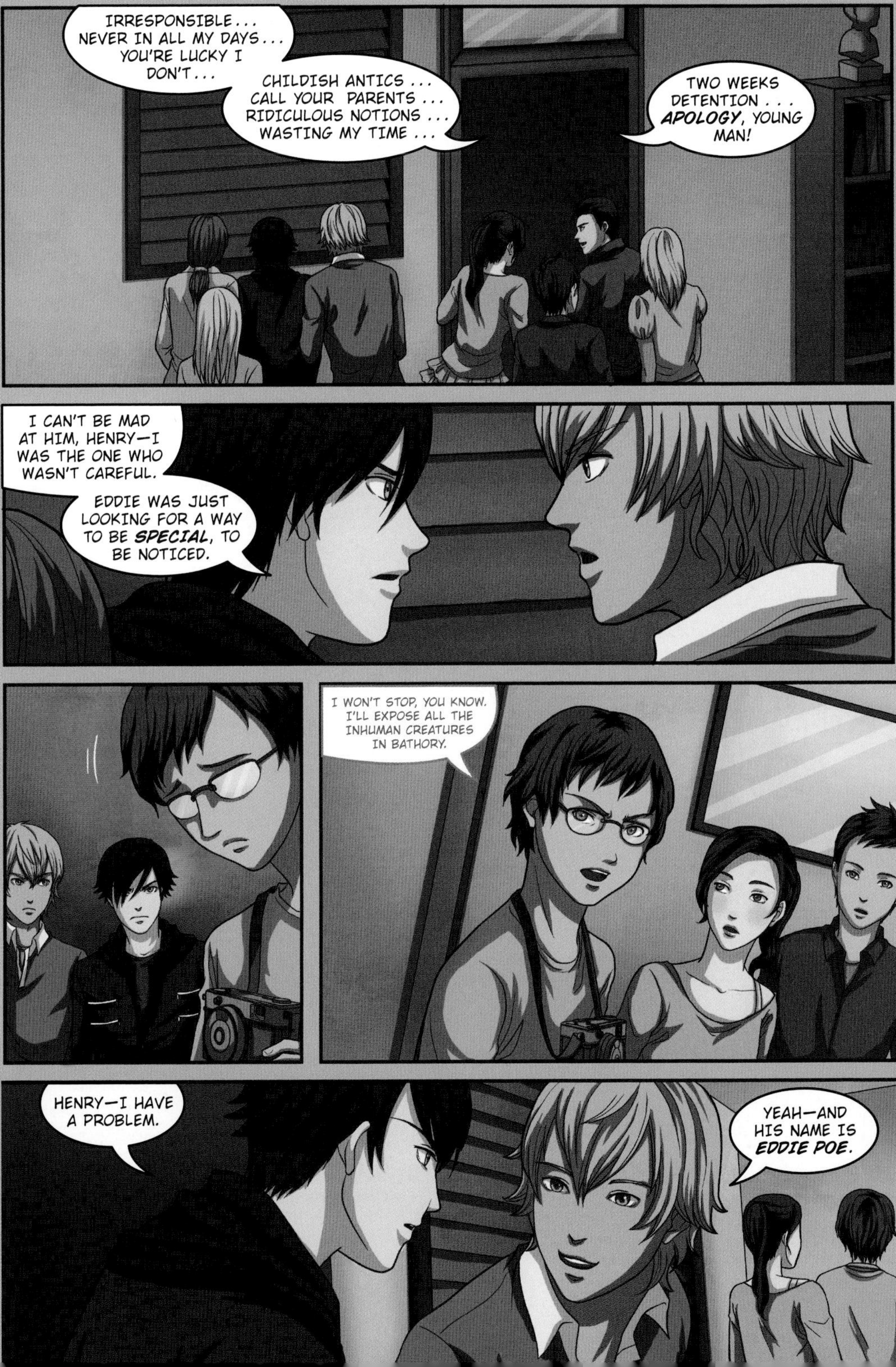
IRRESPONSIBLE... NEVER IN ALL MY DAYS... YOU'RE LUCKY I DON'T...
CHILDISH ANTICS ... CALL YOUR PARENTS ... RIDICULOUS NOTIONS ... WASTING MY TIME ...
TWO WEEKS DETENTION . . . **APOLOGY**, YOUNG MAN!
I CAN'T BE MAD AT HIM, HENRY—I WAS THE ONE WHO WASN'T CAREFUL.
EDDIE WAS JUST LOOKING FOR A WAY TO BE **SPECIAL**, TO BE NOTICED.
I WON'T STOP, YOU KNOW. I'LL EXPOSE ALL THE INHUMAN CREATURES IN BATHORY.
HENRY—I HAVE A PROBLEM.
YEAH—AND HIS NAME IS **EDDIE POE**.

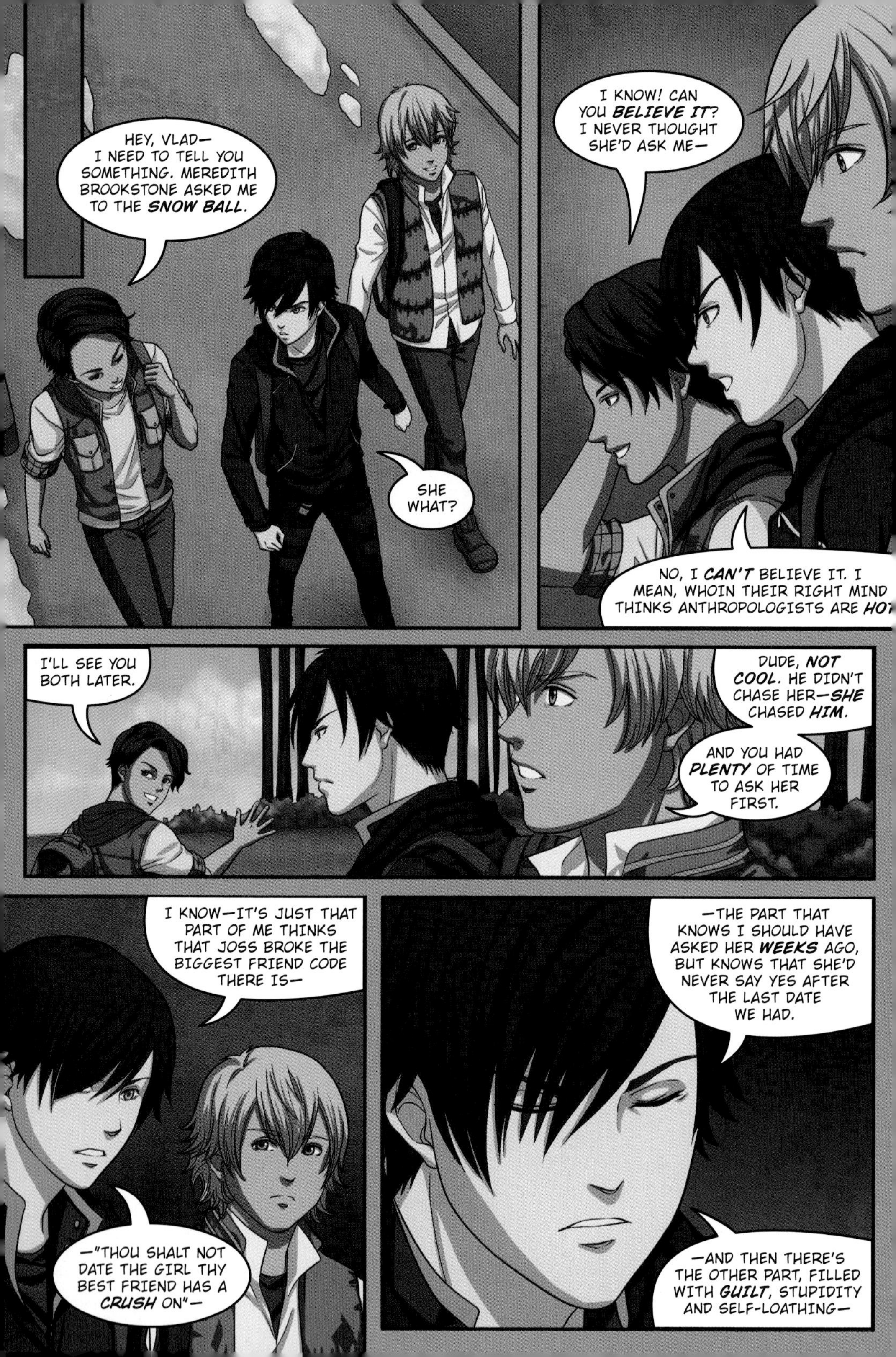
HEY, VLAD—
I NEED TO TELL YOU
SOMETHING. MEREDITH
BROOKSTONE ASKED ME
TO THE SNOW BALL.
SHE WHAT?
I KNOW! CAN YOU BELIEVE IT? I NEVER THOUGHT SHE'D ASK ME—
NO, I CAN'T BELIEVE IT. I MEAN, WHOIN THEIR RIGHT MIND THINKS ANTHROPOLOGISTS ARE HO
I'LL SEE YOU BOTH LATER.
DUDE, NOT COOL. HE DIDN'T CHASE HER—SHE CHASED HIM.
AND YOU HAD PLENTY OF TIME TO ASK HER FIRST.
I KNOW—IT'S JUST THAT PART OF ME THINKS THAT JOSS BROKE THE BIGGEST FRIEND CODE THERE IS—
—"THOU SHALT NOT DATE THE GIRL THY BEST FRIEND HAS A CRUSH ON"—
—THE PART THAT KNOWS I SHOULD HAVE ASKED HER WEEKS AGO, BUT KNOWS THAT SHE'D NEVER SAY YES AFTER THE LAST DATE WE HAD.
—AND THEN THERE'S THE OTHER PART, FILLED WITH GUILT, STUPIDITY AND SELF-LOATHING—

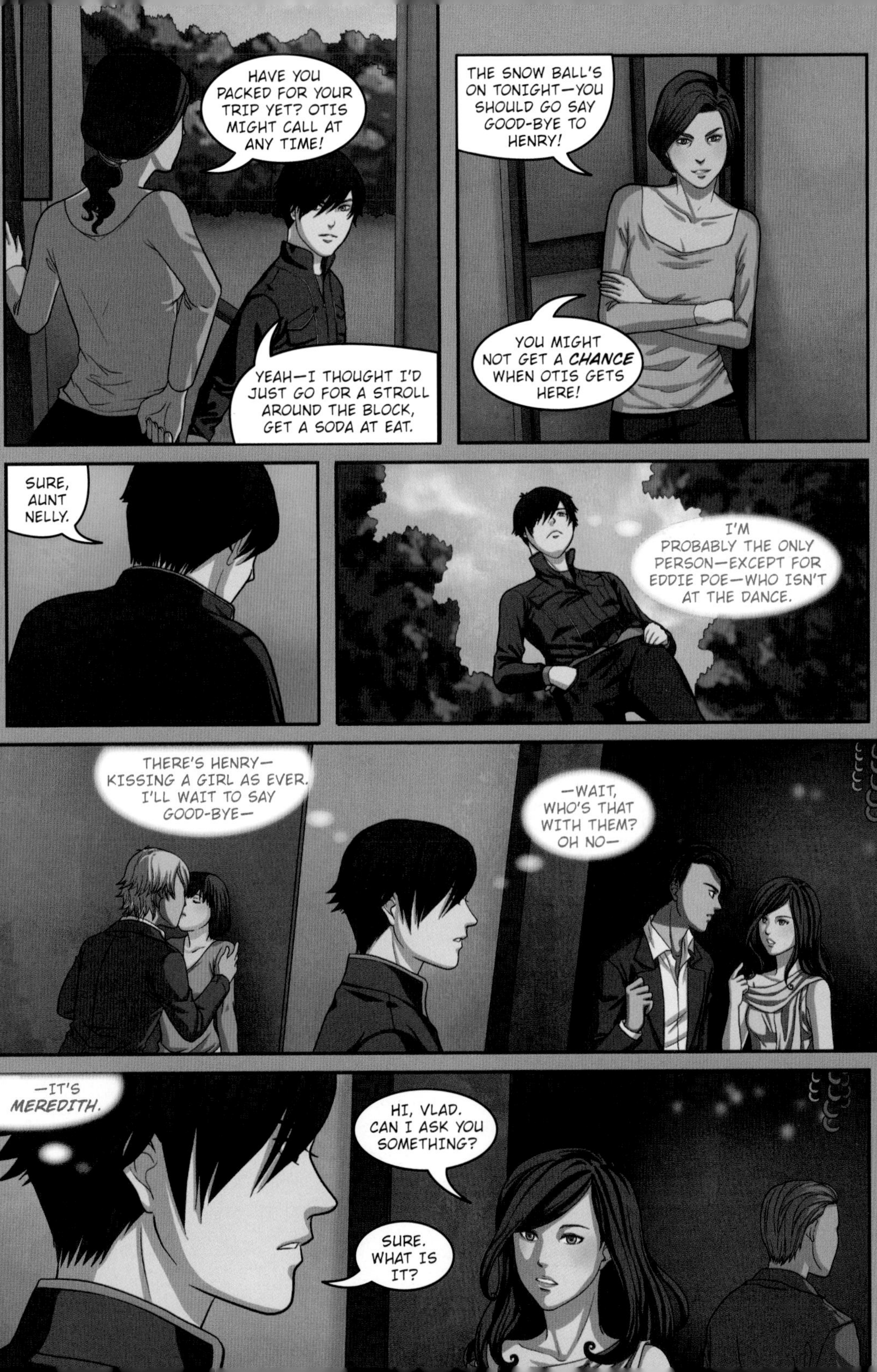
HAVE YOU PACKED FOR YOUR TRIP YET? OTIS MIGHT CALL AT ANY TIME!
YEAH—I THOUGHT I'D JUST GO FOR A STROLL AROUND THE BLOCK, GET A SODA AT EAT.
THE SNOW BALL'S ON TONIGHT—YOU SHOULD GO SAY GOOD-BYE TO HENRY!
YOU MIGHT NOT GET A *CHANCE* WHEN OTIS GETS HERE!
SURE, AUNT NELLY.
I'M PROBABLY THE ONLY PERSON—EXCEPT FOR EDDIE POE—WHO ISN'T AT THE DANCE.
THERE'S HENRY—KISSING A GIRL AS EVER. I'LL WAIT TO SAY GOOD-BYE—
—WAIT, WHO'S THAT WITH THEM? OH NO—
—IT'S *MEREDITH*.
HI, VLAD. CAN I ASK YOU SOMETHING?
SURE. WHAT IS IT?

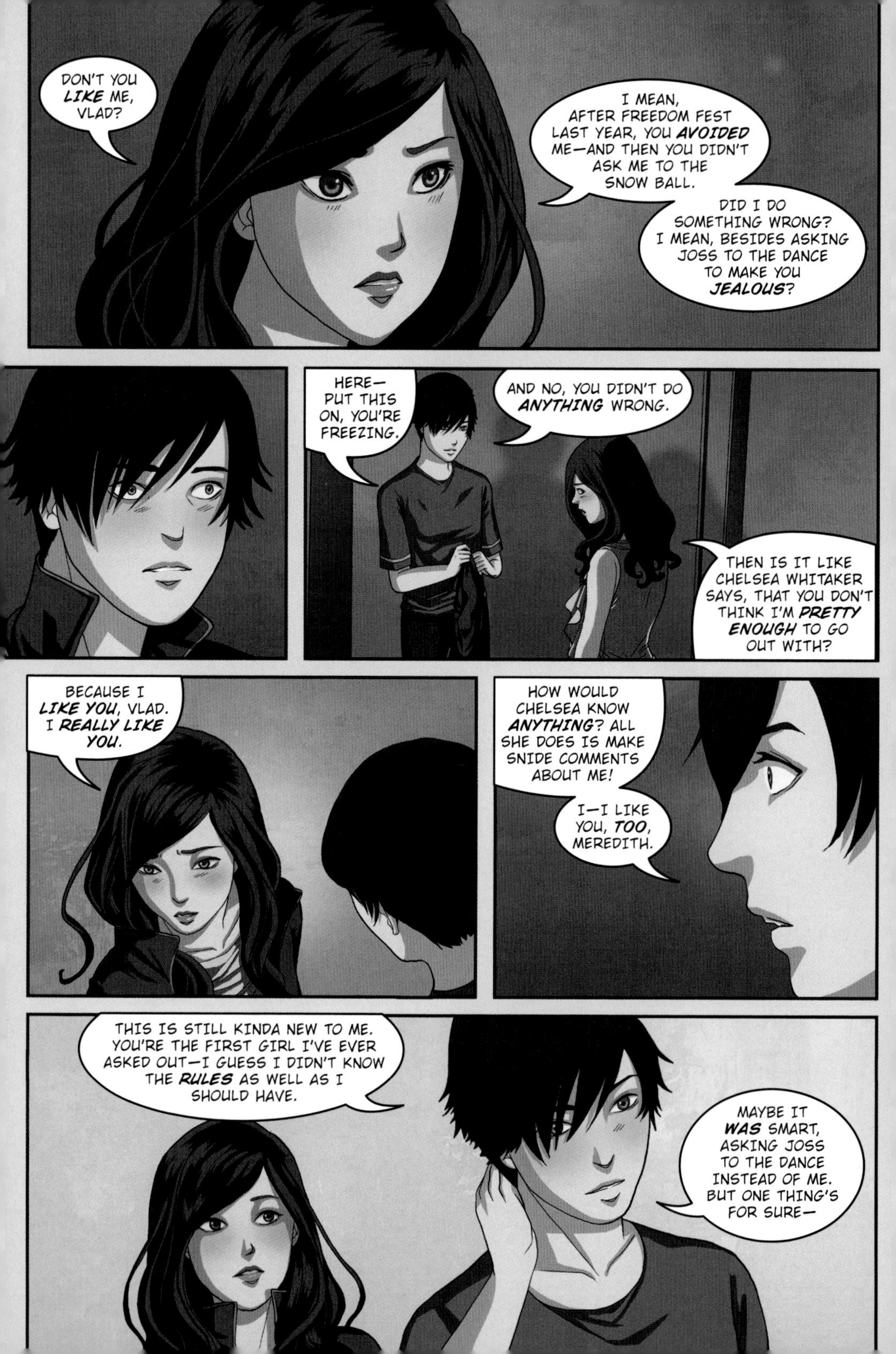
DON'T YOU LIKE ME, VLAD?
I MEAN, AFTER FREEDOM FEST LAST YEAR, YOU AVOIDED ME—AND THEN YOU DIDN'T ASK ME TO THE SNOW BALL.
DID I DO SOMETHING WRONG? I MEAN, BESIDES ASKING JOSS TO THE DANCE TO MAKE YOU JEALOUS?
HERE—PUT THIS ON, YOU'RE FREEZING.
AND NO, YOU DIDN'T DO ANYTHING WRONG.
THEN IS IT LIKE CHELSEA WHITAKER SAYS, THAT YOU DON'T THINK I'M PRETTY ENOUGH TO GO OUT WITH?
BECAUSE I LIKE YOU, VLAD. I REALLY LIKE YOU.
HOW WOULD CHELSEA KNOW ANYTHING? ALL SHE DOES IS MAKE SNIDE COMMENTS ABOUT ME!
I—I LIKE YOU, TOO, MEREDITH.
THIS IS STILL KINDA NEW TO ME. YOU'RE THE FIRST GIRL I'VE EVER ASKED OUT—I GUESS I DIDN'T KNOW THE RULES AS WELL AS I SHOULD HAVE.
MAYBE IT WAS SMART, ASKING JOSS TO THE DANCE INSTEAD OF ME. BUT ONE THING'S FOR SURE—

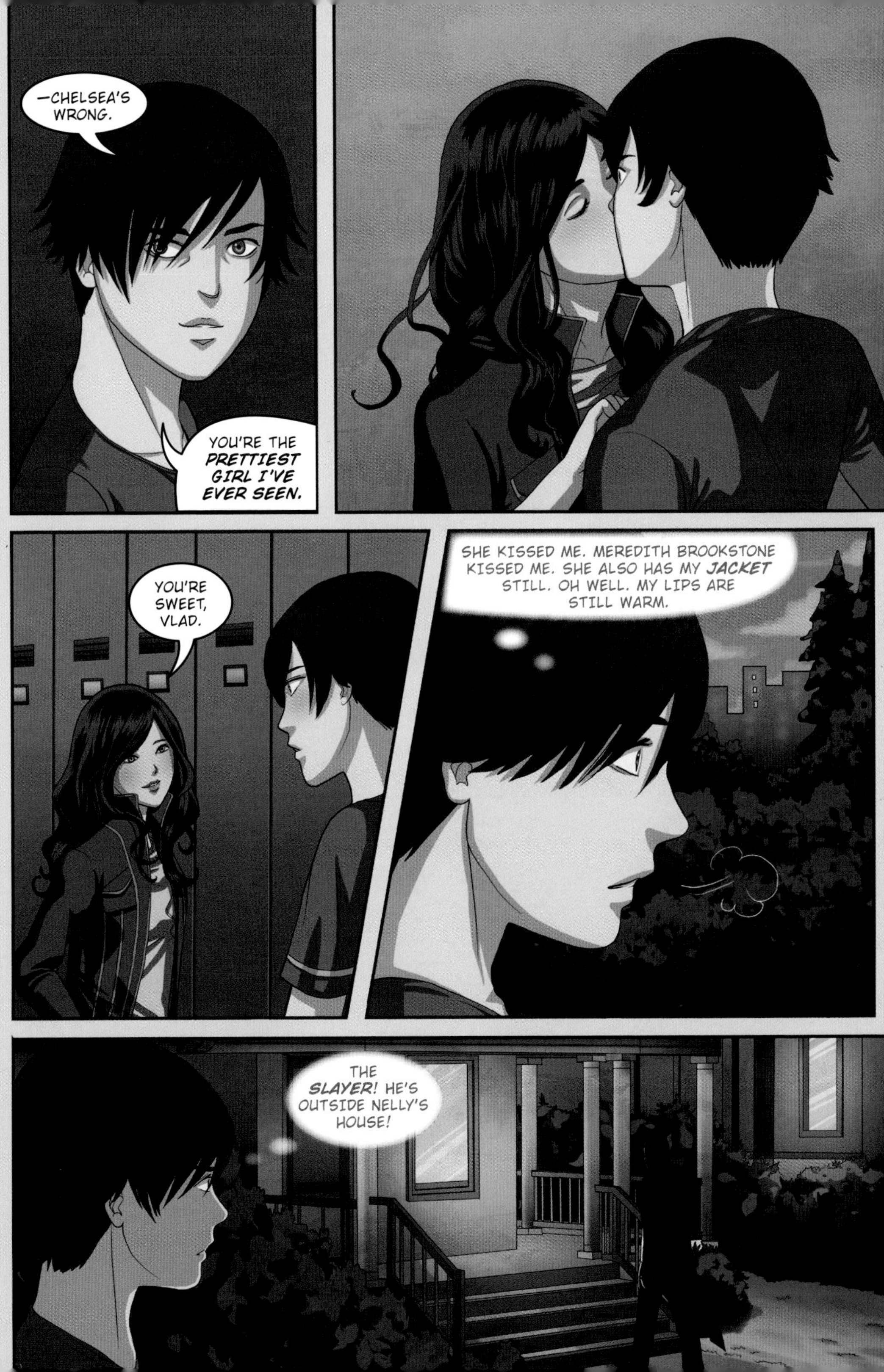
—CHELSEA'S WRONG.
YOU'RE THE *PRETTIEST* GIRL I'VE EVER SEEN.
YOU'RE SWEET, VLAD.
SHE KISSED ME. MEREDITH BROOKSTONE KISSED ME. SHE ALSO HAS MY *JACKET* STILL. OH WELL. MY LIPS ARE STILL WARM.
THE *SLAYER!* HE'S OUTSIDE NELLY'S HOUSE!

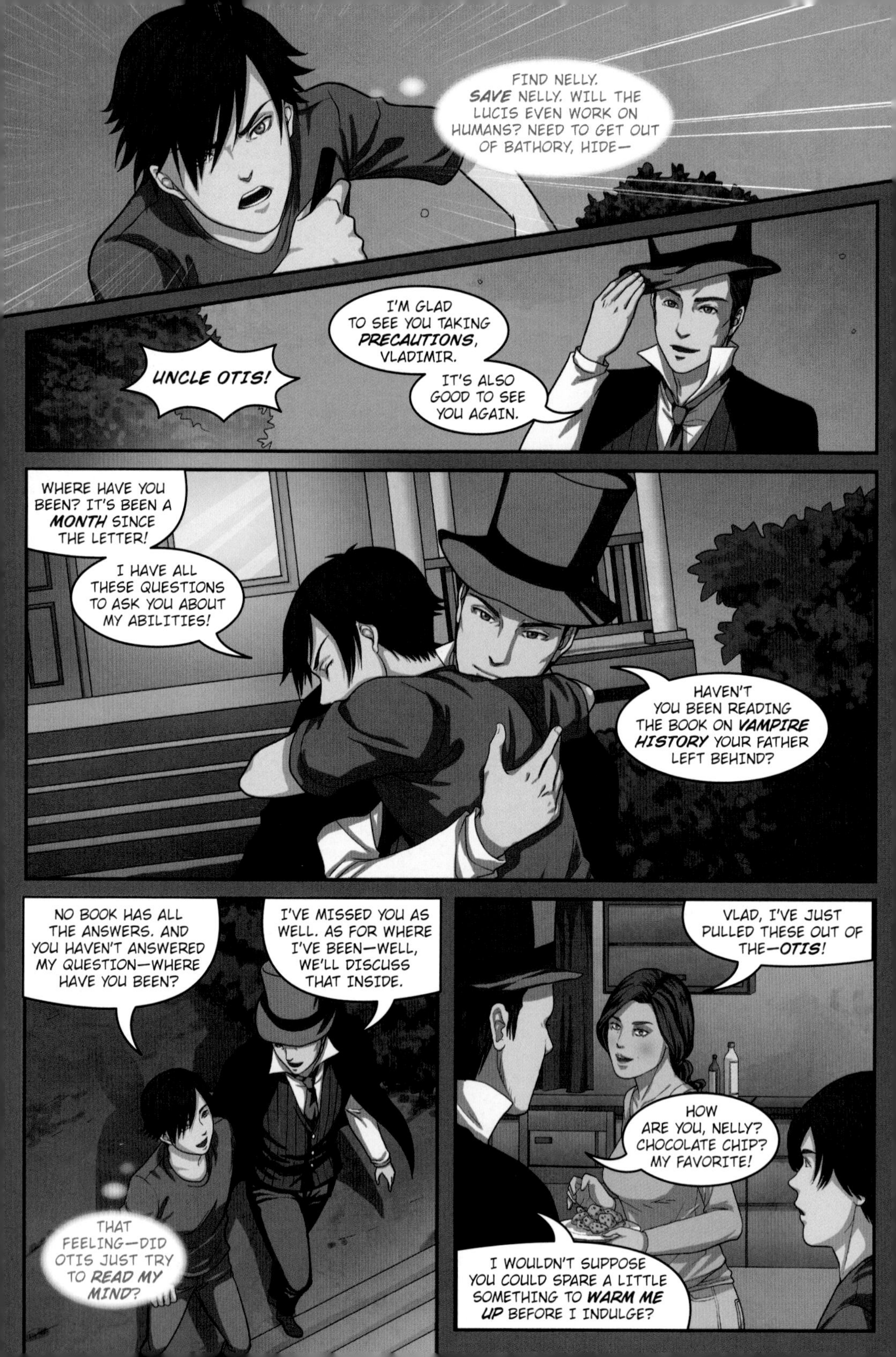
FIND NELLY. SAVE NELLY. WILL THE LUCIS EVEN WORK ON HUMANS? NEED TO GET OUT OF BATHORY, HIDE—
UNCLE OTIS!
I'M GLAD TO SEE YOU TAKING PRECAUTIONS, VLADIMIR.
IT'S ALSO GOOD TO SEE YOU AGAIN.
WHERE HAVE YOU BEEN? IT'S BEEN A MONTH SINCE THE LETTER!
I HAVE ALL THESE QUESTIONS TO ASK YOU ABOUT MY ABILITIES!
HAVEN'T YOU BEEN READING THE BOOK ON VAMPIRE HISTORY YOUR FATHER LEFT BEHIND?
NO BOOK HAS ALL THE ANSWERS. AND YOU HAVEN'T ANSWERED MY QUESTION—WHERE HAVE YOU BEEN?
I'VE MISSED YOU AS WELL. AS FOR WHERE I'VE BEEN—WELL, WE'LL DISCUSS THAT INSIDE.
THAT FEELING—DID OTIS JUST TRY TO READ MY MIND?
VLAD, I'VE JUST PULLED THESE OUT OF THE—OTIS!
HOW ARE YOU, NELLY? CHOCOLATE CHIP? MY FAVORITE!
I WOULDN'T SUPPOSE YOU COULD SPARE A LITTLE SOMETHING TO WARM ME UP BEFORE I INDULGE?

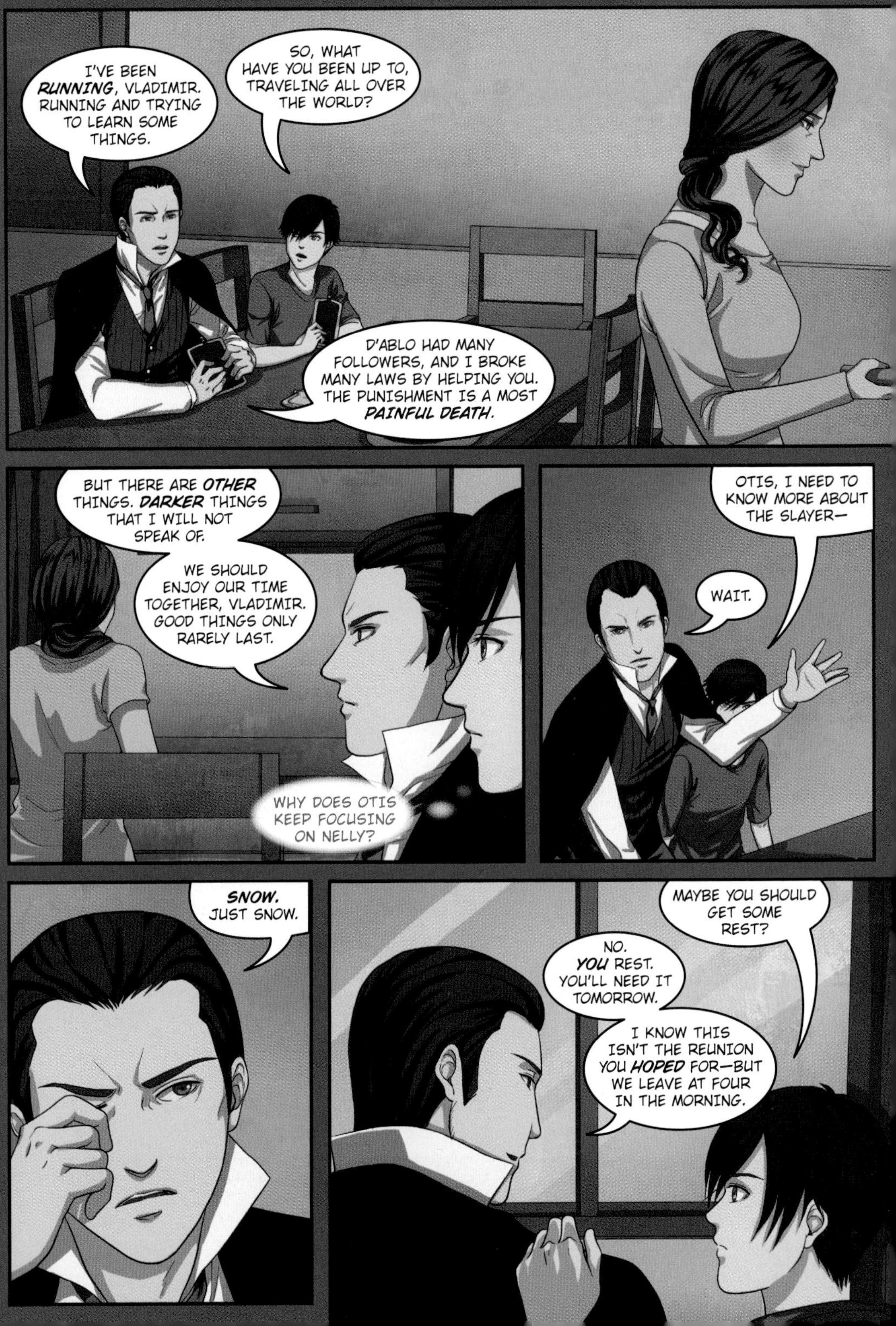
SO, WHAT HAVE YOU BEEN UP TO, TRAVELING ALL OVER THE WORLD?
I'VE BEEN *RUNNING*, VLADIMIR. RUNNING AND TRYING TO LEARN SOME THINGS.
D'ABLO HAD MANY FOLLOWERS, AND I BROKE MANY LAWS BY HELPING YOU. THE PUNISHMENT IS A MOST *PAINFUL DEATH.*
BUT THERE ARE *OTHER* THINGS. *DARKER* THINGS THAT I WILL NOT SPEAK OF.
WE SHOULD ENJOY OUR TIME TOGETHER, VLADIMIR. GOOD THINGS ONLY RARELY LAST.
WHY DOES OTIS KEEP FOCUSING ON NELLY?
OTIS, I NEED TO KNOW MORE ABOUT THE SLAYER—
WAIT.
SNOW. JUST SNOW.
MAYBE YOU SHOULD GET SOME REST?
NO. *YOU* REST. YOU'LL NEED IT TOMORROW.
I KNOW THIS ISN'T THE REUNION YOU *HOPED* FOR—BUT WE LEAVE AT FOUR IN THE MORNING.

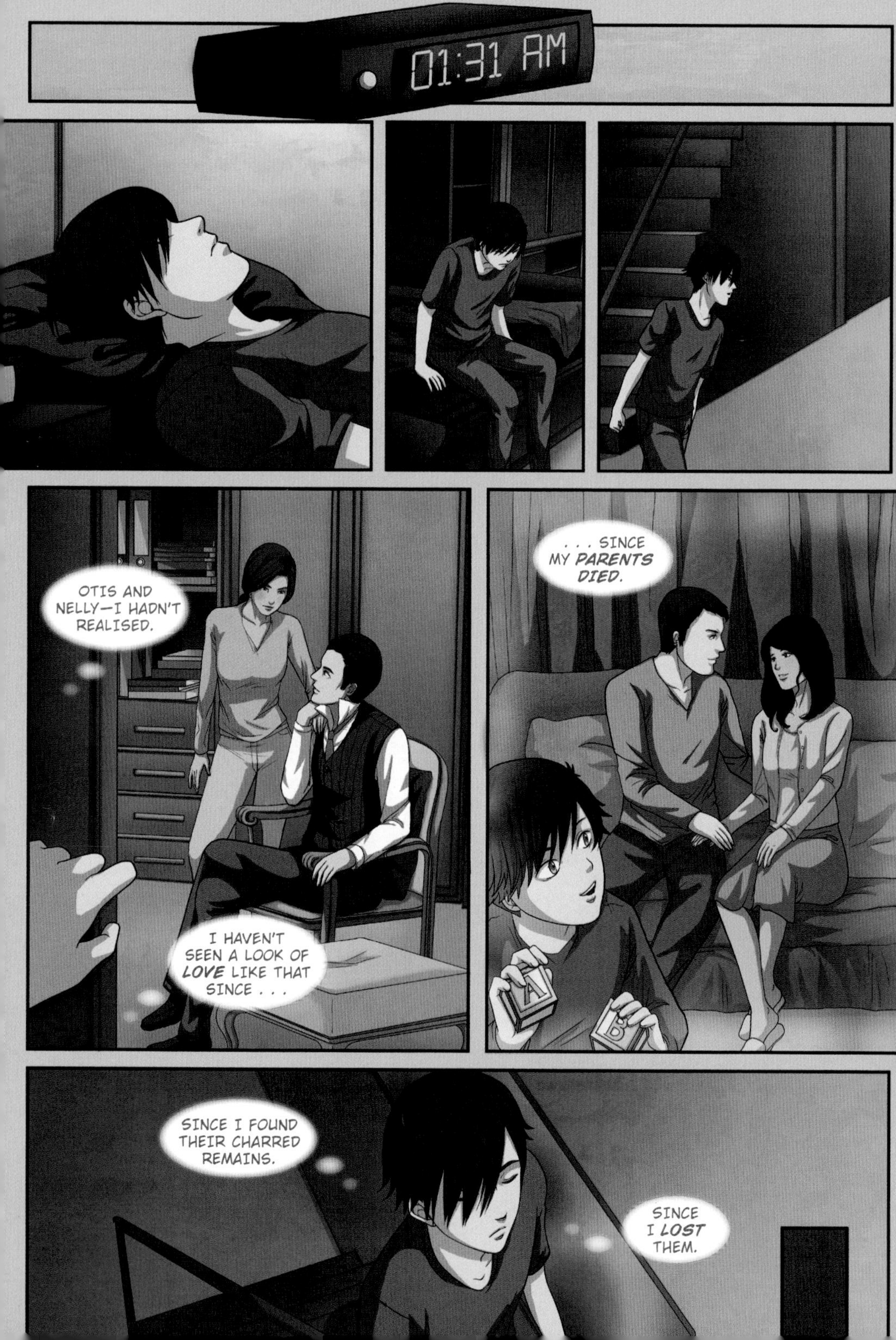
01:31 AM
OTIS AND NELLY—I HADN'T REALISED.
I HAVEN'T SEEN A LOOK OF LOVE LIKE THAT SINCE . . .
. . . SINCE MY PARENTS DIED.
SINCE I FOUND THEIR CHARRED REMAINS.
SINCE I LOST THEM.

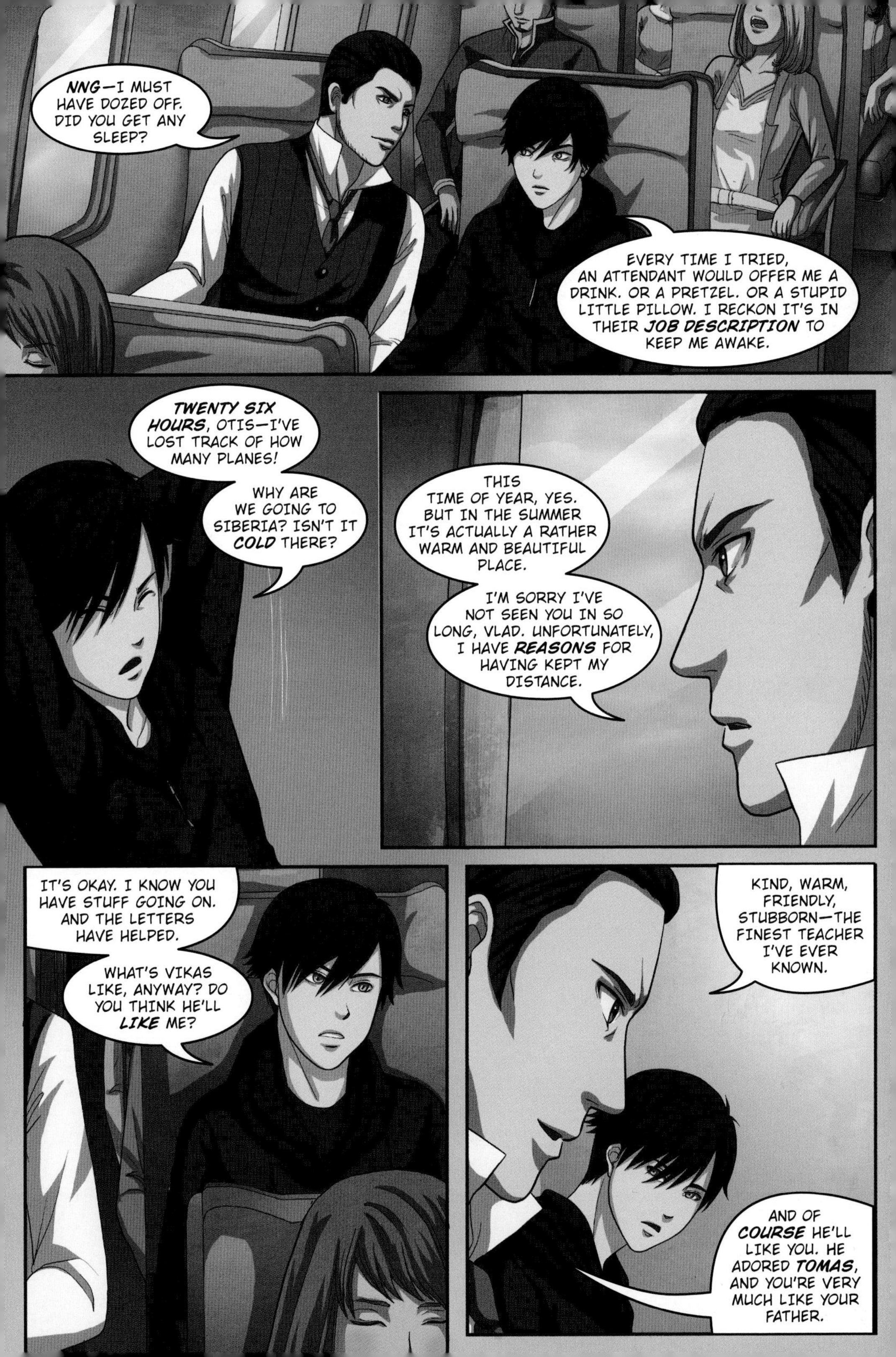

NNG—I MUST HAVE DOZED OFF. DID YOU GET ANY SLEEP?
EVERY TIME I TRIED, AN ATTENDANT WOULD OFFER ME A DRINK. OR A PRETZEL. OR A STUPID LITTLE PILLOW. I RECKON IT'S IN THEIR *JOB DESCRIPTION* TO KEEP ME AWAKE.
TWENTY SIX HOURS, OTIS—I'VE LOST TRACK OF HOW MANY PLANES!
WHY ARE WE GOING TO SIBERIA? ISN'T IT *COLD* THERE?
THIS TIME OF YEAR, YES. BUT IN THE SUMMER IT'S ACTUALLY A RATHER WARM AND BEAUTIFUL PLACE.
I'M SORRY I'VE NOT SEEN YOU IN SO LONG, VLAD. UNFORTUNATELY, I HAVE *REASONS* FOR HAVING KEPT MY DISTANCE.
IT'S OKAY. I KNOW YOU HAVE STUFF GOING ON. AND THE LETTERS HAVE HELPED.
WHAT'S VIKAS LIKE, ANYWAY? DO YOU THINK HE'LL *LIKE* ME?
KIND, WARM, FRIENDLY, STUBBORN—THE FINEST TEACHER I'VE EVER KNOWN.
AND OF *COURSE* HE'LL LIKE YOU. HE ADORED *TOMAS*, AND YOU'RE VERY MUCH LIKE YOUR FATHER.

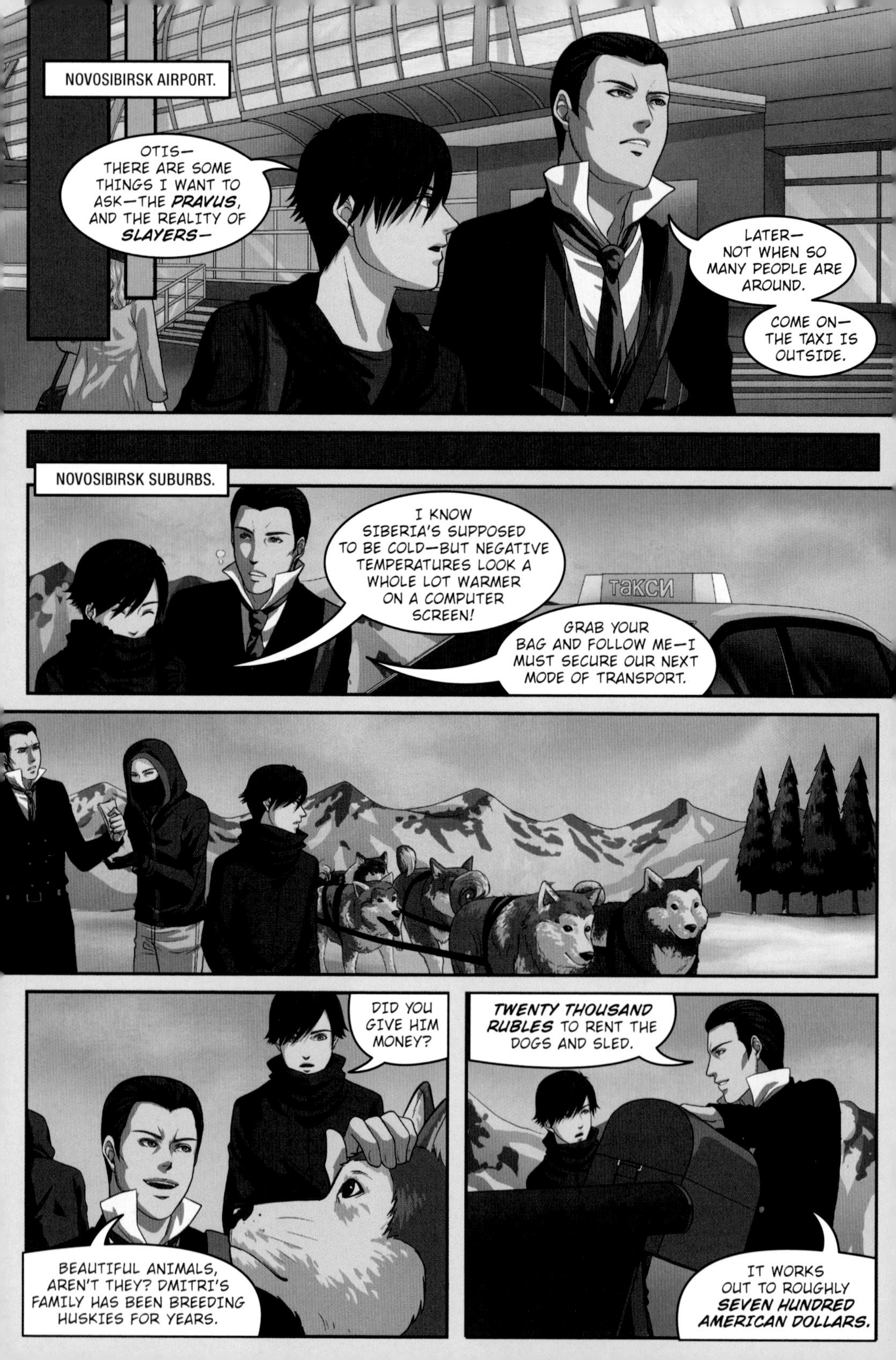
NOVOSIBIRSK AIRPORT.
OTIS— THERE ARE SOME THINGS I WANT TO ASK—THE PRAVUS, AND THE REALITY OF SLAYERS—
LATER— NOT WHEN SO MANY PEOPLE ARE AROUND.
COME ON— THE TAXI IS OUTSIDE.
NOVOSIBIRSK SUBURBS.
I KNOW SIBERIA'S SUPPOSED TO BE COLD—BUT NEGATIVE TEMPERATURES LOOK A WHOLE LOT WARMER ON A COMPUTER SCREEN!
ТАКСИ
GRAB YOUR BAG AND FOLLOW ME—I MUST SECURE OUR NEXT MODE OF TRANSPORT.
DID YOU GIVE HIM MONEY?
BEAUTIFUL ANIMALS, AREN'T THEY? DMITRI'S FAMILY HAS BEEN BREEDING HUSKIES FOR YEARS.
TWENTY THOUSAND RUBLES TO RENT THE DOGS AND SLED.
IT WORKS OUT TO ROUGHLY SEVEN HUNDRED AMERICAN DOLLARS.

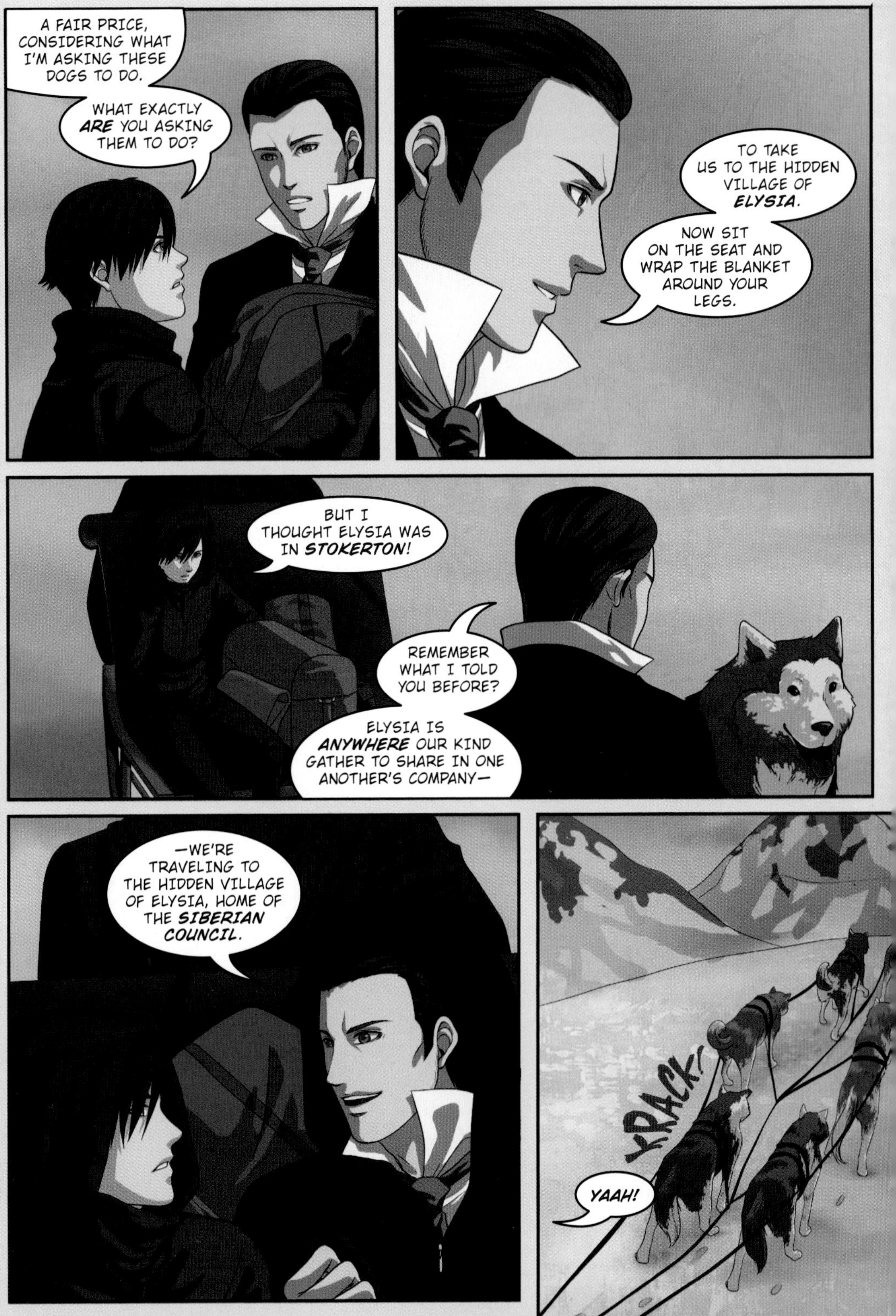
A FAIR PRICE, CONSIDERING WHAT I'M ASKING THESE DOGS TO DO.
WHAT EXACTLY **ARE** YOU ASKING THEM TO DO?
TO TAKE US TO THE HIDDEN VILLAGE OF **ELYSIA**.
NOW SIT ON THE SEAT AND WRAP THE BLANKET AROUND YOUR LEGS.
BUT I THOUGHT ELYSIA WAS IN **STOKERTON**!
REMEMBER WHAT I TOLD YOU BEFORE?
ELYSIA IS **ANYWHERE** OUR KIND GATHER TO SHARE IN ONE ANOTHER'S COMPANY—
—WE'RE TRAVELING TO THE HIDDEN VILLAGE OF ELYSIA, HOME OF THE **SIBERIAN COUNCIL**.
KRACK!
YAAH!

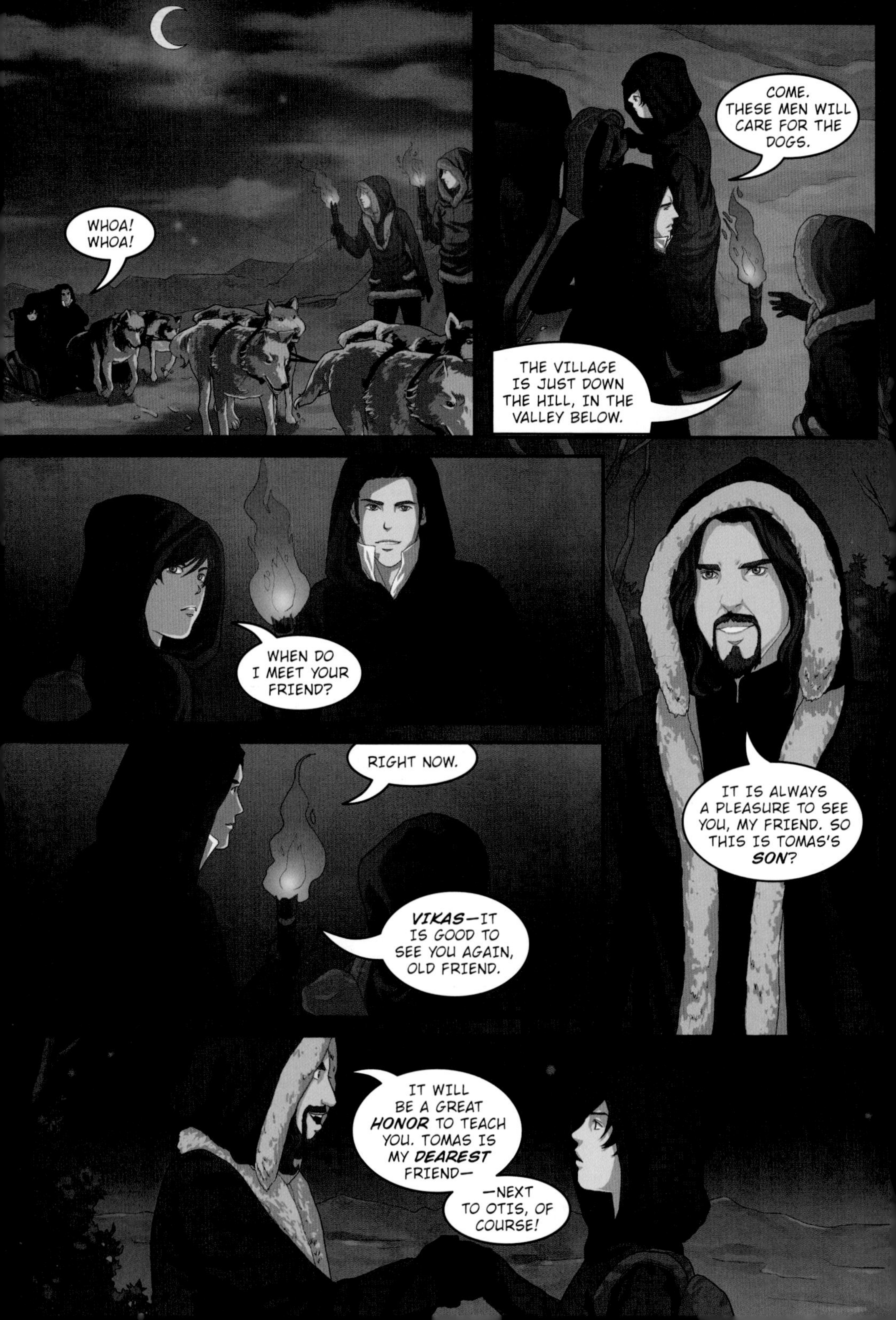
WHOA! WHOA!
COME. THESE MEN WILL CARE FOR THE DOGS.
THE VILLAGE IS JUST DOWN THE HILL, IN THE VALLEY BELOW.
WHEN DO I MEET YOUR FRIEND?
RIGHT NOW.
VIKAS—IT IS GOOD TO SEE YOU AGAIN, OLD FRIEND.
IT IS ALWAYS A PLEASURE TO SEE YOU, MY FRIEND. SO THIS IS TOMAS'S SON?
IT WILL BE A GREAT HONOR TO TEACH YOU. TOMAS IS MY DEAREST FRIEND—
—NEXT TO OTIS, OF COURSE!

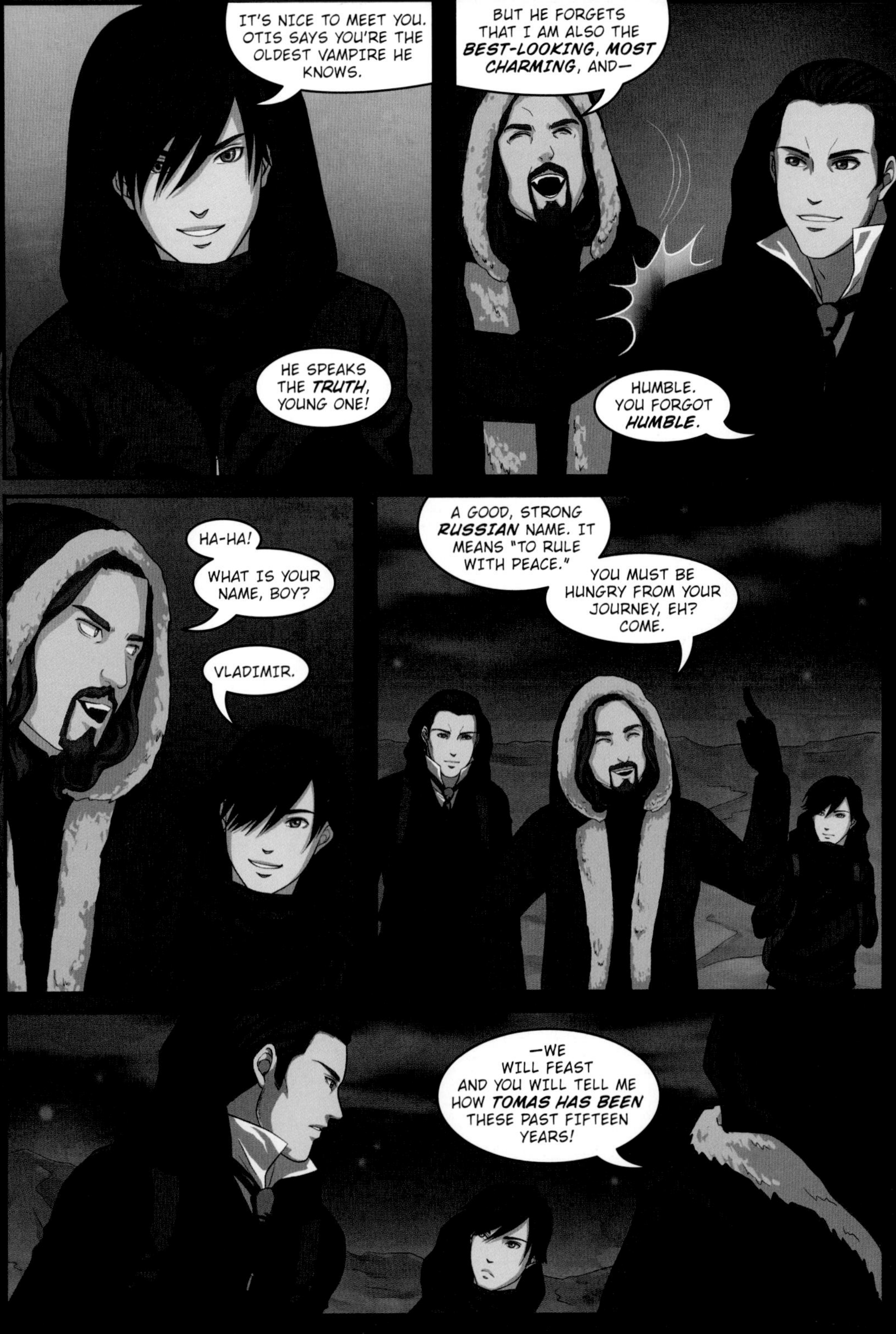
IT'S NICE TO MEET YOU. OTIS SAYS YOU'RE THE OLDEST VAMPIRE HE KNOWS.
HE SPEAKS THE **TRUTH**, YOUNG ONE!
BUT HE FORGETS THAT I AM ALSO THE **BEST-LOOKING, MOST CHARMING**, AND—
HUMBLE. YOU FORGOT **HUMBLE**.
HA-HA!
WHAT IS YOUR NAME, BOY?
VLADIMIR.
A GOOD, STRONG **RUSSIAN** NAME. IT MEANS "TO RULE WITH PEACE."
YOU MUST BE HUNGRY FROM YOUR JOURNEY, EH? COME.
—WE WILL FEAST AND YOU WILL TELL ME HOW **TOMAS HAS BEEN** THESE PAST FIFTEEN YEARS!

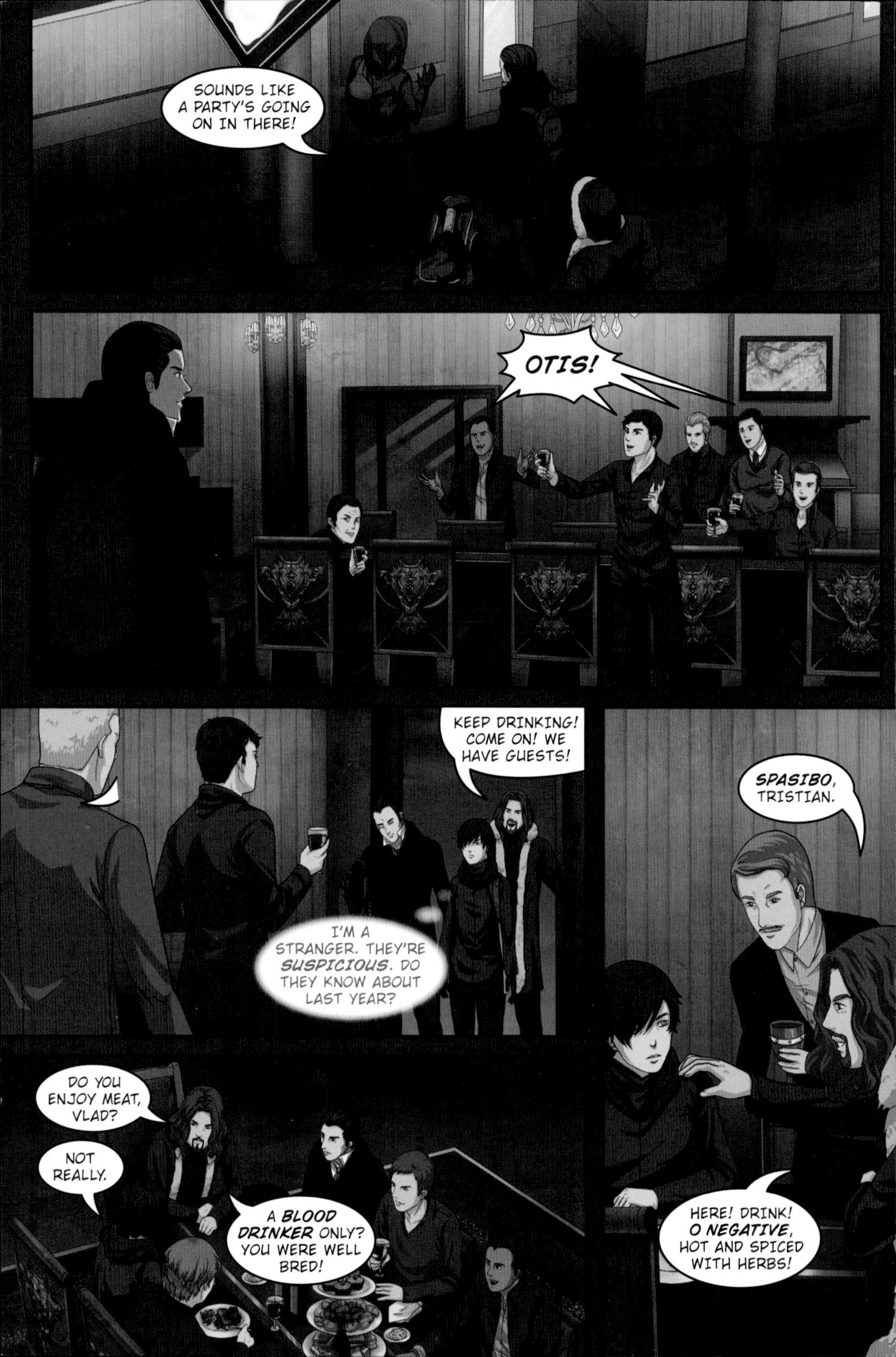
SOUNDS LIKE A PARTY'S GOING ON IN THERE!
OTIS!
KEEP DRINKING! COME ON! WE HAVE GUESTS!
I'M A STRANGER. THEY'RE SUSPICIOUS. DO THEY KNOW ABOUT LAST YEAR?
SPASIBO, TRISTIAN.
DO YOU ENJOY MEAT, VLAD?
NOT REALLY.
A BLOOD DRINKER ONLY? YOU WERE WELL BRED!
HERE! DRINK! O NEGATIVE, HOT AND SPICED WITH HERBS!

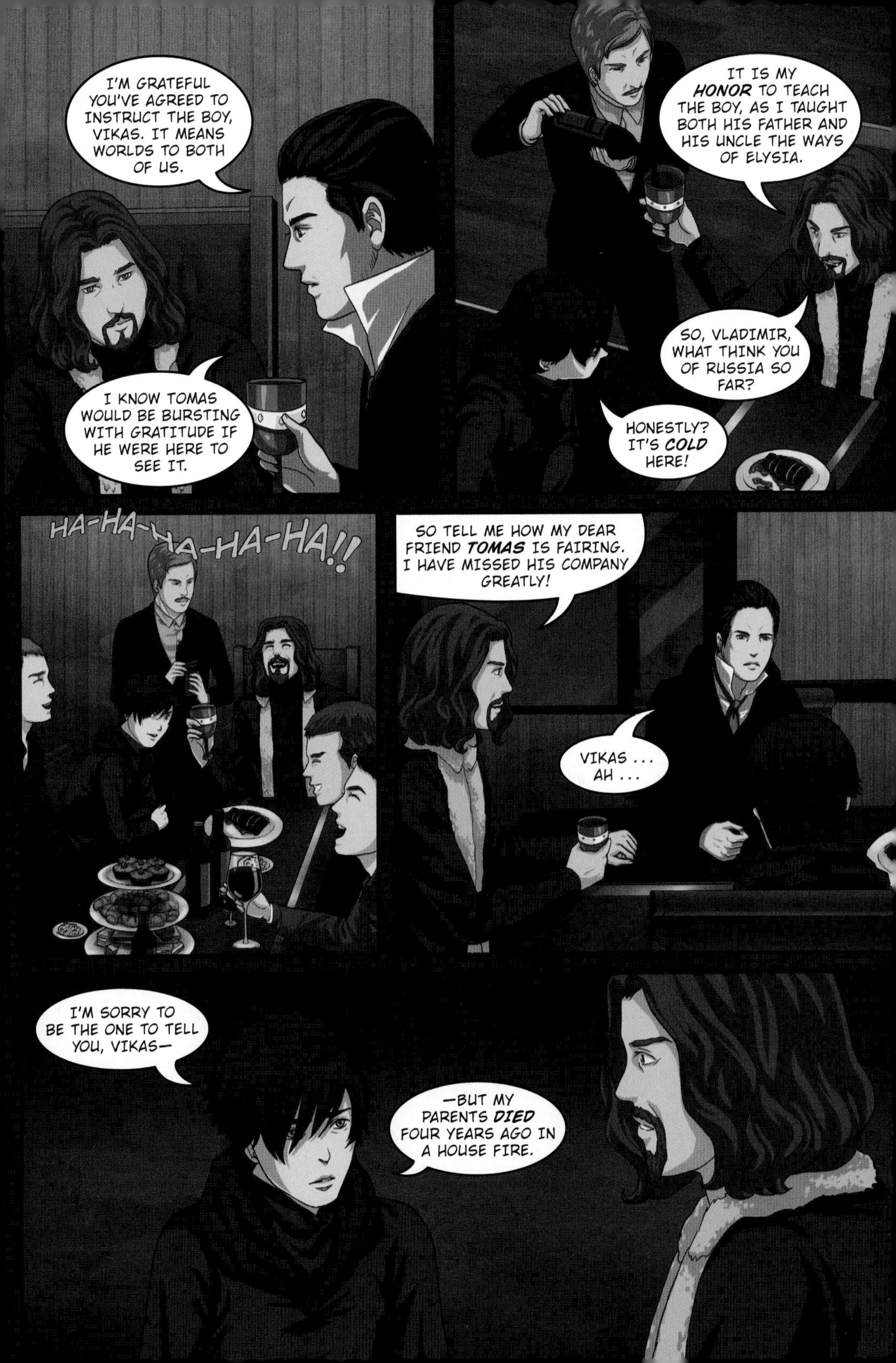
I'M GRATEFUL YOU'VE AGREED TO INSTRUCT THE BOY, VIKAS. IT MEANS WORLDS TO BOTH OF US.
I KNOW TOMAS WOULD BE BURSTING WITH GRATITUDE IF HE WERE HERE TO SEE IT.
IT IS MY **HONOR** TO TEACH THE BOY, AS I TAUGHT BOTH HIS FATHER AND HIS UNCLE THE WAYS OF ELYSIA.
SO, VLADIMIR, WHAT THINK YOU OF RUSSIA SO FAR?
HONESTLY? IT'S **COLD** HERE!
HA-HA-HA-HA-HA!!
SO TELL ME HOW MY DEAR FRIEND **TOMAS** IS FAIRING. I HAVE MISSED HIS COMPANY GREATLY!
VIKAS . . . AH . . .
I'M SORRY TO BE THE ONE TO TELL YOU, VIKAS—
—BUT MY PARENTS **DIED** FOUR YEARS AGO IN A HOUSE FIRE.

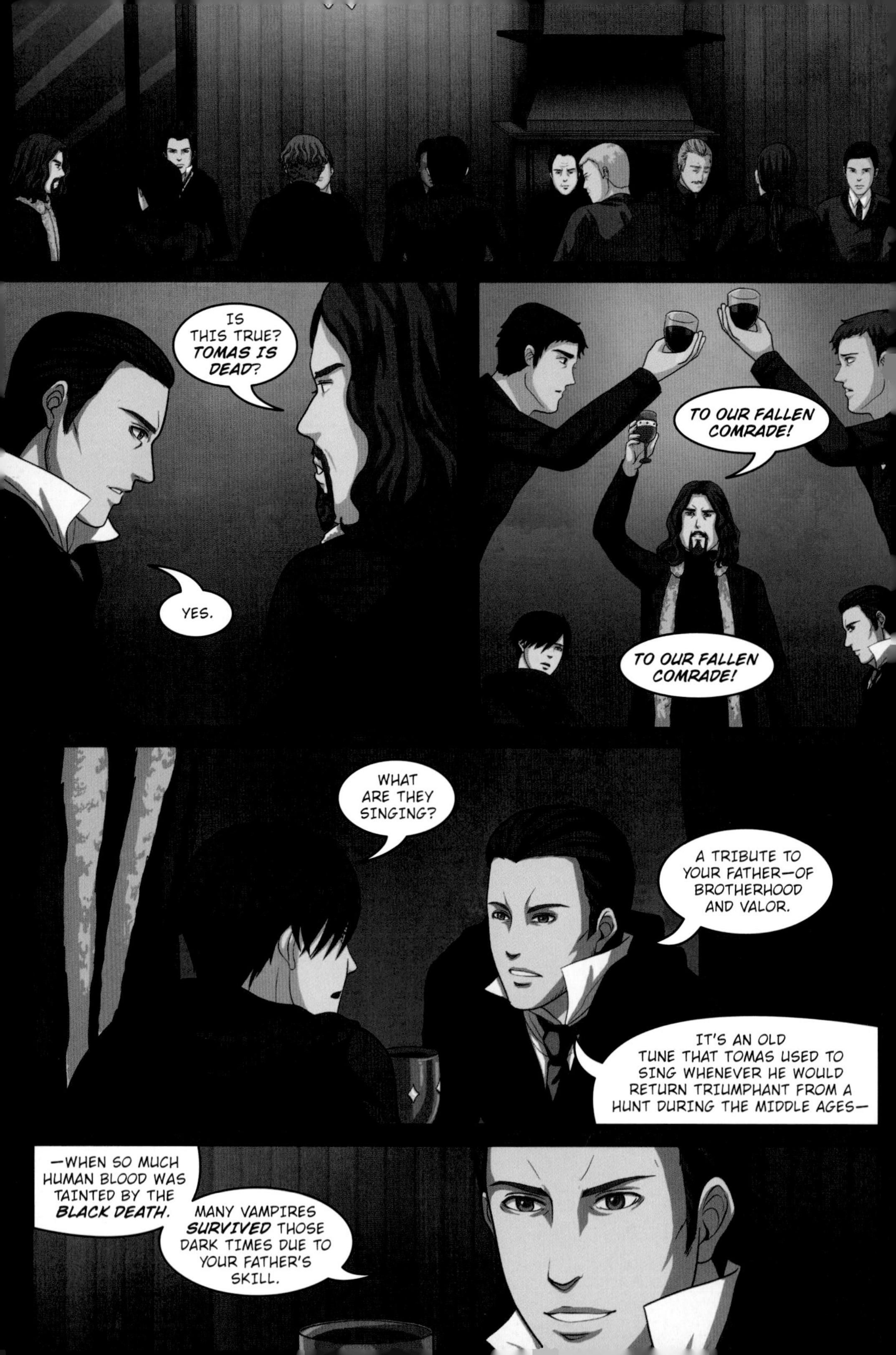
IS THIS TRUE? TOMAS IS DEAD?
YES.
TO OUR FALLEN COMRADE!
TO OUR FALLEN COMRADE!
WHAT ARE THEY SINGING?
A TRIBUTE TO YOUR FATHER—OF BROTHERHOOD AND VALOR.
IT'S AN OLD TUNE THAT TOMAS USED TO SING WHENEVER HE WOULD RETURN TRIUMPHANT FROM A HUNT DURING THE MIDDLE AGES—
—WHEN SO MUCH HUMAN BLOOD WAS TAINTED BY THE BLACK DEATH.
MANY VAMPIRES SURVIVED THOSE DARK TIMES DUE TO YOUR FATHER'S SKILL.

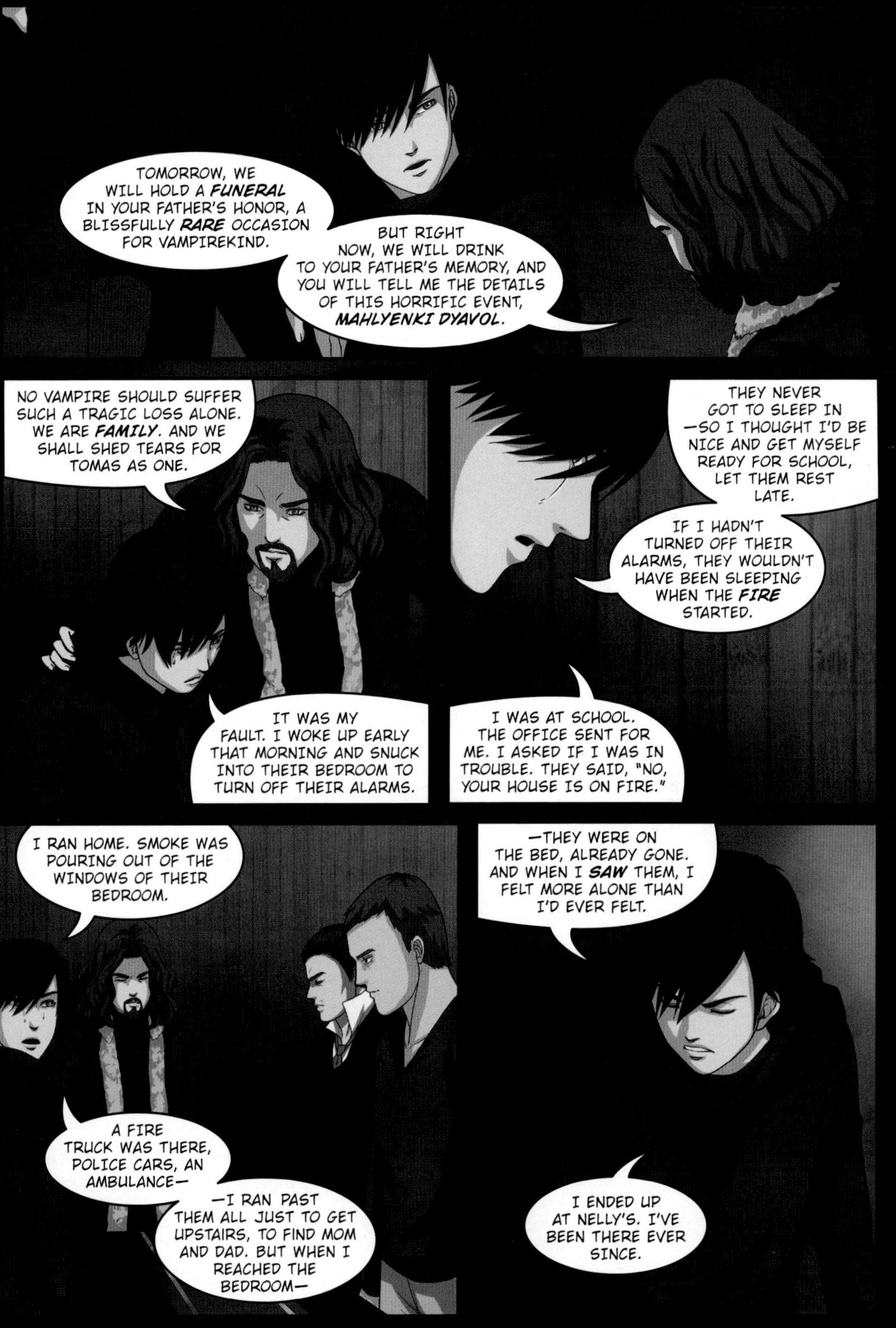
TOMORROW, WE WILL HOLD A FUNERAL IN YOUR FATHER'S HONOR, A BLISSFULLY RARE OCCASION FOR VAMPIREKIND.
BUT RIGHT NOW, WE WILL DRINK TO YOUR FATHER'S MEMORY, AND YOU WILL TELL ME THE DETAILS OF THIS HORRIFIC EVENT, MAHLYENKI DYAVOL.
NO VAMPIRE SHOULD SUFFER SUCH A TRAGIC LOSS ALONE. WE ARE FAMILY. AND WE SHALL SHED TEARS FOR TOMAS AS ONE.
IT WAS MY FAULT. I WOKE UP EARLY THAT MORNING AND SNUCK INTO THEIR BEDROOM TO TURN OFF THEIR ALARMS.
THEY NEVER GOT TO SLEEP IN —SO I THOUGHT I'D BE NICE AND GET MYSELF READY FOR SCHOOL, LET THEM REST LATE.
IF I HADN'T TURNED OFF THEIR ALARMS, THEY WOULDN'T HAVE BEEN SLEEPING WHEN THE FIRE STARTED.
I WAS AT SCHOOL. THE OFFICE SENT FOR ME. I ASKED IF I WAS IN TROUBLE. THEY SAID, "NO, YOUR HOUSE IS ON FIRE."
I RAN HOME. SMOKE WAS POURING OUT OF THE WINDOWS OF THEIR BEDROOM.
A FIRE TRUCK WAS THERE, POLICE CARS, AN AMBULANCE—
—I RAN PAST THEM ALL JUST TO GET UPSTAIRS, TO FIND MOM AND DAD. BUT WHEN I REACHED THE BEDROOM—
—THEY WERE ON THE BED, ALREADY GONE. AND WHEN I SAW THEM, I FELT MORE ALONE THAN I'D EVER FELT.
I ENDED UP AT NELLY'S. I'VE BEEN THERE EVER SINCE.

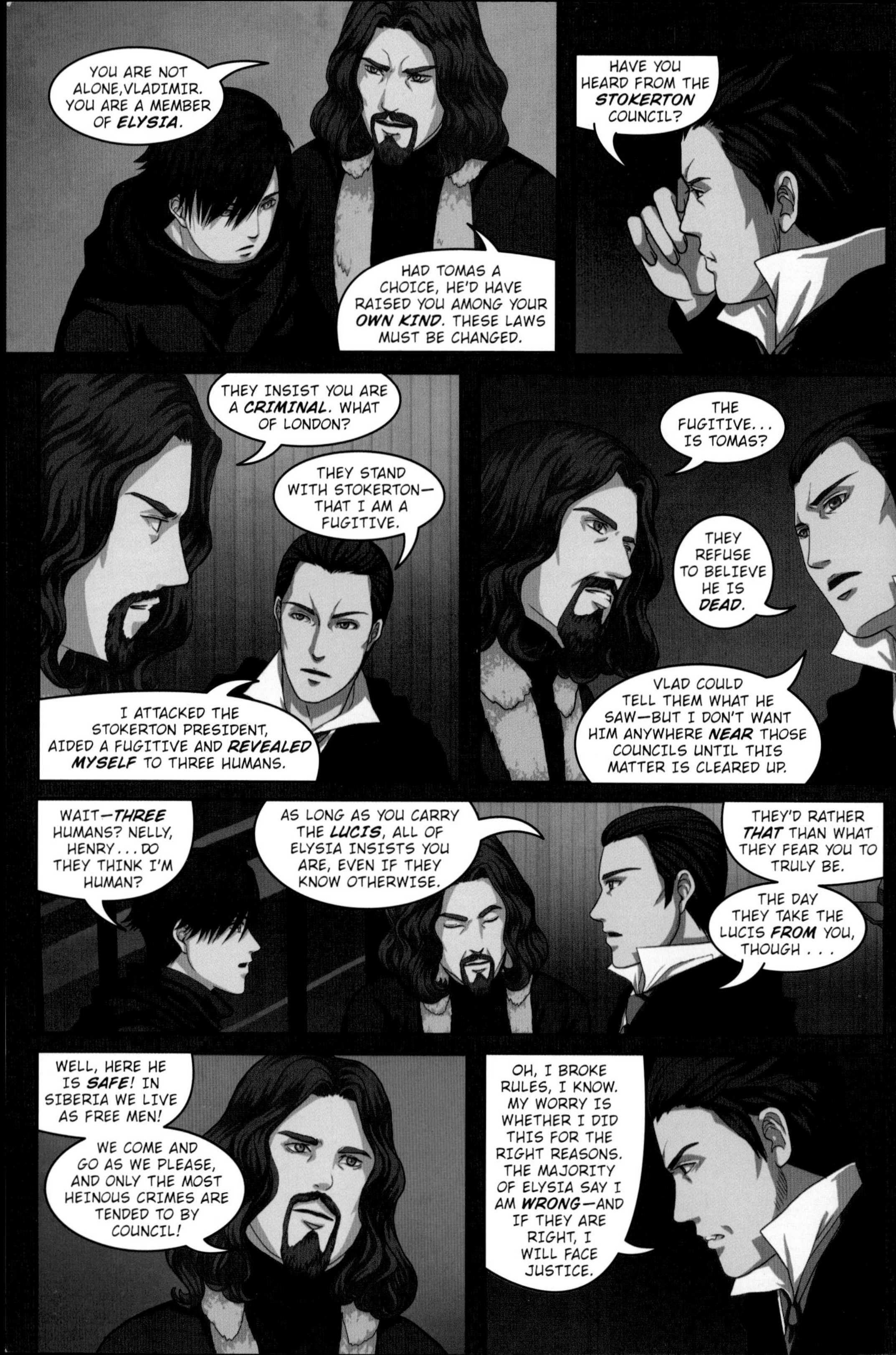
YOU ARE NOT ALONE, VLADIMIR. YOU ARE A MEMBER OF ELYSIA.
HAD TOMAS A CHOICE, HE'D HAVE RAISED YOU AMONG YOUR OWN KIND. THESE LAWS MUST BE CHANGED.
HAVE YOU HEARD FROM THE STOKERTON COUNCIL?
THEY INSIST YOU ARE A CRIMINAL. WHAT OF LONDON?
THEY STAND WITH STOKERTON—THAT I AM A FUGITIVE.
I ATTACKED THE STOKERTON PRESIDENT, AIDED A FUGITIVE AND REVEALED MYSELF TO THREE HUMANS.
THE FUGITIVE . . . IS TOMAS?
THEY REFUSE TO BELIEVE HE IS DEAD.
VLAD COULD TELL THEM WHAT HE SAW—BUT I DON'T WANT HIM ANYWHERE NEAR THOSE COUNCILS UNTIL THIS MATTER IS CLEARED UP.
WAIT—THREE HUMANS? NELLY, HENRY . . . DO THEY THINK I'M HUMAN?
AS LONG AS YOU CARRY THE LUCIS, ALL OF ELYSIA INSISTS YOU ARE, EVEN IF THEY KNOW OTHERWISE.
THEY'D RATHER THAT THAN WHAT THEY FEAR YOU TO TRULY BE.
THE DAY THEY TAKE THE LUCIS FROM YOU, THOUGH . . .
WELL, HERE HE IS SAFE! IN SIBERIA WE LIVE AS FREE MEN!
WE COME AND GO AS WE PLEASE, AND ONLY THE MOST HEINOUS CRIMES ARE TENDED TO BY COUNCIL!
OH, I BROKE RULES, I KNOW. MY WORRY IS WHETHER I DID THIS FOR THE RIGHT REASONS. THE MAJORITY OF ELYSIA SAY I AM WRONG—AND IF THEY ARE RIGHT, I WILL FACE JUSTICE.

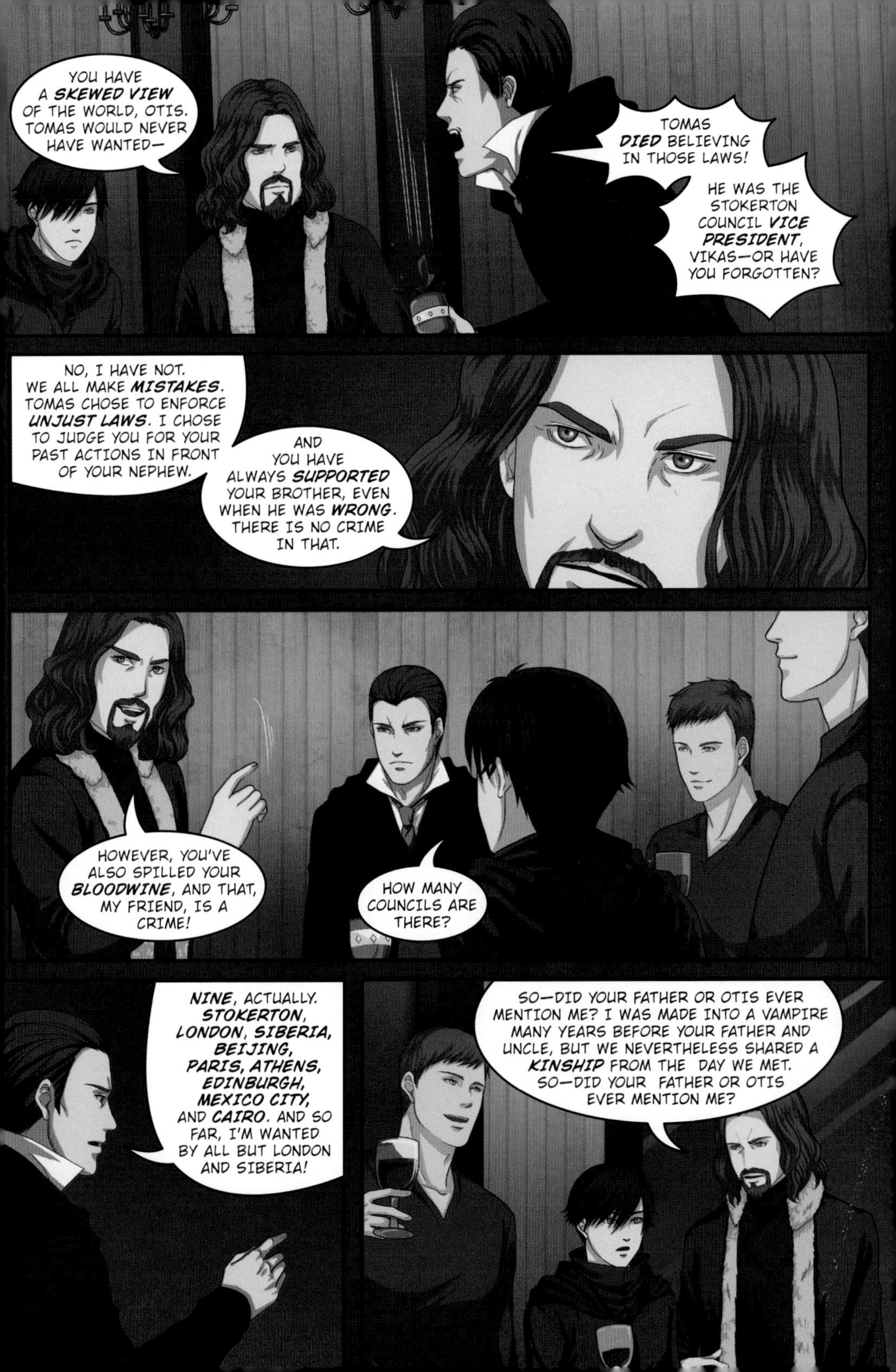
YOU HAVE A SKEWED VIEW OF THE WORLD, OTIS. TOMAS WOULD NEVER HAVE WANTED—
TOMAS DIED BELIEVING IN THOSE LAWS!
HE WAS THE STOKERTON COUNCIL VICE PRESIDENT, VIKAS—OR HAVE YOU FORGOTTEN?
NO, I HAVE NOT. WE ALL MAKE MISTAKES. TOMAS CHOSE TO ENFORCE UNJUST LAWS. I CHOSE TO JUDGE YOU FOR YOUR PAST ACTIONS IN FRONT OF YOUR NEPHEW.
AND YOU HAVE ALWAYS SUPPORTED YOUR BROTHER, EVEN WHEN HE WAS WRONG. THERE IS NO CRIME IN THAT.
HOWEVER, YOU'VE ALSO SPILLED YOUR BLOODWINE, AND THAT, MY FRIEND, IS A CRIME!
HOW MANY COUNCILS ARE THERE?
NINE, ACTUALLY. STOKERTON, LONDON, SIBERIA, BEIJING, PARIS, ATHENS, EDINBURGH, MEXICO CITY, AND CAIRO. AND SO FAR, I'M WANTED BY ALL BUT LONDON AND SIBERIA!
SO—DID YOUR FATHER OR OTIS EVER MENTION ME? I WAS MADE INTO A VAMPIRE MANY YEARS BEFORE YOUR FATHER AND UNCLE, BUT WE NEVERTHELESS SHARED A KINSHIP FROM THE DAY WE MET. SO—DID YOUR FATHER OR OTIS EVER MENTION ME?

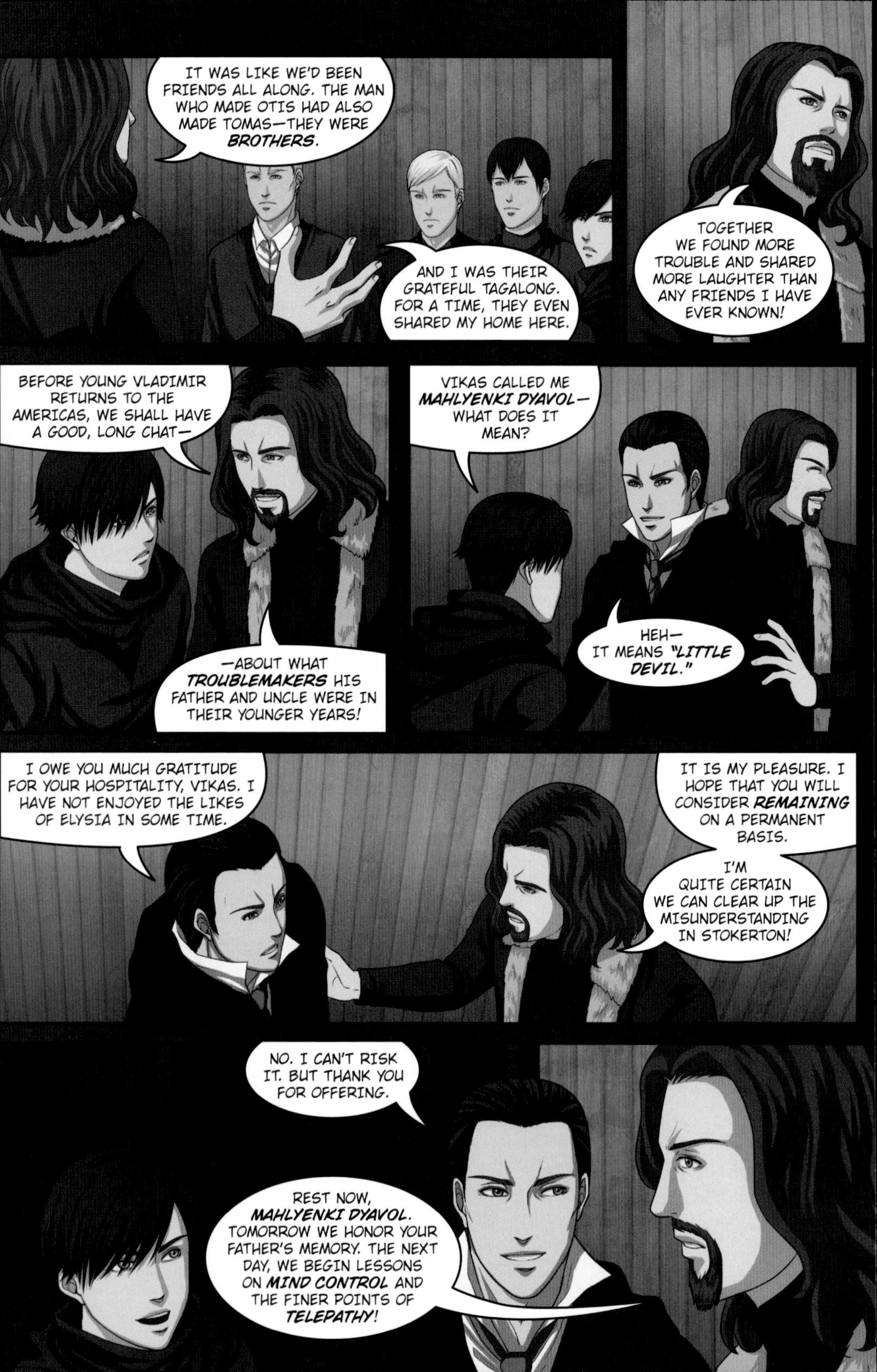
IT WAS LIKE WE'D BEEN FRIENDS ALL ALONG. THE MAN WHO MADE OTIS HAD ALSO MADE TOMAS—THEY WERE **BROTHERS**.
AND I WAS THEIR GRATEFUL TAGALONG. FOR A TIME, THEY EVEN SHARED MY HOME HERE.
TOGETHER WE FOUND MORE TROUBLE AND SHARED MORE LAUGHTER THAN ANY FRIENDS I HAVE EVER KNOWN!
BEFORE YOUNG VLADIMIR RETURNS TO THE AMERICAS, WE SHALL HAVE A GOOD, LONG CHAT—
—ABOUT WHAT **TROUBLEMAKERS** HIS FATHER AND UNCLE WERE IN THEIR YOUNGER YEARS!
VIKAS CALLED ME ***MAHLYENKI DYAVOL***—WHAT DOES IT MEAN?
HEH—IT MEANS ***"LITTLE DEVIL."***
I OWE YOU MUCH GRATITUDE FOR YOUR HOSPITALITY, VIKAS. I HAVE NOT ENJOYED THE LIKES OF ELYSIA IN SOME TIME.
IT IS MY PLEASURE. I HOPE THAT YOU WILL CONSIDER ***REMAINING*** ON A PERMANENT BASIS.
I'M QUITE CERTAIN WE CAN CLEAR UP THE MISUNDERSTANDING IN STOKERTON!
NO. I CAN'T RISK IT. BUT THANK YOU FOR OFFERING.
REST NOW, ***MAHLYENKI DYAVOL***. TOMORROW WE HONOR YOUR FATHER'S MEMORY. THE NEXT DAY, WE BEGIN LESSONS ON ***MIND CONTROL*** AND THE FINER POINTS OF ***TELEPATHY***!

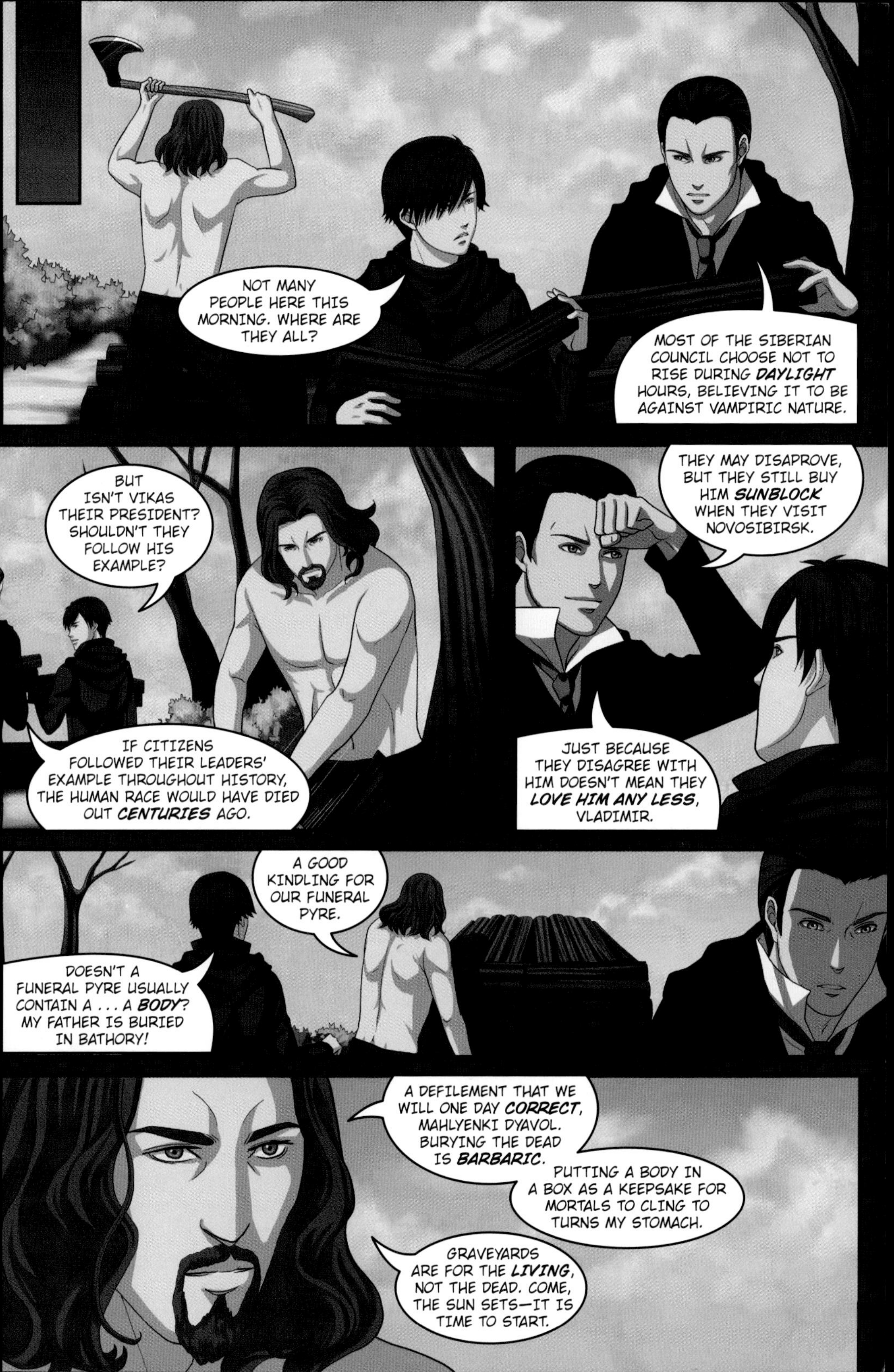
NOT MANY PEOPLE HERE THIS MORNING. WHERE ARE THEY ALL?
MOST OF THE SIBERIAN COUNCIL CHOOSE NOT TO RISE DURING DAYLIGHT HOURS, BELIEVING IT TO BE AGAINST VAMPIRIC NATURE.
BUT ISN'T VIKAS THEIR PRESIDENT? SHOULDN'T THEY FOLLOW HIS EXAMPLE?
IF CITIZENS FOLLOWED THEIR LEADERS' EXAMPLE THROUGHOUT HISTORY, THE HUMAN RACE WOULD HAVE DIED OUT CENTURIES AGO.
THEY MAY DISAPROVE, BUT THEY STILL BUY HIM SUNBLOCK WHEN THEY VISIT NOVOSIBIRSK.
JUST BECAUSE THEY DISAGREE WITH HIM DOESN'T MEAN THEY LOVE HIM ANY LESS, VLADIMIR.
A GOOD KINDLING FOR OUR FUNERAL PYRE.
DOESN'T A FUNERAL PYRE USUALLY CONTAIN A . . . A BODY? MY FATHER IS BURIED IN BATHORY!
A DEFILEMENT THAT WE WILL ONE DAY CORRECT, MAHLYENKI DYAVOL. BURYING THE DEAD IS BARBARIC.
PUTTING A BODY IN A BOX AS A KEEPSAKE FOR MORTALS TO CLING TO TURNS MY STOMACH.
GRAVEYARDS ARE FOR THE LIVING, NOT THE DEAD. COME, THE SUN SETS—IT IS TIME TO START.

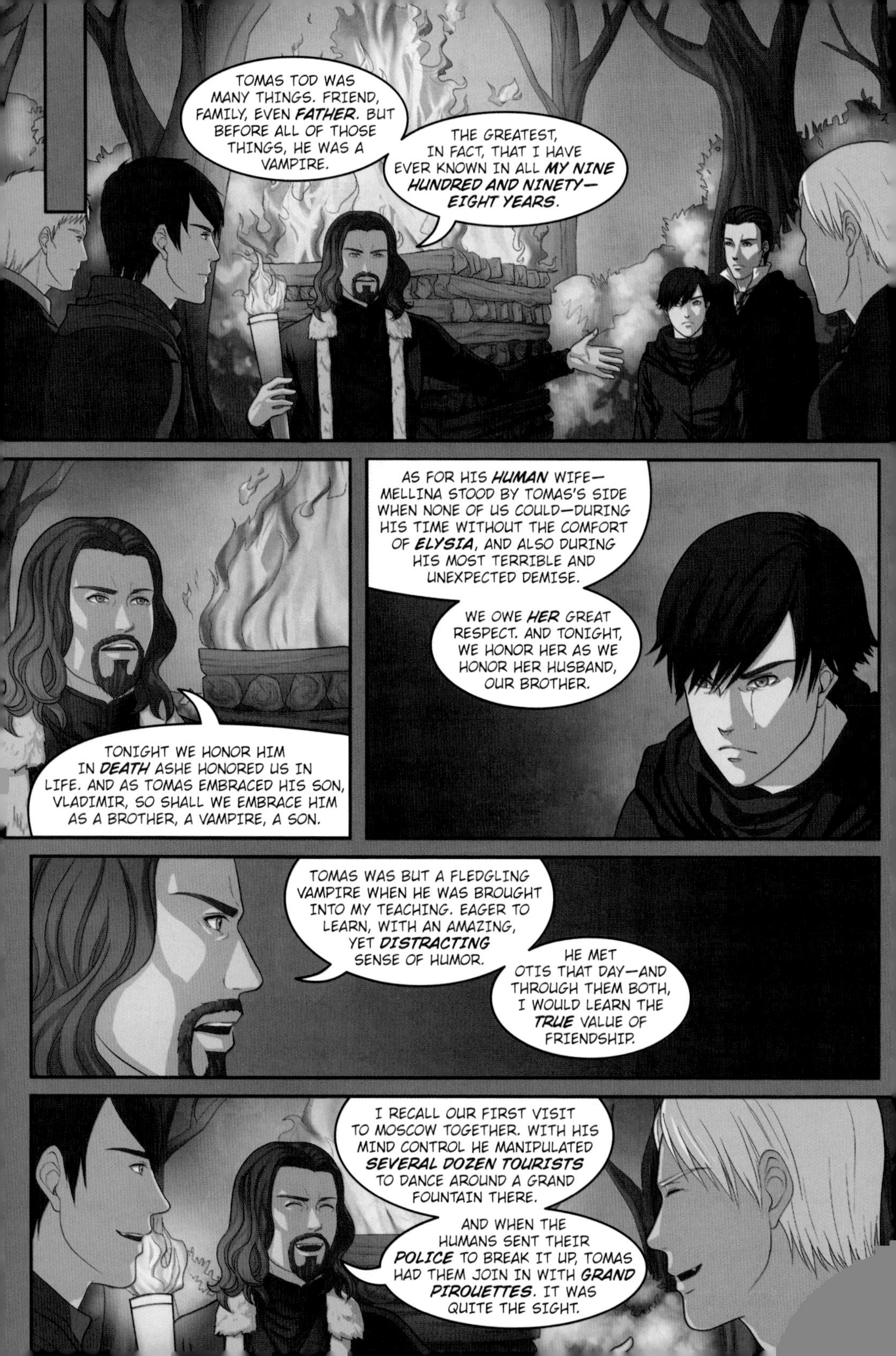
TOMAS TOD WAS MANY THINGS. FRIEND, FAMILY, EVEN FATHER. BUT BEFORE ALL OF THOSE THINGS, HE WAS A VAMPIRE.
THE GREATEST, IN FACT, THAT I HAVE EVER KNOWN IN ALL MY NINE HUNDRED AND NINETY—EIGHT YEARS.
TONIGHT WE HONOR HIM IN DEATH ASHE HONORED US IN LIFE. AND AS TOMAS EMBRACED HIS SON, VLADIMIR, SO SHALL WE EMBRACE HIM AS A BROTHER, A VAMPIRE, A SON.
AS FOR HIS HUMAN WIFE—MELLINA STOOD BY TOMAS'S SIDE WHEN NONE OF US COULD—DURING HIS TIME WITHOUT THE COMFORT OF ELYSIA, AND ALSO DURING HIS MOST TERRIBLE AND UNEXPECTED DEMISE.
WE OWE HER GREAT RESPECT. AND TONIGHT, WE HONOR HER AS WE HONOR HER HUSBAND, OUR BROTHER.
TOMAS WAS BUT A FLEDGLING VAMPIRE WHEN HE WAS BROUGHT INTO MY TEACHING. EAGER TO LEARN, WITH AN AMAZING, YET DISTRACTING SENSE OF HUMOR.
HE MET OTIS THAT DAY—AND THROUGH THEM BOTH, I WOULD LEARN THE TRUE VALUE OF FRIENDSHIP.
I RECALL OUR FIRST VISIT TO MOSCOW TOGETHER. WITH HIS MIND CONTROL HE MANIPULATED SEVERAL DOZEN TOURISTS TO DANCE AROUND A GRAND FOUNTAIN THERE.
AND WHEN THE HUMANS SENT THEIR POLICE TO BREAK IT UP, TOMAS HAD THEM JOIN IN WITH GRAND PIROUETTES. IT WAS QUITE THE SIGHT.

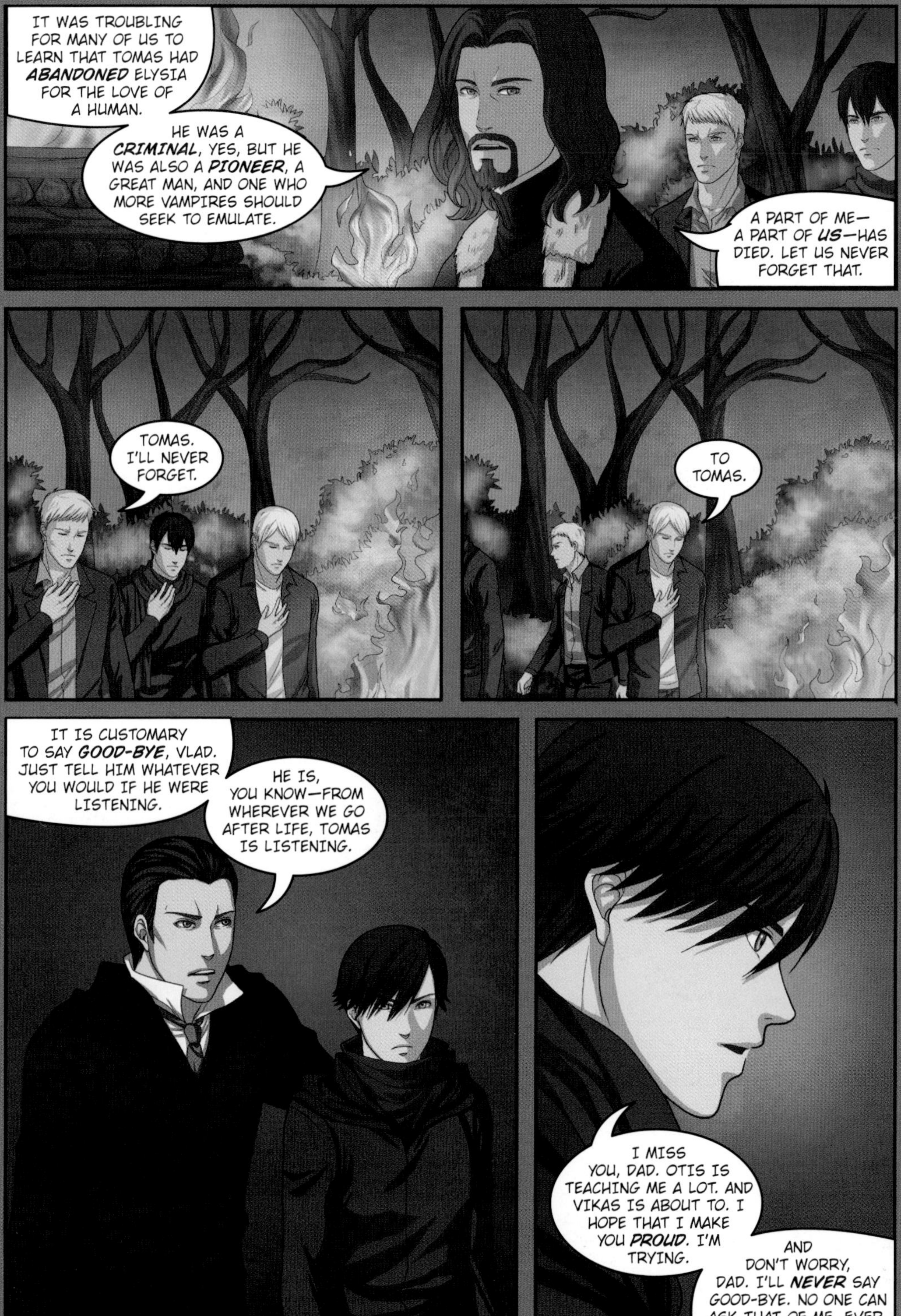
IT WAS TROUBLING FOR MANY OF US TO LEARN THAT TOMAS HAD ***ABANDONED*** ELYSIA FOR THE LOVE OF A HUMAN.
HE WAS A ***CRIMINAL***, YES, BUT HE WAS ALSO A ***PIONEER***, A GREAT MAN, AND ONE WHO MORE VAMPIRES SHOULD SEEK TO EMULATE.
A PART OF ME—A PART OF ***US***—HAS DIED. LET US NEVER FORGET THAT.
TOMAS. I'LL NEVER FORGET.
TO TOMAS.
IT IS CUSTOMARY TO SAY ***GOOD-BYE***, VLAD. JUST TELL HIM WHATEVER YOU WOULD IF HE WERE LISTENING.
HE IS, YOU KNOW—FROM WHEREVER WE GO AFTER LIFE, TOMAS IS LISTENING.
I MISS YOU, DAD. OTIS IS TEACHING ME A LOT. AND VIKAS IS ABOUT TO. I HOPE THAT I MAKE YOU ***PROUD***. I'M TRYING.
AND DON'T WORRY, DAD. I'LL ***NEVER*** SAY GOOD-BYE. NO ONE CAN ASK THAT OF ME. EVER.

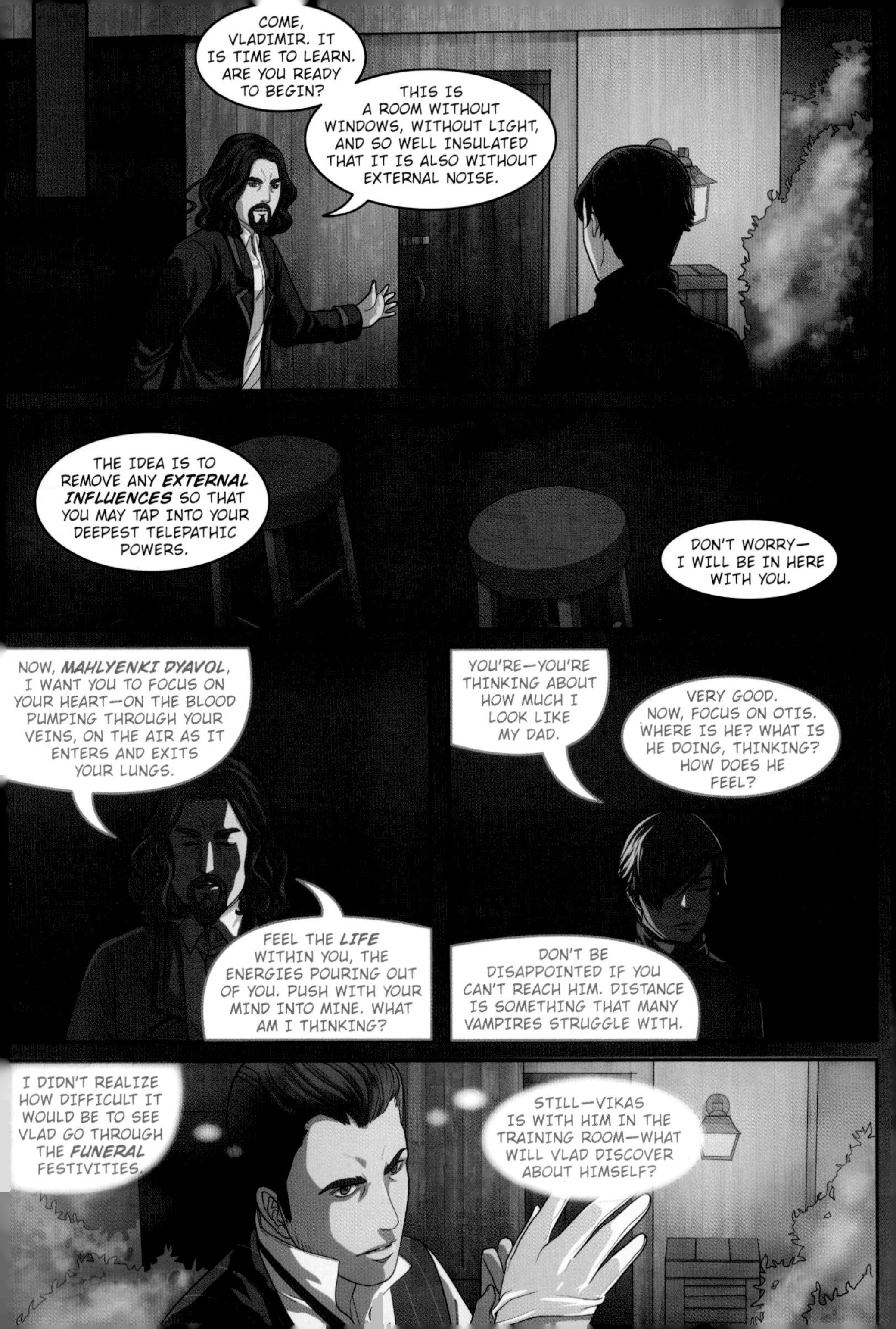
COME, VLADIMIR. IT IS TIME TO LEARN. ARE YOU READY TO BEGIN?
THIS IS A ROOM WITHOUT WINDOWS, WITHOUT LIGHT, AND SO WELL INSULATED THAT IT IS ALSO WITHOUT EXTERNAL NOISE.
THE IDEA IS TO REMOVE ANY *EXTERNAL INFLUENCES* SO THAT YOU MAY TAP INTO YOUR DEEPEST TELEPATHIC POWERS.
DON'T WORRY— I WILL BE IN HERE WITH YOU.
NOW, *MAHLYENKI DYAVOL*, I WANT YOU TO FOCUS ON YOUR HEART—ON THE BLOOD PUMPING THROUGH YOUR VEINS, ON THE AIR AS IT ENTERS AND EXITS YOUR LUNGS.
FEEL THE *LIFE* WITHIN YOU, THE ENERGIES POURING OUT OF YOU. PUSH WITH YOUR MIND INTO MINE. WHAT AM I THINKING?
YOU'RE—YOU'RE THINKING ABOUT HOW MUCH I LOOK LIKE MY DAD.
VERY GOOD. NOW, FOCUS ON OTIS. WHERE IS HE? WHAT IS HE DOING, THINKING? HOW DOES HE FEEL?
DON'T BE DISAPPOINTED IF YOU CAN'T REACH HIM. DISTANCE IS SOMETHING THAT MANY VAMPIRES STRUGGLE WITH.
I DIDN'T REALIZE HOW DIFFICULT IT WOULD BE TO SEE VLAD GO THROUGH THE *FUNERAL* FESTIVITIES.
STILL—VIKAS IS WITH HIM IN THE TRAINING ROOM—WHAT WILL VLAD DISCOVER ABOUT HIMSELF?

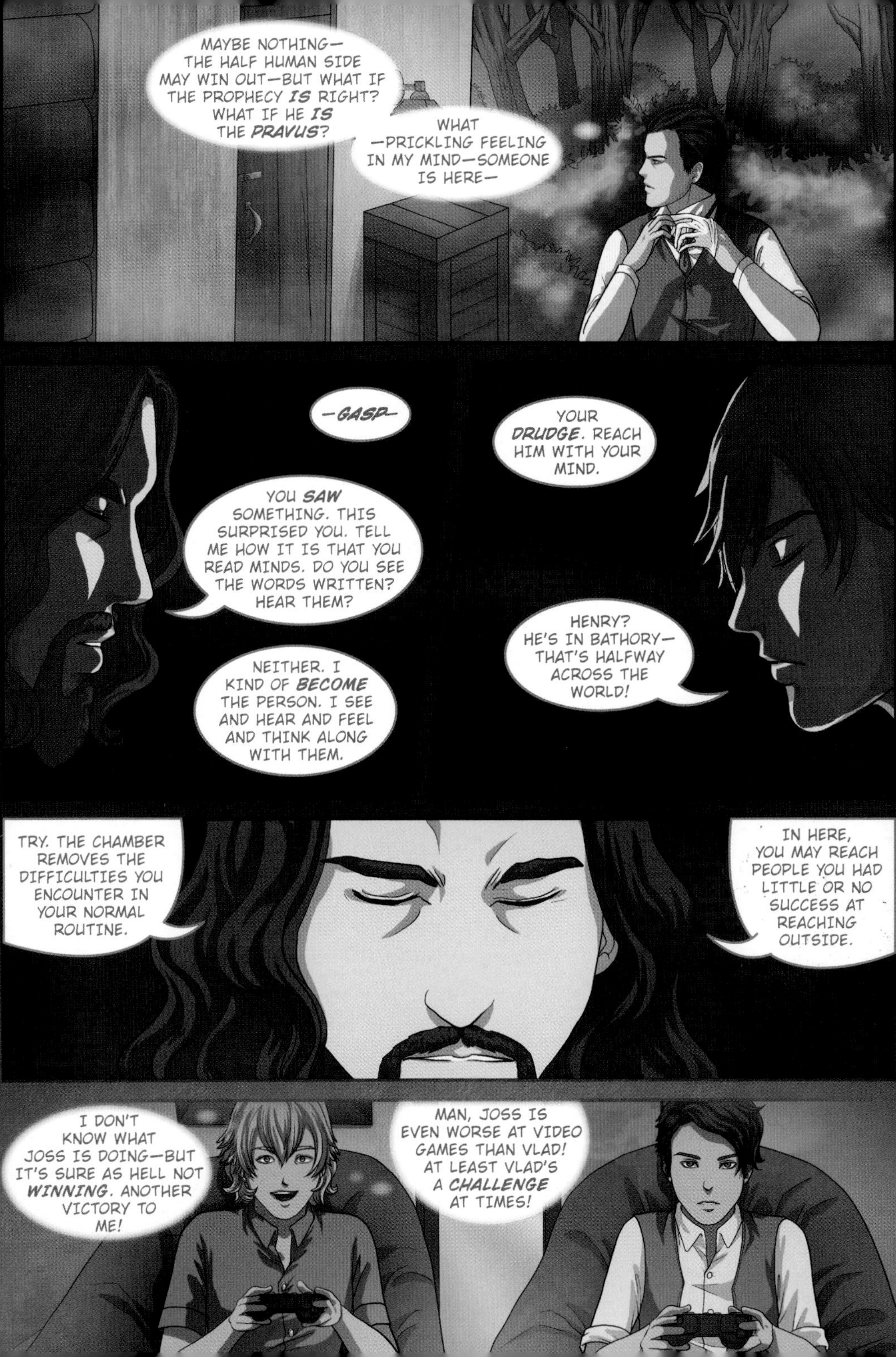

MAYBE NOTHING— THE HALF HUMAN SIDE MAY WIN OUT—BUT WHAT IF THE PROPHECY IS RIGHT? WHAT IF HE IS THE PRAVUS?
WHAT —PRICKLING FEELING IN MY MIND—SOMEONE IS HERE—
—GASP—
YOUR DRUDGE. REACH HIM WITH YOUR MIND.
YOU SAW SOMETHING. THIS SURPRISED YOU. TELL ME HOW IT IS THAT YOU READ MINDS. DO YOU SEE THE WORDS WRITTEN? HEAR THEM?
HENRY? HE'S IN BATHORY— THAT'S HALFWAY ACROSS THE WORLD!
NEITHER. I KIND OF BECOME THE PERSON. I SEE AND HEAR AND FEEL AND THINK ALONG WITH THEM.
TRY. THE CHAMBER REMOVES THE DIFFICULTIES YOU ENCOUNTER IN YOUR NORMAL ROUTINE.
IN HERE, YOU MAY REACH PEOPLE YOU HAD LITTLE OR NO SUCCESS AT REACHING OUTSIDE.
I DON'T KNOW WHAT JOSS IS DOING—BUT IT'S SURE AS HELL NOT WINNING. ANOTHER VICTORY TO ME!
MAN, JOSS IS EVEN WORSE AT VIDEO GAMES THAN VLAD! AT LEAST VLAD'S A CHALLENGE AT TIMES!

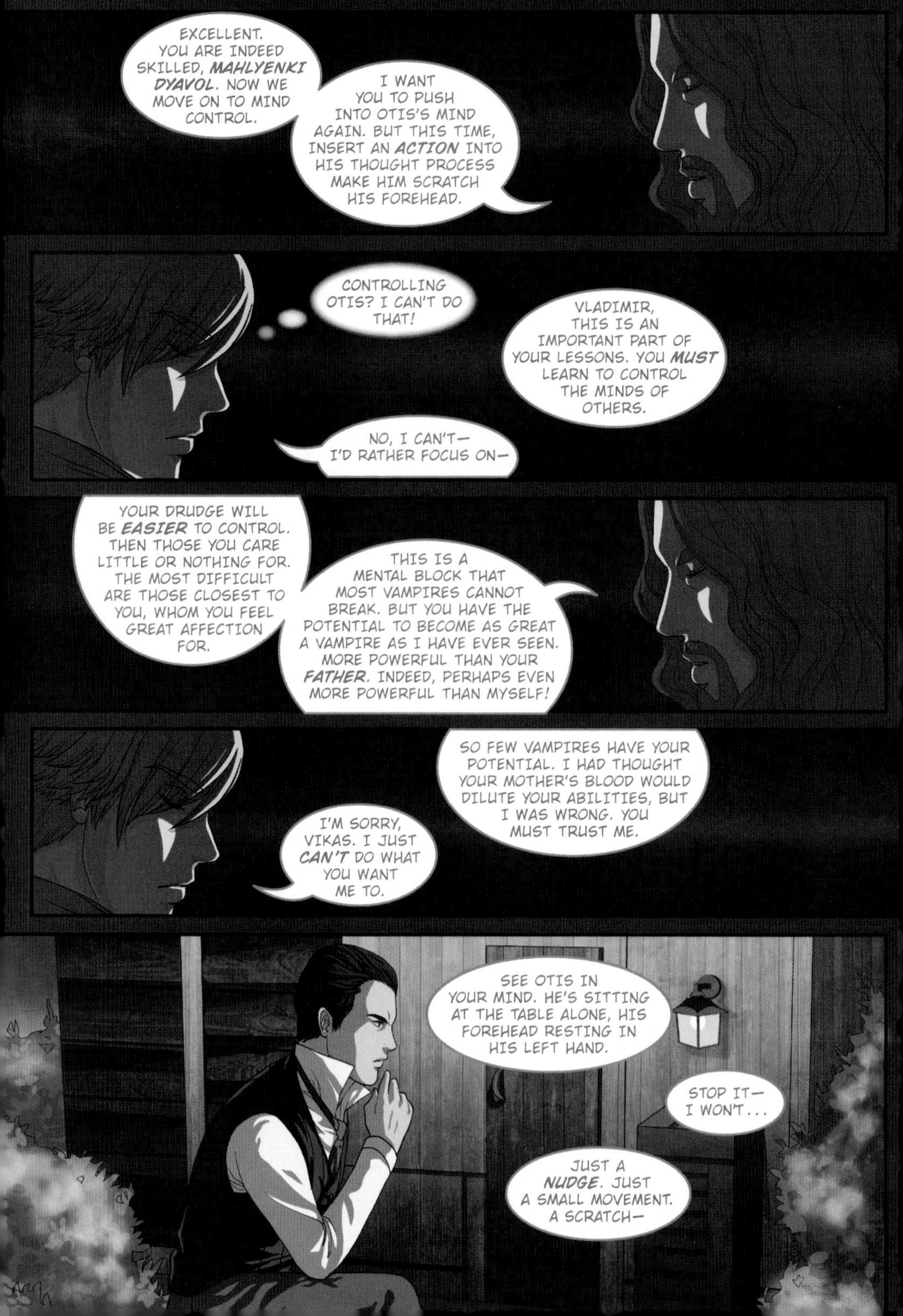
EXCELLENT. YOU ARE INDEED SKILLED, MAHLYENKI DYAVOL. NOW WE MOVE ON TO MIND CONTROL.
I WANT YOU TO PUSH INTO OTIS'S MIND AGAIN. BUT THIS TIME, INSERT AN ACTION INTO HIS THOUGHT PROCESS MAKE HIM SCRATCH HIS FOREHEAD.
CONTROLLING OTIS? I CAN'T DO THAT!
VLADIMIR, THIS IS AN IMPORTANT PART OF YOUR LESSONS. YOU MUST LEARN TO CONTROL THE MINDS OF OTHERS.
NO, I CAN'T— I'D RATHER FOCUS ON—
YOUR DRUDGE WILL BE EASIER TO CONTROL. THEN THOSE YOU CARE LITTLE OR NOTHING FOR. THE MOST DIFFICULT ARE THOSE CLOSEST TO YOU, WHOM YOU FEEL GREAT AFFECTION FOR.
THIS IS A MENTAL BLOCK THAT MOST VAMPIRES CANNOT BREAK. BUT YOU HAVE THE POTENTIAL TO BECOME AS GREAT A VAMPIRE AS I HAVE EVER SEEN. MORE POWERFUL THAN YOUR FATHER. INDEED, PERHAPS EVEN MORE POWERFUL THAN MYSELF!
SO FEW VAMPIRES HAVE YOUR POTENTIAL. I HAD THOUGHT YOUR MOTHER'S BLOOD WOULD DILUTE YOUR ABILITIES, BUT I WAS WRONG. YOU MUST TRUST ME.
I'M SORRY, VIKAS. I JUST CAN'T DO WHAT YOU WANT ME TO.
SEE OTIS IN YOUR MIND. HE'S SITTING AT THE TABLE ALONE, HIS FOREHEAD RESTING IN HIS LEFT HAND.
STOP IT— I WON'T . . .
JUST A NUDGE. JUST A SMALL MOVEMENT. A SCRATCH—

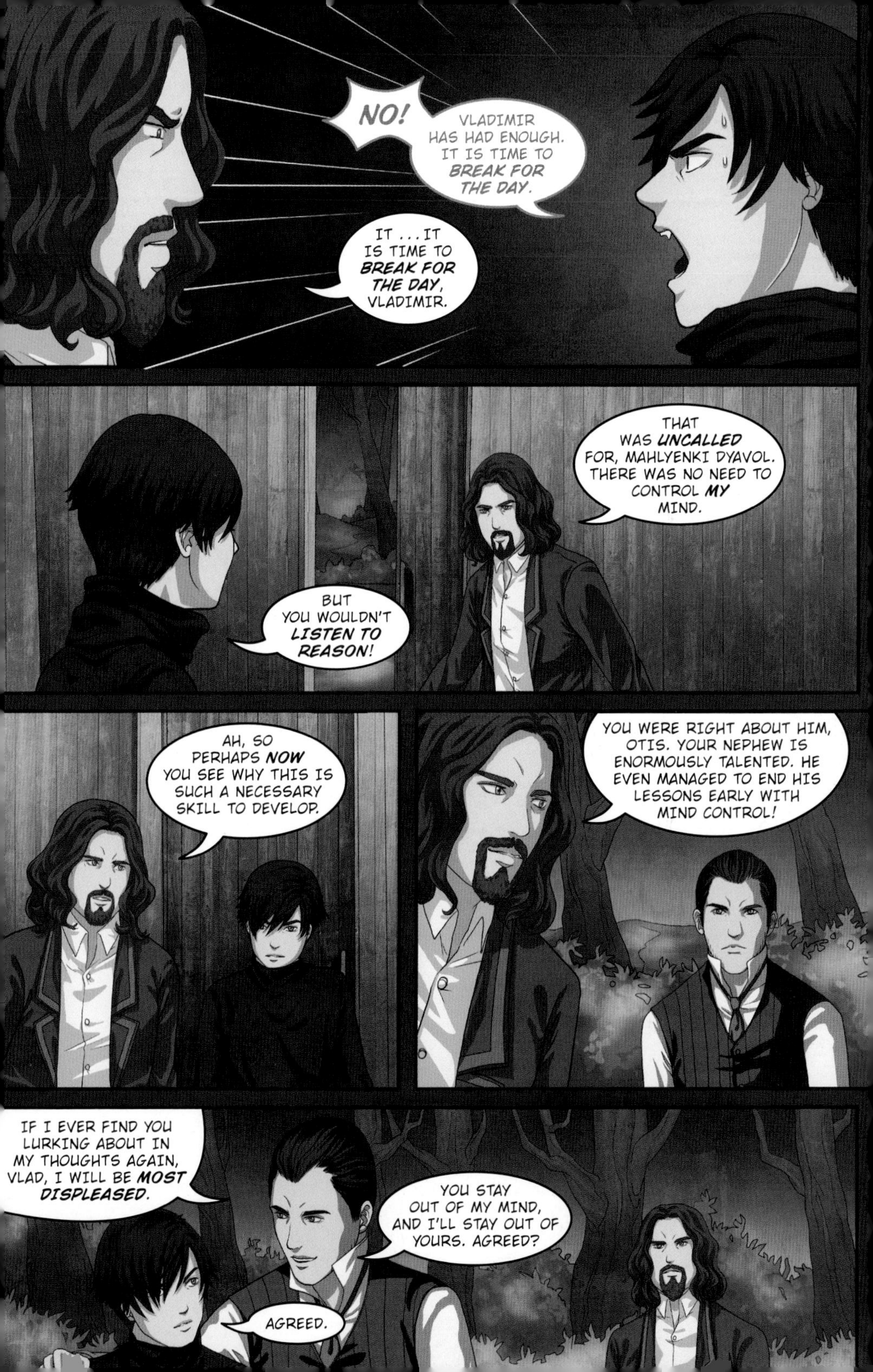

NO!
VLADIMIR HAS HAD ENOUGH. IT IS TIME TO BREAK FOR THE DAY.
IT . . . IT IS TIME TO BREAK FOR THE DAY, VLADIMIR.
THAT WAS UNCALLED FOR, MAHLYENKI DYAVOL. THERE WAS NO NEED TO CONTROL MY MIND.
BUT YOU WOULDN'T LISTEN TO REASON!
AH, SO PERHAPS NOW YOU SEE WHY THIS IS SUCH A NECESSARY SKILL TO DEVELOP.
YOU WERE RIGHT ABOUT HIM, OTIS. YOUR NEPHEW IS ENORMOUSLY TALENTED. HE EVEN MANAGED TO END HIS LESSONS EARLY WITH MIND CONTROL!
IF I EVER FIND YOU LURKING ABOUT IN MY THOUGHTS AGAIN, VLAD, I WILL BE MOST DISPLEASED.
YOU STAY OUT OF MY MIND, AND I'LL STAY OUT OF YOURS. AGREED?
AGREED.

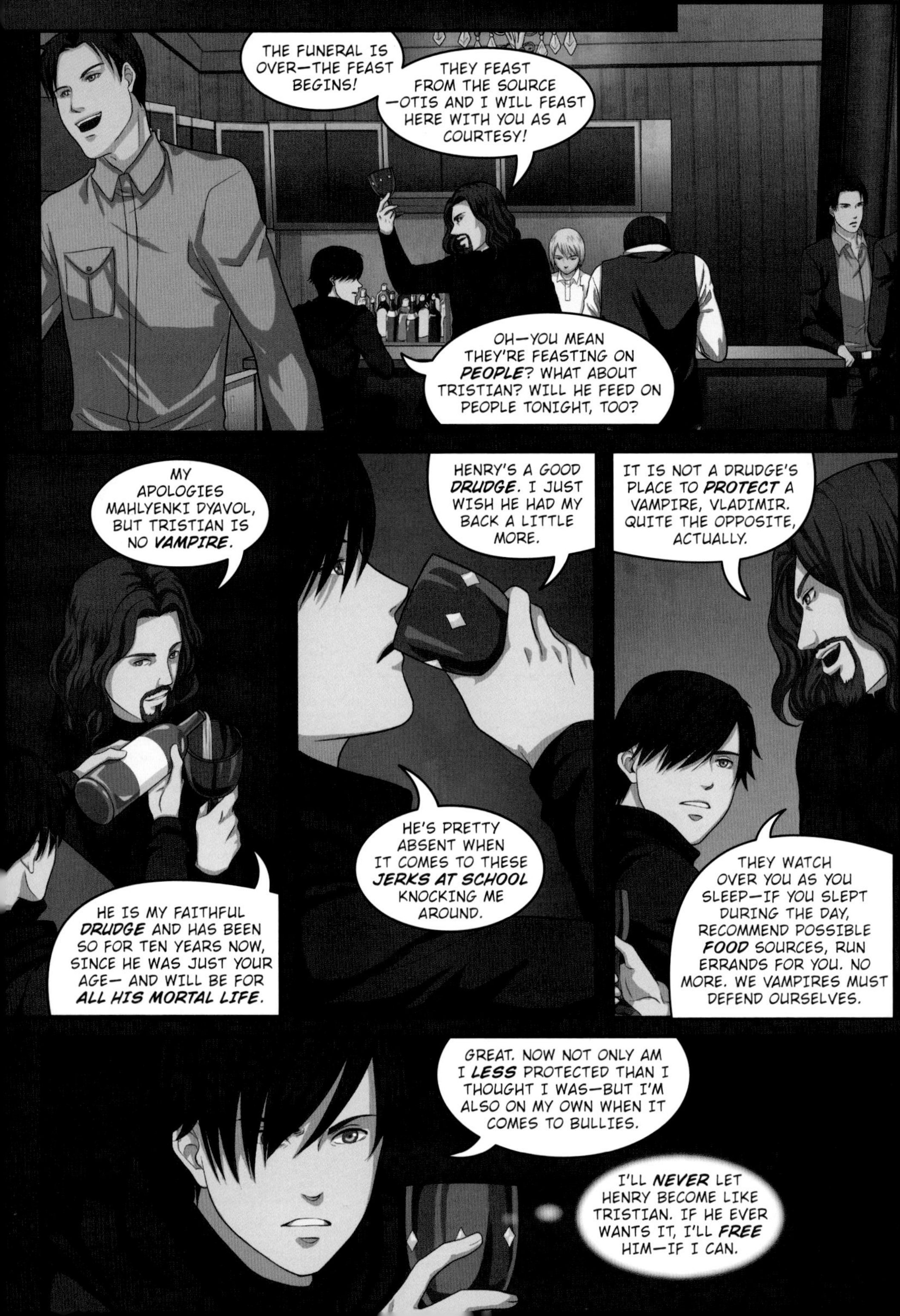
THE FUNERAL IS OVER—THE FEAST BEGINS!
THEY FEAST FROM THE SOURCE —OTIS AND I WILL FEAST HERE WITH YOU AS A COURTESY!
OH—YOU MEAN THEY'RE FEASTING ON PEOPLE? WHAT ABOUT TRISTIAN? WILL HE FEED ON PEOPLE TONIGHT, TOO?
MY APOLOGIES MAHLYENKI DYAVOL, BUT TRISTIAN IS NO VAMPIRE.
HE IS MY FAITHFUL DRUDGE AND HAS BEEN SO FOR TEN YEARS NOW, SINCE HE WAS JUST YOUR AGE— AND WILL BE FOR ALL HIS MORTAL LIFE.
HENRY'S A GOOD DRUDGE. I JUST WISH HE HAD MY BACK A LITTLE MORE.
HE'S PRETTY ABSENT WHEN IT COMES TO THESE JERKS AT SCHOOL KNOCKING ME AROUND.
IT IS NOT A DRUDGE'S PLACE TO PROTECT A VAMPIRE, VLADIMIR. QUITE THE OPPOSITE, ACTUALLY.
THEY WATCH OVER YOU AS YOU SLEEP—IF YOU SLEPT DURING THE DAY, RECOMMEND POSSIBLE FOOD SOURCES, RUN ERRANDS FOR YOU. NO MORE. WE VAMPIRES MUST DEFEND OURSELVES.
GREAT. NOW NOT ONLY AM I LESS PROTECTED THAN I THOUGHT I WAS—BUT I'M ALSO ON MY OWN WHEN IT COMES TO BULLIES.
I'LL NEVER LET HENRY BECOME LIKE TRISTIAN. IF HE EVER WANTS IT, I'LL FREE HIM—IF I CAN.

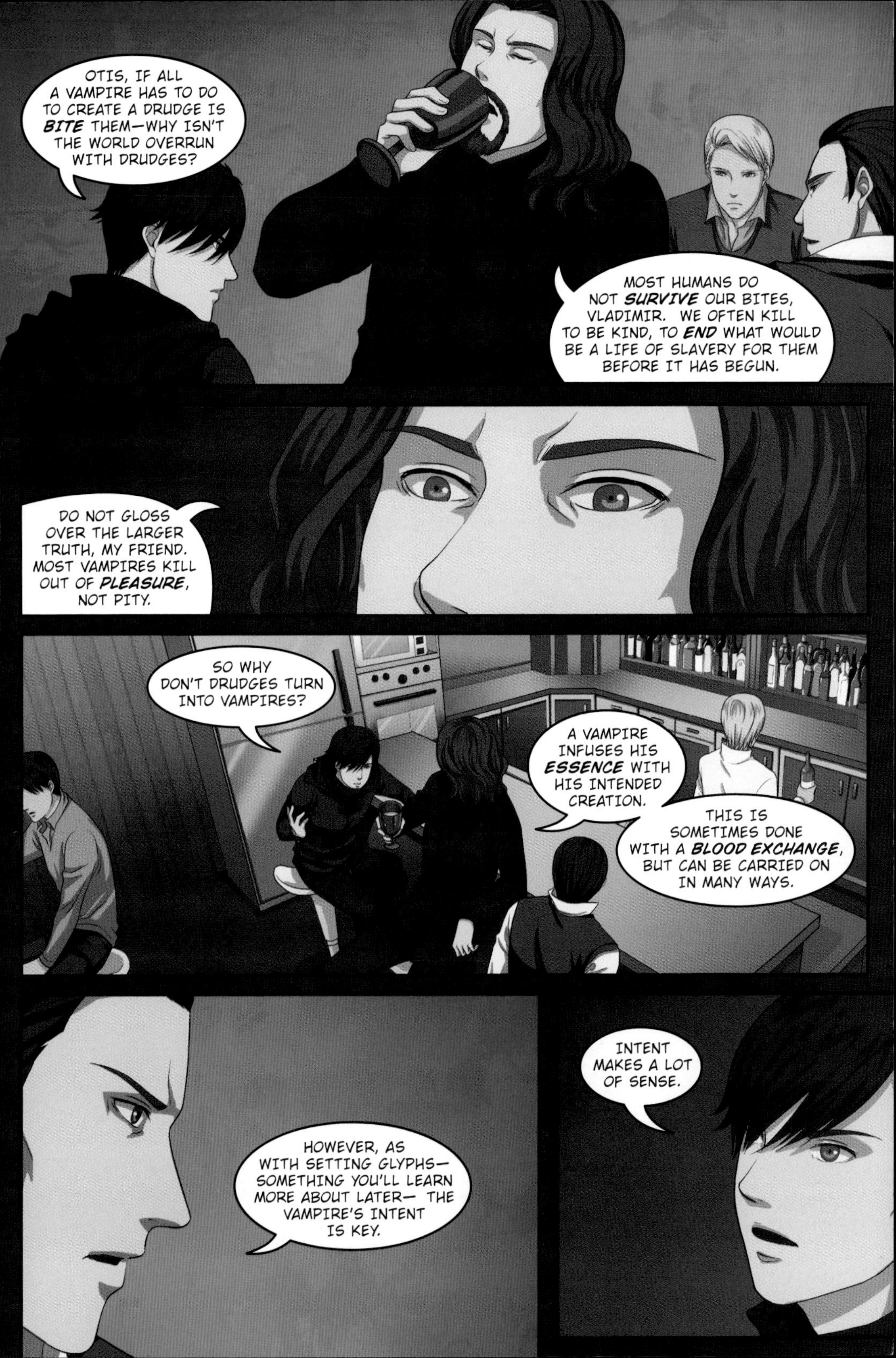
OTIS, IF ALL A VAMPIRE HAS TO DO TO CREATE A DRUDGE IS BITE THEM—WHY ISN'T THE WORLD OVERRUN WITH DRUDGES?
MOST HUMANS DO NOT SURVIVE OUR BITES, VLADIMIR. WE OFTEN KILL TO BE KIND, TO END WHAT WOULD BE A LIFE OF SLAVERY FOR THEM BEFORE IT HAS BEGUN.
DO NOT GLOSS OVER THE LARGER TRUTH, MY FRIEND. MOST VAMPIRES KILL OUT OF PLEASURE, NOT PITY.
SO WHY DON'T DRUDGES TURN INTO VAMPIRES?
A VAMPIRE INFUSES HIS ESSENCE WITH HIS INTENDED CREATION.
THIS IS SOMETIMES DONE WITH A BLOOD EXCHANGE, BUT CAN BE CARRIED ON IN MANY WAYS.
HOWEVER, AS WITH SETTING GLYPHS— SOMETHING YOU'LL LEARN MORE ABOUT LATER— THE VAMPIRE'S INTENT IS KEY.
INTENT MAKES A LOT OF SENSE.

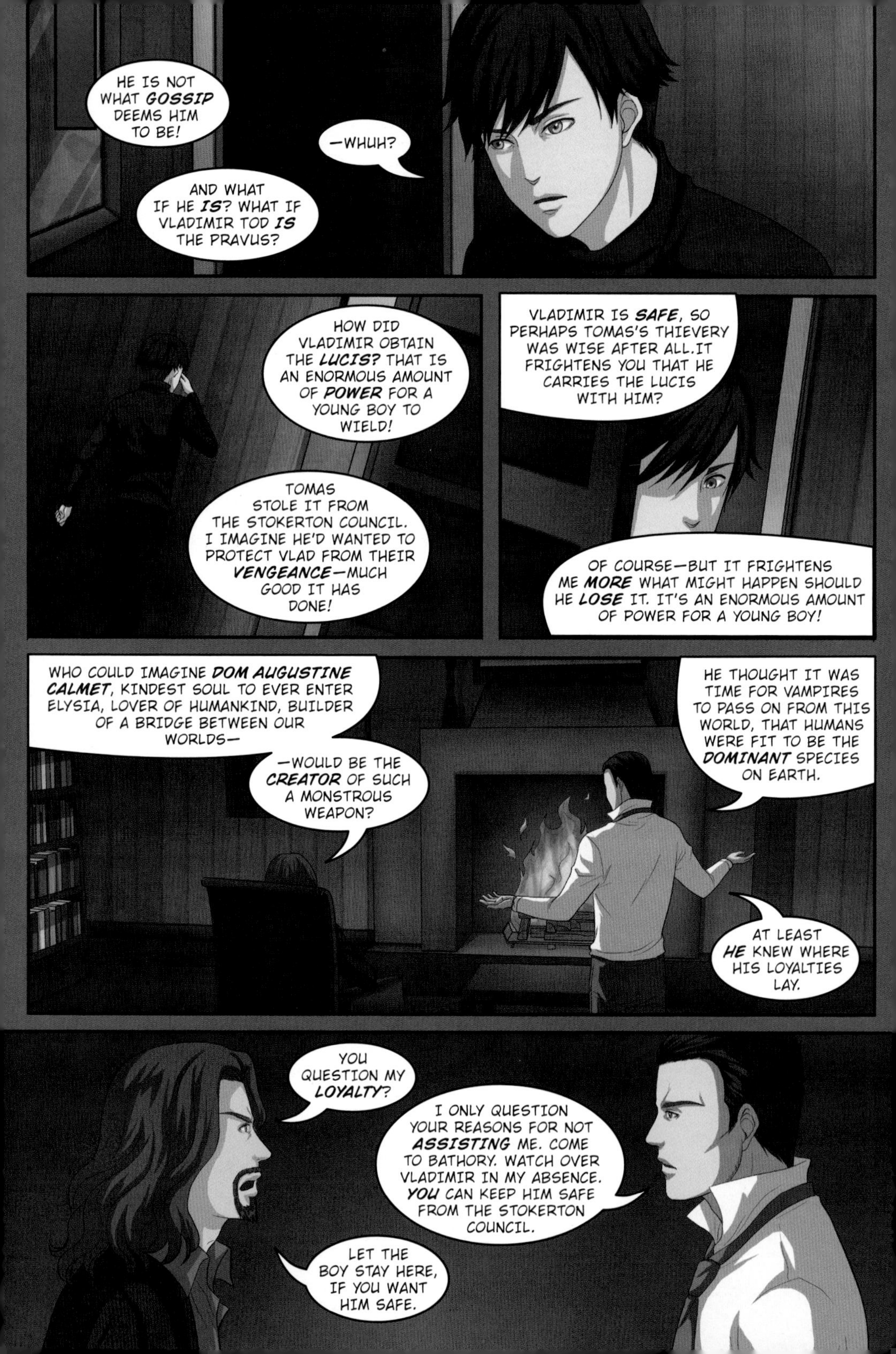
HE IS NOT WHAT GOSSIP DEEMS HIM TO BE!
—WHUH?
AND WHAT IF HE IS? WHAT IF VLADIMIR TOD IS THE PRAVUS?
HOW DID VLADIMIR OBTAIN THE LUCIS? THAT IS AN ENORMOUS AMOUNT OF POWER FOR A YOUNG BOY TO WIELD!
TOMAS STOLE IT FROM THE STOKERTON COUNCIL. I IMAGINE HE'D WANTED TO PROTECT VLAD FROM THEIR VENGEANCE—MUCH GOOD IT HAS DONE!
VLADIMIR IS SAFE, SO PERHAPS TOMAS'S THIEVERY WAS WISE AFTER ALL.IT FRIGHTENS YOU THAT HE CARRIES THE LUCIS WITH HIM?
OF COURSE—BUT IT FRIGHTENS ME MORE WHAT MIGHT HAPPEN SHOULD HE LOSE IT. IT'S AN ENORMOUS AMOUNT OF POWER FOR A YOUNG BOY!
WHO COULD IMAGINE DOM AUGUSTINE CALMET, KINDEST SOUL TO EVER ENTER ELYSIA, LOVER OF HUMANKIND, BUILDER OF A BRIDGE BETWEEN OUR WORLDS—
—WOULD BE THE CREATOR OF SUCH A MONSTROUS WEAPON?
HE THOUGHT IT WAS TIME FOR VAMPIRES TO PASS ON FROM THIS WORLD, THAT HUMANS WERE FIT TO BE THE DOMINANT SPECIES ON EARTH.
AT LEAST HE KNEW WHERE HIS LOYALTIES LAY.
YOU QUESTION MY LOYALTY?
I ONLY QUESTION YOUR REASONS FOR NOT ASSISTING ME. COME TO BATHORY. WATCH OVER VLADIMIR IN MY ABSENCE. YOU CAN KEEP HIM SAFE FROM THE STOKERTON COUNCIL.
LET THE BOY STAY HERE, IF YOU WANT HIM SAFE.

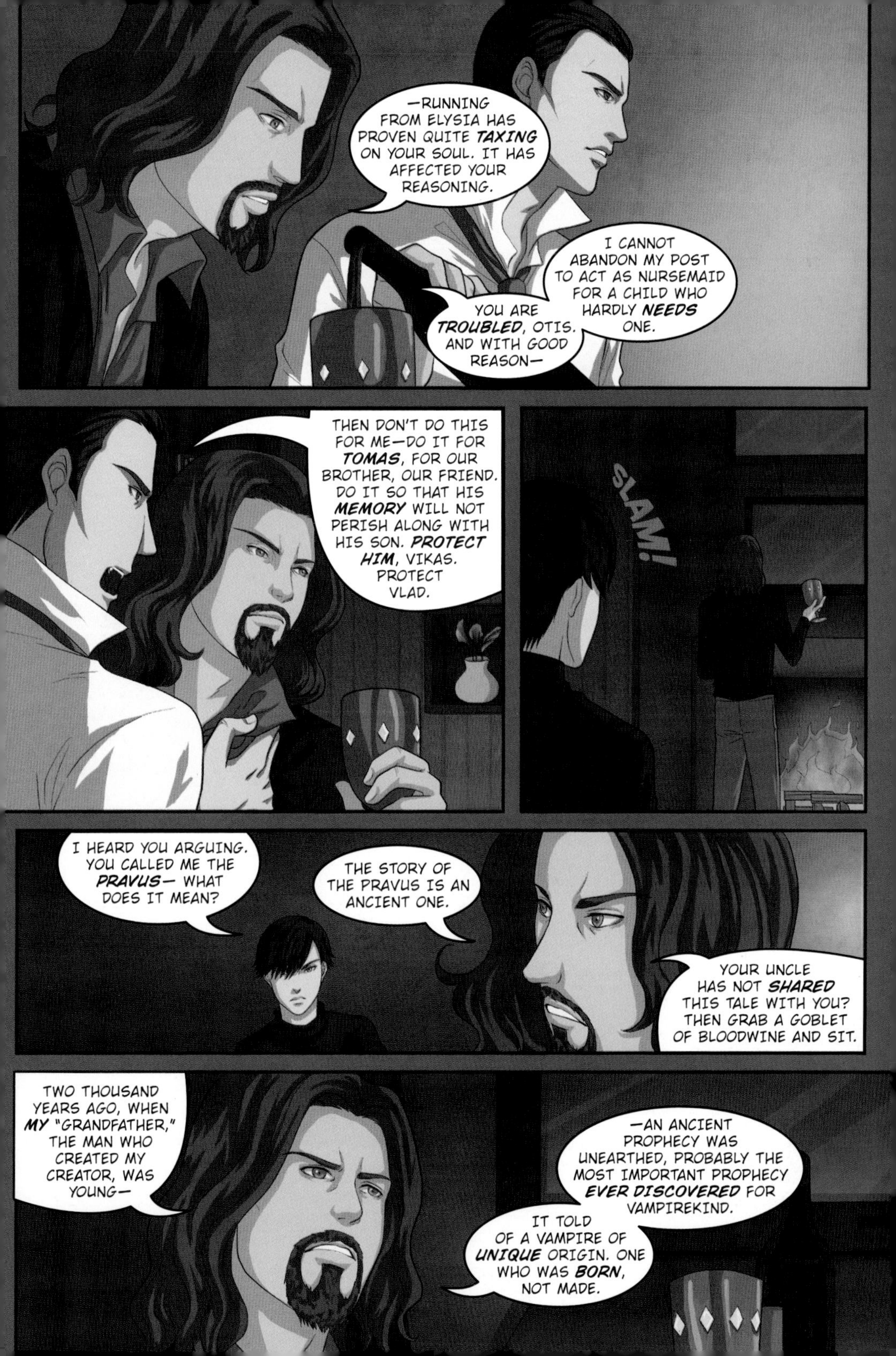
—RUNNING FROM ELYSIA HAS PROVEN QUITE TAXING ON YOUR SOUL. IT HAS AFFECTED YOUR REASONING.
I CANNOT ABANDON MY POST TO ACT AS NURSEMAID FOR A CHILD WHO HARDLY NEEDS ONE.
YOU ARE TROUBLED, OTIS. AND WITH GOOD REASON—
THEN DON'T DO THIS FOR ME—DO IT FOR TOMAS, FOR OUR BROTHER, OUR FRIEND. DO IT SO THAT HIS MEMORY WILL NOT PERISH ALONG WITH HIS SON. PROTECT HIM, VIKAS. PROTECT VLAD.
SLAM!
I HEARD YOU ARGUING. YOU CALLED ME THE PRAVUS— WHAT DOES IT MEAN?
THE STORY OF THE PRAVUS IS AN ANCIENT ONE.
YOUR UNCLE HAS NOT SHARED THIS TALE WITH YOU? THEN GRAB A GOBLET OF BLOODWINE AND SIT.
TWO THOUSAND YEARS AGO, WHEN MY "GRANDFATHER," THE MAN WHO CREATED MY CREATOR, WAS YOUNG—
—AN ANCIENT PROPHECY WAS UNEARTHED, PROBABLY THE MOST IMPORTANT PROPHECY EVER DISCOVERED FOR VAMPIREKIND.
IT TOLD OF A VAMPIRE OF UNIQUE ORIGIN. ONE WHO WAS BORN, NOT MADE.

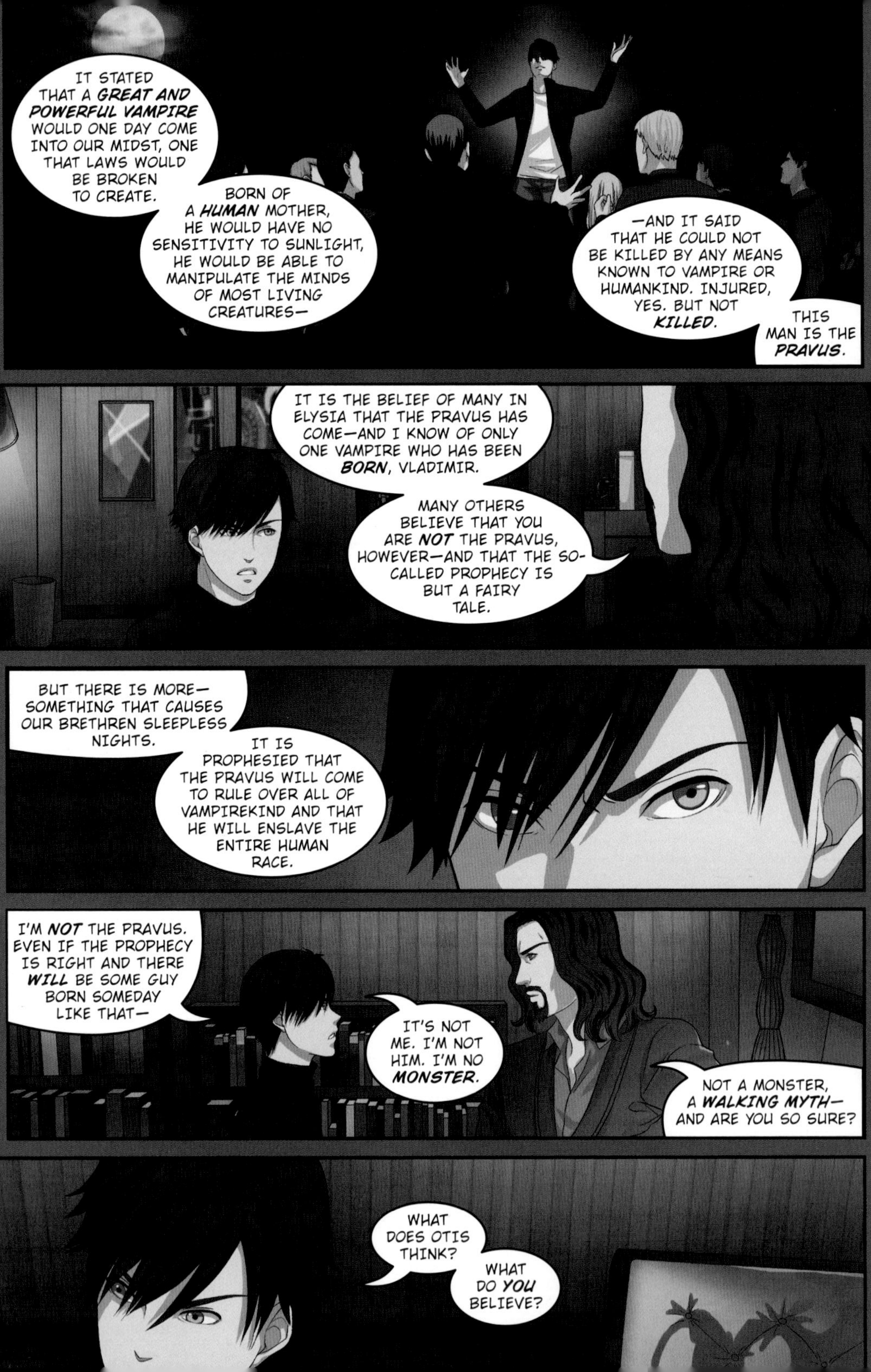
IT STATED THAT A GREAT AND POWERFUL VAMPIRE WOULD ONE DAY COME INTO OUR MIDST, ONE THAT LAWS WOULD BE BROKEN TO CREATE.
BORN OF A HUMAN MOTHER, HE WOULD HAVE NO SENSITIVITY TO SUNLIGHT, HE WOULD BE ABLE TO MANIPULATE THE MINDS OF MOST LIVING CREATURES—
—AND IT SAID THAT HE COULD NOT BE KILLED BY ANY MEANS KNOWN TO VAMPIRE OR HUMANKIND. INJURED, YES. BUT NOT KILLED.
THIS MAN IS THE PRAVUS.
IT IS THE BELIEF OF MANY IN ELYSIA THAT THE PRAVUS HAS COME—AND I KNOW OF ONLY ONE VAMPIRE WHO HAS BEEN BORN, VLADIMIR.
MANY OTHERS BELIEVE THAT YOU ARE NOT THE PRAVUS, HOWEVER—AND THAT THE SO-CALLED PROPHECY IS BUT A FAIRY TALE.
BUT THERE IS MORE—SOMETHING THAT CAUSES OUR BRETHREN SLEEPLESS NIGHTS.
IT IS PROPHESIED THAT THE PRAVUS WILL COME TO RULE OVER ALL OF VAMPIREKIND AND THAT HE WILL ENSLAVE THE ENTIRE HUMAN RACE.
I'M NOT THE PRAVUS. EVEN IF THE PROPHECY IS RIGHT AND THERE WILL BE SOME GUY BORN SOMEDAY LIKE THAT—
IT'S NOT ME. I'M NOT HIM. I'M NO MONSTER.
NOT A MONSTER, A WALKING MYTH—AND ARE YOU SO SURE?
WHAT DOES OTIS THINK?
WHAT DO YOU BELIEVE?

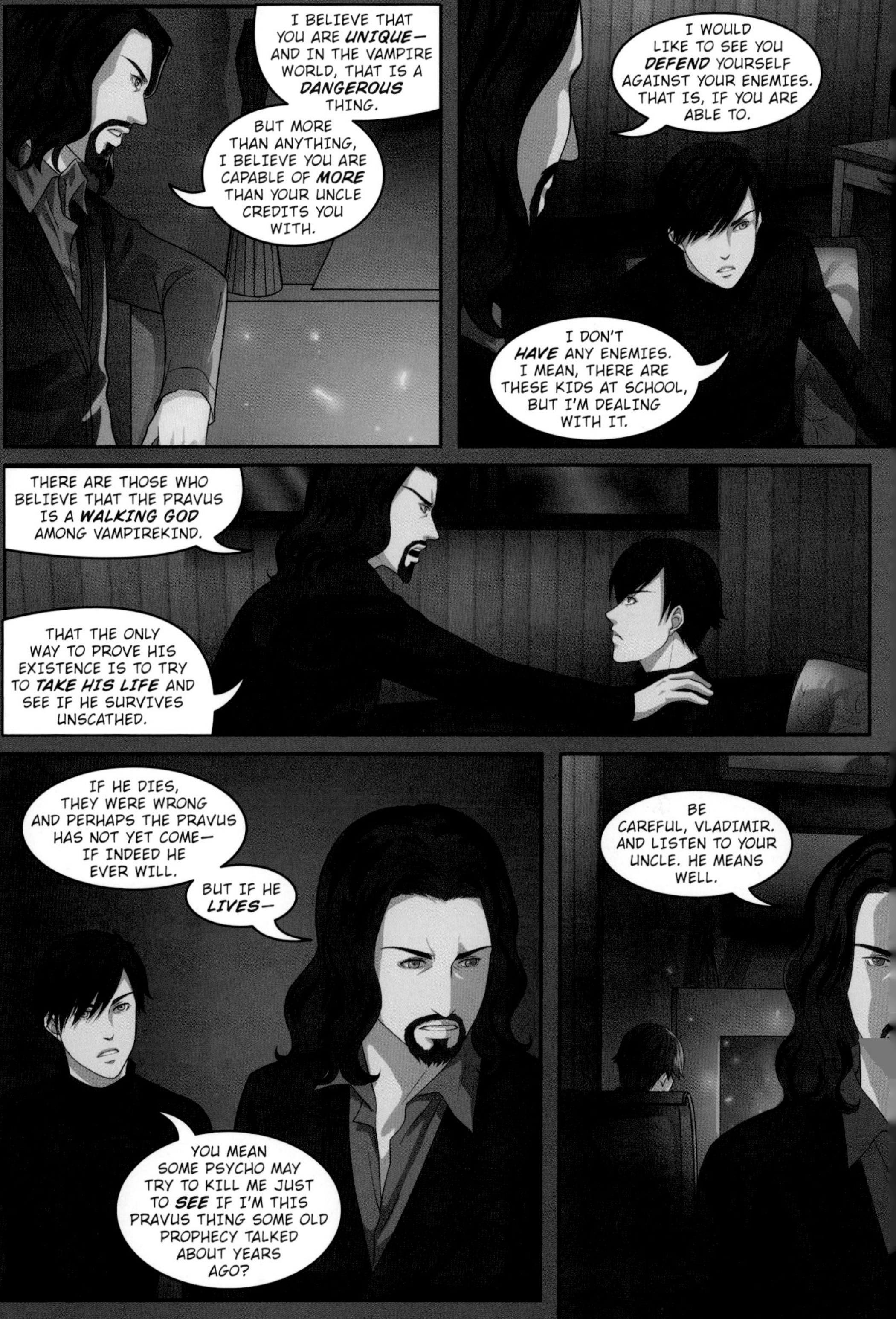
I BELIEVE THAT YOU ARE *UNIQUE*— AND IN THE VAMPIRE WORLD, THAT IS A *DANGEROUS* THING.
BUT MORE THAN ANYTHING, I BELIEVE YOU ARE CAPABLE OF *MORE* THAN YOUR UNCLE CREDITS YOU WITH.
I WOULD LIKE TO SEE YOU *DEFEND* YOURSELF AGAINST YOUR ENEMIES. THAT IS, IF YOU ARE ABLE TO.
I DON'T *HAVE* ANY ENEMIES. I MEAN, THERE ARE THESE KIDS AT SCHOOL, BUT I'M DEALING WITH IT.
THERE ARE THOSE WHO BELIEVE THAT THE PRAVUS IS A *WALKING GOD* AMONG VAMPIREKIND.
THAT THE ONLY WAY TO PROVE HIS EXISTENCE IS TO TRY TO *TAKE HIS LIFE* AND SEE IF HE SURVIVES UNSCATHED.
IF HE DIES, THEY WERE WRONG AND PERHAPS THE PRAVUS HAS NOT YET COME— IF INDEED HE EVER WILL.
BUT IF HE *LIVES*—
YOU MEAN SOME PSYCHO MAY TRY TO KILL ME JUST TO *SEE* IF I'M THIS PRAVUS THING SOME OLD PROPHECY TALKED ABOUT YEARS AGO?
BE CAREFUL, VLADIMIR. AND LISTEN TO YOUR UNCLE. HE MEANS WELL.

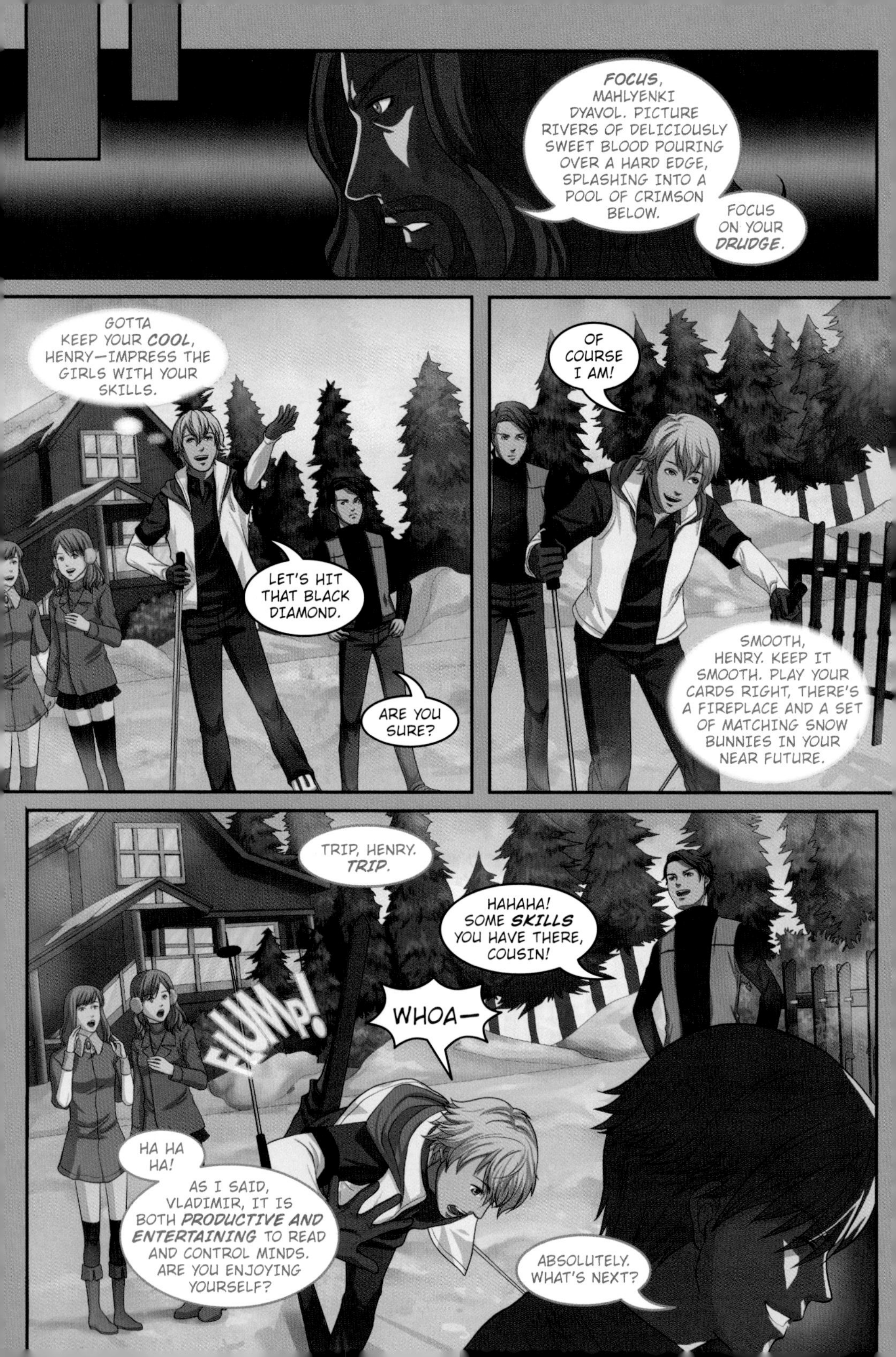
FOCUS, MAHLYENKI DYAVOL. PICTURE RIVERS OF DELICIOUSLY SWEET BLOOD POURING OVER A HARD EDGE, SPLASHING INTO A POOL OF CRIMSON BELOW.
FOCUS ON YOUR DRUDGE.
GOTTA KEEP YOUR COOL, HENRY—IMPRESS THE GIRLS WITH YOUR SKILLS.
LET'S HIT THAT BLACK DIAMOND.
ARE YOU SURE?
OF COURSE I AM!
SMOOTH, HENRY. KEEP IT SMOOTH. PLAY YOUR CARDS RIGHT, THERE'S A FIREPLACE AND A SET OF MATCHING SNOW BUNNIES IN YOUR NEAR FUTURE.
TRIP, HENRY. TRIP.
HAHAHA! SOME SKILLS YOU HAVE THERE, COUSIN!
WHOA—
FLUMP!
HA HA HA!
AS I SAID, VLADIMIR, IT IS BOTH PRODUCTIVE AND ENTERTAINING TO READ AND CONTROL MINDS. ARE YOU ENJOYING YOURSELF?
ABSOLUTELY. WHAT'S NEXT?

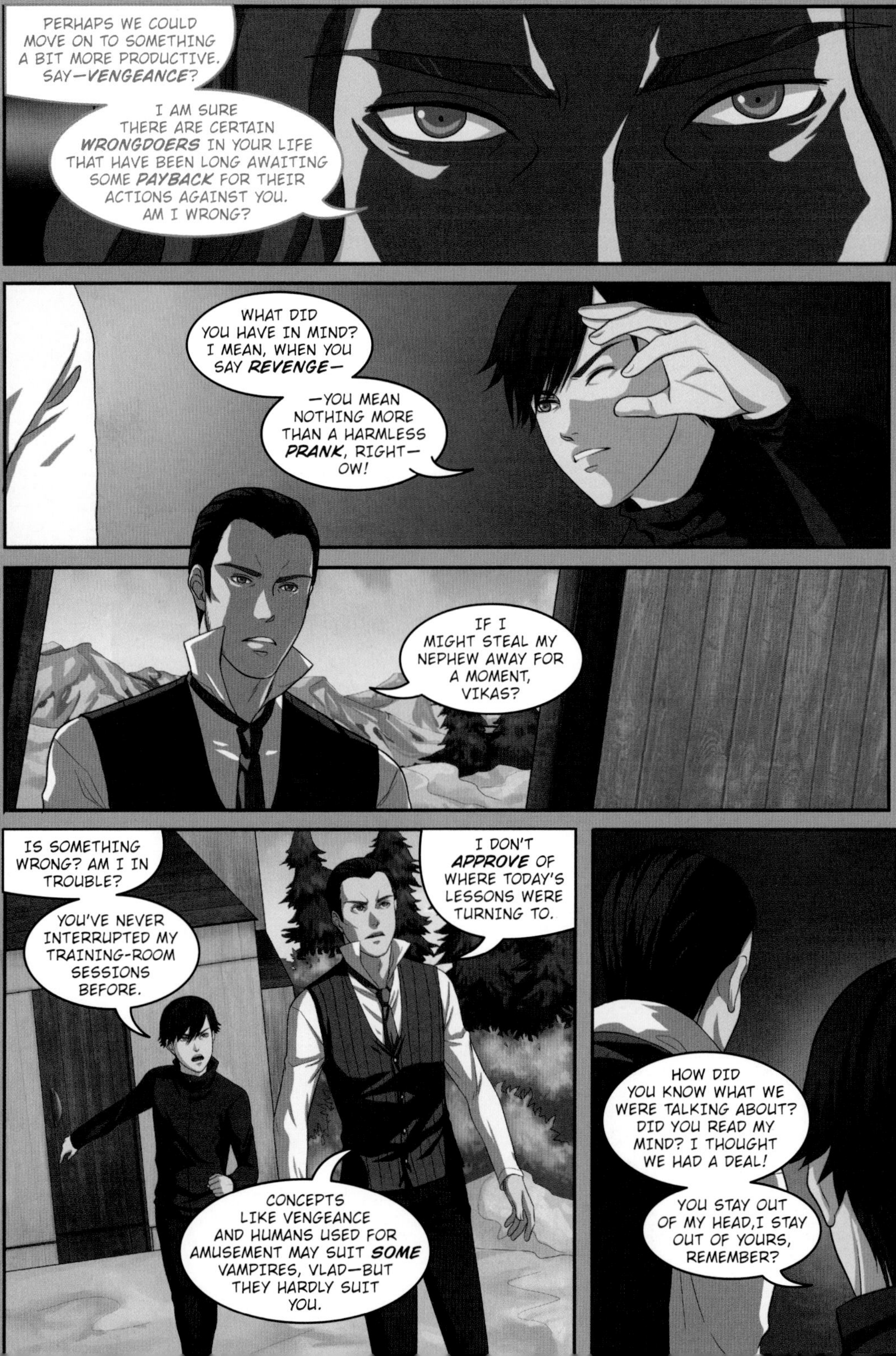
PERHAPS WE COULD MOVE ON TO SOMETHING A BIT MORE PRODUCTIVE. SAY—*VENGEANCE*?
I AM SURE THERE ARE CERTAIN *WRONGDOERS* IN YOUR LIFE THAT HAVE BEEN LONG AWAITING SOME *PAYBACK* FOR THEIR ACTIONS AGAINST YOU. AM I WRONG?
WHAT DID YOU HAVE IN MIND? I MEAN, WHEN YOU SAY *REVENGE*—
—YOU MEAN NOTHING MORE THAN A HARMLESS *PRANK*, RIGHT—OW!
IF I MIGHT STEAL MY NEPHEW AWAY FOR A MOMENT, VIKAS?
IS SOMETHING WRONG? AM I IN TROUBLE?
YOU'VE NEVER INTERRUPTED MY TRAINING-ROOM SESSIONS BEFORE.
I DON'T *APPROVE* OF WHERE TODAY'S LESSONS WERE TURNING TO.
CONCEPTS LIKE VENGEANCE AND HUMANS USED FOR AMUSEMENT MAY SUIT *SOME* VAMPIRES, VLAD—BUT THEY HARDLY SUIT YOU.
HOW DID YOU KNOW WHAT WE WERE TALKING ABOUT? DID YOU READ MY MIND? I THOUGHT WE HAD A DEAL!
YOU STAY OUT OF MY HEAD, I STAY OUT OF YOURS, REMEMBER?

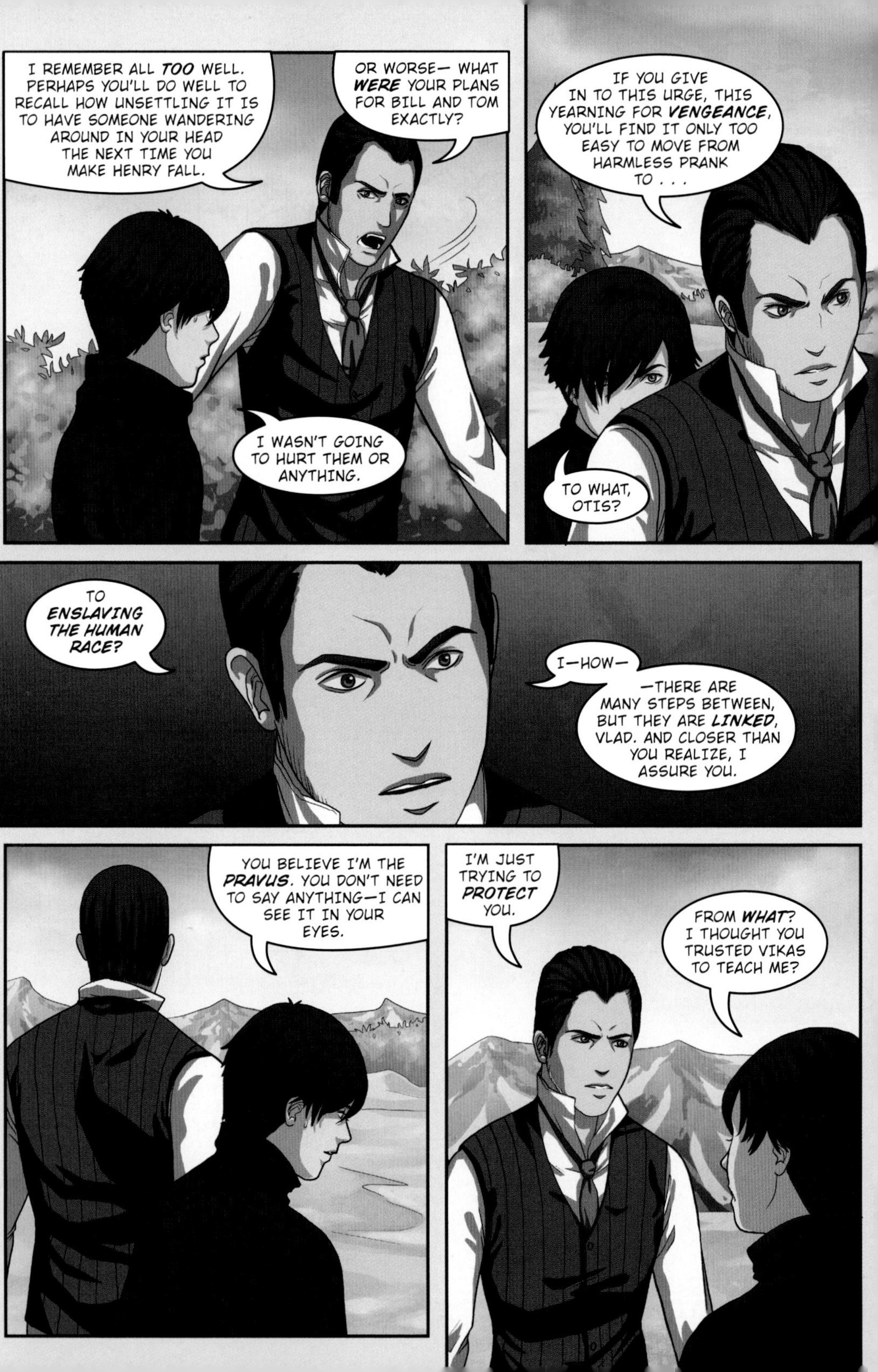
I REMEMBER ALL TOO WELL. PERHAPS YOU'LL DO WELL TO RECALL HOW UNSETTLING IT IS TO HAVE SOMEONE WANDERING AROUND IN YOUR HEAD THE NEXT TIME YOU MAKE HENRY FALL.
OR WORSE— WHAT WERE YOUR PLANS FOR BILL AND TOM EXACTLY?
I WASN'T GOING TO HURT THEM OR ANYTHING.
IF YOU GIVE IN TO THIS URGE, THIS YEARNING FOR VENGEANCE, YOU'LL FIND IT ONLY TOO EASY TO MOVE FROM HARMLESS PRANK TO . . .
TO WHAT, OTIS?
TO ENSLAVING THE HUMAN RACE?
I—HOW—
—THERE ARE MANY STEPS BETWEEN, BUT THEY ARE LINKED, VLAD. AND CLOSER THAN YOU REALIZE, I ASSURE YOU.
YOU BELIEVE I'M THE PRAVUS. YOU DON'T NEED TO SAY ANYTHING—I CAN SEE IT IN YOUR EYES.
I'M JUST TRYING TO PROTECT YOU.
FROM WHAT? I THOUGHT YOU TRUSTED VIKAS TO TEACH ME?

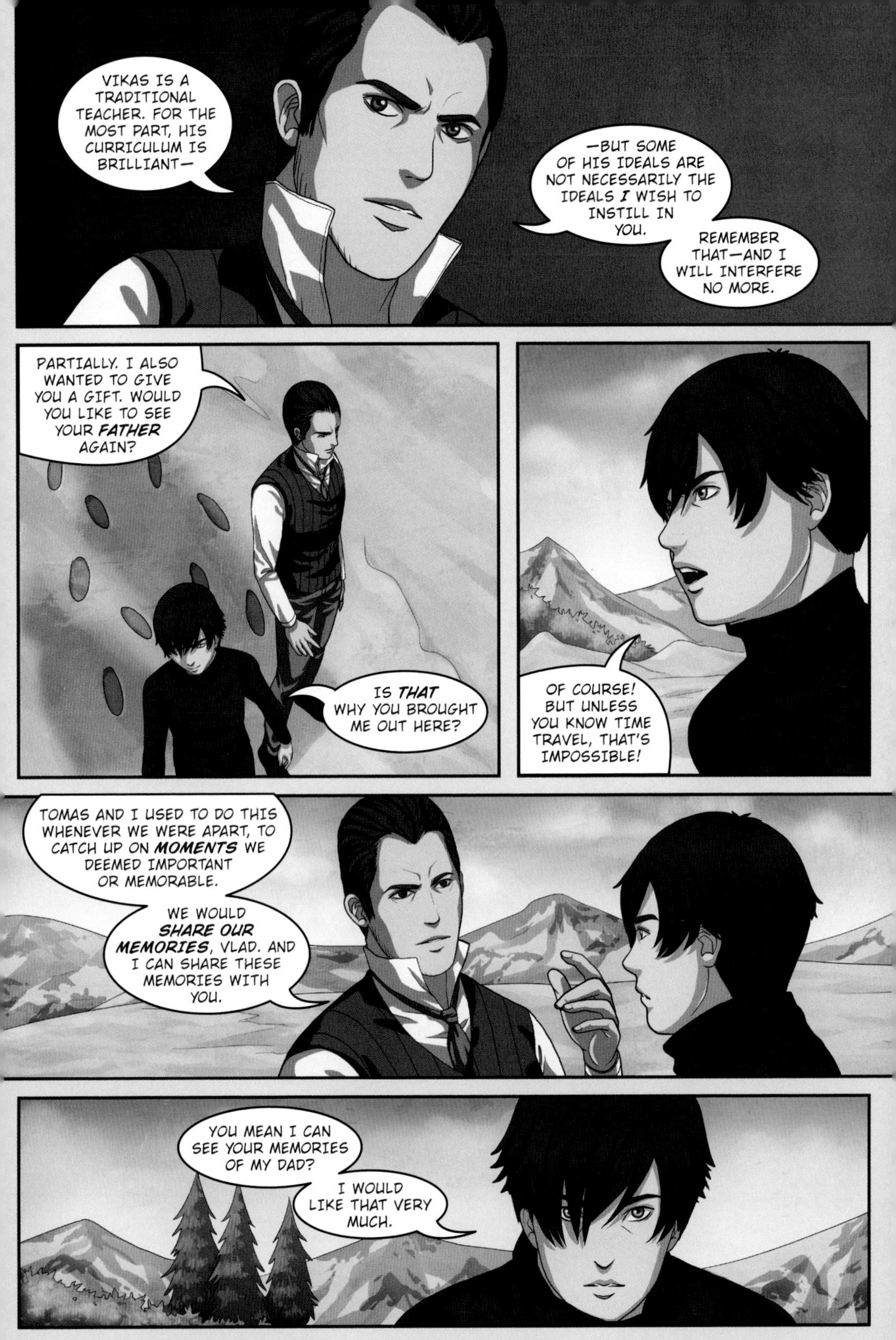
VIKAS IS A TRADITIONAL TEACHER. FOR THE MOST PART, HIS CURRICULUM IS BRILLIANT—
—BUT SOME OF HIS IDEALS ARE NOT NECESSARILY THE IDEALS *I* WISH TO INSTILL IN YOU.
REMEMBER THAT—AND I WILL INTERFERE NO MORE.
PARTIALLY. I ALSO WANTED TO GIVE YOU A GIFT. WOULD YOU LIKE TO SEE YOUR ***FATHER*** AGAIN?
IS ***THAT*** WHY YOU BROUGHT ME OUT HERE?
OF COURSE! BUT UNLESS YOU KNOW TIME TRAVEL, THAT'S IMPOSSIBLE!
TOMAS AND I USED TO DO THIS WHENEVER WE WERE APART, TO CATCH UP ON ***MOMENTS*** WE DEEMED IMPORTANT OR MEMORABLE.
WE WOULD ***SHARE OUR MEMORIES***, VLAD. AND I CAN SHARE THESE MEMORIES WITH YOU.
YOU MEAN I CAN SEE YOUR MEMORIES OF MY DAD?
I WOULD LIKE THAT VERY MUCH.

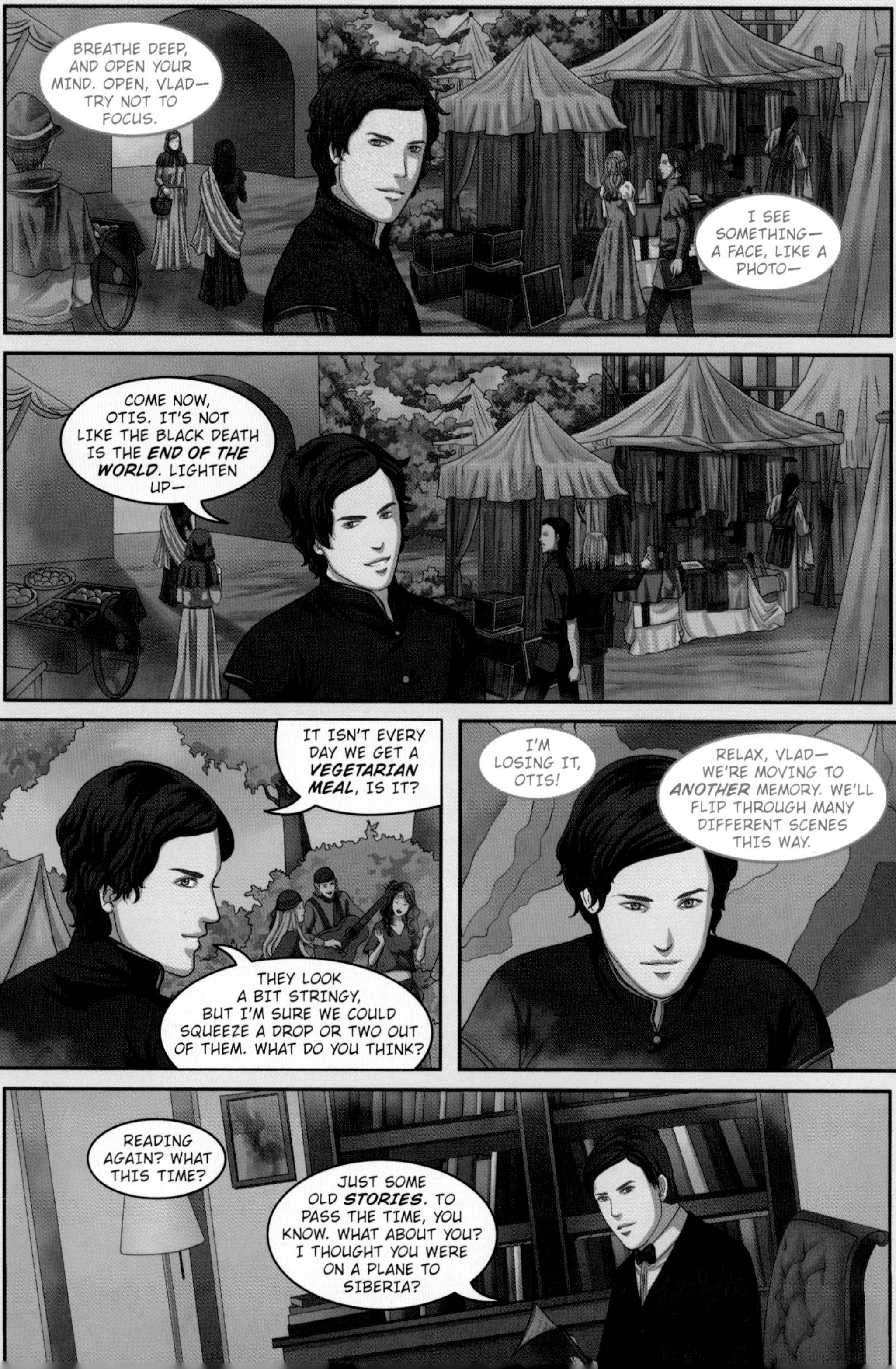
BREATHE DEEP, AND OPEN YOUR MIND. OPEN, VLAD— TRY NOT TO FOCUS.
I SEE SOMETHING— A FACE, LIKE A PHOTO—
COME NOW, OTIS. IT'S NOT LIKE THE BLACK DEATH IS THE END OF THE WORLD. LIGHTEN UP—
IT ISN'T EVERY DAY WE GET A VEGETARIAN MEAL, IS IT?
THEY LOOK A BIT STRINGY, BUT I'M SURE WE COULD SQUEEZE A DROP OR TWO OUT OF THEM. WHAT DO YOU THINK?
I'M LOSING IT, OTIS!
RELAX, VLAD— WE'RE MOVING TO ANOTHER MEMORY. WE'LL FLIP THROUGH MANY DIFFERENT SCENES THIS WAY.
READING AGAIN? WHAT THIS TIME?
JUST SOME OLD STORIES. TO PASS THE TIME, YOU KNOW. WHAT ABOUT YOU? I THOUGHT YOU WERE ON A PLANE TO SIBERIA?

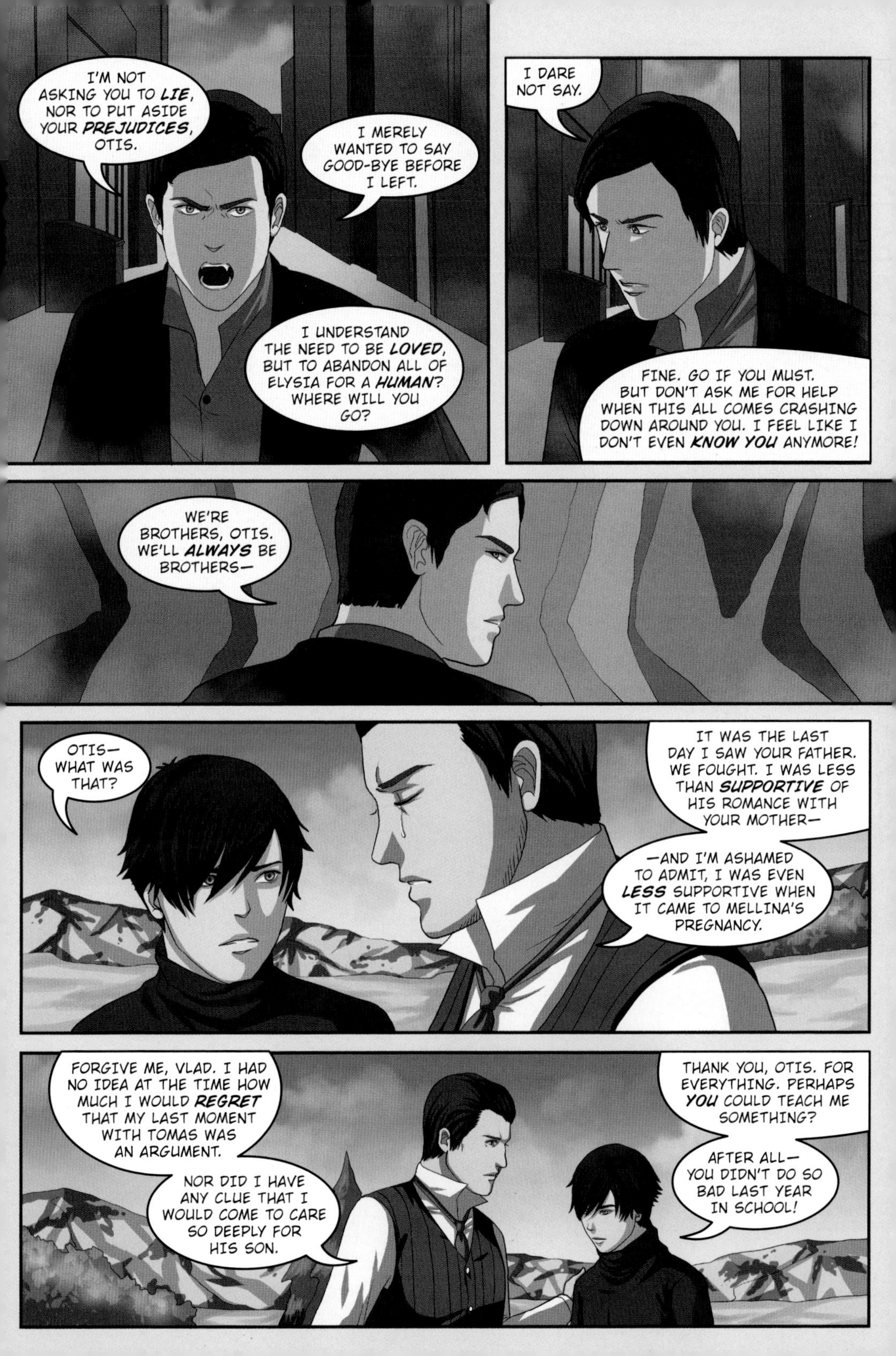

I'M NOT ASKING YOU TO *LIE*, NOR TO PUT ASIDE YOUR *PREJUDICES*, OTIS.
I MERELY WANTED TO SAY GOOD-BYE BEFORE I LEFT.
I UNDERSTAND THE NEED TO BE *LOVED*, BUT TO ABANDON ALL OF ELYSIA FOR A *HUMAN*? WHERE WILL YOU GO?
I DARE NOT SAY.
FINE. GO IF YOU MUST. BUT DON'T ASK ME FOR HELP WHEN THIS ALL COMES CRASHING DOWN AROUND YOU. I FEEL LIKE I DON'T EVEN *KNOW YOU* ANYMORE!
WE'RE BROTHERS, OTIS. WE'LL *ALWAYS* BE BROTHERS—
OTIS— WHAT WAS THAT?
IT WAS THE LAST DAY I SAW YOUR FATHER. WE FOUGHT. I WAS LESS THAN *SUPPORTIVE* OF HIS ROMANCE WITH YOUR MOTHER—
—AND I'M ASHAMED TO ADMIT, I WAS EVEN *LESS* SUPPORTIVE WHEN IT CAME TO MELLINA'S PREGNANCY.
FORGIVE ME, VLAD. I HAD NO IDEA AT THE TIME HOW MUCH I WOULD *REGRET* THAT MY LAST MOMENT WITH TOMAS WAS AN ARGUMENT.
NOR DID I HAVE ANY CLUE THAT I WOULD COME TO CARE SO DEEPLY FOR HIS SON.
THANK YOU, OTIS. FOR EVERYTHING. PERHAPS *YOU* COULD TEACH ME SOMETHING?
AFTER ALL— YOU DIDN'T DO SO BAD LAST YEAR IN SCHOOL!

ALL RIGHT. HAS VIKAS TAUGHT YOU *TELEPATHIC COMMUNICATION* YET?

YOUR FATHER AND I USED TO COMMUNICATE BY THOUGHT QUITE OFTEN.

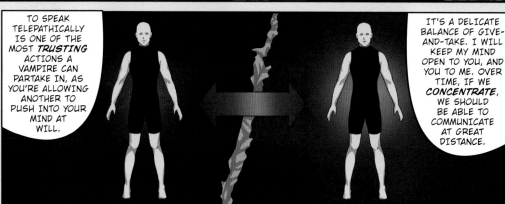

TO SPEAK TELEPATHICALLY IS ONE OF THE MOST *TRUSTING* ACTIONS A VAMPIRE CAN PARTAKE IN, AS YOU'RE ALLOWING ANOTHER TO PUSH INTO YOUR MIND AT WILL.

IT'S A DELICATE BALANCE OF GIVE-AND-TAKE. I WILL KEEP MY MIND OPEN TO YOU, AND YOU TO ME. OVER TIME, IF WE *CONCENTRATE*, WE SHOULD BE ABLE TO COMMUNICATE AT GREAT DISTANCE.

OPEN YOUR MIND TO ME. GOOD.

NOW, FOCUS ON THE MEANING OF YOUR WORDS AND PUSH THEM INTO MY MIND GENTLY.

LIKE THIS?

ABSOLUTELY. IT COMES IN HANDY WHEN HUMANS ARE AROUND AND WE WANT TO DISCUSS THINGS OF *VAMPIRIC* NATURE. PRETTY NEAT, EH?

REMEMBER—ONLY *VAMPIRES* CAN DO THIS. HUMANS LIKE HENRY CANNOT.

YOU CAN ONLY READ, OR GUIDE HIS MIND.

THAT SUCKS.

IS THERE ANYTHING *ELSE* I'M MISSING OUT ON? I MEAN, BESIDES LEARNING ABOUT TELEPATHY AND MEMORY SHARING?

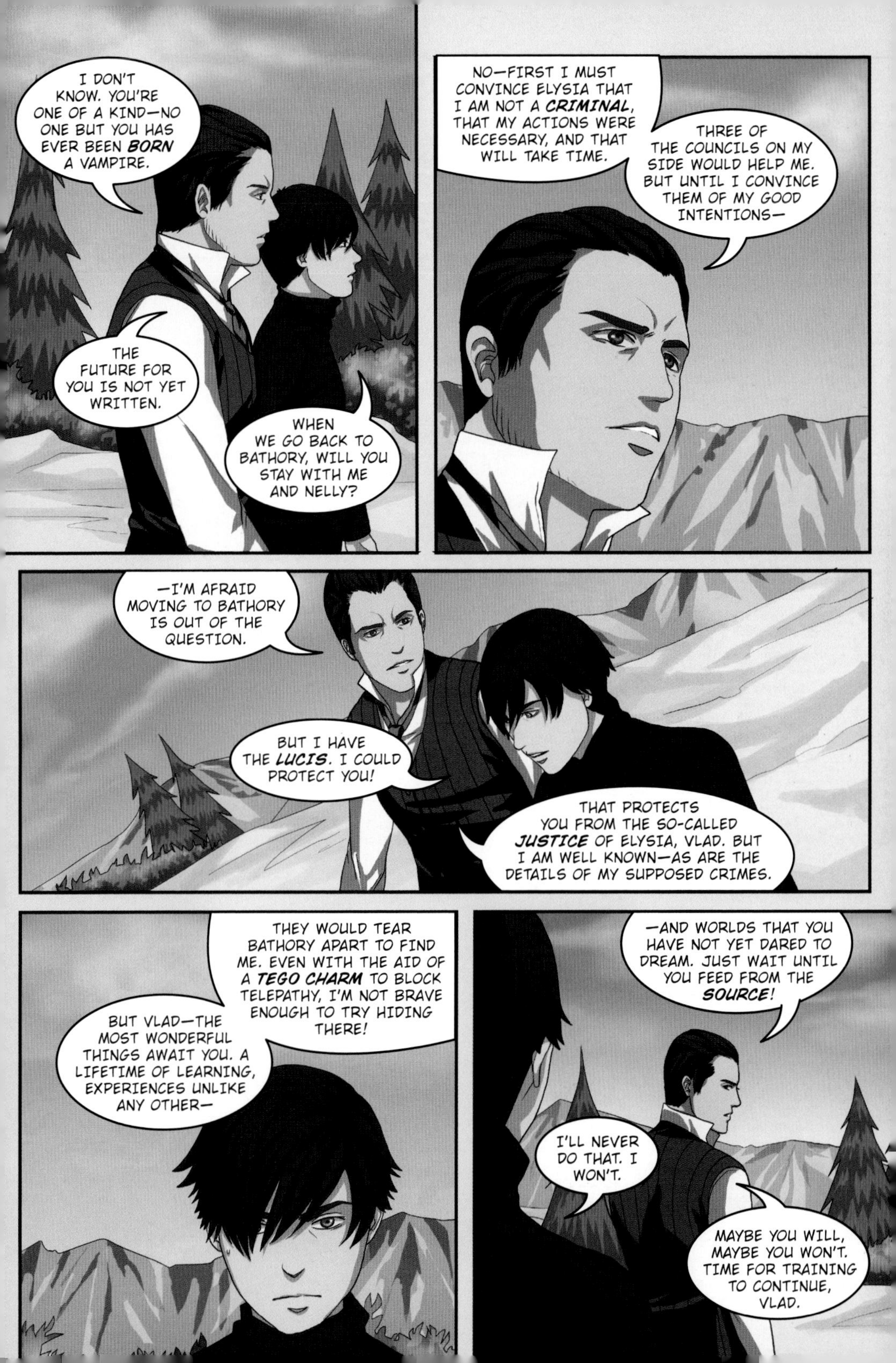
I DON'T KNOW. YOU'RE ONE OF A KIND—NO ONE BUT YOU HAS EVER BEEN *BORN* A VAMPIRE.
THE FUTURE FOR YOU IS NOT YET WRITTEN.
WHEN WE GO BACK TO BATHORY, WILL YOU STAY WITH ME AND NELLY?
NO—FIRST I MUST CONVINCE ELYSIA THAT I AM NOT A *CRIMINAL*, THAT MY ACTIONS WERE NECESSARY, AND THAT WILL TAKE TIME.
THREE OF THE COUNCILS ON MY SIDE WOULD HELP ME. BUT UNTIL I CONVINCE THEM OF MY GOOD INTENTIONS—
—I'M AFRAID MOVING TO BATHORY IS OUT OF THE QUESTION.
BUT I HAVE THE *LUCIS*. I COULD PROTECT YOU!
THAT PROTECTS YOU FROM THE SO-CALLED *JUSTICE* OF ELYSIA, VLAD. BUT I AM WELL KNOWN—AS ARE THE DETAILS OF MY SUPPOSED CRIMES.
THEY WOULD TEAR BATHORY APART TO FIND ME. EVEN WITH THE AID OF A *TEGO CHARM* TO BLOCK TELEPATHY, I'M NOT BRAVE ENOUGH TO TRY HIDING THERE!
BUT VLAD—THE MOST WONDERFUL THINGS AWAIT YOU. A LIFETIME OF LEARNING, EXPERIENCES UNLIKE ANY OTHER—
—AND WORLDS THAT YOU HAVE NOT YET DARED TO DREAM. JUST WAIT UNTIL YOU FEED FROM THE *SOURCE*!
I'LL NEVER DO THAT. I WON'T.
MAYBE YOU WILL, MAYBE YOU WON'T. TIME FOR TRAINING TO CONTINUE, VLAD.

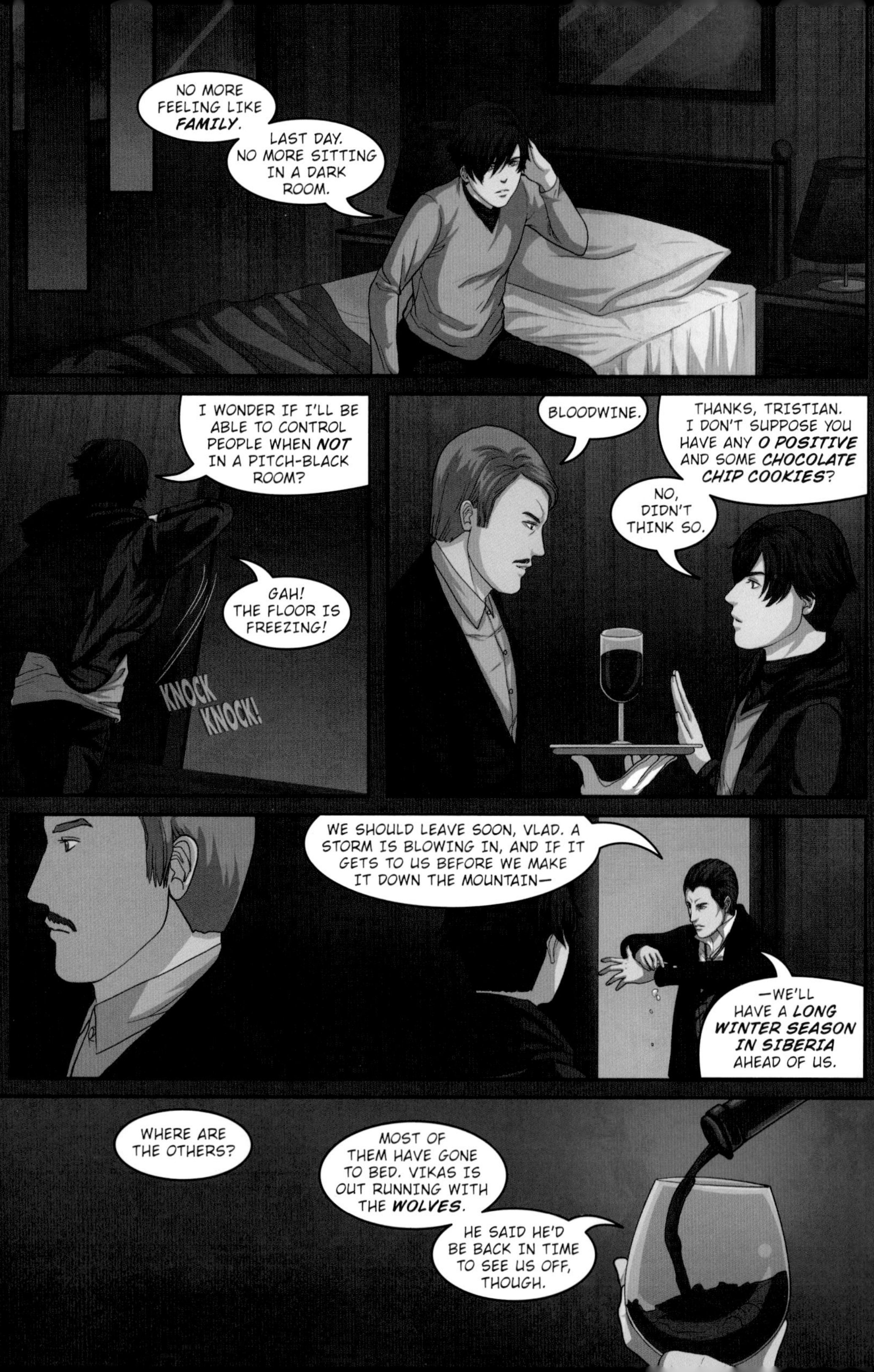
NO MORE FEELING LIKE ***FAMILY***.
LAST DAY. NO MORE SITTING IN A DARK ROOM.
I WONDER IF I'LL BE ABLE TO CONTROL PEOPLE WHEN ***NOT*** IN A PITCH-BLACK ROOM?
GAH! THE FLOOR IS FREEZING!
KNOCK KNOCK!
BLOODWINE.
THANKS, TRISTIAN. I DON'T SUPPOSE YOU HAVE ANY ***O POSITIVE*** AND SOME ***CHOCOLATE CHIP COOKIES***?
NO, DIDN'T THINK SO.
WE SHOULD LEAVE SOON, VLAD. A STORM IS BLOWING IN, AND IF IT GETS TO US BEFORE WE MAKE IT DOWN THE MOUNTAIN—
—WE'LL HAVE A ***LONG WINTER SEASON IN SIBERIA*** AHEAD OF US.
WHERE ARE THE OTHERS?
MOST OF THEM HAVE GONE TO BED. VIKAS IS OUT RUNNING WITH THE ***WOLVES***.
HE SAID HE'D BE BACK IN TIME TO SEE US OFF, THOUGH.

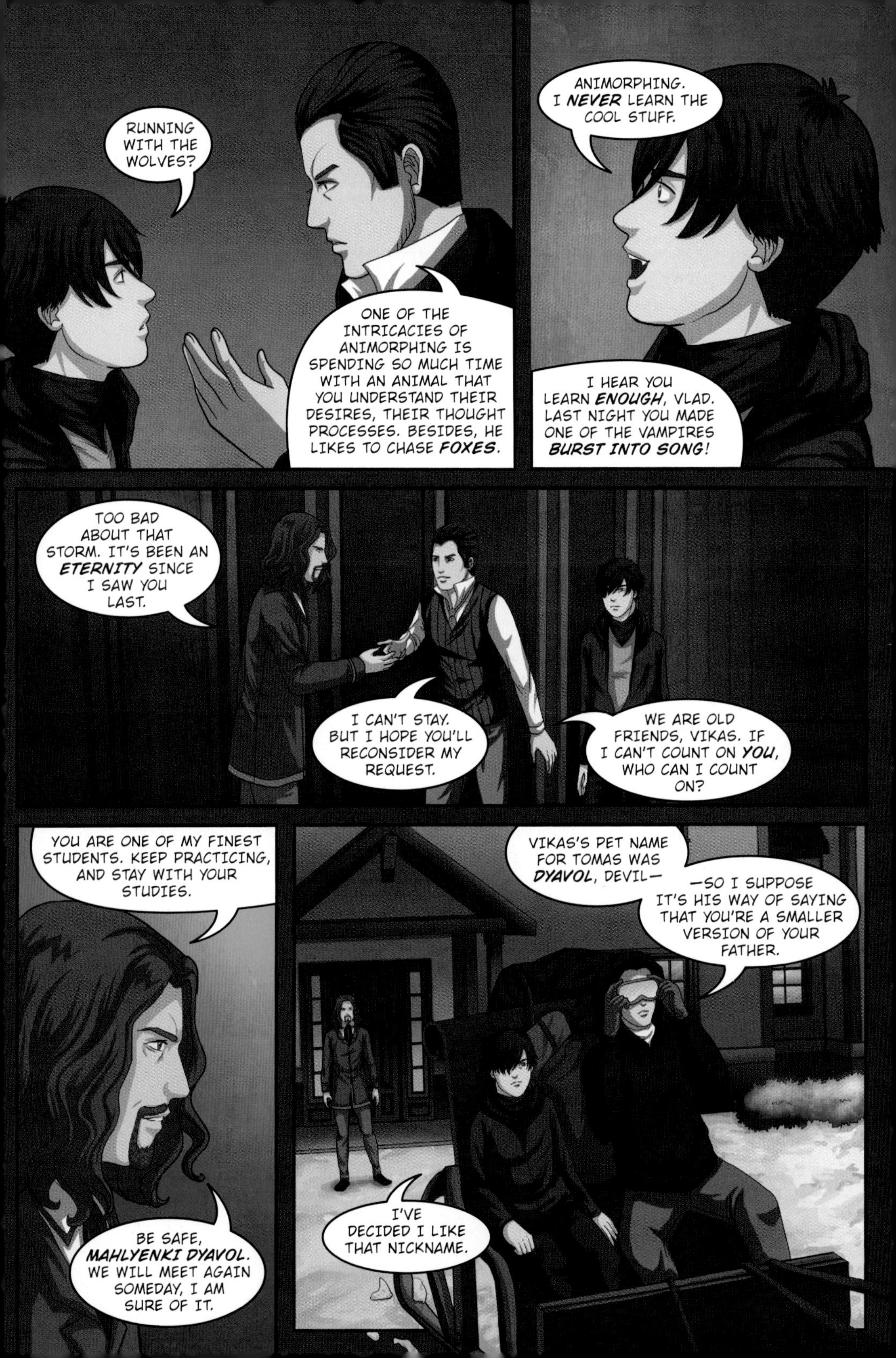
RUNNING WITH THE WOLVES?
ONE OF THE INTRICACIES OF ANIMORPHING IS SPENDING SO MUCH TIME WITH AN ANIMAL THAT YOU UNDERSTAND THEIR DESIRES, THEIR THOUGHT PROCESSES. BESIDES, HE LIKES TO CHASE FOXES.
ANIMORPHING. I NEVER LEARN THE COOL STUFF.
I HEAR YOU LEARN ENOUGH, VLAD. LAST NIGHT YOU MADE ONE OF THE VAMPIRES BURST INTO SONG!
TOO BAD ABOUT THAT STORM. IT'S BEEN AN ETERNITY SINCE I SAW YOU LAST.
I CAN'T STAY. BUT I HOPE YOU'LL RECONSIDER MY REQUEST.
WE ARE OLD FRIENDS, VIKAS. IF I CAN'T COUNT ON YOU, WHO CAN I COUNT ON?
YOU ARE ONE OF MY FINEST STUDENTS. KEEP PRACTICING, AND STAY WITH YOUR STUDIES.
BE SAFE, MAHLYENKI DYAVOL. WE WILL MEET AGAIN SOMEDAY, I AM SURE OF IT.
VIKAS'S PET NAME FOR TOMAS WAS DYAVOL, DEVIL—
—SO I SUPPOSE IT'S HIS WAY OF SAYING THAT YOU'RE A SMALLER VERSION OF YOUR FATHER.
I'VE DECIDED I LIKE THAT NICKNAME.

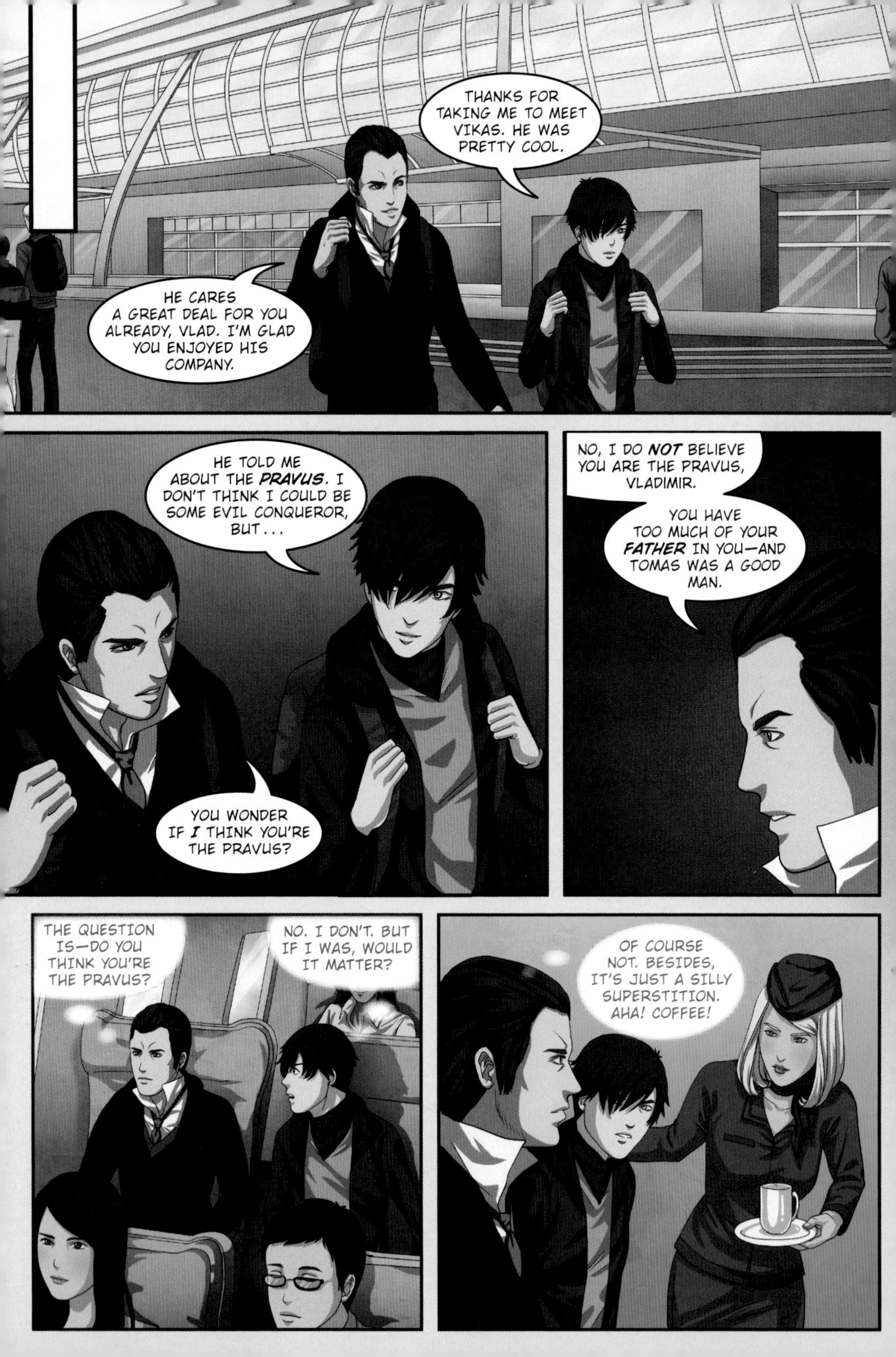
THANKS FOR TAKING ME TO MEET VIKAS. HE WAS PRETTY COOL.
HE CARES A GREAT DEAL FOR YOU ALREADY, VLAD. I'M GLAD YOU ENJOYED HIS COMPANY.
HE TOLD ME ABOUT THE PRAVUS. I DON'T THINK I COULD BE SOME EVIL CONQUEROR, BUT . . .
YOU WONDER IF I THINK YOU'RE THE PRAVUS?
NO, I DO NOT BELIEVE YOU ARE THE PRAVUS, VLADIMIR.
YOU HAVE TOO MUCH OF YOUR FATHER IN YOU—AND TOMAS WAS A GOOD MAN.
THE QUESTION IS—DO YOU THINK YOU'RE THE PRAVUS?
NO. I DON'T. BUT IF I WAS, WOULD IT MATTER?
OF COURSE NOT. BESIDES, IT'S JUST A SILLY SUPERSTITION. AHA! COFFEE!

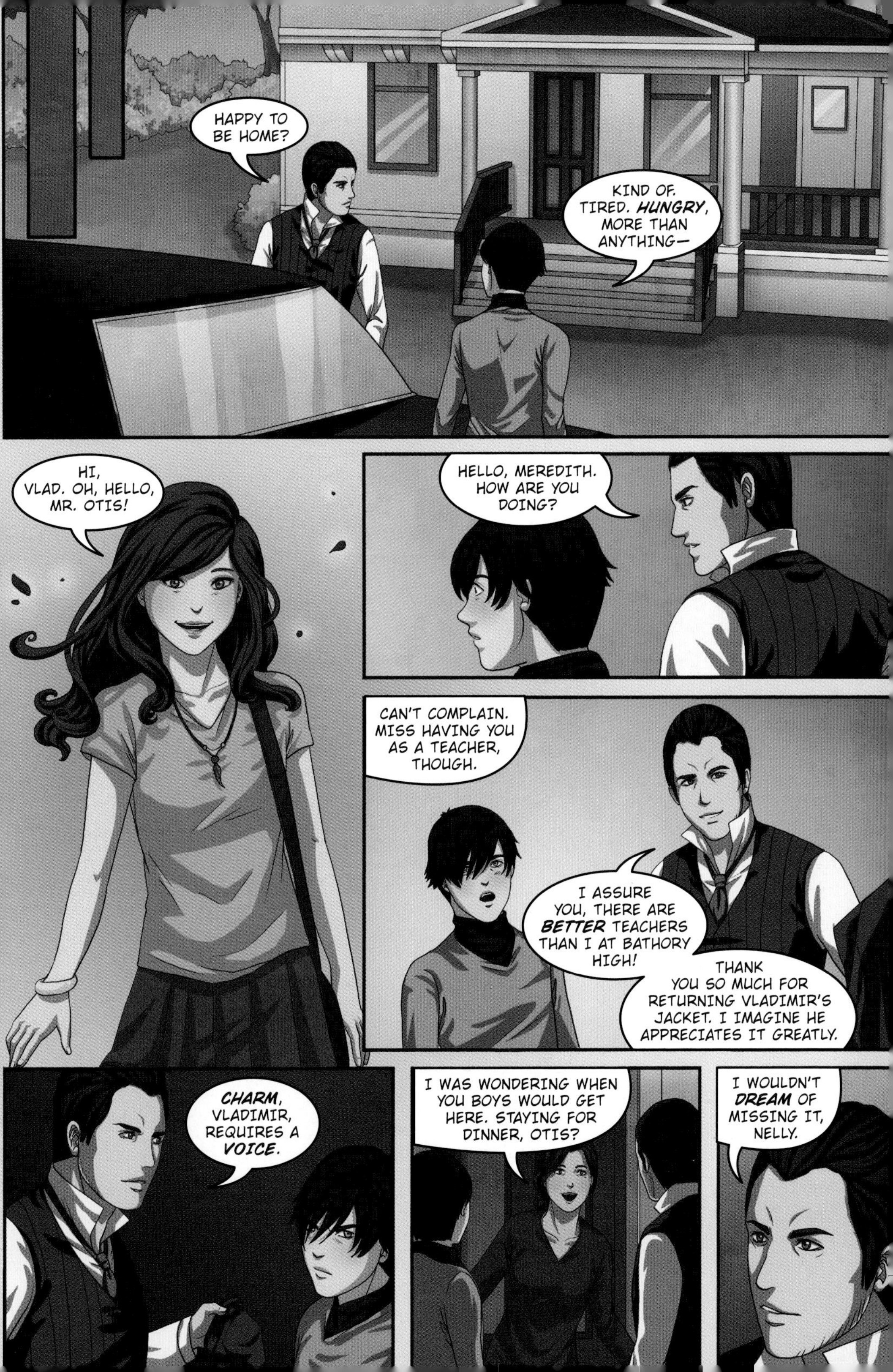
HAPPY TO BE HOME?
KIND OF. TIRED. HUNGRY, MORE THAN ANYTHING—
HI, VLAD. OH, HELLO, MR. OTIS!
HELLO, MEREDITH. HOW ARE YOU DOING?
CAN'T COMPLAIN. MISS HAVING YOU AS A TEACHER, THOUGH.
I ASSURE YOU, THERE ARE BETTER TEACHERS THAN I AT BATHORY HIGH!
THANK YOU SO MUCH FOR RETURNING VLADIMIR'S JACKET. I IMAGINE HE APPRECIATES IT GREATLY.
CHARM, VLADIMIR, REQUIRES A VOICE.
I WAS WONDERING WHEN YOU BOYS WOULD GET HERE. STAYING FOR DINNER, OTIS?
I WOULDN'T DREAM OF MISSING IT, NELLY.

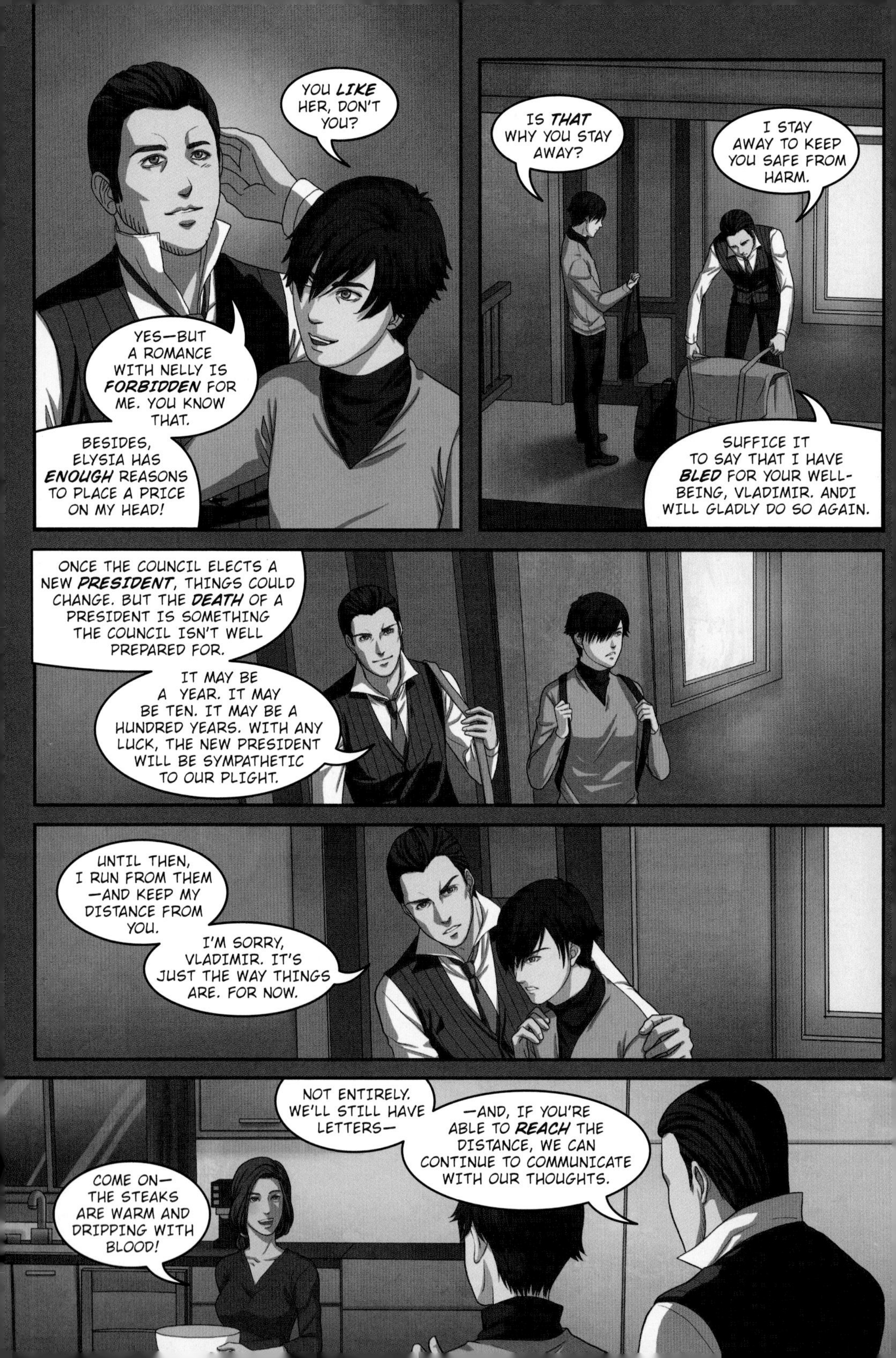
YOU *LIKE* HER, DON'T YOU?
YES—BUT A ROMANCE WITH NELLY IS *FORBIDDEN* FOR ME. YOU KNOW THAT.
BESIDES, ELYSIA HAS *ENOUGH* REASONS TO PLACE A PRICE ON MY HEAD!
IS *THAT* WHY YOU STAY AWAY?
I STAY AWAY TO KEEP YOU SAFE FROM HARM.
SUFFICE IT TO SAY THAT I HAVE *BLED* FOR YOUR WELL-BEING, VLADIMIR. ANDI WILL GLADLY DO SO AGAIN.
ONCE THE COUNCIL ELECTS A NEW *PRESIDENT*, THINGS COULD CHANGE. BUT THE *DEATH* OF A PRESIDENT IS SOMETHING THE COUNCIL ISN'T WELL PREPARED FOR.
IT MAY BE A YEAR. IT MAY BE TEN. IT MAY BE A HUNDRED YEARS. WITH ANY LUCK, THE NEW PRESIDENT WILL BE SYMPATHETIC TO OUR PLIGHT.
UNTIL THEN, I RUN FROM THEM —AND KEEP MY DISTANCE FROM YOU.
I'M SORRY, VLADIMIR. IT'S JUST THE WAY THINGS ARE. FOR NOW.
NOT ENTIRELY. WE'LL STILL HAVE LETTERS—
—AND, IF YOU'RE ABLE TO *REACH* THE DISTANCE, WE CAN CONTINUE TO COMMUNICATE WITH OUR THOUGHTS.
COME ON—THE STEAKS ARE WARM AND DRIPPING WITH BLOOD!

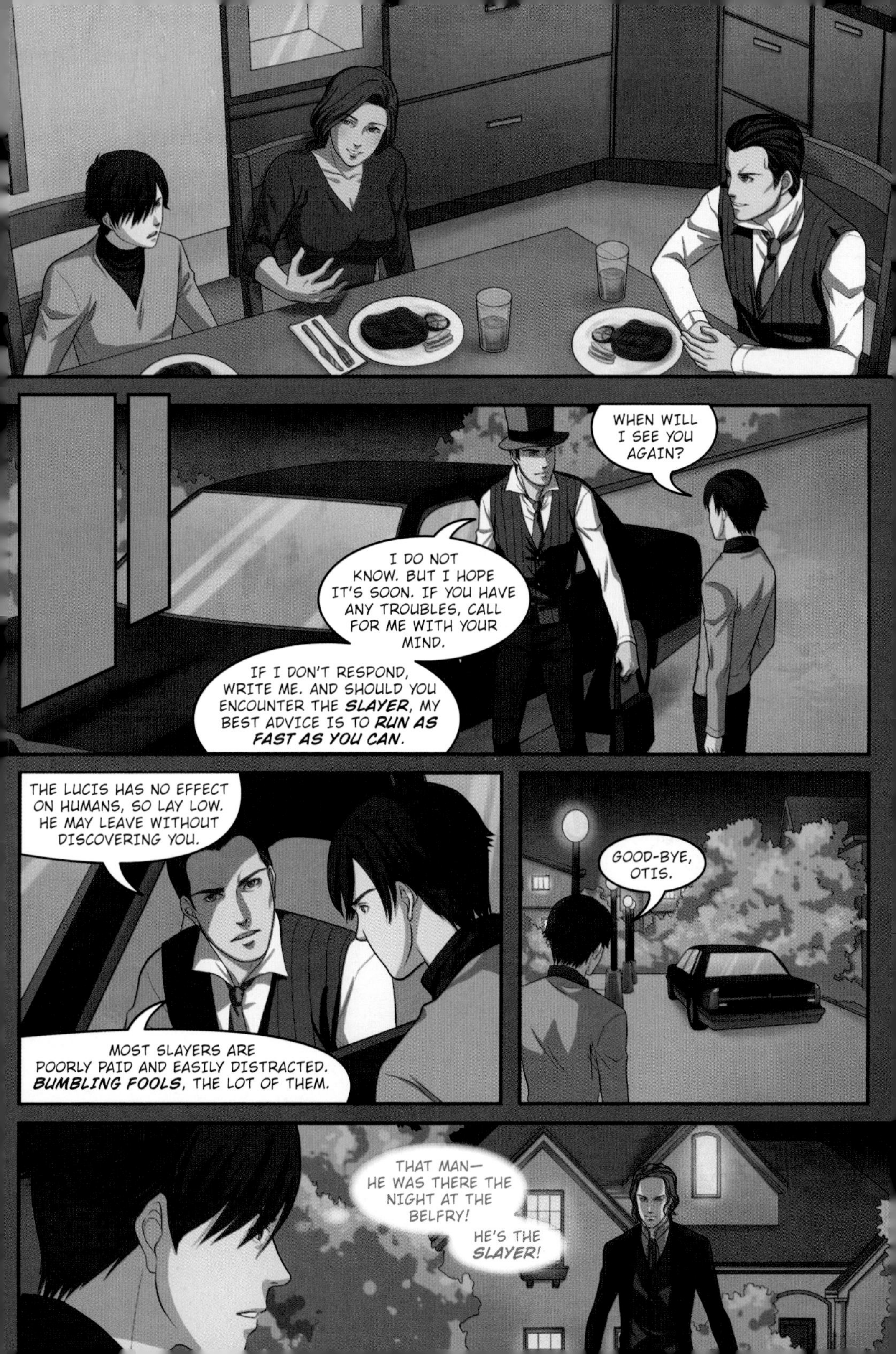
WHEN WILL I SEE YOU AGAIN?
I DO NOT KNOW. BUT I HOPE IT'S SOON. IF YOU HAVE ANY TROUBLES, CALL FOR ME WITH YOUR MIND.
IF I DON'T RESPOND, WRITE ME. AND SHOULD YOU ENCOUNTER THE ***SLAYER***, MY BEST ADVICE IS TO ***RUN AS FAST AS YOU CAN***.
THE LUCIS HAS NO EFFECT ON HUMANS, SO LAY LOW. HE MAY LEAVE WITHOUT DISCOVERING YOU.
MOST SLAYERS ARE POORLY PAID AND EASILY DISTRACTED. ***BUMBLING FOOLS***, THE LOT OF THEM.
GOOD-BYE, OTIS.
THAT MAN— HE WAS THERE THE NIGHT AT THE BELFRY!
HE'S THE ***SLAYER***!

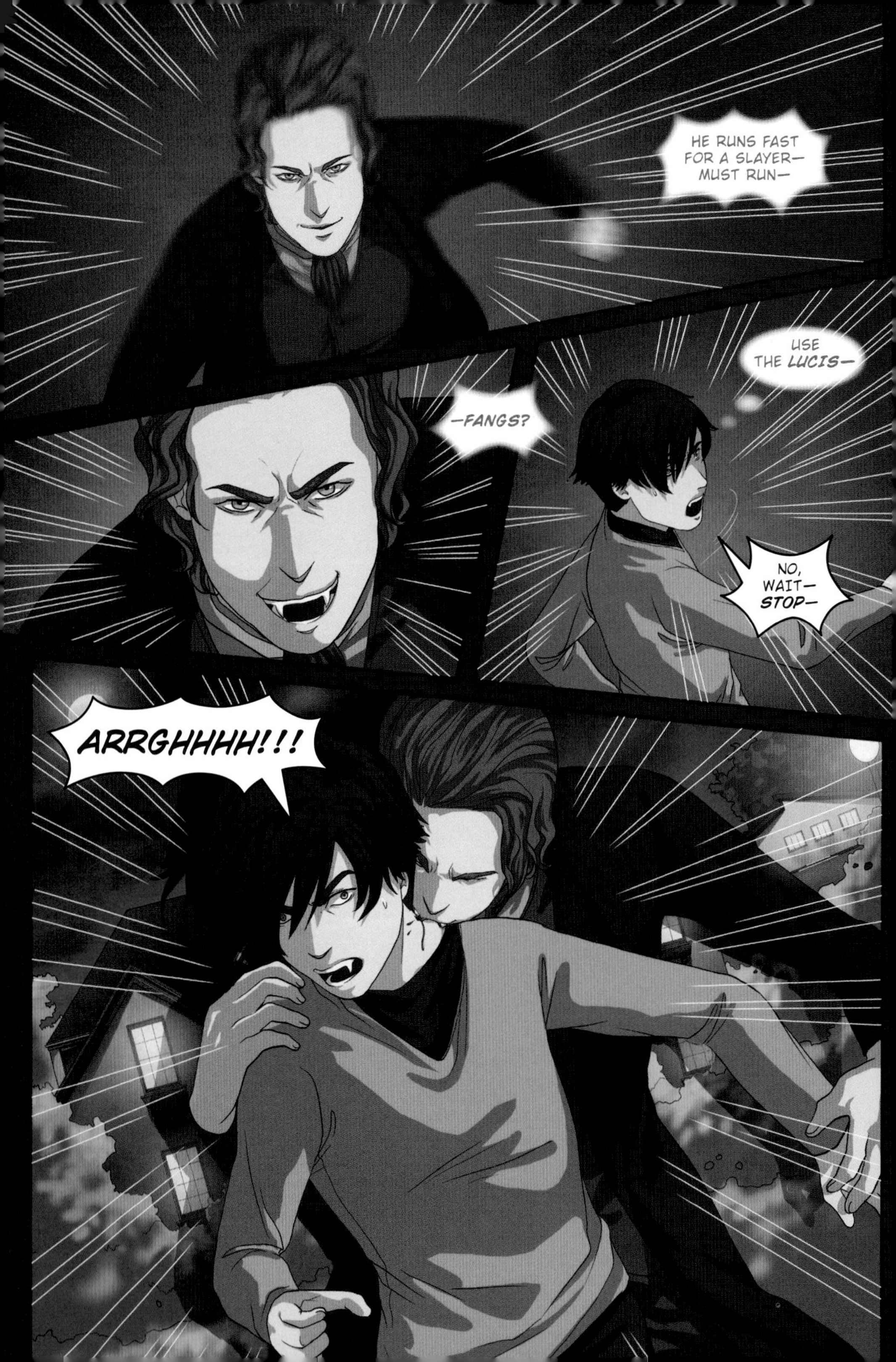
HE RUNS FAST
FOR A SLAYER—
MUST RUN—
USE
THE LUCIS—
—FANGS?
NO,
WAIT—
STOP—
ARRGHHHH!!!

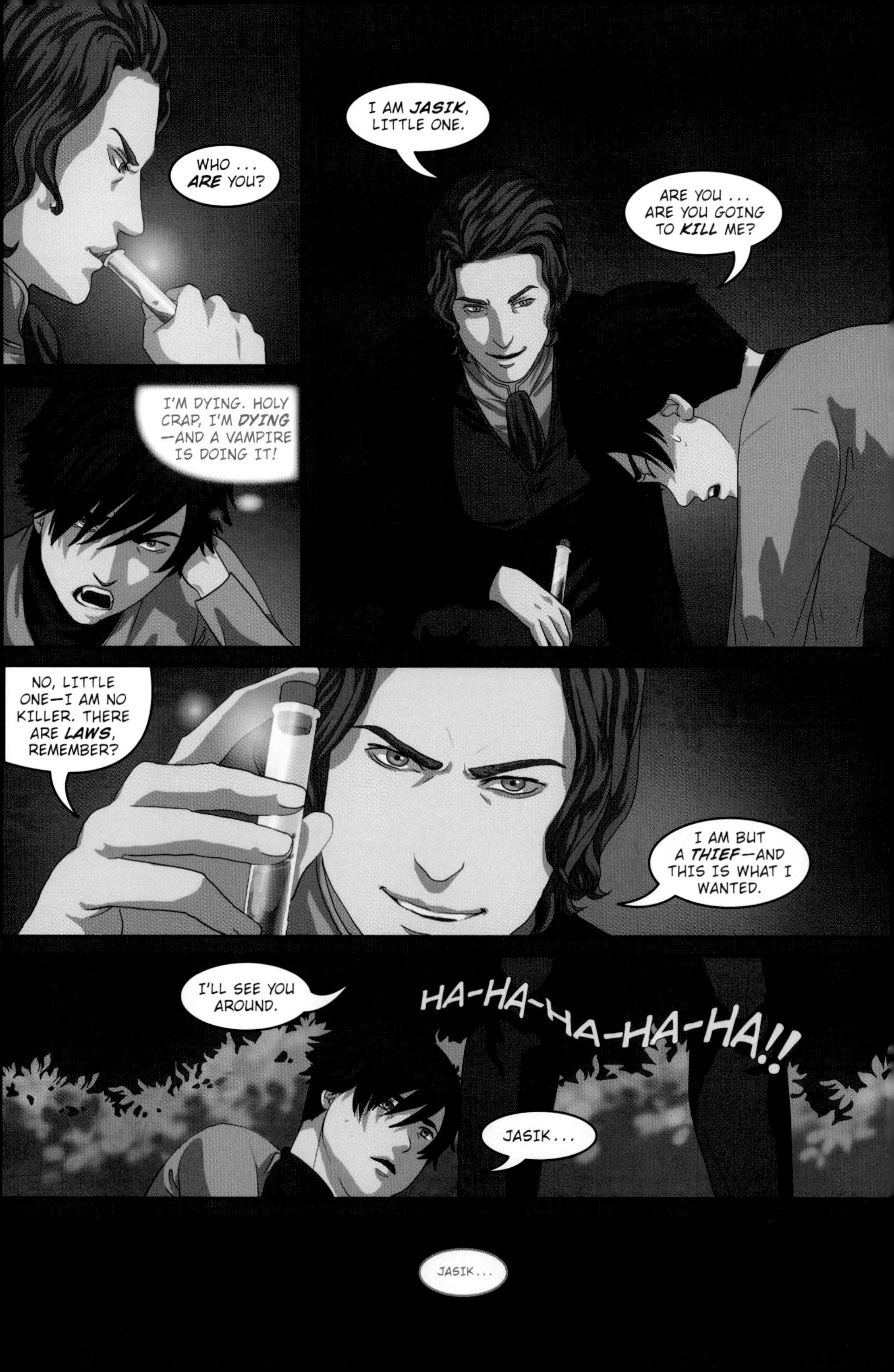
WHO . . . ARE YOU?
I AM JASIK, LITTLE ONE.
ARE YOU . . . ARE YOU GOING TO KILL ME?
I'M DYING. HOLY CRAP, I'M DYING—AND A VAMPIRE IS DOING IT!
NO, LITTLE ONE—I AM NO KILLER. THERE ARE LAWS, REMEMBER?
I AM BUT A THIEF—AND THIS IS WHAT I WANTED.
I'LL SEE YOU AROUND.
HA-HA-HA-HA-HA!!
JASIK . . .
JASIK . . .

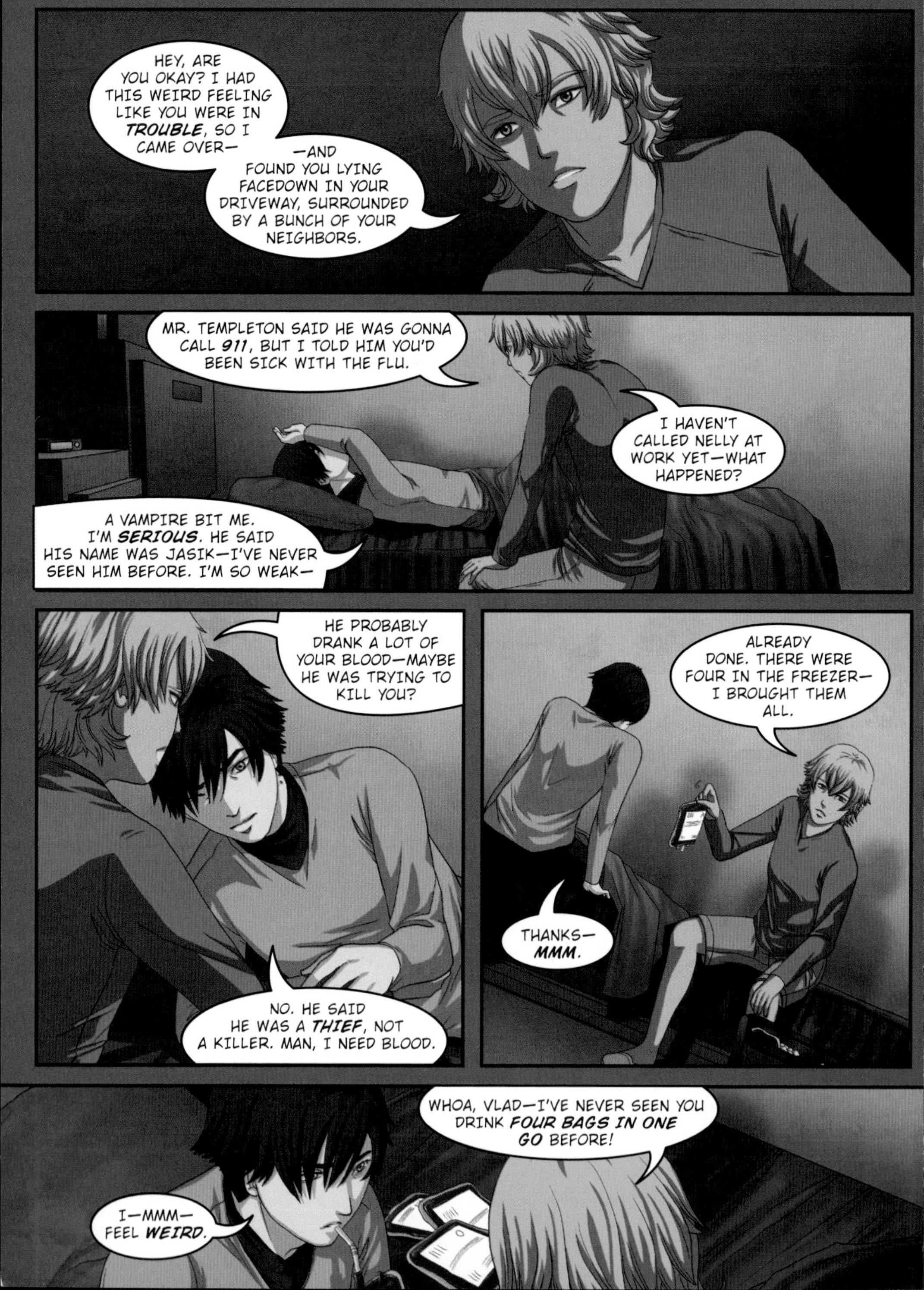
HEY, ARE YOU OKAY? I HAD THIS WEIRD FEELING LIKE YOU WERE IN ***TROUBLE***, SO I CAME OVER—
—AND FOUND YOU LYING FACEDOWN IN YOUR DRIVEWAY, SURROUNDED BY A BUNCH OF YOUR NEIGHBORS.
MR. TEMPLETON SAID HE WAS GONNA CALL ***911***, BUT I TOLD HIM YOU'D BEEN SICK WITH THE FLU.
I HAVEN'T CALLED NELLY AT WORK YET—WHAT HAPPENED?
A VAMPIRE BIT ME. I'M ***SERIOUS***. HE SAID HIS NAME WAS JASIK—I'VE NEVER SEEN HIM BEFORE. I'M SO WEAK—
HE PROBABLY DRANK A LOT OF YOUR BLOOD—MAYBE HE WAS TRYING TO KILL YOU?
NO. HE SAID HE WAS A ***THIEF***, NOT A KILLER. MAN, I NEED BLOOD.
ALREADY DONE. THERE WERE FOUR IN THE FREEZER—I BROUGHT THEM ALL.
THANKS—***MMM***.
WHOA, VLAD—I'VE NEVER SEEN YOU DRINK ***FOUR BAGS IN ONE GO*** BEFORE!
I—MMM—FEEL ***WEIRD***.

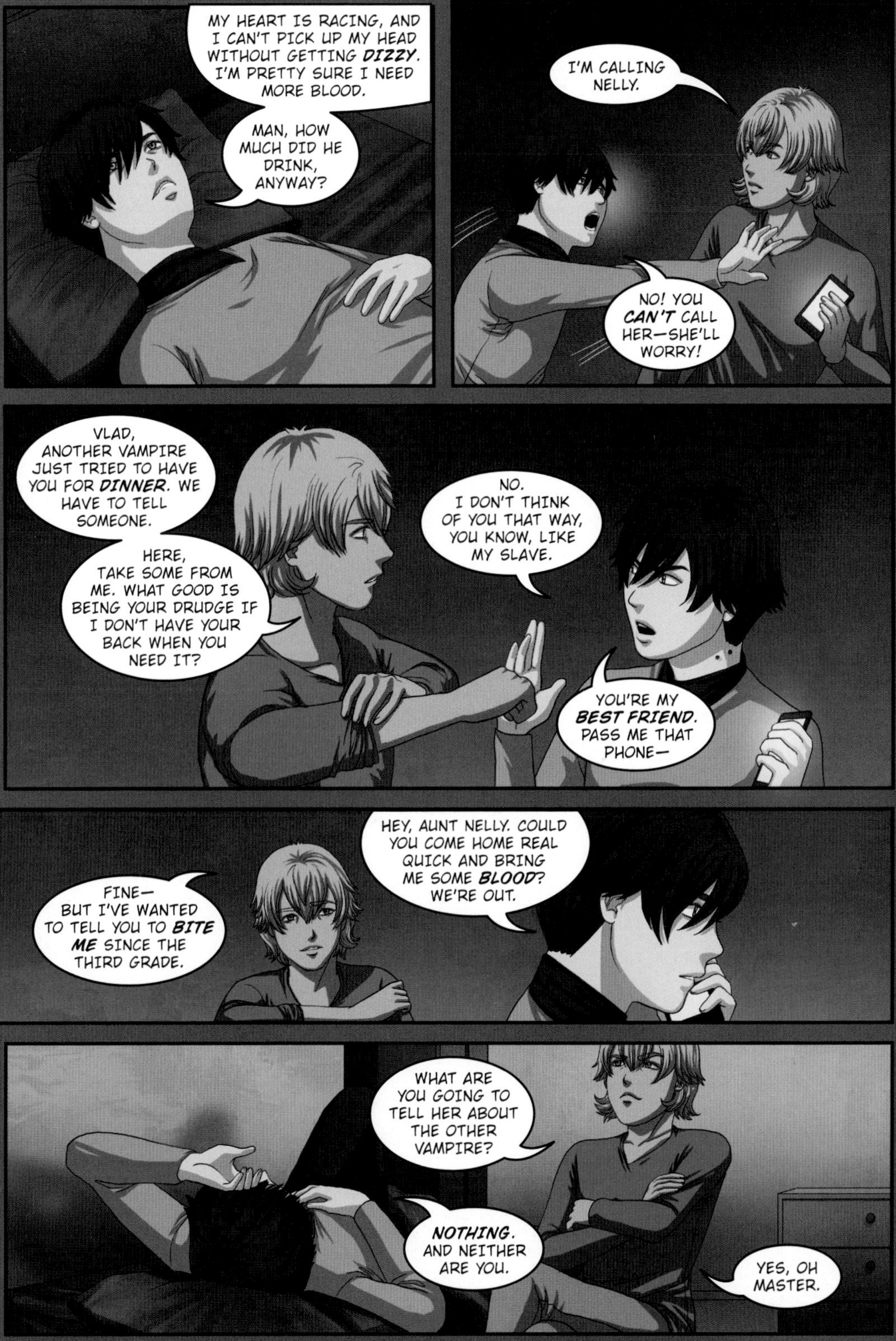
MY HEART IS RACING, AND I CAN'T PICK UP MY HEAD WITHOUT GETTING DIZZY. I'M PRETTY SURE I NEED MORE BLOOD.
MAN, HOW MUCH DID HE DRINK, ANYWAY?
I'M CALLING NELLY.
NO! YOU CAN'T CALL HER—SHE'LL WORRY!
VLAD, ANOTHER VAMPIRE JUST TRIED TO HAVE YOU FOR DINNER. WE HAVE TO TELL SOMEONE.
HERE, TAKE SOME FROM ME. WHAT GOOD IS BEING YOUR DRUDGE IF I DON'T HAVE YOUR BACK WHEN YOU NEED IT?
NO. I DON'T THINK OF YOU THAT WAY, YOU KNOW, LIKE MY SLAVE.
YOU'RE MY BEST FRIEND. PASS ME THAT PHONE—
FINE— BUT I'VE WANTED TO TELL YOU TO BITE ME SINCE THE THIRD GRADE.
HEY, AUNT NELLY. COULD YOU COME HOME REAL QUICK AND BRING ME SOME BLOOD? WE'RE OUT.
WHAT ARE YOU GOING TO TELL HER ABOUT THE OTHER VAMPIRE?
NOTHING. AND NEITHER ARE YOU.
YES, OH MASTER.

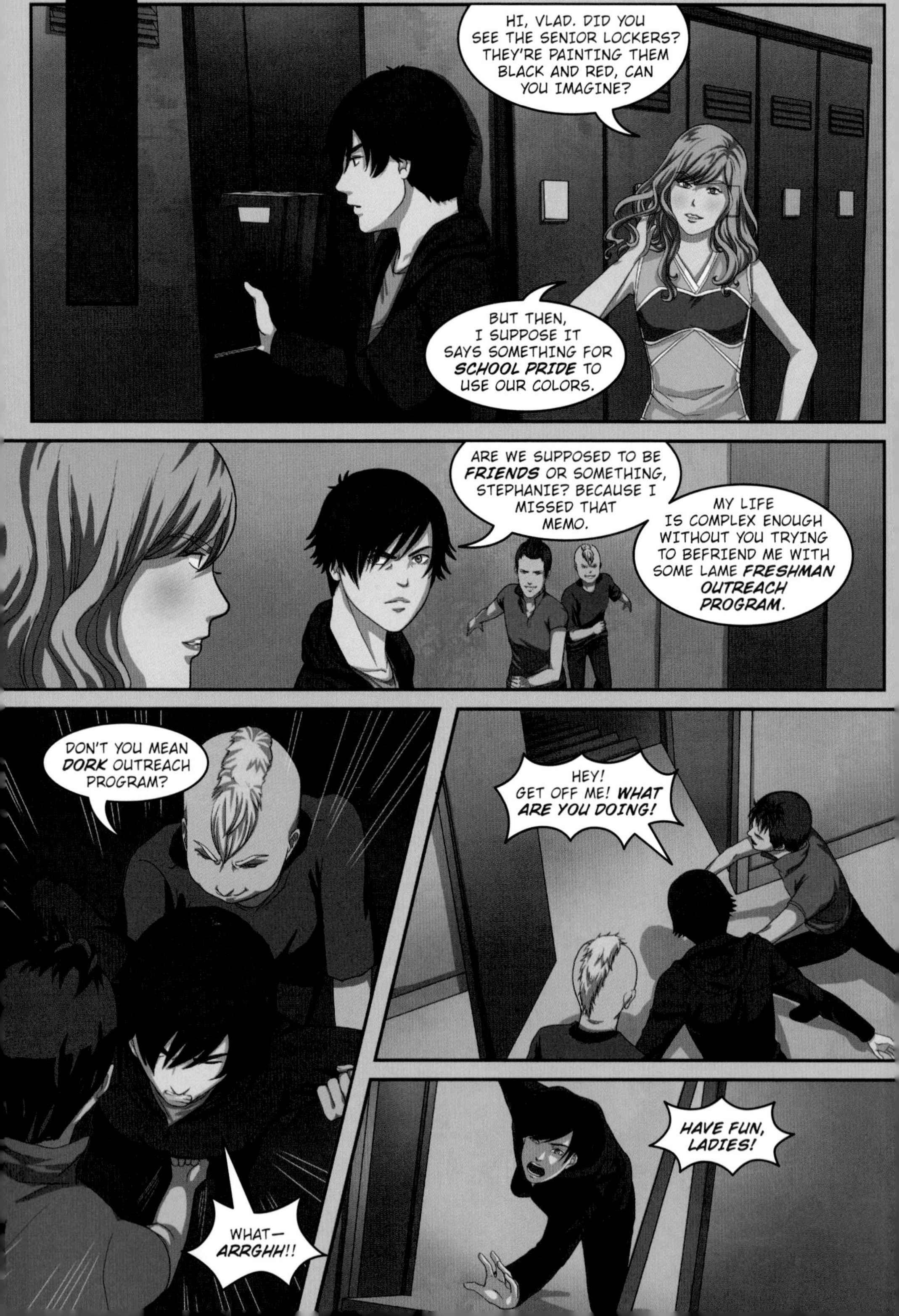
HI, VLAD. DID YOU SEE THE SENIOR LOCKERS? THEY'RE PAINTING THEM BLACK AND RED, CAN YOU IMAGINE?
BUT THEN, I SUPPOSE IT SAYS SOMETHING FOR **SCHOOL PRIDE** TO USE OUR COLORS.
ARE WE SUPPOSED TO BE **FRIENDS** OR SOMETHING, STEPHANIE? BECAUSE I MISSED THAT MEMO.
MY LIFE IS COMPLEX ENOUGH WITHOUT YOU TRYING TO BEFRIEND ME WITH SOME LAME **FRESHMAN OUTREACH PROGRAM**.
DON'T YOU MEAN **DORK** OUTREACH PROGRAM?
WHAT— **ARRGHH**!!
HEY! GET OFF ME! **WHAT ARE YOU DOING!**
HAVE FUN, LADIES!

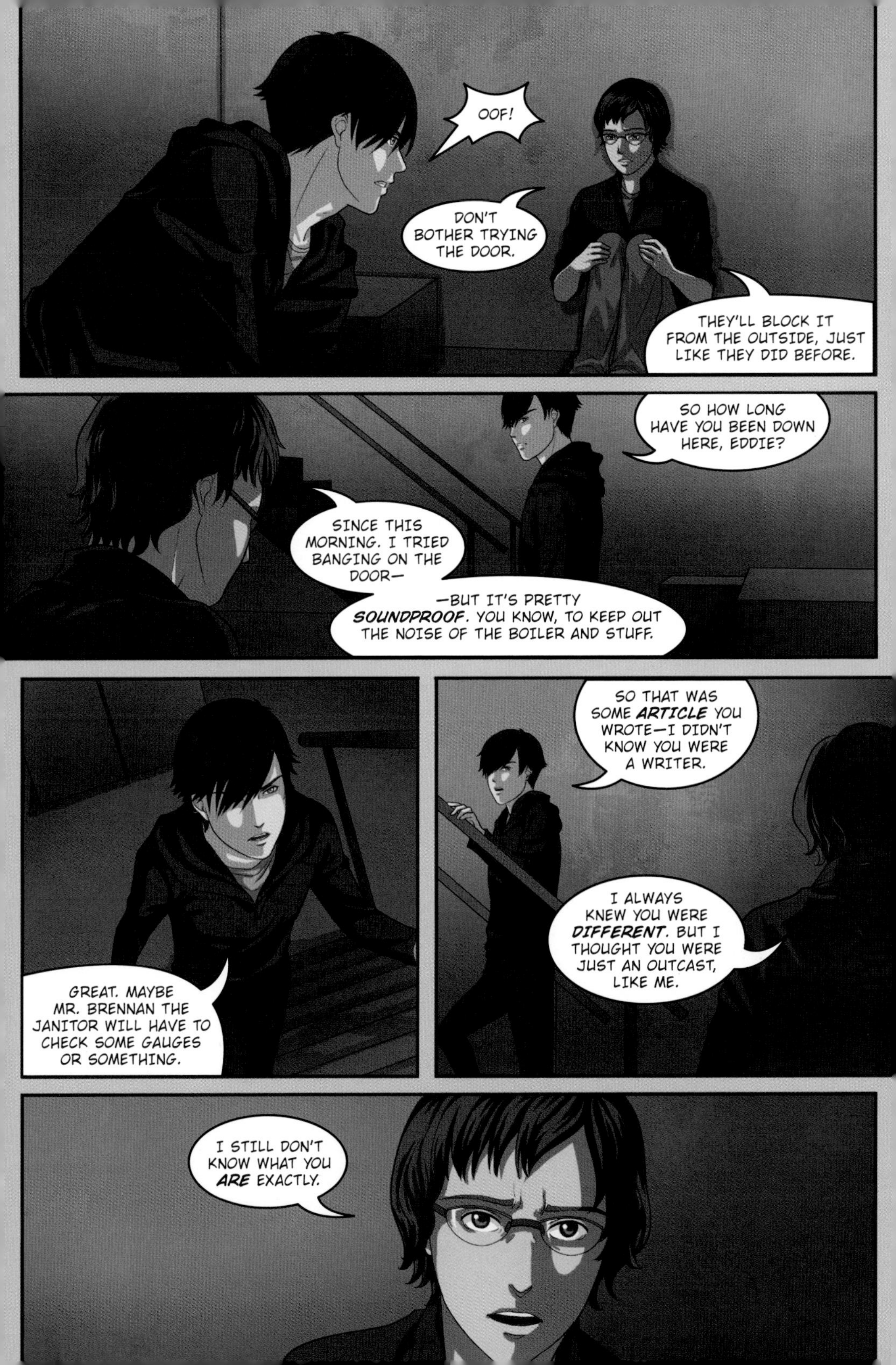
OOF!
DON'T BOTHER TRYING THE DOOR.
THEY'LL BLOCK IT FROM THE OUTSIDE, JUST LIKE THEY DID BEFORE.
SO HOW LONG HAVE YOU BEEN DOWN HERE, EDDIE?
SINCE THIS MORNING. I TRIED BANGING ON THE DOOR—
—BUT IT'S PRETTY SOUNDPROOF. YOU KNOW, TO KEEP OUT THE NOISE OF THE BOILER AND STUFF.
GREAT. MAYBE MR. BRENNAN THE JANITOR WILL HAVE TO CHECK SOME GAUGES OR SOMETHING.
SO THAT WAS SOME ARTICLE YOU WROTE—I DIDN'T KNOW YOU WERE A WRITER.
I ALWAYS KNEW YOU WERE DIFFERENT. BUT I THOUGHT YOU WERE JUST AN OUTCAST, LIKE ME.
I STILL DON'T KNOW WHAT YOU ARE EXACTLY.

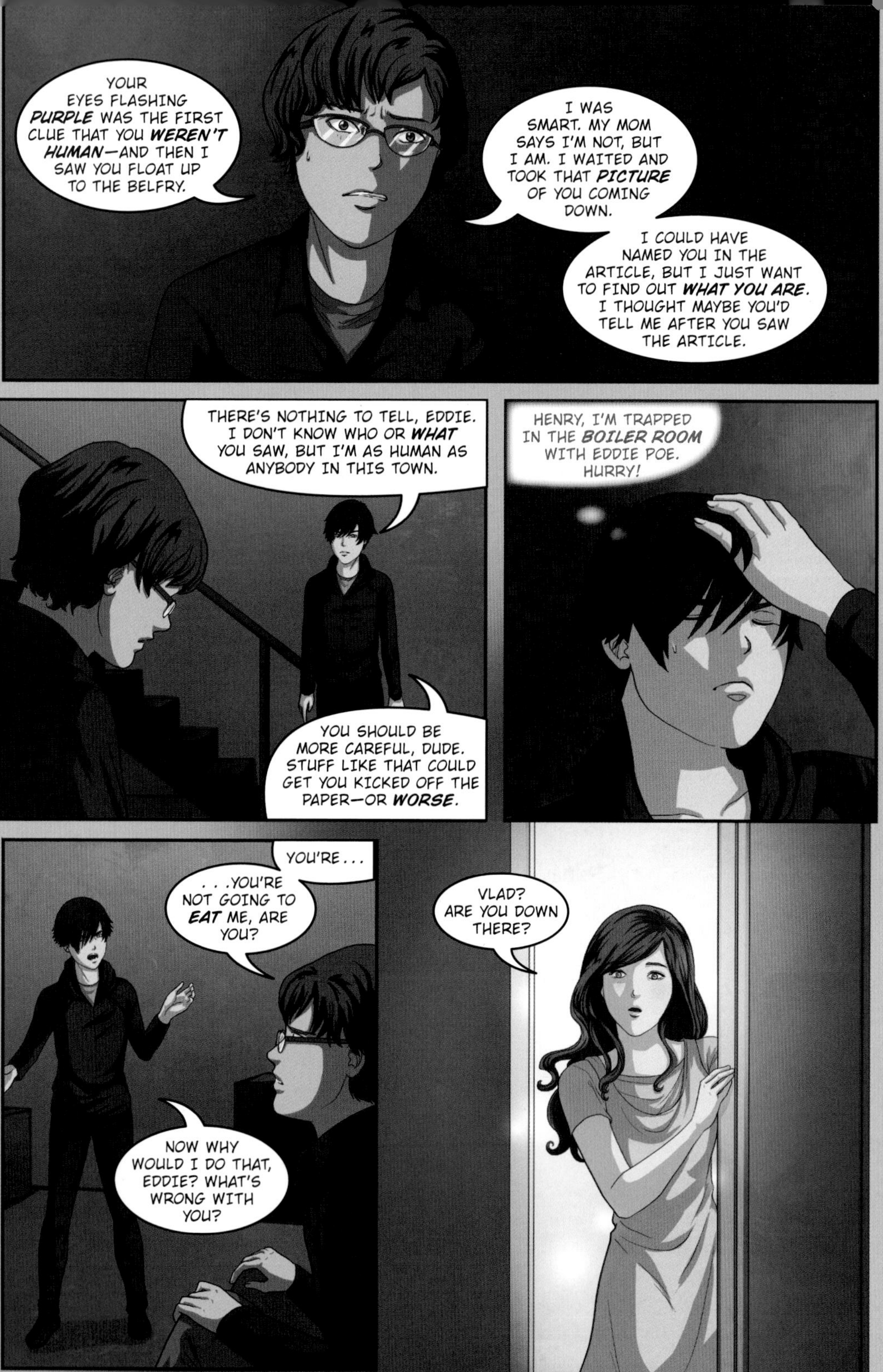
YOUR EYES FLASHING PURPLE WAS THE FIRST CLUE THAT YOU WEREN'T HUMAN—AND THEN I SAW YOU FLOAT UP TO THE BELFRY.
I WAS SMART. MY MOM SAYS I'M NOT, BUT I AM. I WAITED AND TOOK THAT PICTURE OF YOU COMING DOWN.
I COULD HAVE NAMED YOU IN THE ARTICLE, BUT I JUST WANT TO FIND OUT WHAT YOU ARE. I THOUGHT MAYBE YOU'D TELL ME AFTER YOU SAW THE ARTICLE.
THERE'S NOTHING TO TELL, EDDIE. I DON'T KNOW WHO OR WHAT YOU SAW, BUT I'M AS HUMAN AS ANYBODY IN THIS TOWN.
YOU SHOULD BE MORE CAREFUL, DUDE. STUFF LIKE THAT COULD GET YOU KICKED OFF THE PAPER—OR WORSE.
HENRY, I'M TRAPPED IN THE BOILER ROOM WITH EDDIE POE. HURRY!
YOU'RE . . .
. . .YOU'RE NOT GOING TO EAT ME, ARE YOU?
NOW WHY WOULD I DO THAT, EDDIE? WHAT'S WRONG WITH YOU?
VLAD? ARE YOU DOWN THERE?

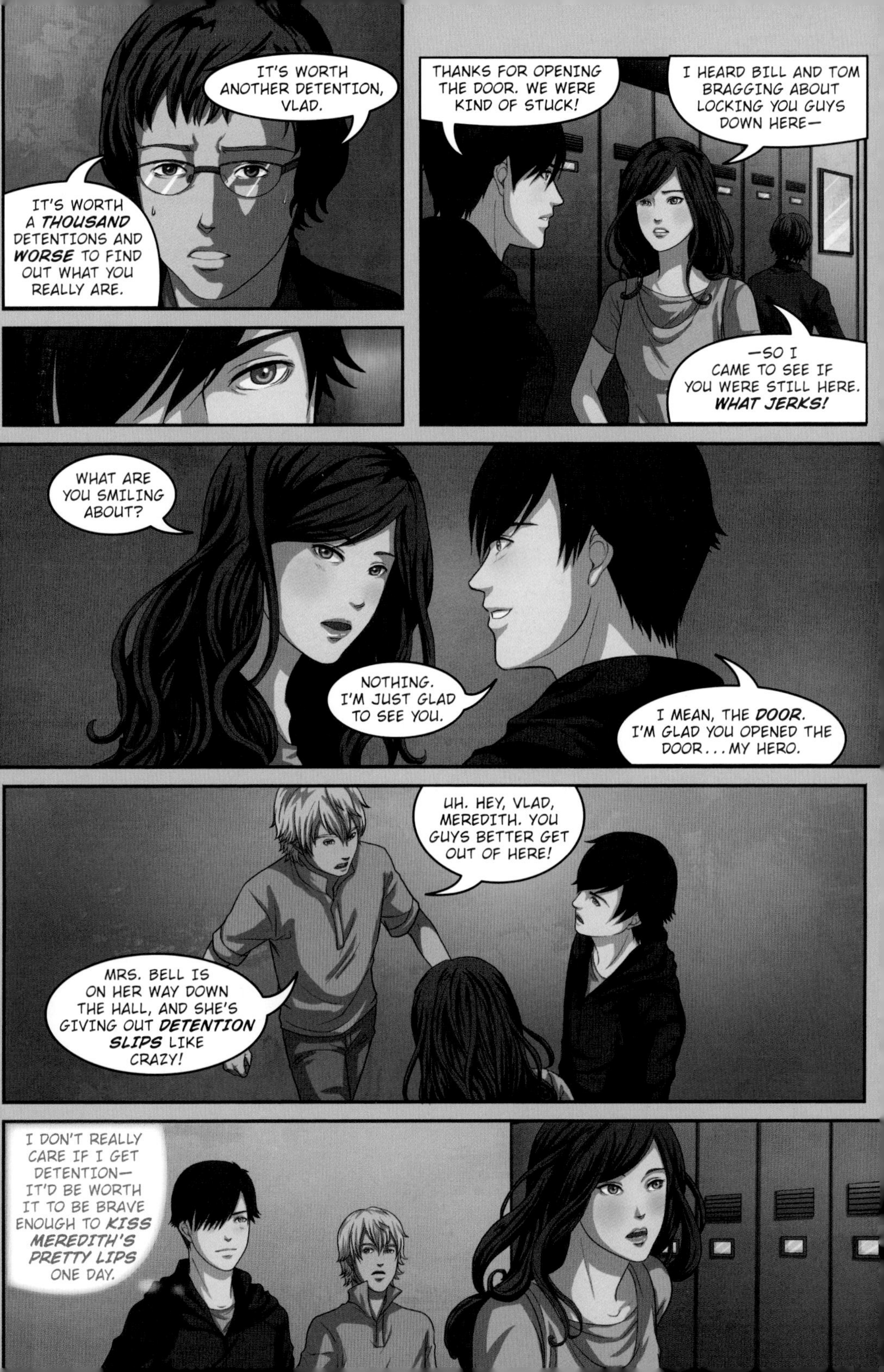
IT'S WORTH ANOTHER DETENTION, VLAD.
IT'S WORTH A **THOUSAND** DETENTIONS AND **WORSE** TO FIND OUT WHAT YOU REALLY ARE.
THANKS FOR OPENING THE DOOR. WE WERE KIND OF STUCK!
I HEARD BILL AND TOM BRAGGING ABOUT LOCKING YOU GUYS DOWN HERE—
—SO I CAME TO SEE IF YOU WERE STILL HERE. **WHAT JERKS!**
WHAT ARE YOU SMILING ABOUT?
NOTHING. I'M JUST GLAD TO SEE YOU.
I MEAN, THE **DOOR**. I'M GLAD YOU OPENED THE DOOR . . . MY HERO.
UH. HEY, VLAD, MEREDITH. YOU GUYS BETTER GET OUT OF HERE!
MRS. BELL IS ON HER WAY DOWN THE HALL, AND SHE'S GIVING OUT **DETENTION SLIPS** LIKE CRAZY!
I DON'T REALLY CARE IF I GET DETENTION— IT'D BE WORTH IT TO BE BRAVE ENOUGH TO **KISS MEREDITH'S PRETTY LIPS** ONE DAY.

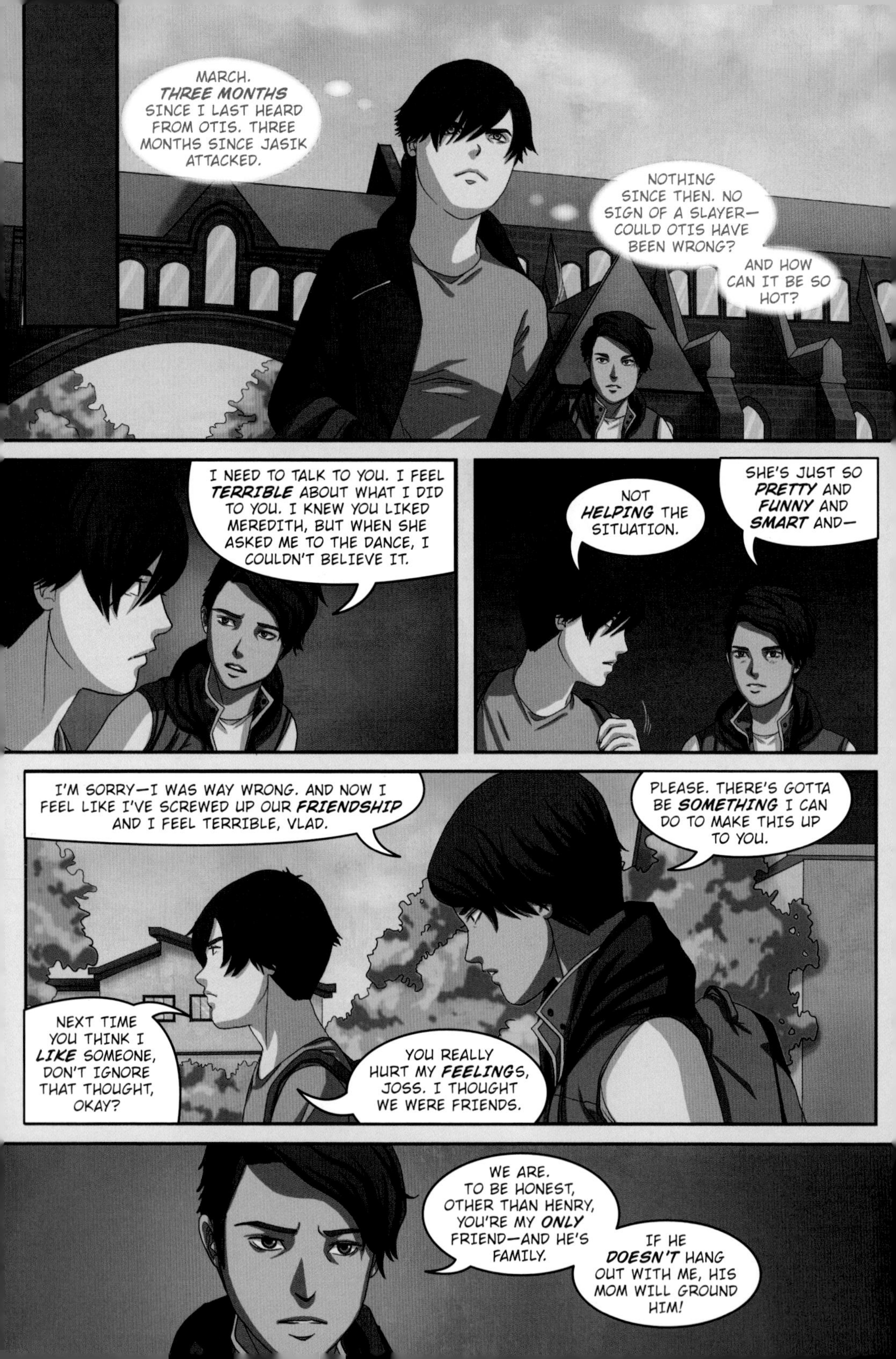
MARCH. THREE MONTHS SINCE I LAST HEARD FROM OTIS. THREE MONTHS SINCE JASIK ATTACKED.
NOTHING SINCE THEN. NO SIGN OF A SLAYER— COULD OTIS HAVE BEEN WRONG?
AND HOW CAN IT BE SO HOT?
I NEED TO TALK TO YOU. I FEEL TERRIBLE ABOUT WHAT I DID TO YOU. I KNEW YOU LIKED MEREDITH, BUT WHEN SHE ASKED ME TO THE DANCE, I COULDN'T BELIEVE IT.
SHE'S JUST SO PRETTY AND FUNNY AND SMART AND—
NOT HELPING THE SITUATION.
I'M SORRY—I WAS WAY WRONG. AND NOW I FEEL LIKE I'VE SCREWED UP OUR FRIENDSHIP AND I FEEL TERRIBLE, VLAD.
PLEASE. THERE'S GOTTA BE SOMETHING I CAN DO TO MAKE THIS UP TO YOU.
NEXT TIME YOU THINK I LIKE SOMEONE, DON'T IGNORE THAT THOUGHT, OKAY?
YOU REALLY HURT MY FEELINGS, JOSS. I THOUGHT WE WERE FRIENDS.
WE ARE. TO BE HONEST, OTHER THAN HENRY, YOU'RE MY ONLY FRIEND—AND HE'S FAMILY.
IF HE DOESN'T HANG OUT WITH ME, HIS MOM WILL GROUND HIM!

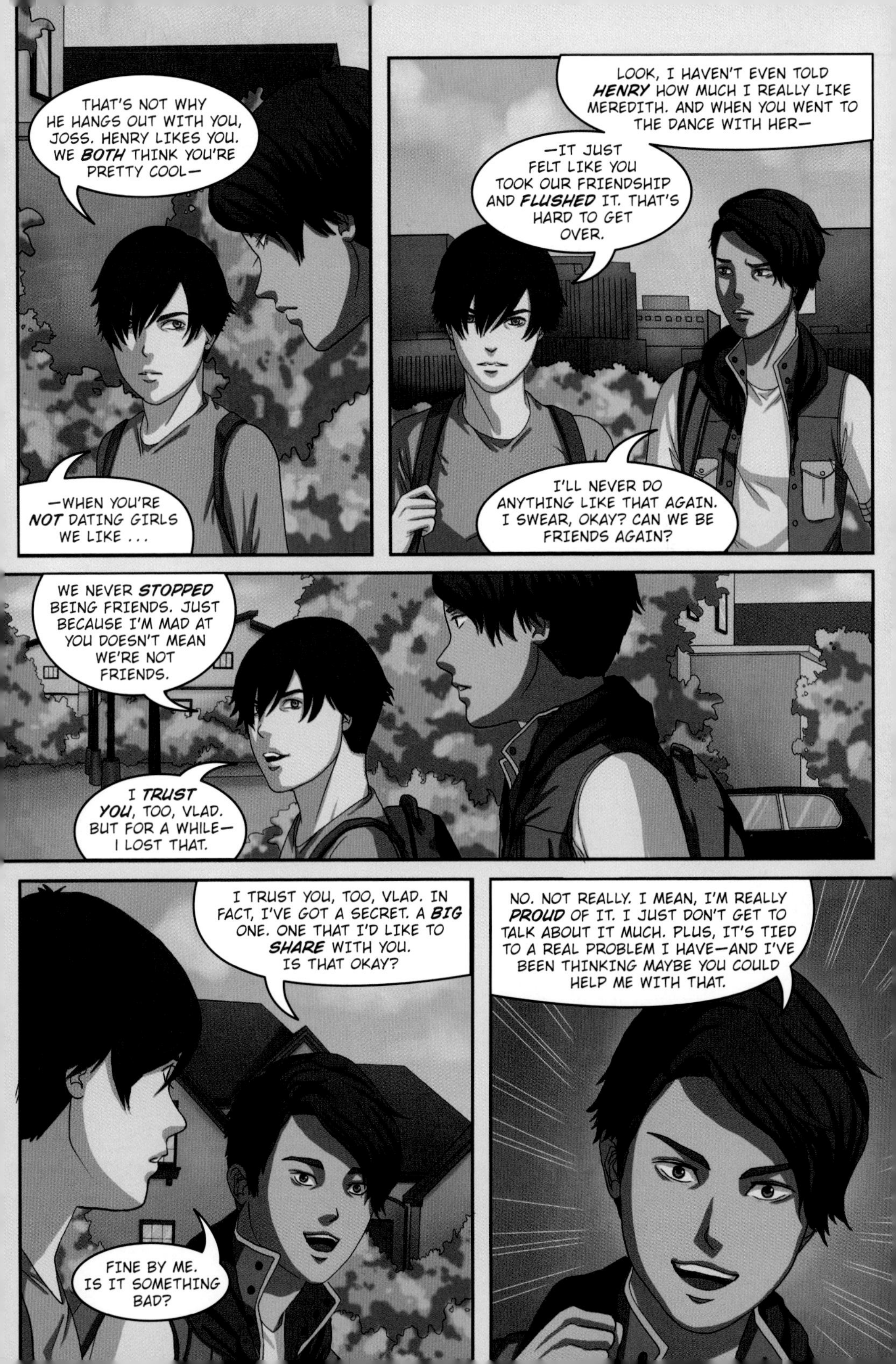
THAT'S NOT WHY HE HANGS OUT WITH YOU, JOSS. HENRY LIKES YOU. WE BOTH THINK YOU'RE PRETTY COOL—
—WHEN YOU'RE NOT DATING GIRLS WE LIKE . . .
LOOK, I HAVEN'T EVEN TOLD HENRY HOW MUCH I REALLY LIKE MEREDITH. AND WHEN YOU WENT TO THE DANCE WITH HER—
—IT JUST FELT LIKE YOU TOOK OUR FRIENDSHIP AND FLUSHED IT. THAT'S HARD TO GET OVER.
I'LL NEVER DO ANYTHING LIKE THAT AGAIN. I SWEAR, OKAY? CAN WE BE FRIENDS AGAIN?
WE NEVER STOPPED BEING FRIENDS. JUST BECAUSE I'M MAD AT YOU DOESN'T MEAN WE'RE NOT FRIENDS.
I TRUST YOU, TOO, VLAD. BUT FOR A WHILE— I LOST THAT.
I TRUST YOU, TOO, VLAD. IN FACT, I'VE GOT A SECRET. A BIG ONE. ONE THAT I'D LIKE TO SHARE WITH YOU. IS THAT OKAY?
FINE BY ME. IS IT SOMETHING BAD?
NO. NOT REALLY. I MEAN, I'M REALLY PROUD OF IT. I JUST DON'T GET TO TALK ABOUT IT MUCH. PLUS, IT'S TIED TO A REAL PROBLEM I HAVE—AND I'VE BEEN THINKING MAYBE YOU COULD HELP ME WITH THAT.

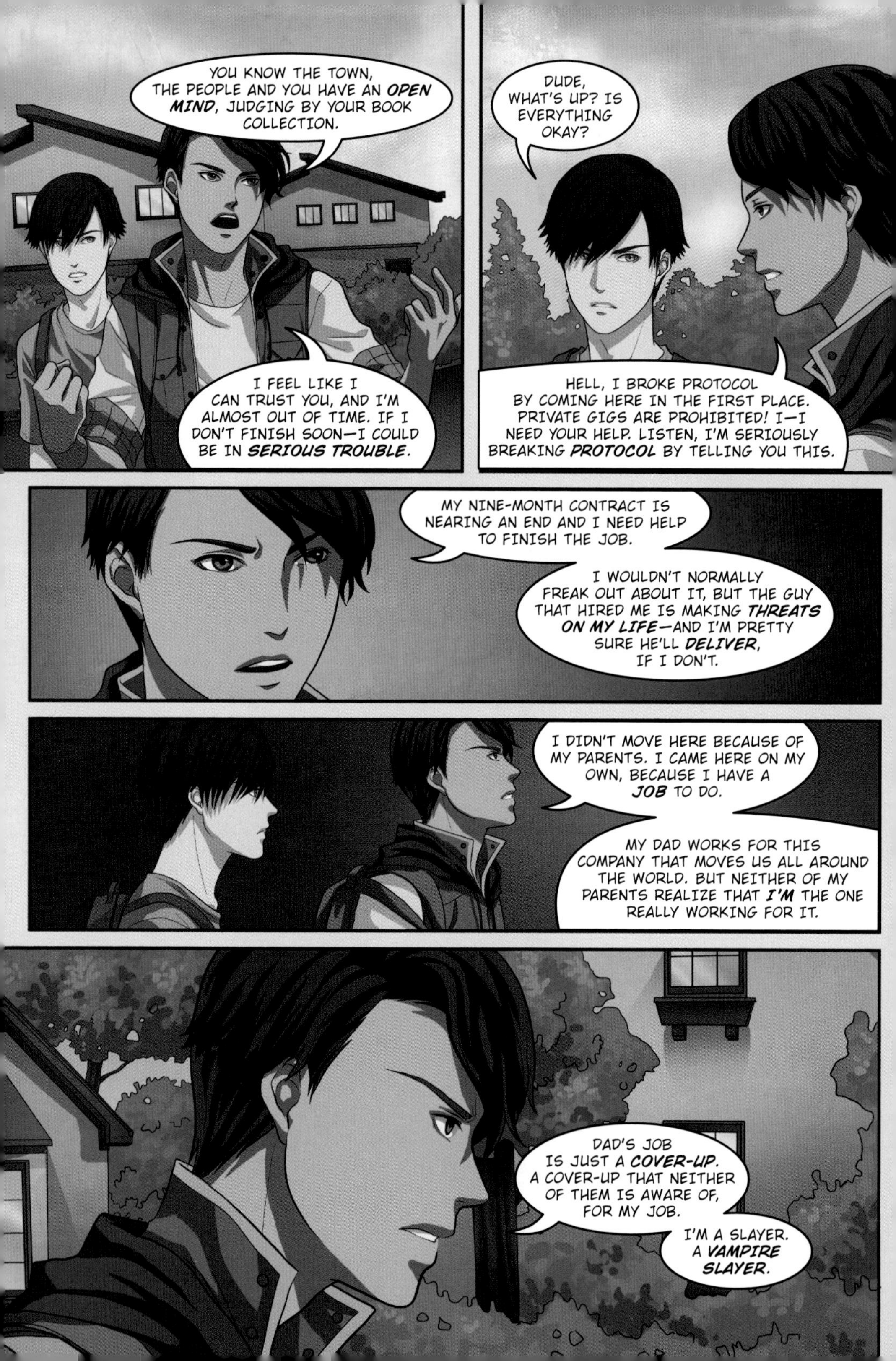

YOU KNOW THE TOWN, THE PEOPLE AND YOU HAVE AN OPEN MIND, JUDGING BY YOUR BOOK COLLECTION.
I FEEL LIKE I CAN TRUST YOU, AND I'M ALMOST OUT OF TIME. IF I DON'T FINISH SOON—I COULD BE IN SERIOUS TROUBLE.
DUDE, WHAT'S UP? IS EVERYTHING OKAY?
HELL, I BROKE PROTOCOL BY COMING HERE IN THE FIRST PLACE. PRIVATE GIGS ARE PROHIBITED! I—I NEED YOUR HELP. LISTEN, I'M SERIOUSLY BREAKING PROTOCOL BY TELLING YOU THIS.
MY NINE-MONTH CONTRACT IS NEARING AN END AND I NEED HELP TO FINISH THE JOB.
I WOULDN'T NORMALLY FREAK OUT ABOUT IT, BUT THE GUY THAT HIRED ME IS MAKING THREATS ON MY LIFE—AND I'M PRETTY SURE HE'LL DELIVER, IF I DON'T.
I DIDN'T MOVE HERE BECAUSE OF MY PARENTS. I CAME HERE ON MY OWN, BECAUSE I HAVE A JOB TO DO.
MY DAD WORKS FOR THIS COMPANY THAT MOVES US ALL AROUND THE WORLD. BUT NEITHER OF MY PARENTS REALIZE THAT I'M THE ONE REALLY WORKING FOR IT.
DAD'S JOB IS JUST A COVER-UP. A COVER-UP THAT NEITHER OF THEM IS AWARE OF, FOR MY JOB.
I'M A SLAYER. A VAMPIRE SLAYER.

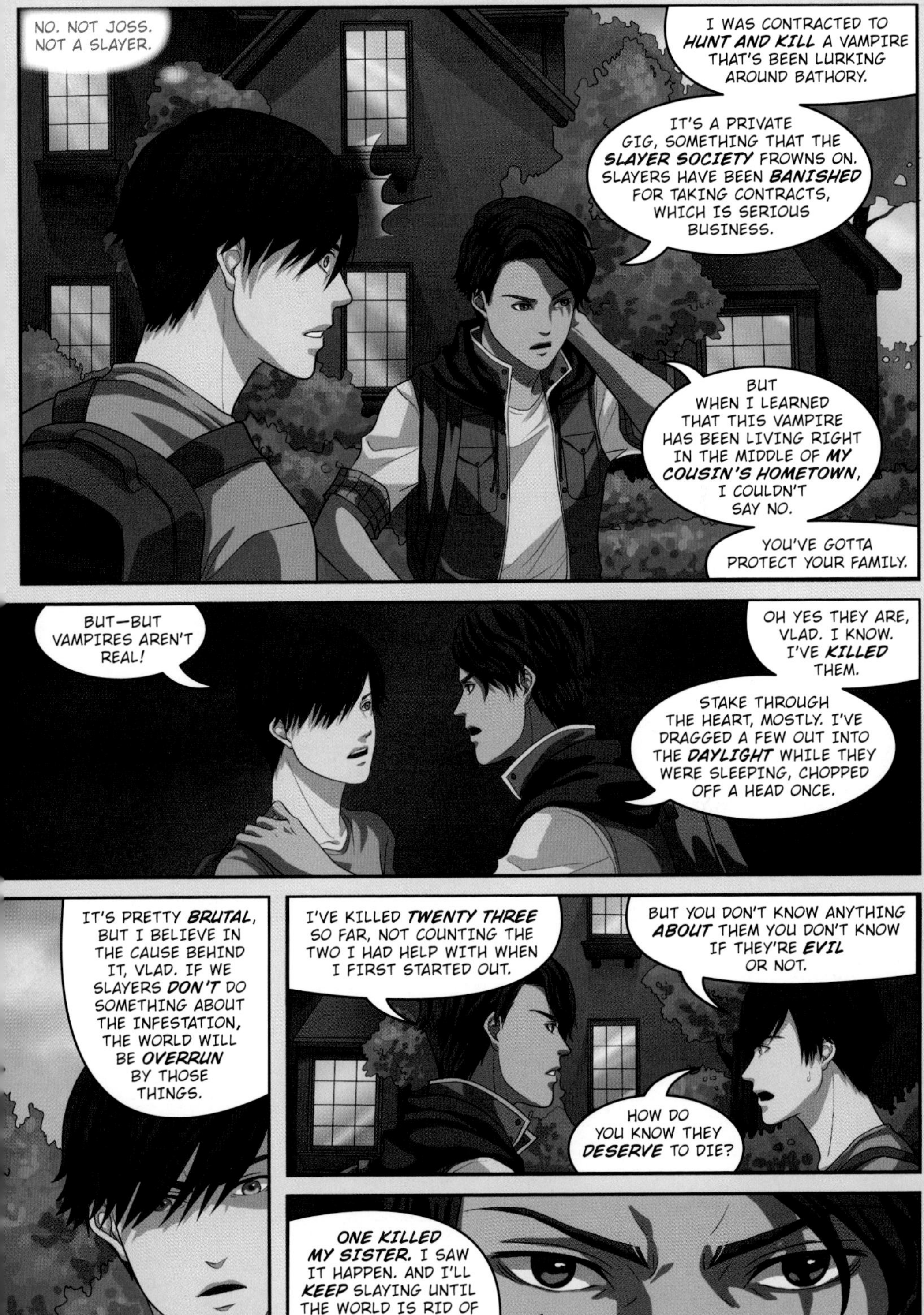
NO. NOT JOSS. NOT A SLAYER.
I WAS CONTRACTED TO *HUNT AND KILL* A VAMPIRE THAT'S BEEN LURKING AROUND BATHORY.
IT'S A PRIVATE GIG, SOMETHING THAT THE *SLAYER SOCIETY* FROWNS ON. SLAYERS HAVE BEEN *BANISHED* FOR TAKING CONTRACTS, WHICH IS SERIOUS BUSINESS.
BUT WHEN I LEARNED THAT THIS VAMPIRE HAS BEEN LIVING RIGHT IN THE MIDDLE OF *MY COUSIN'S HOMETOWN*, I COULDN'T SAY NO.
YOU'VE GOTTA PROTECT YOUR FAMILY.
BUT—BUT VAMPIRES AREN'T REAL!
OH YES THEY ARE, VLAD. I KNOW. I'VE *KILLED* THEM.
STAKE THROUGH THE HEART, MOSTLY. I'VE DRAGGED A FEW OUT INTO THE *DAYLIGHT* WHILE THEY WERE SLEEPING, CHOPPED OFF A HEAD ONCE.
IT'S PRETTY *BRUTAL*, BUT I BELIEVE IN THE CAUSE BEHIND IT, VLAD. IF WE SLAYERS *DON'T* DO SOMETHING ABOUT THE INFESTATION, THE WORLD WILL BE *OVERRUN* BY THOSE THINGS.
I'VE KILLED *TWENTY THREE* SO FAR, NOT COUNTING THE TWO I HAD HELP WITH WHEN I FIRST STARTED OUT.
BUT YOU DON'T KNOW ANYTHING *ABOUT* THEM YOU DON'T KNOW IF THEY'RE *EVIL* OR NOT.
HOW DO YOU KNOW THEY *DESERVE* TO DIE?
ONE KILLED MY SISTER. I SAW IT HAPPEN. AND I'LL *KEEP* SLAYING UNTIL THE WORLD IS RID OF THOSE *MONSTERS*.

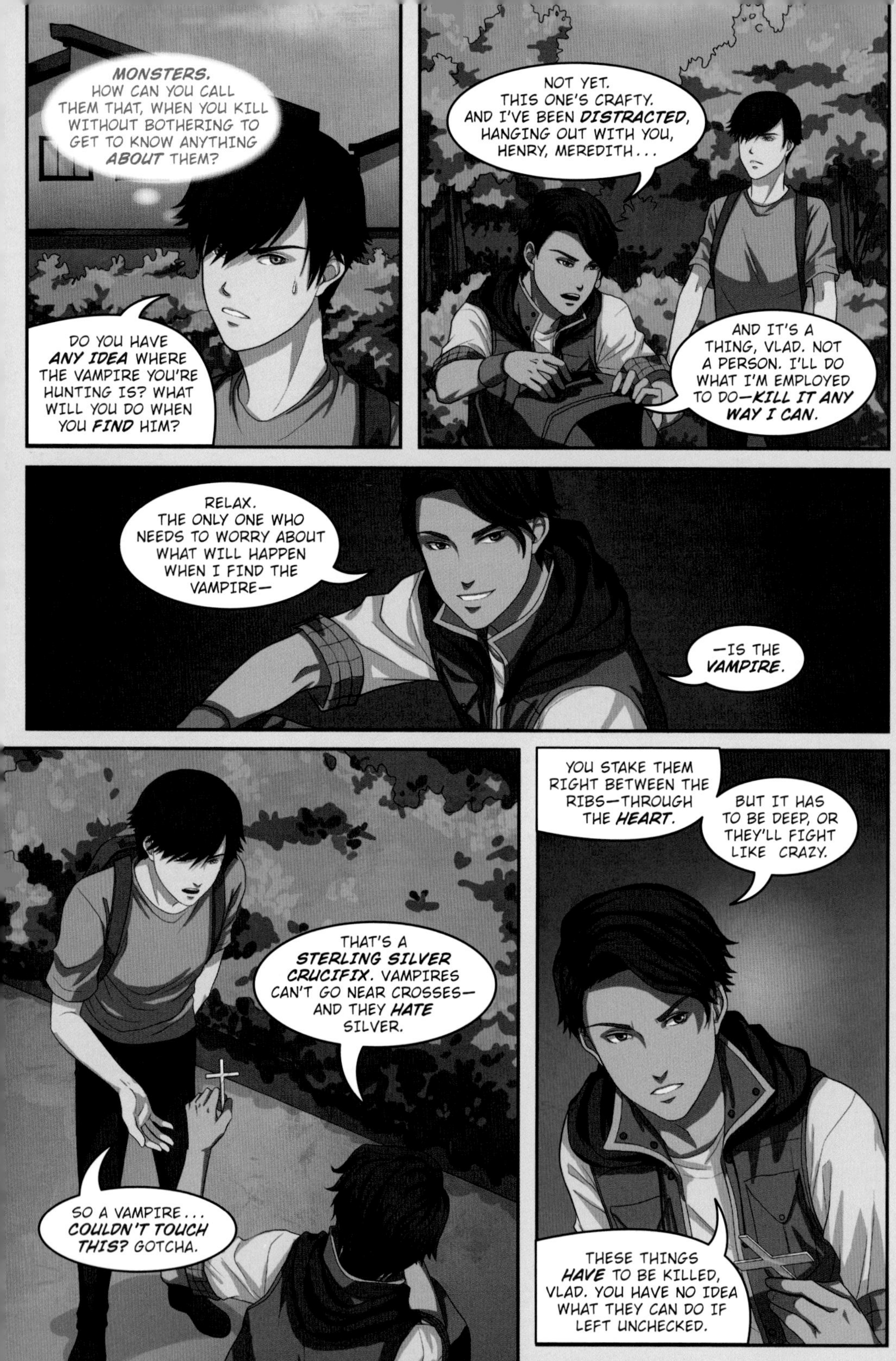
MONSTERS. HOW CAN YOU CALL THEM THAT, WHEN YOU KILL WITHOUT BOTHERING TO GET TO KNOW ANYTHING ABOUT THEM?
DO YOU HAVE ANY IDEA WHERE THE VAMPIRE YOU'RE HUNTING IS? WHAT WILL YOU DO WHEN YOU FIND HIM?
NOT YET. THIS ONE'S CRAFTY. AND I'VE BEEN DISTRACTED, HANGING OUT WITH YOU, HENRY, MEREDITH . . .
AND IT'S A THING, VLAD. NOT A PERSON. I'LL DO WHAT I'M EMPLOYED TO DO—KILL IT ANY WAY I CAN.
RELAX. THE ONLY ONE WHO NEEDS TO WORRY ABOUT WHAT WILL HAPPEN WHEN I FIND THE VAMPIRE—
—IS THE VAMPIRE.
THAT'S A STERLING SILVER CRUCIFIX. VAMPIRES CAN'T GO NEAR CROSSES—AND THEY HATE SILVER.
SO A VAMPIRE . . . COULDN'T TOUCH THIS? GOTCHA.
YOU STAKE THEM RIGHT BETWEEN THE RIBS—THROUGH THE HEART.
BUT IT HAS TO BE DEEP, OR THEY'LL FIGHT LIKE CRAZY.
THESE THINGS HAVE TO BE KILLED, VLAD. YOU HAVE NO IDEA WHAT THEY CAN DO IF LEFT UNCHECKED.

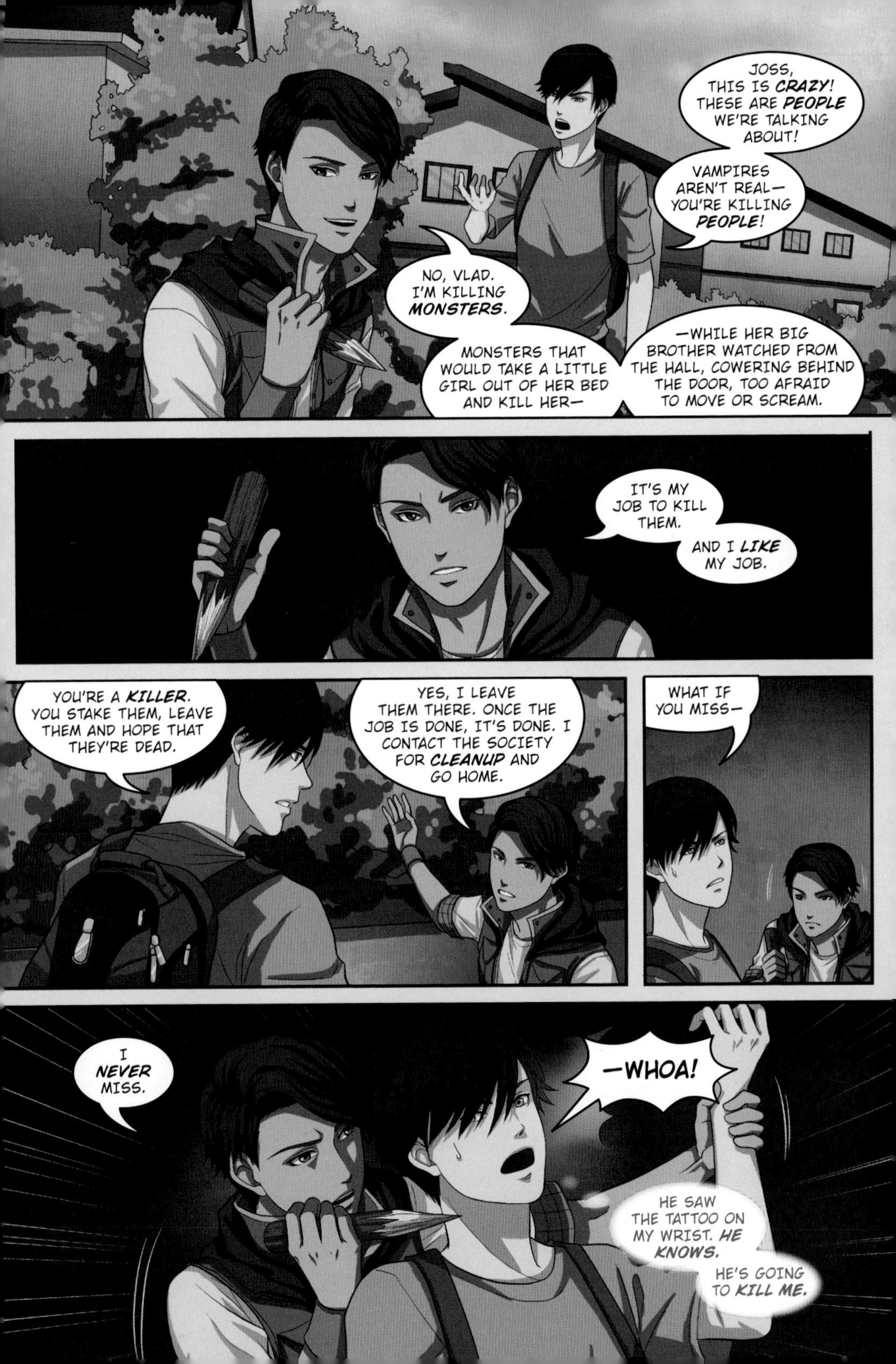
JOSS, THIS IS *CRAZY*! THESE ARE *PEOPLE* WE'RE TALKING ABOUT!
VAMPIRES AREN'T REAL—YOU'RE KILLING *PEOPLE*!
NO, VLAD. I'M KILLING *MONSTERS*.
MONSTERS THAT WOULD TAKE A LITTLE GIRL OUT OF HER BED AND KILL HER—
—WHILE HER BIG BROTHER WATCHED FROM THE HALL, COWERING BEHIND THE DOOR, TOO AFRAID TO MOVE OR SCREAM.
IT'S MY JOB TO KILL THEM.
AND I *LIKE* MY JOB.
YOU'RE A *KILLER*. YOU STAKE THEM, LEAVE THEM AND HOPE THAT THEY'RE DEAD.
YES, I LEAVE THEM THERE. ONCE THE JOB IS DONE, IT'S DONE. I CONTACT THE SOCIETY FOR *CLEANUP* AND GO HOME.
WHAT IF YOU MISS—
I *NEVER* MISS.
—WHOA!
HE SAW THE TATTOO ON MY WRIST. *HE KNOWS.*
HE'S GOING TO *KILL ME.*

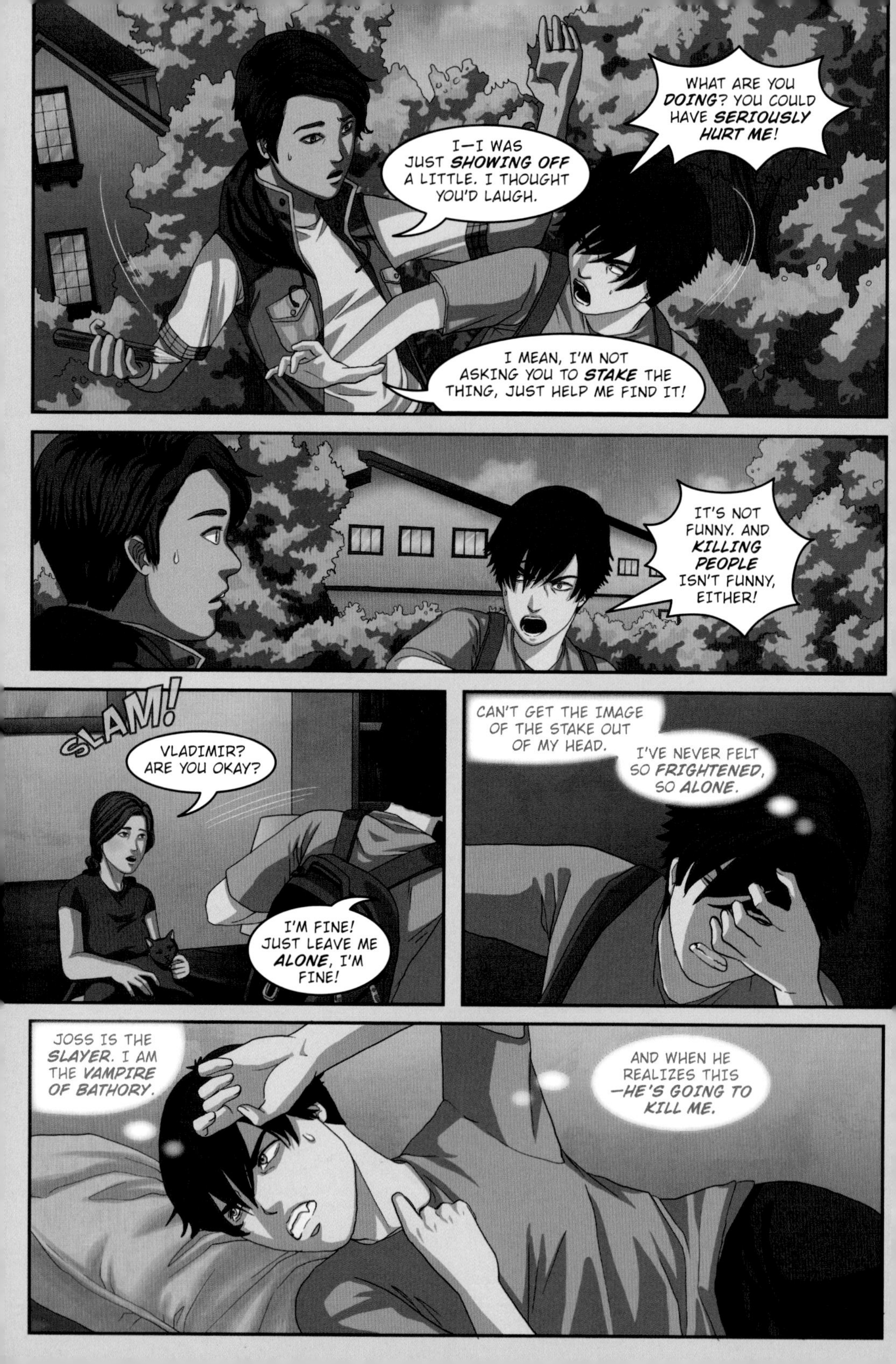
I—I WAS JUST SHOWING OFF A LITTLE. I THOUGHT YOU'D LAUGH.
WHAT ARE YOU DOING? YOU COULD HAVE SERIOUSLY HURT ME!
I MEAN, I'M NOT ASKING YOU TO STAKE THE THING, JUST HELP ME FIND IT!
IT'S NOT FUNNY. AND KILLING PEOPLE ISN'T FUNNY, EITHER!
SLAM!
VLADIMIR? ARE YOU OKAY?
I'M FINE! JUST LEAVE ME ALONE, I'M FINE!
CAN'T GET THE IMAGE OF THE STAKE OUT OF MY HEAD.
I'VE NEVER FELT SO FRIGHTENED, SO ALONE.
JOSS IS THE SLAYER. I AM THE VAMPIRE OF BATHORY.
AND WHEN HE REALIZES THIS —HE'S GOING TO KILL ME.

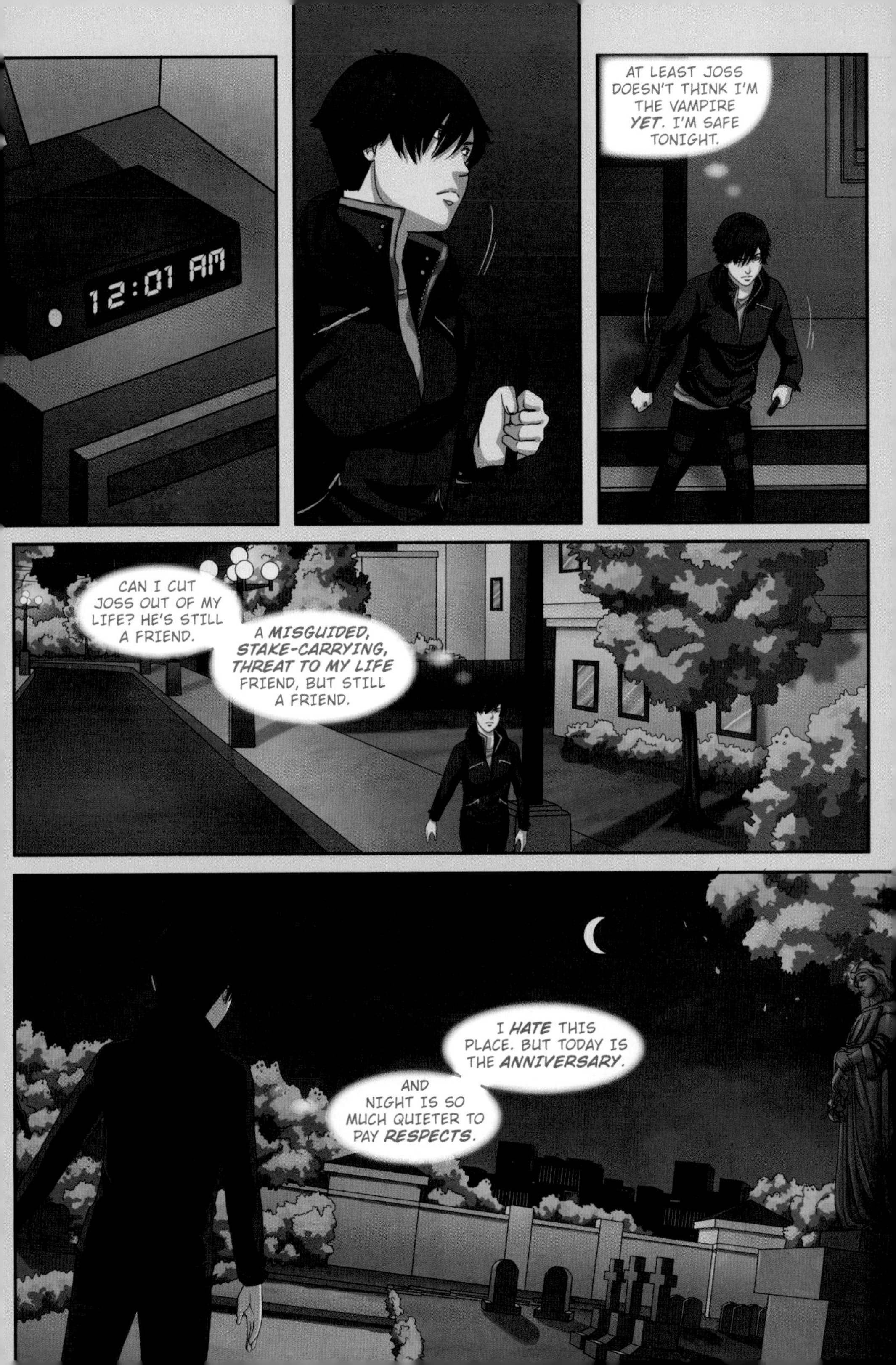
12:01 AM
AT LEAST JOSS DOESN'T THINK I'M THE VAMPIRE YET. I'M SAFE TONIGHT.
CAN I CUT JOSS OUT OF MY LIFE? HE'S STILL A FRIEND.
A MISGUIDED, STAKE-CARRYING, THREAT TO MY LIFE FRIEND, BUT STILL A FRIEND.
I HATE THIS PLACE. BUT TODAY IS THE ANNIVERSARY.
AND NIGHT IS SO MUCH QUIETER TO PAY RESPECTS.

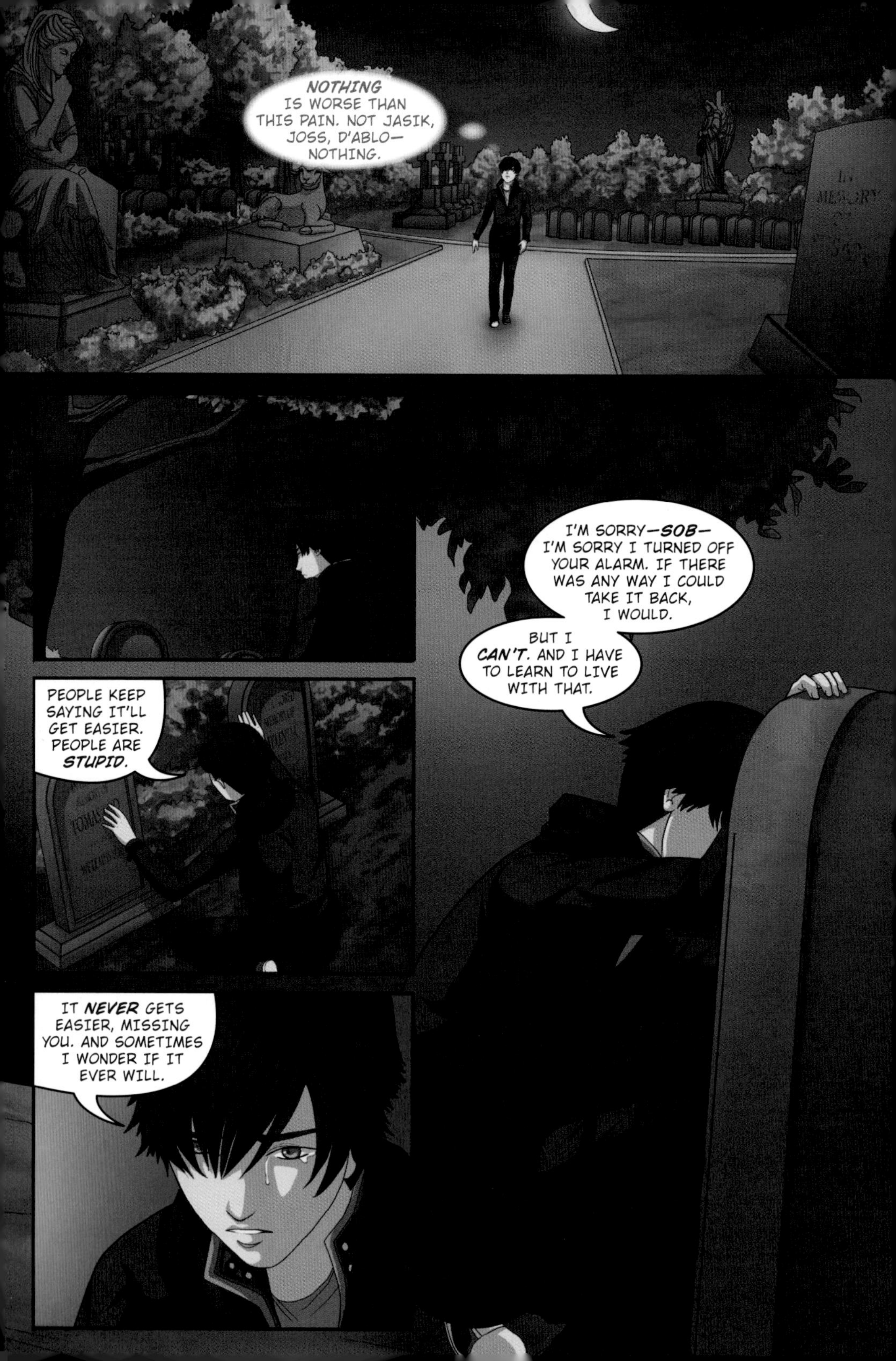
NOTHING IS WORSE THAN THIS PAIN. NOT JASIK, JOSS, D'ABLO—NOTHING.
IN MEMORY
I'M SORRY—SOB—I'M SORRY I TURNED OFF YOUR ALARM. IF THERE WAS ANY WAY I COULD TAKE IT BACK, I WOULD.
BUT I CAN'T. AND I HAVE TO LEARN TO LIVE WITH THAT.
PEOPLE KEEP SAYING IT'LL GET EASIER. PEOPLE ARE STUPID.
IT NEVER GETS EASIER, MISSING YOU. AND SOMETIMES I WONDER IF IT EVER WILL.

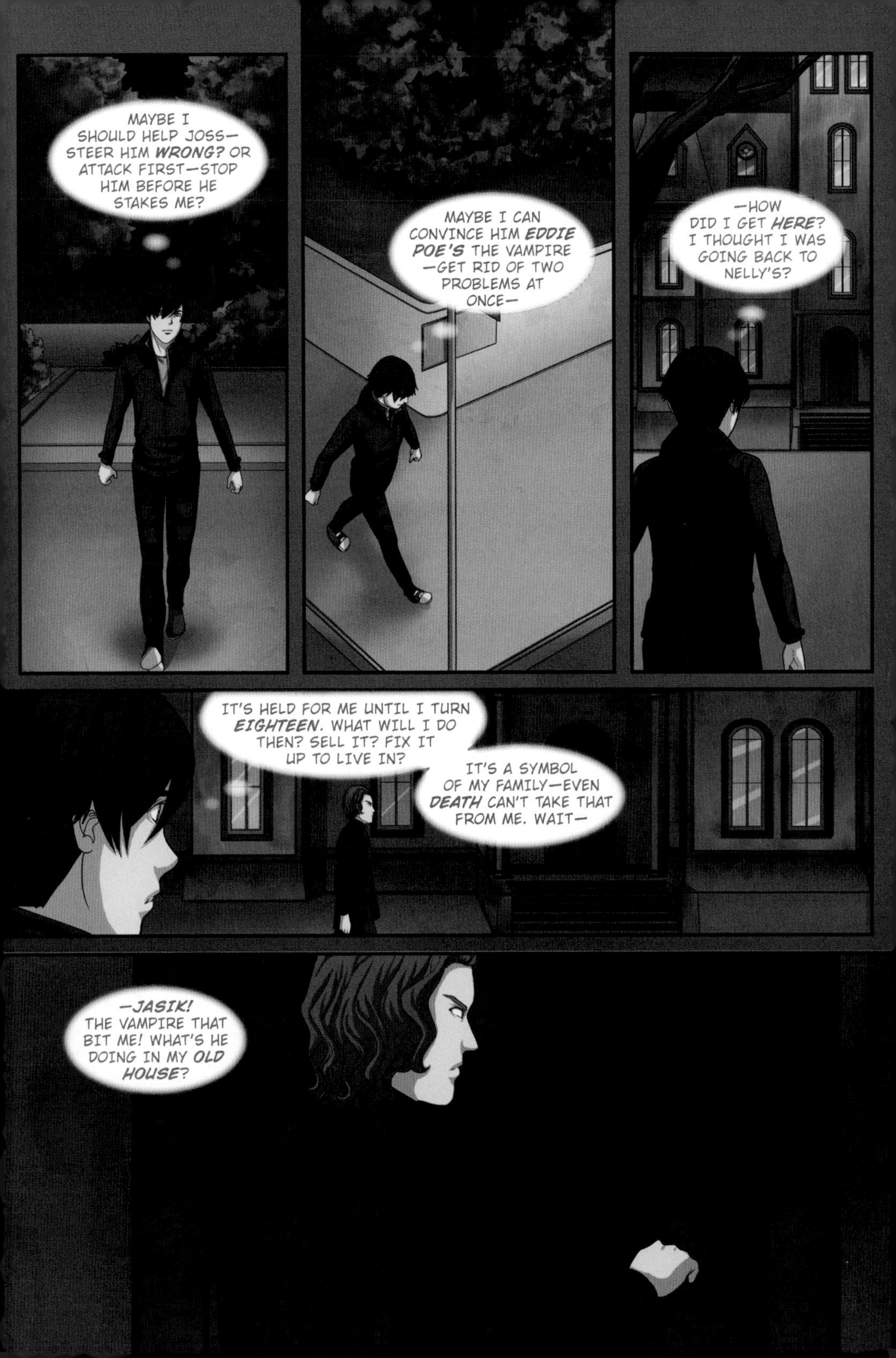
MAYBE I SHOULD HELP JOSS—STEER HIM WRONG? OR ATTACK FIRST—STOP HIM BEFORE HE STAKES ME?
MAYBE I CAN CONVINCE HIM EDDIE POE'S THE VAMPIRE—GET RID OF TWO PROBLEMS AT ONCE—
—HOW DID I GET HERE? I THOUGHT I WAS GOING BACK TO NELLY'S?
IT'S HELD FOR ME UNTIL I TURN EIGHTEEN. WHAT WILL I DO THEN? SELL IT? FIX IT UP TO LIVE IN?
IT'S A SYMBOL OF MY FAMILY—EVEN DEATH CAN'T TAKE THAT FROM ME. WAIT—
—JASIK! THE VAMPIRE THAT BIT ME! WHAT'S HE DOING IN MY OLD HOUSE?

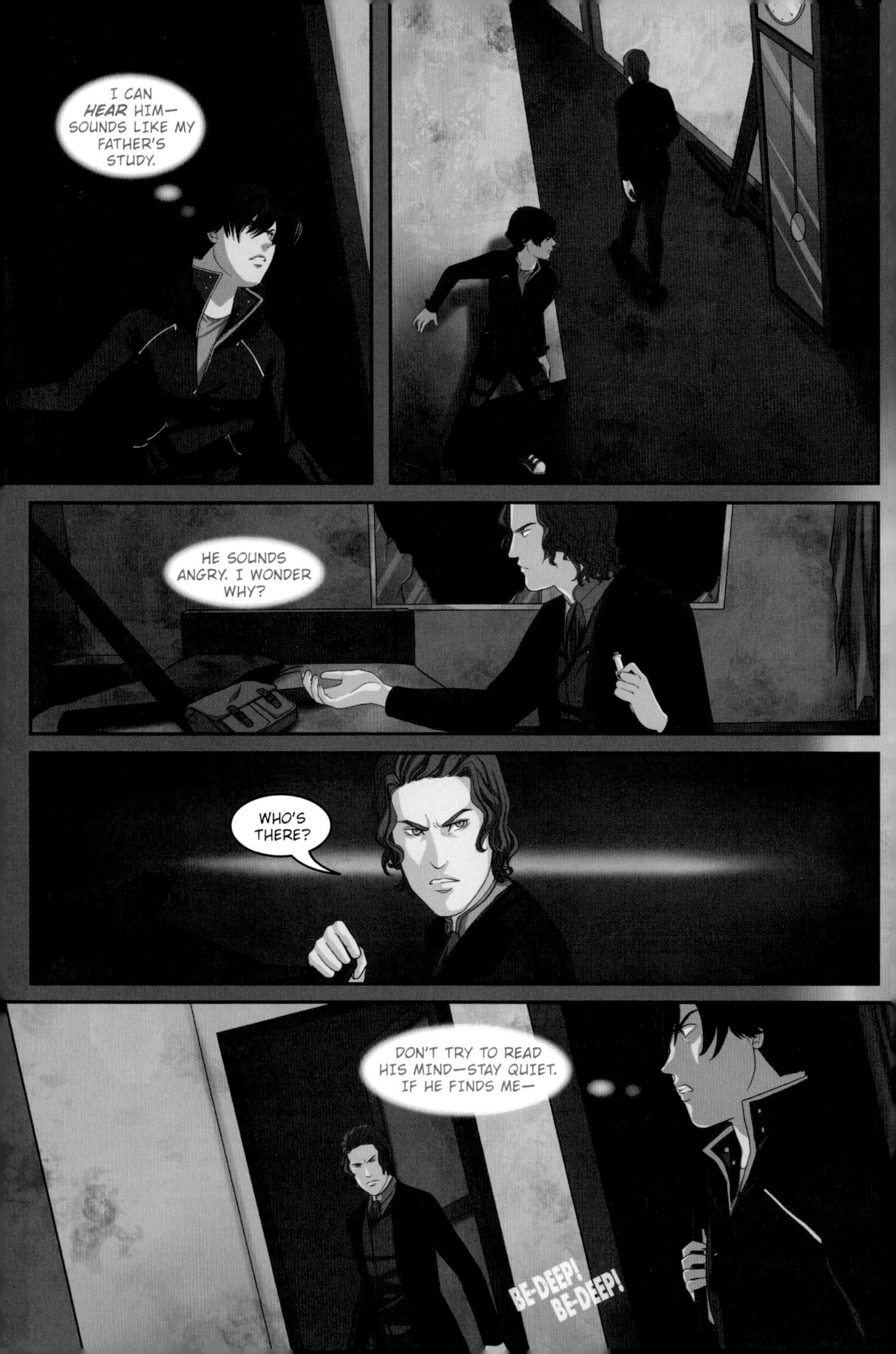
I CAN HEAR HIM—SOUNDS LIKE MY FATHER'S STUDY.
HE SOUNDS ANGRY. I WONDER WHY?
WHO'S THERE?
DON'T TRY TO READ HIS MIND—STAY QUIET. IF HE FINDS ME—
BE-DEEP! BE-DEEP!

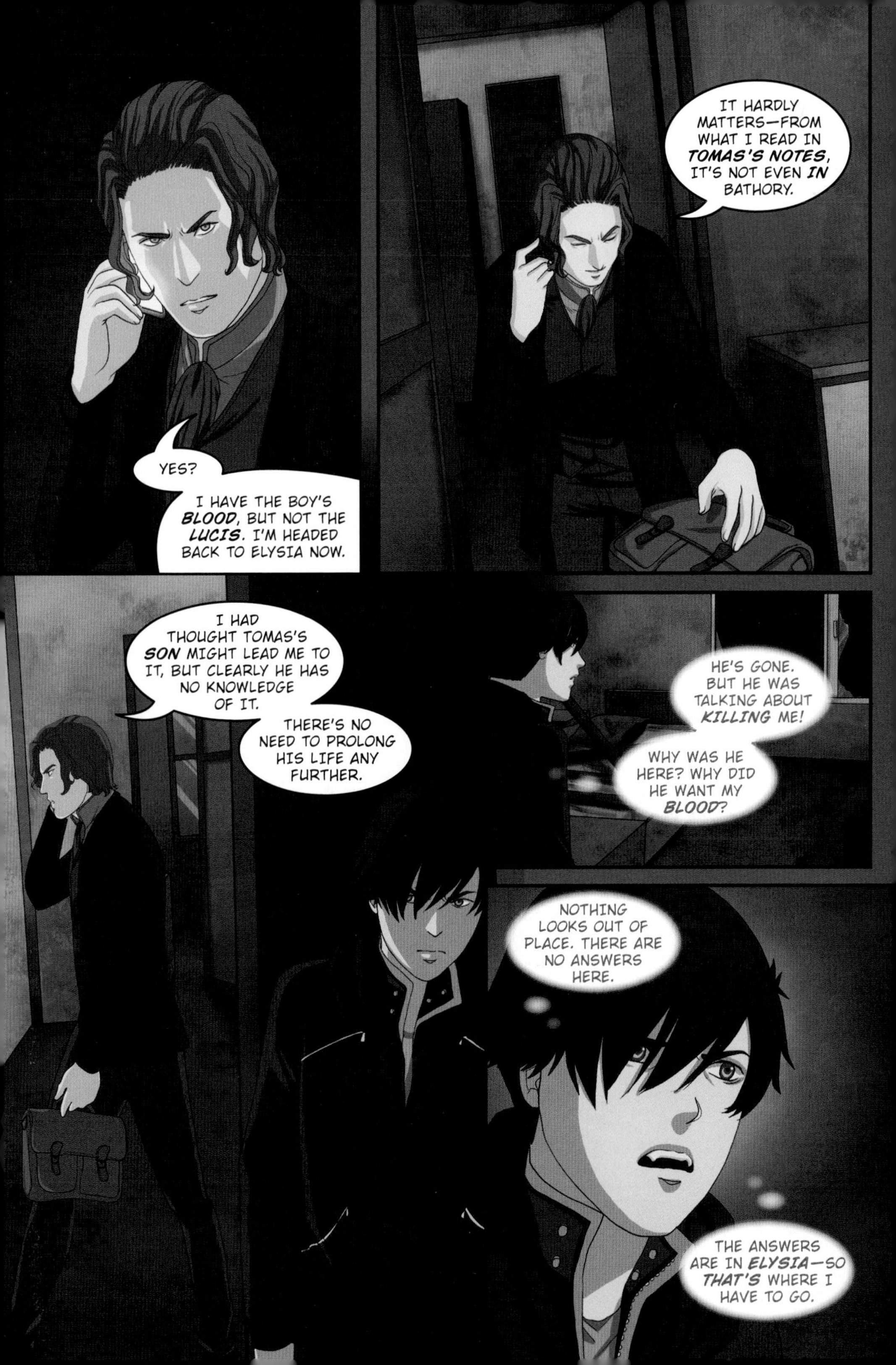
YES?
I HAVE THE BOY'S **BLOOD**, BUT NOT THE **LUCIS**. I'M HEADED BACK TO ELYSIA NOW.
IT HARDLY MATTERS—FROM WHAT I READ IN **TOMAS'S NOTES**, IT'S NOT EVEN **IN** BATHORY.
I HAD THOUGHT TOMAS'S **SON** MIGHT LEAD ME TO IT, BUT CLEARLY HE HAS NO KNOWLEDGE OF IT.
THERE'S NO NEED TO PROLONG HIS LIFE ANY FURTHER.
HE'S GONE. BUT HE WAS TALKING ABOUT **KILLING** ME!
WHY WAS HE HERE? WHY DID HE WANT MY **BLOOD**?
NOTHING LOOKS OUT OF PLACE. THERE ARE NO ANSWERS HERE.
THE ANSWERS ARE IN **ELYSIA**—SO **THAT'S** WHERE I HAVE TO GO.

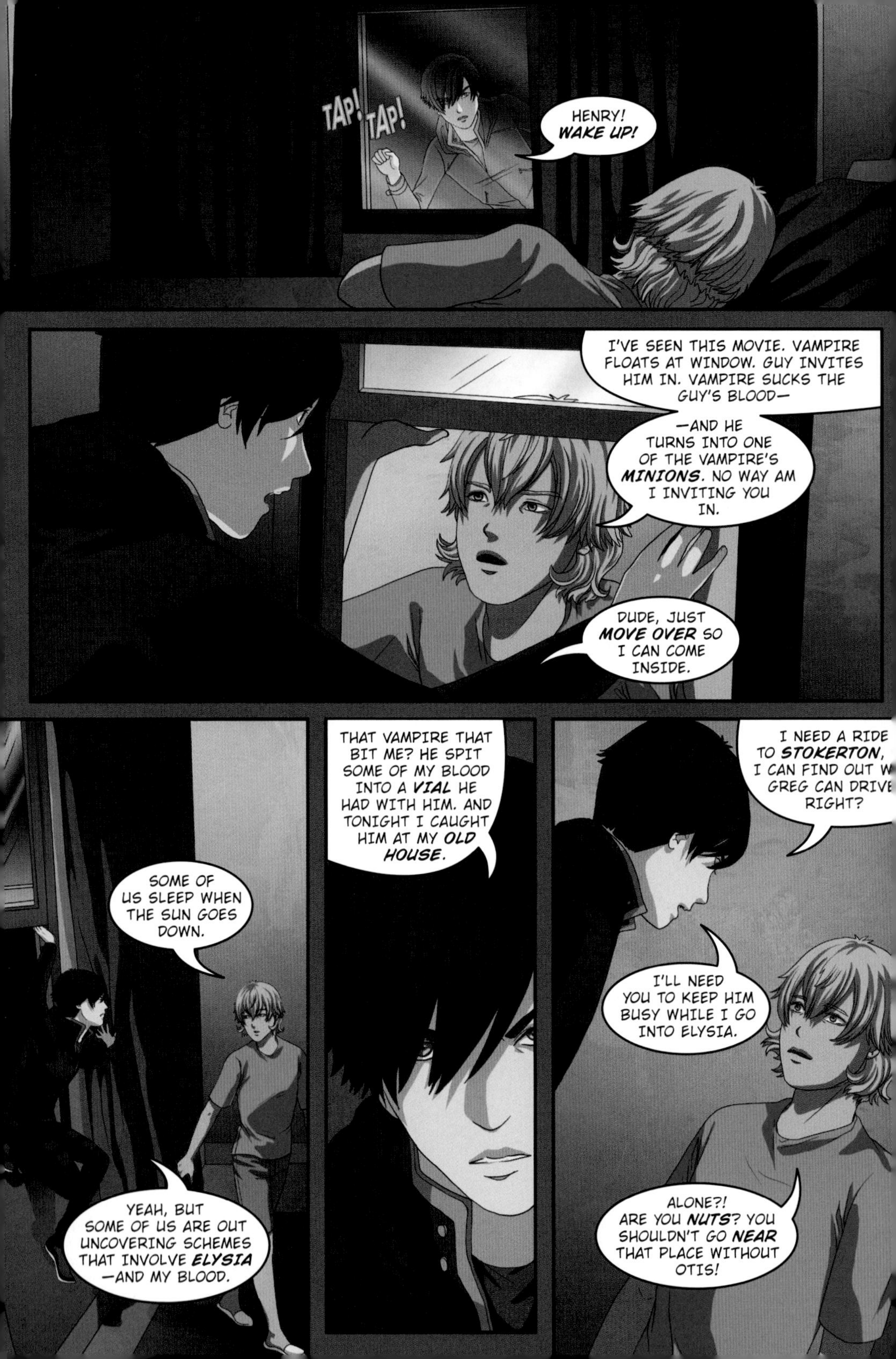
TAP! TAP!
HENRY! WAKE UP!
I'VE SEEN THIS MOVIE. VAMPIRE FLOATS AT WINDOW. GUY INVITES HIM IN. VAMPIRE SUCKS THE GUY'S BLOOD—
—AND HE TURNS INTO ONE OF THE VAMPIRE'S MINIONS. NO WAY AM I INVITING YOU IN.
DUDE, JUST MOVE OVER SO I CAN COME INSIDE.
SOME OF US SLEEP WHEN THE SUN GOES DOWN.
YEAH, BUT SOME OF US ARE OUT UNCOVERING SCHEMES THAT INVOLVE ELYSIA —AND MY BLOOD.
THAT VAMPIRE THAT BIT ME? HE SPIT SOME OF MY BLOOD INTO A VIAL HE HAD WITH HIM. AND TONIGHT I CAUGHT HIM AT MY OLD HOUSE.
I NEED A RIDE TO STOKERTON, I CAN FIND OUT W GREG CAN DRIVE RIGHT?
I'LL NEED YOU TO KEEP HIM BUSY WHILE I GO INTO ELYSIA.
ALONE?! ARE YOU NUTS? YOU SHOULDN'T GO NEAR THAT PLACE WITHOUT OTIS!

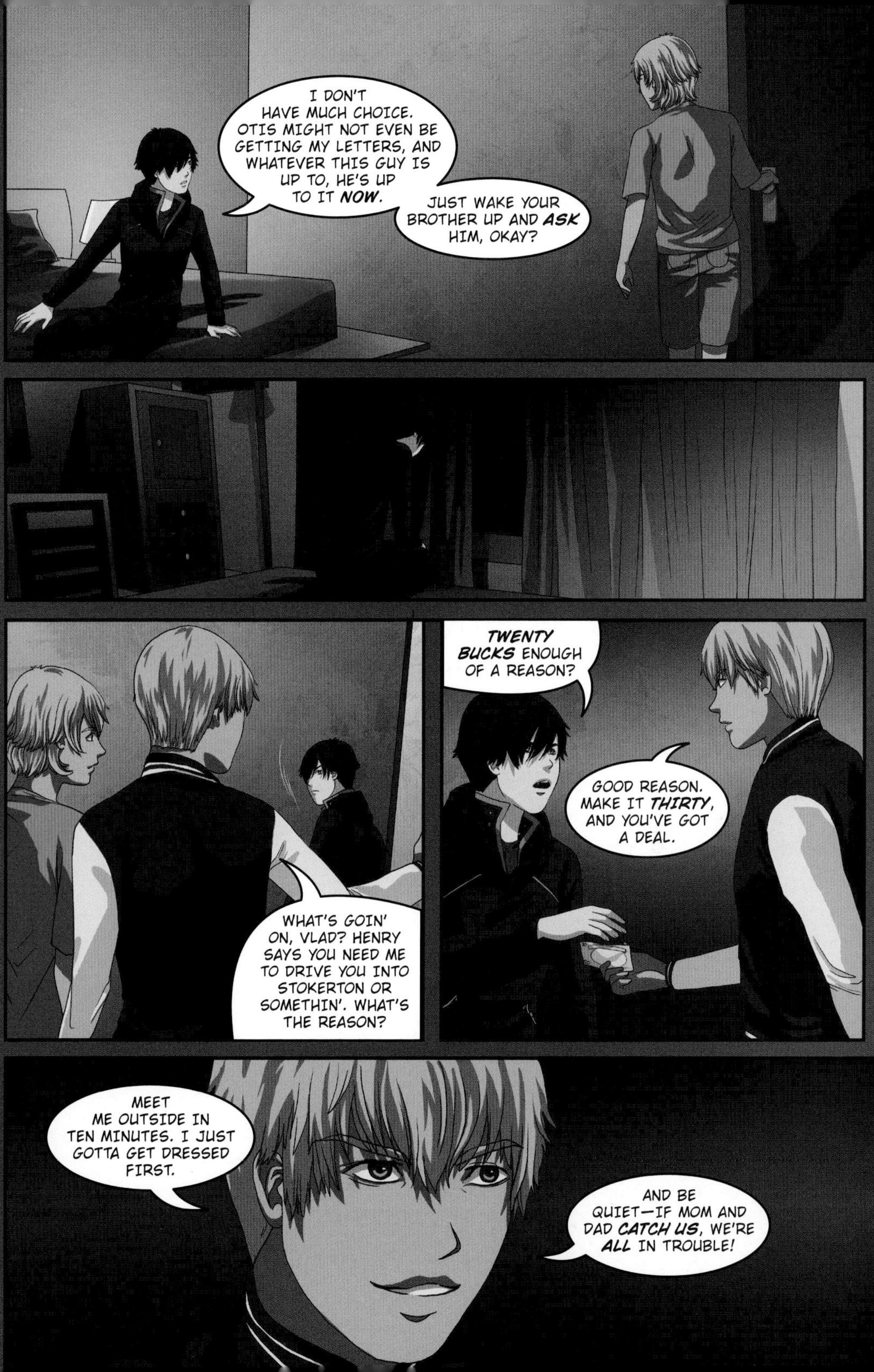
I DON'T HAVE MUCH CHOICE. OTIS MIGHT NOT EVEN BE GETTING MY LETTERS, AND WHATEVER THIS GUY IS UP TO, HE'S UP TO IT **NOW**.
JUST WAKE YOUR BROTHER UP AND **ASK** HIM, OKAY?
WHAT'S GOIN' ON, VLAD? HENRY SAYS YOU NEED ME TO DRIVE YOU INTO STOKERTON OR SOMETHIN'. WHAT'S THE REASON?
TWENTY BUCKS ENOUGH OF A REASON?
GOOD REASON. MAKE IT **THIRTY**, AND YOU'VE GOT A DEAL.
MEET ME OUTSIDE IN TEN MINUTES. I JUST GOTTA GET DRESSED FIRST.
AND BE QUIET—IF MOM AND DAD **CATCH US**, WE'RE **ALL** IN TROUBLE!

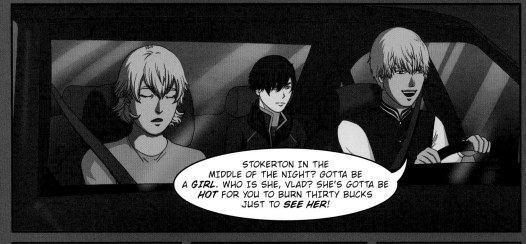

STOKERTON IN THE MIDDLE OF THE NIGHT? GOTTA BE A *GIRL.* WHO IS SHE, VLAD? SHE'S GOTTA BE *HOT* FOR YOU TO BURN THIRTY BUCKS JUST TO *SEE HER!*

JUST WAIT HERE.

I HAVEN'T BEEN HERE SINCE I *KILLED D'ABLO.*

THIS TUNNEL WAS MADE BY MY FATHER AND OTIS—IT LEADS TO ONE OF THE HOLDING CELLS.

OF COURSE, IF THE CELL IS *LOCKED,* THIS WILL HAVE BEEN A *STUPID* VENTURE.

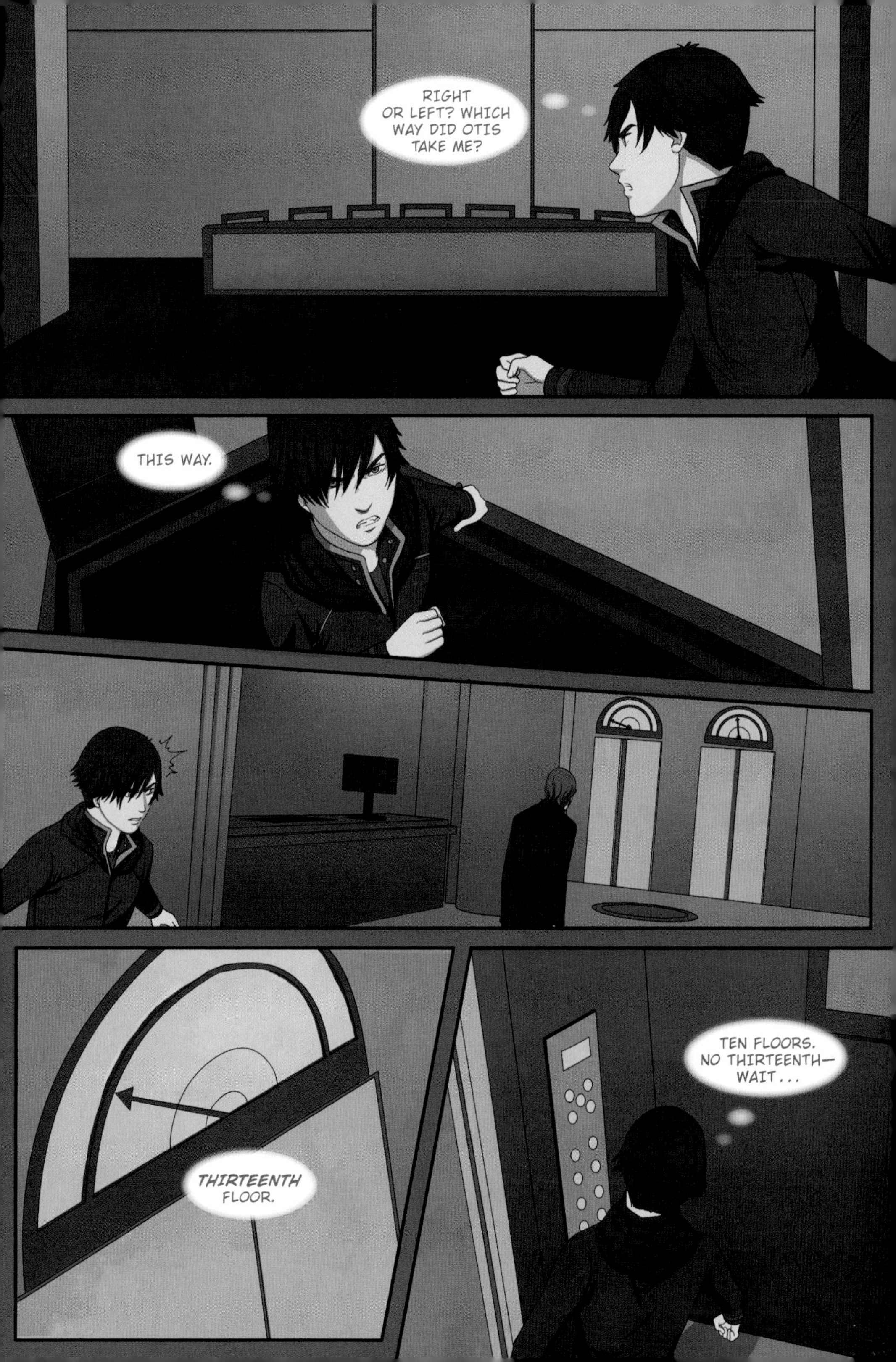
RIGHT OR LEFT? WHICH WAY DID OTIS TAKE ME?
THIS WAY.
THIRTEENTH FLOOR.
TEN FLOORS. NO THIRTEENTH— WAIT . . .

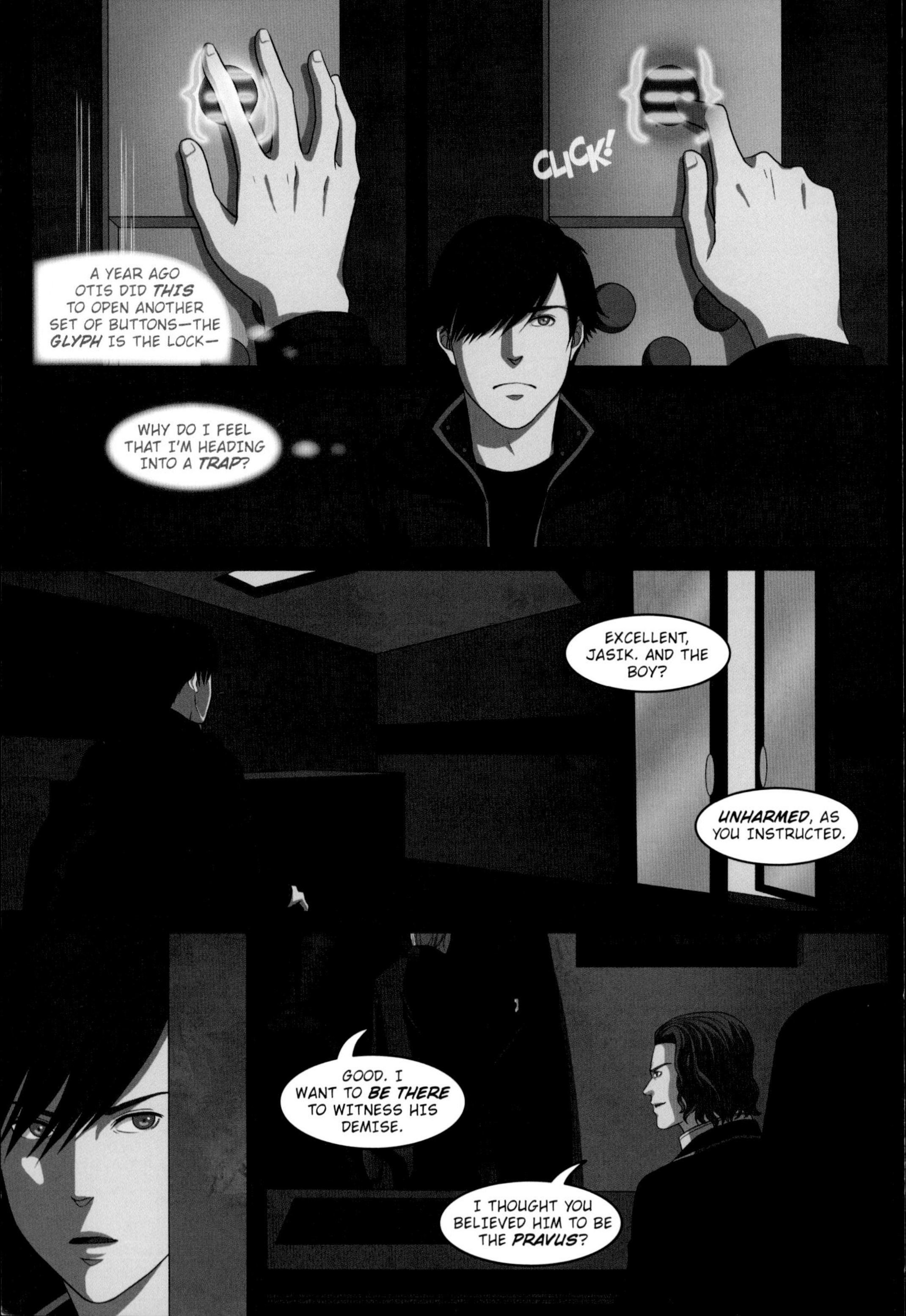
CLICK!
A YEAR AGO OTIS DID *THIS* TO OPEN ANOTHER SET OF BUTTONS—THE *GLYPH* IS THE LOCK—
WHY DO I FEEL THAT I'M HEADING INTO A *TRAP*?
EXCELLENT, JASIK. AND THE BOY?
UNHARMED, AS YOU INSTRUCTED.
GOOD. I WANT TO *BE THERE* TO WITNESS HIS DEMISE.
I THOUGHT YOU BELIEVED HIM TO BE THE *PRAVUS*?

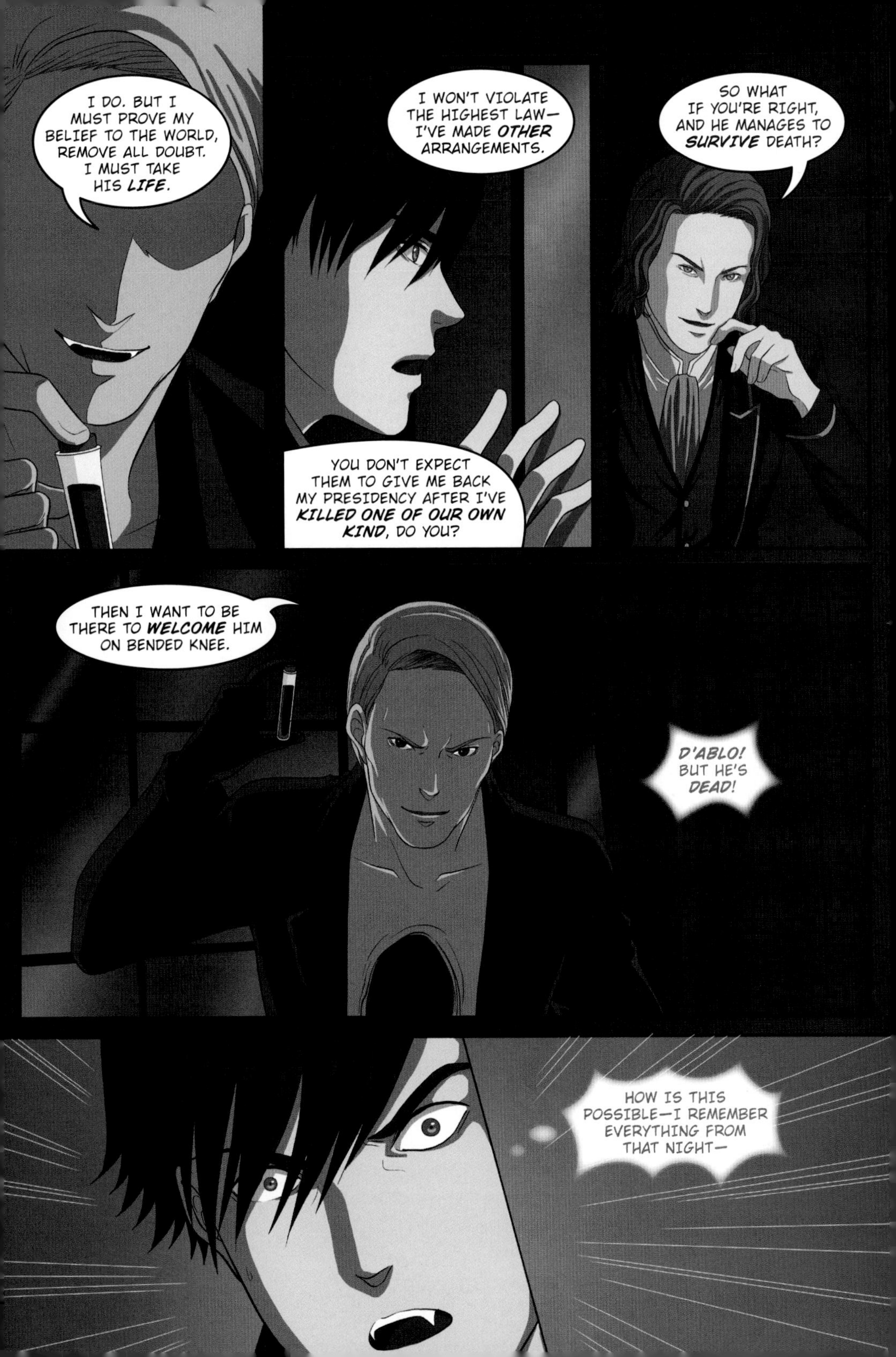
I DO. BUT I MUST PROVE MY BELIEF TO THE WORLD, REMOVE ALL DOUBT. I MUST TAKE HIS LIFE.
I WON'T VIOLATE THE HIGHEST LAW— I'VE MADE OTHER ARRANGEMENTS.
YOU DON'T EXPECT THEM TO GIVE ME BACK MY PRESIDENCY AFTER I'VE KILLED ONE OF OUR OWN KIND, DO YOU?
SO WHAT IF YOU'RE RIGHT, AND HE MANAGES TO SURVIVE DEATH?
THEN I WANT TO BE THERE TO WELCOME HIM ON BENDED KNEE.
D'ABLO! BUT HE'S DEAD!
HOW IS THIS POSSIBLE—I REMEMBER EVERYTHING FROM THAT NIGHT—

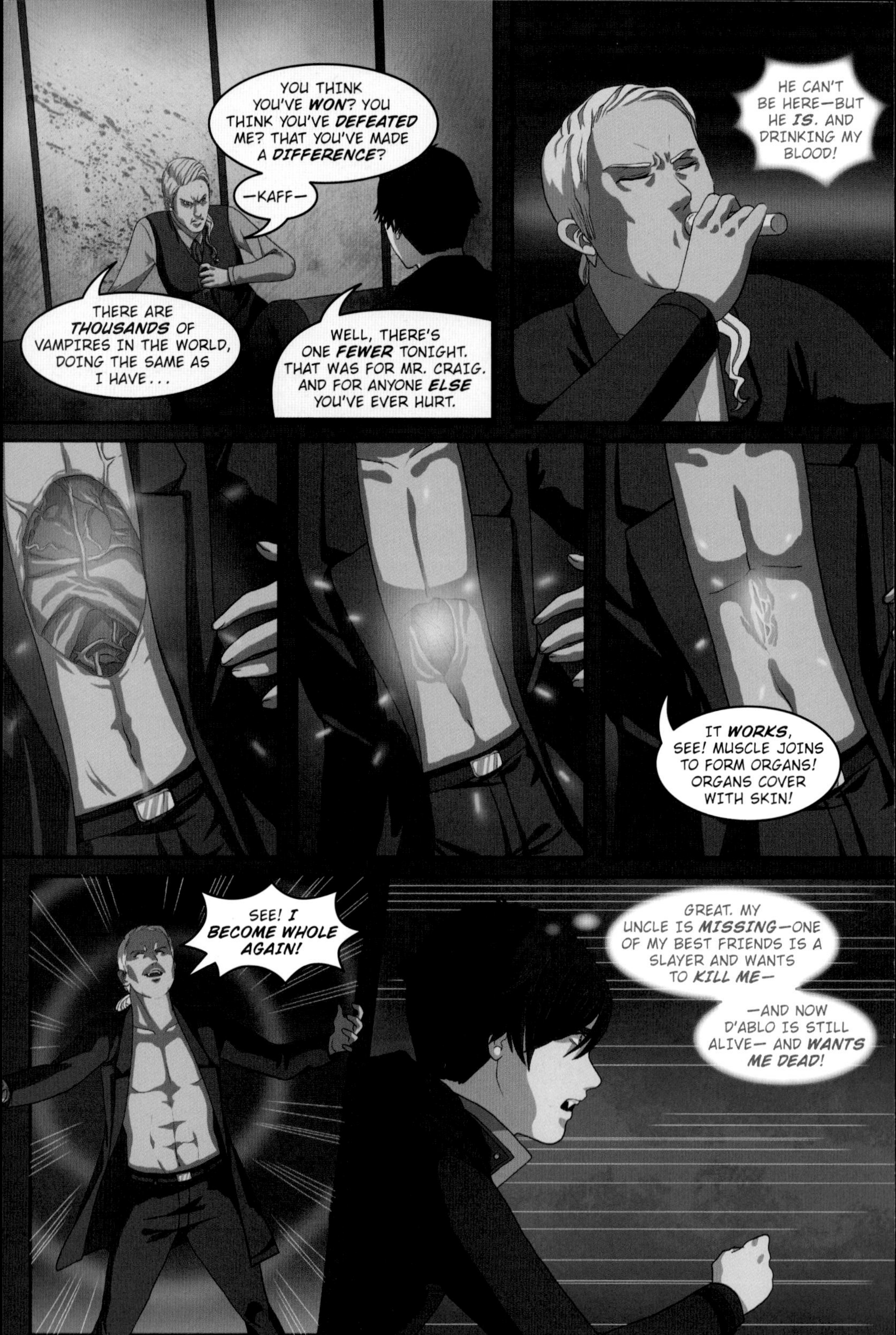
YOU THINK YOU'VE WON? YOU THINK YOU'VE DEFEATED ME? THAT YOU'VE MADE A DIFFERENCE?
—KAFF—
THERE ARE THOUSANDS OF VAMPIRES IN THE WORLD, DOING THE SAME AS I HAVE...
WELL, THERE'S ONE FEWER TONIGHT. THAT WAS FOR MR. CRAIG. AND FOR ANYONE ELSE YOU'VE EVER HURT.
HE CAN'T BE HERE—BUT HE IS. AND DRINKING MY BLOOD!
IT WORKS, SEE! MUSCLE JOINS TO FORM ORGANS! ORGANS COVER WITH SKIN!
SEE! I BECOME WHOLE AGAIN!
GREAT. MY UNCLE IS MISSING—ONE OF MY BEST FRIENDS IS A SLAYER AND WANTS TO KILL ME—
—AND NOW D'ABLO IS STILL ALIVE— AND WANTS ME DEAD!

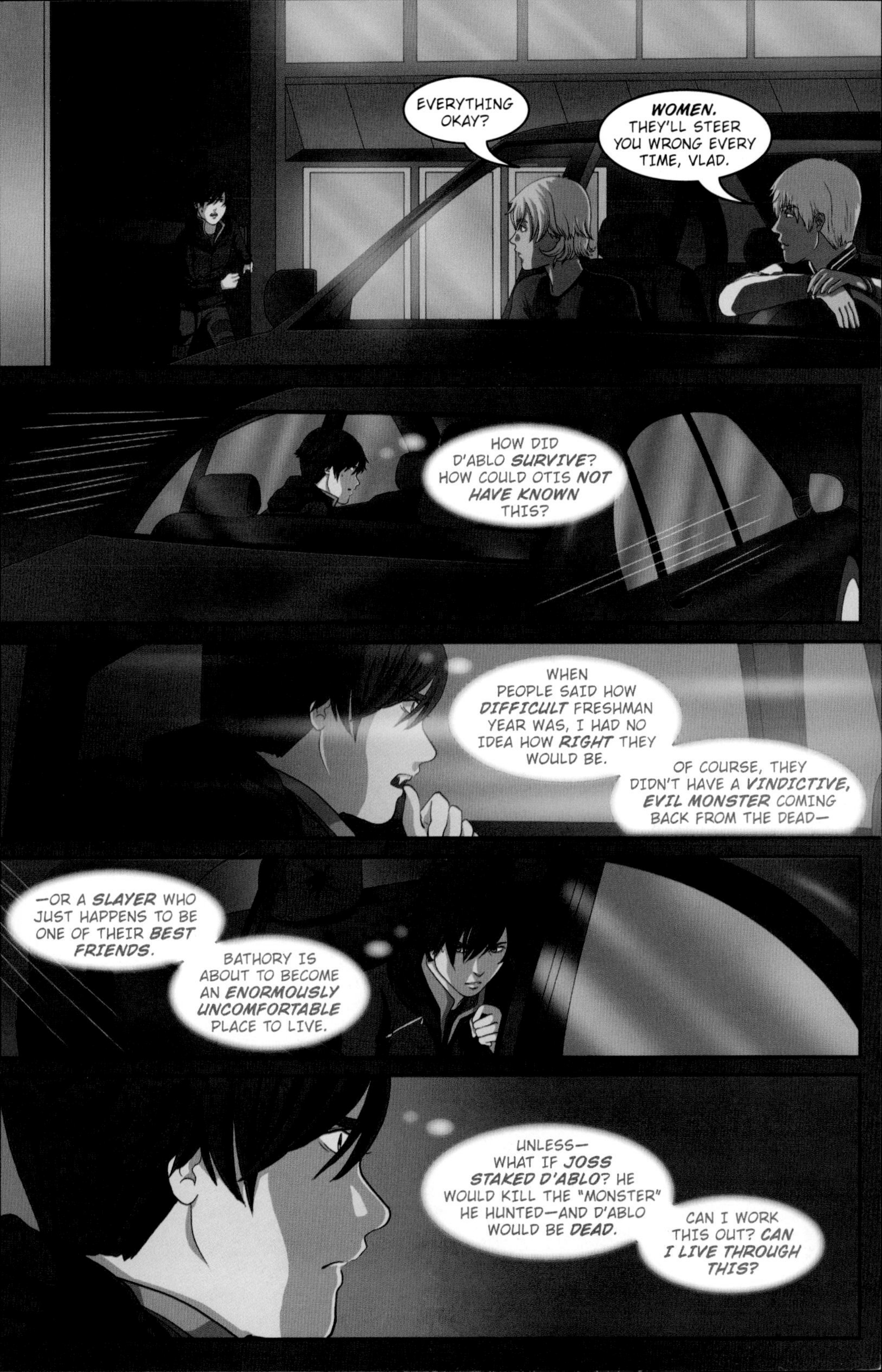
EVERYTHING OKAY?
WOMEN. THEY'LL STEER YOU WRONG EVERY TIME, VLAD.
HOW DID D'ABLO SURVIVE? HOW COULD OTIS NOT HAVE KNOWN THIS?
WHEN PEOPLE SAID HOW DIFFICULT FRESHMAN YEAR WAS, I HAD NO IDEA HOW RIGHT THEY WOULD BE.
OF COURSE, THEY DIDN'T HAVE A VINDICTIVE, EVIL MONSTER COMING BACK FROM THE DEAD—
—OR A SLAYER WHO JUST HAPPENS TO BE ONE OF THEIR BEST FRIENDS.
BATHORY IS ABOUT TO BECOME AN ENORMOUSLY UNCOMFORTABLE PLACE TO LIVE.
UNLESS— WHAT IF JOSS STAKED D'ABLO? HE WOULD KILL THE "MONSTER" HE HUNTED—AND D'ABLO WOULD BE DEAD.
CAN I WORK THIS OUT? CAN I LIVE THROUGH THIS?

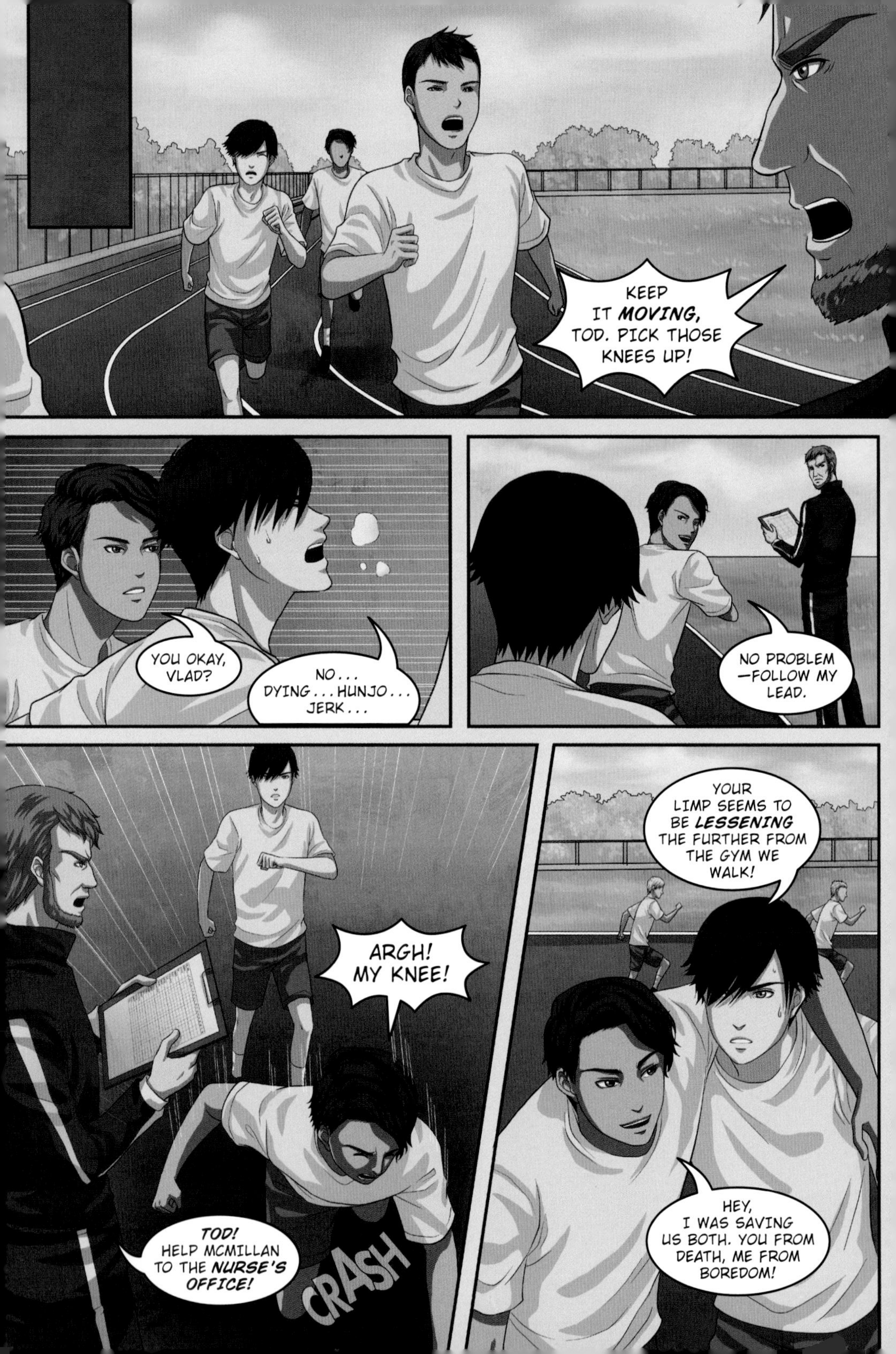
KEEP IT **MOVING**, TOD. PICK THOSE KNEES UP!
YOU OKAY, VLAD?
NO... DYING... HUNJO... JERK...
NO PROBLEM —FOLLOW MY LEAD.
ARGH! MY KNEE!
CRASH
TOD! HELP MCMILLAN TO THE **NURSE'S OFFICE!**
YOUR LIMP SEEMS TO BE **LESSENING** THE FURTHER FROM THE GYM WE WALK!
HEY, I WAS SAVING US BOTH. YOU FROM DEATH, ME FROM BOREDOM!

LISTEN, JOSS, CAN I TALK TO YOU FOR A SECOND? ARE WE COOL?

I MEAN, AFTER I RAN OFF THE OTHER DAY, I THOUGHT I MIGHT HAVE MESSED UP THE *TRUST* WE'VE BEEN BUILDING.

WE'RE COOL, VLAD. IT'S NO BIG DEAL. I JUST DIDN'T WANT YOU THINKING I WAS SOME *NUTCASE*, GOING AROUND KILLING PEOPLE.

WELL, WHAT YOU TOLD ME A FEW WEEKS AGO ABOUT *VAMPIRES* AND *SLAYERS* HAD ME CONVINCED YOU BELONGED IN THE LOONY BIN. BUT AFTER *LAST NIGHT*—I KIND OF *BELIEVE* YOU.

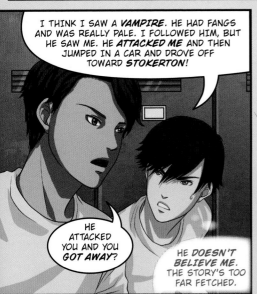

I THINK I SAW A *VAMPIRE*. HE HAD FANGS AND WAS REALLY PALE. I FOLLOWED HIM, BUT HE SAW ME. HE *ATTACKED ME* AND THEN JUMPED IN A CAR AND DROVE OFF TOWARD *STOKERTON*!

HE ATTACKED YOU AND YOU *GOT AWAY*?

HE *DOESN'T BELIEVE ME*. THE STORY'S TOO FAR FETCHED.

I'M *IMPRESSED*. YOU MIGHT HAVE WHAT IT TAKES TO BE A SLAYER AFTER ALL.

YOU SAID HE DROVE TOWARD *STOKERTON*? I'LL GET MY AUNT TO DROP US OFF THERE TOMORROW AFTERNOON AND WE'LL GO HUNTING!

UM...WE?

WELL YEAH, YOU KNOW WHAT IT *LOOKS* LIKE. BESIDES, NOT OFTEN DO I GET TO SHOW OFF MY MOVES.

I'LL COME OVER AFTER DINNER TONIGHT AND WE CAN GO OVER THE *DETAILS*.

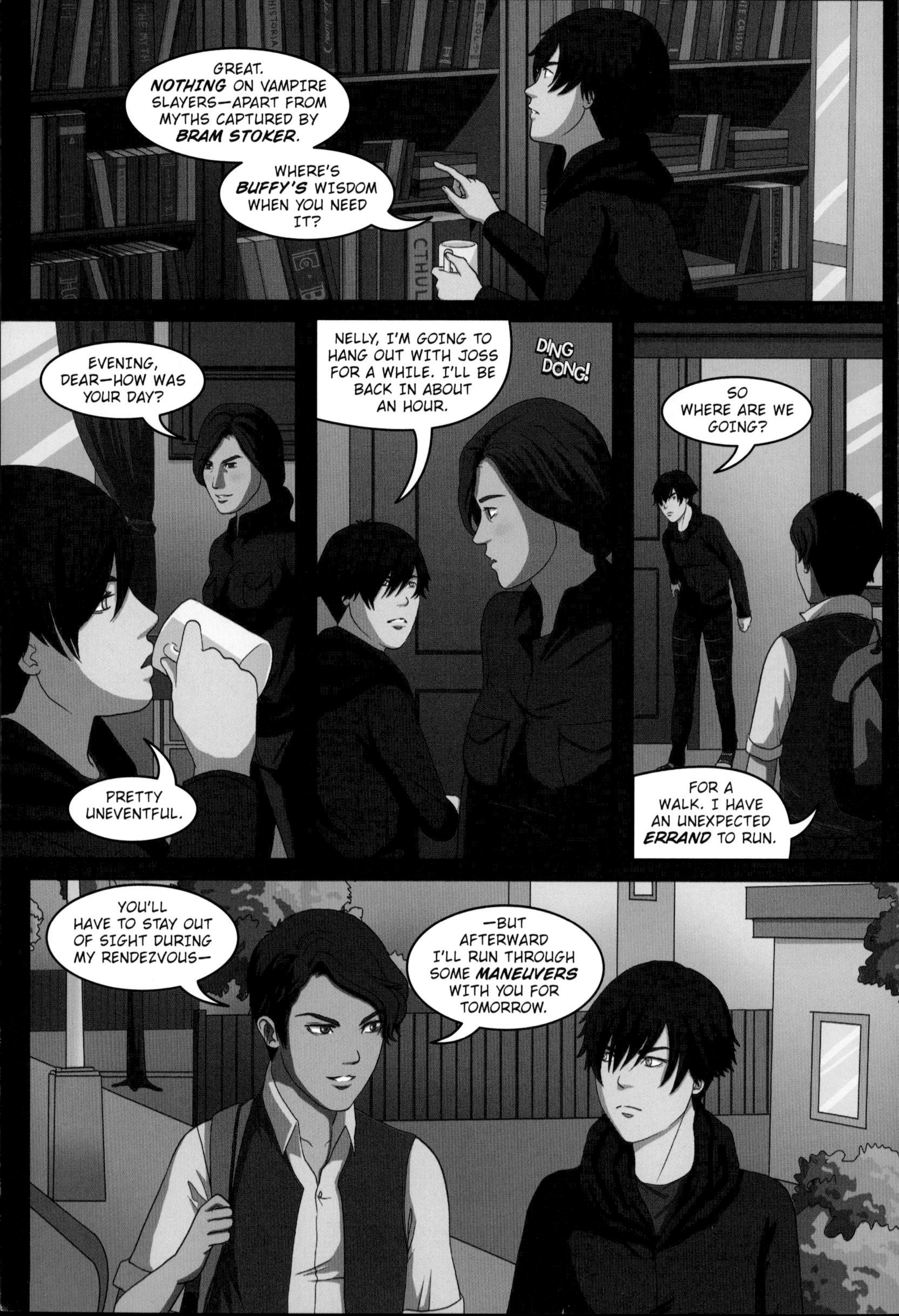
GREAT. NOTHING ON VAMPIRE SLAYERS—APART FROM MYTHS CAPTURED BY BRAM STOKER.
WHERE'S BUFFY'S WISDOM WHEN YOU NEED IT?
EVENING, DEAR—HOW WAS YOUR DAY?
PRETTY UNEVENTFUL.
NELLY, I'M GOING TO HANG OUT WITH JOSS FOR A WHILE. I'LL BE BACK IN ABOUT AN HOUR.
DING DONG!
SO WHERE ARE WE GOING?
FOR A WALK. I HAVE AN UNEXPECTED ERRAND TO RUN.
YOU'LL HAVE TO STAY OUT OF SIGHT DURING MY RENDEZVOUS—
—BUT AFTERWARD I'LL RUN THROUGH SOME MANEUVERS WITH YOU FOR TOMORROW.

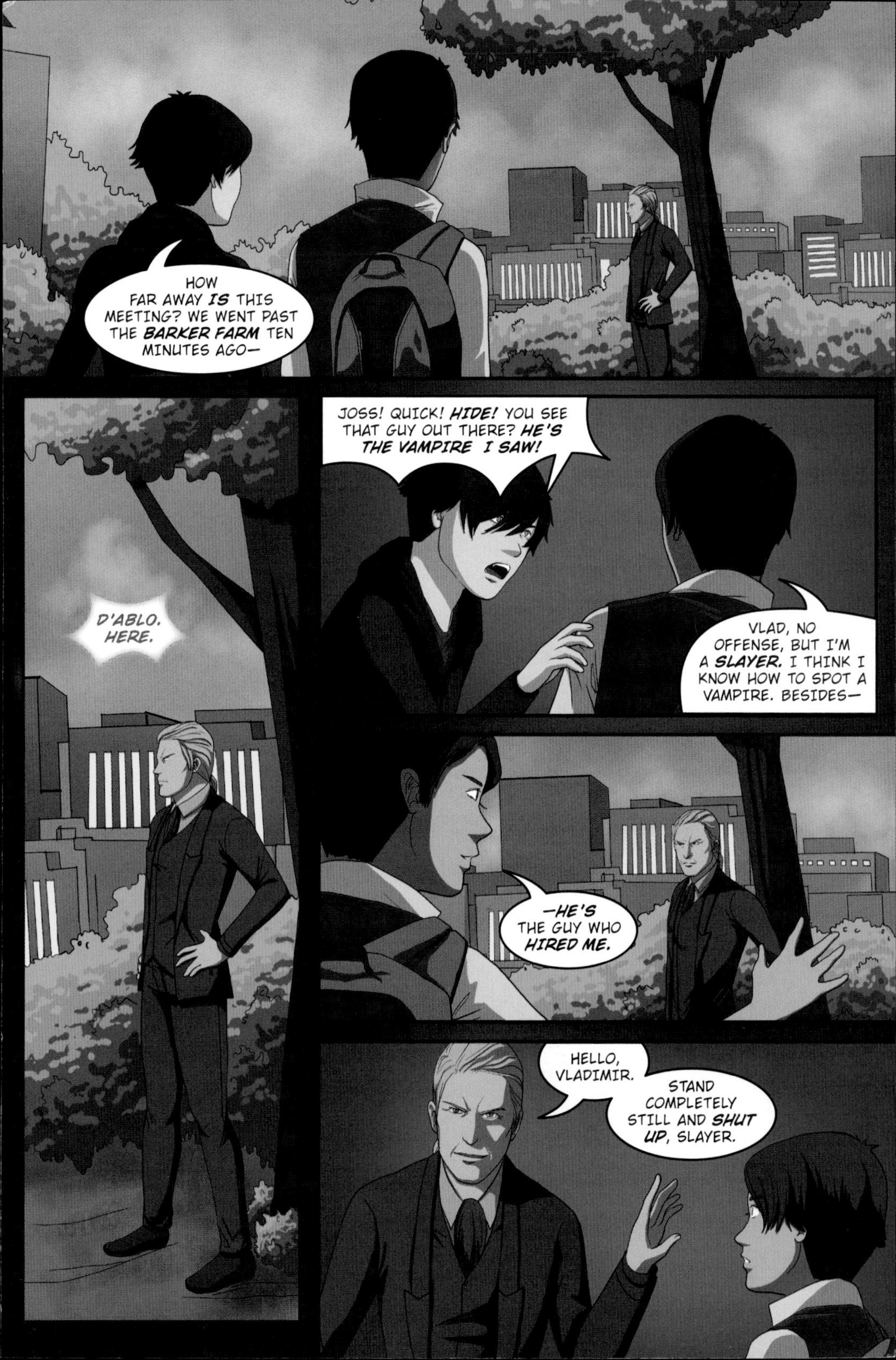
HOW FAR AWAY IS THIS MEETING? WE WENT PAST THE BARKER FARM TEN MINUTES AGO—
D'ABLO. HERE.
JOSS! QUICK! HIDE! YOU SEE THAT GUY OUT THERE? HE'S THE VAMPIRE I SAW!
VLAD, NO OFFENSE, BUT I'M A SLAYER. I THINK I KNOW HOW TO SPOT A VAMPIRE. BESIDES—
—HE'S THE GUY WHO HIRED ME.
HELLO, VLADIMIR.
STAND COMPLETELY STILL AND SHUT UP, SLAYER.

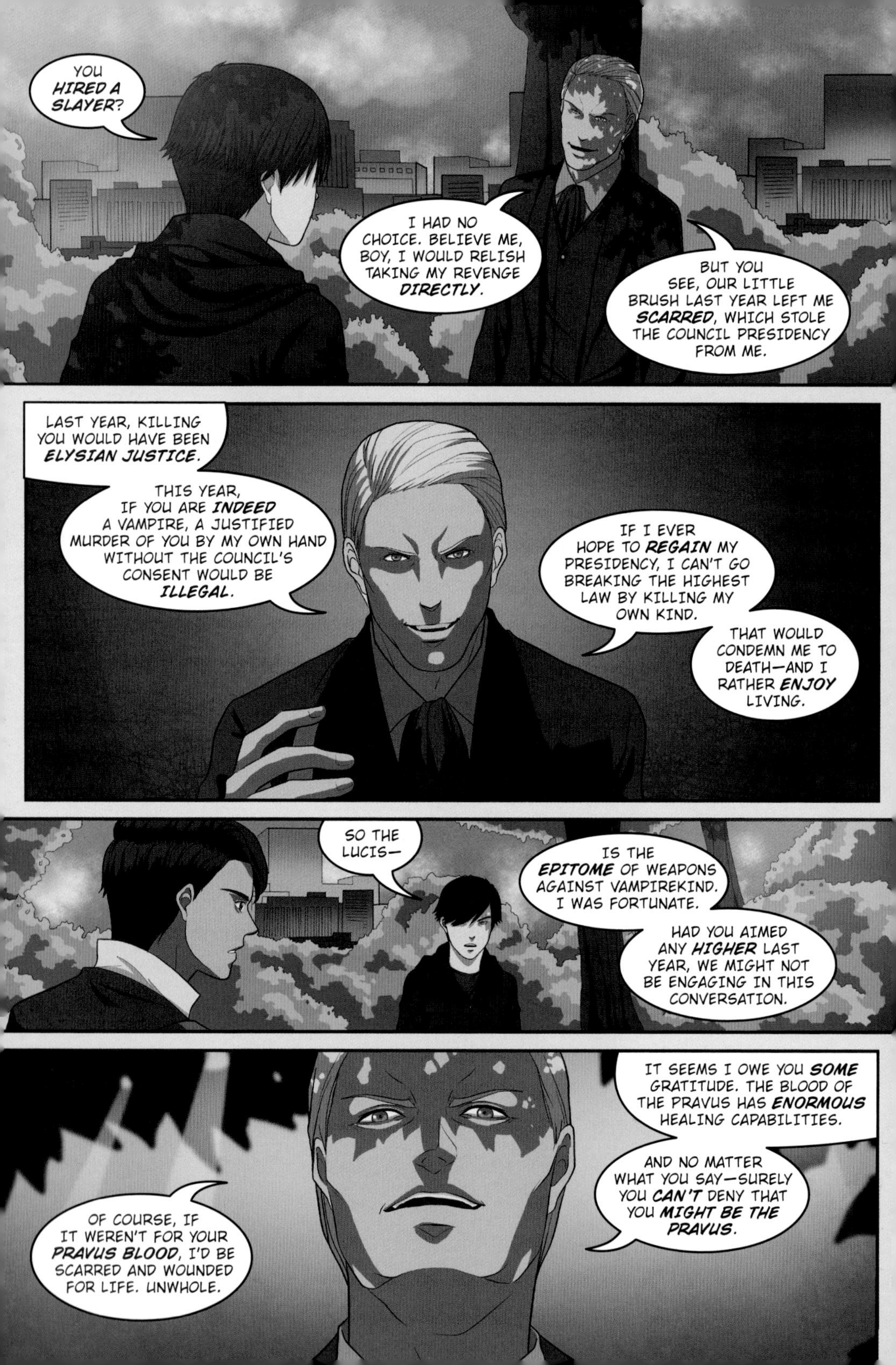
YOU HIRED A SLAYER?
I HAD NO CHOICE. BELIEVE ME, BOY, I WOULD RELISH TAKING MY REVENGE DIRECTLY.
BUT YOU SEE, OUR LITTLE BRUSH LAST YEAR LEFT ME SCARRED, WHICH STOLE THE COUNCIL PRESIDENCY FROM ME.
LAST YEAR, KILLING YOU WOULD HAVE BEEN ELYSIAN JUSTICE.
THIS YEAR, IF YOU ARE INDEED A VAMPIRE, A JUSTIFIED MURDER OF YOU BY MY OWN HAND WITHOUT THE COUNCIL'S CONSENT WOULD BE ILLEGAL.
IF I EVER HOPE TO REGAIN MY PRESIDENCY, I CAN'T GO BREAKING THE HIGHEST LAW BY KILLING MY OWN KIND.
THAT WOULD CONDEMN ME TO DEATH—AND I RATHER ENJOY LIVING.
SO THE LUCIS—
IS THE EPITOME OF WEAPONS AGAINST VAMPIREKIND. I WAS FORTUNATE.
HAD YOU AIMED ANY HIGHER LAST YEAR, WE MIGHT NOT BE ENGAGING IN THIS CONVERSATION.
IT SEEMS I OWE YOU SOME GRATITUDE. THE BLOOD OF THE PRAVUS HAS ENORMOUS HEALING CAPABILITIES.
AND NO MATTER WHAT YOU SAY—SURELY YOU CAN'T DENY THAT YOU MIGHT BE THE PRAVUS.
OF COURSE, IF IT WEREN'T FOR YOUR PRAVUS BLOOD, I'D BE SCARRED AND WOUNDED FOR LIFE. UNWHOLE.

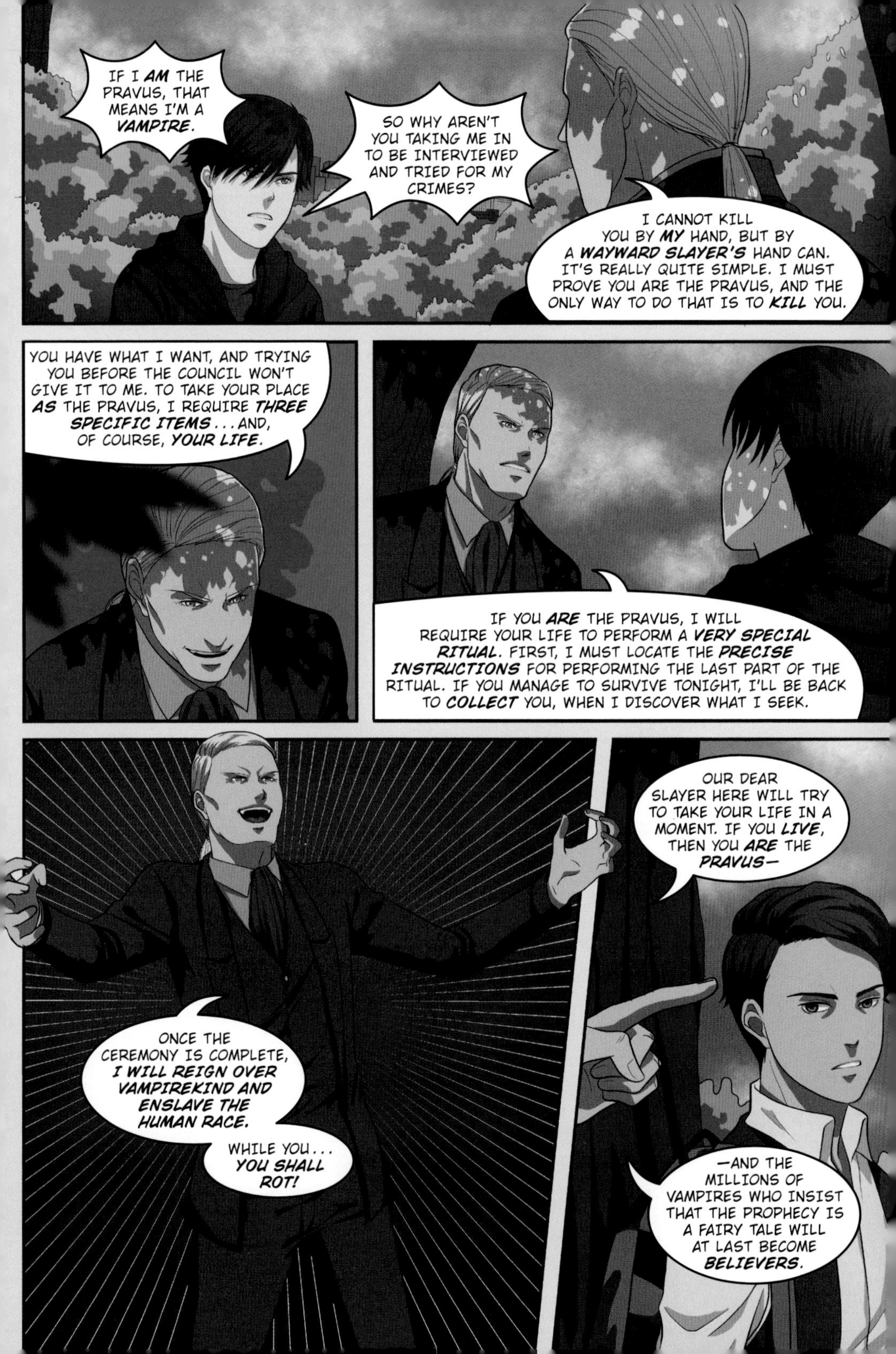
IF I AM THE PRAVUS, THAT MEANS I'M A VAMPIRE.
SO WHY AREN'T YOU TAKING ME IN TO BE INTERVIEWED AND TRIED FOR MY CRIMES?
I CANNOT KILL YOU BY MY HAND, BUT BY A WAYWARD SLAYER'S HAND CAN. IT'S REALLY QUITE SIMPLE. I MUST PROVE YOU ARE THE PRAVUS, AND THE ONLY WAY TO DO THAT IS TO KILL YOU.
YOU HAVE WHAT I WANT, AND TRYING YOU BEFORE THE COUNCIL WON'T GIVE IT TO ME. TO TAKE YOUR PLACE AS THE PRAVUS, I REQUIRE THREE SPECIFIC ITEMS . . . AND, OF COURSE, YOUR LIFE.
IF YOU ARE THE PRAVUS, I WILL REQUIRE YOUR LIFE TO PERFORM A VERY SPECIAL RITUAL. FIRST, I MUST LOCATE THE PRECISE INSTRUCTIONS FOR PERFORMING THE LAST PART OF THE RITUAL. IF YOU MANAGE TO SURVIVE TONIGHT, I'LL BE BACK TO COLLECT YOU, WHEN I DISCOVER WHAT I SEEK.
ONCE THE CEREMONY IS COMPLETE, I WILL REIGN OVER VAMPIREKIND AND ENSLAVE THE HUMAN RACE.
WHILE YOU . . . YOU SHALL ROT!
OUR DEAR SLAYER HERE WILL TRY TO TAKE YOUR LIFE IN A MOMENT. IF YOU LIVE, THEN YOU ARE THE PRAVUS—
—AND THE MILLIONS OF VAMPIRES WHO INSIST THAT THE PROPHECY IS A FAIRY TALE WILL AT LAST BECOME BELIEVERS.

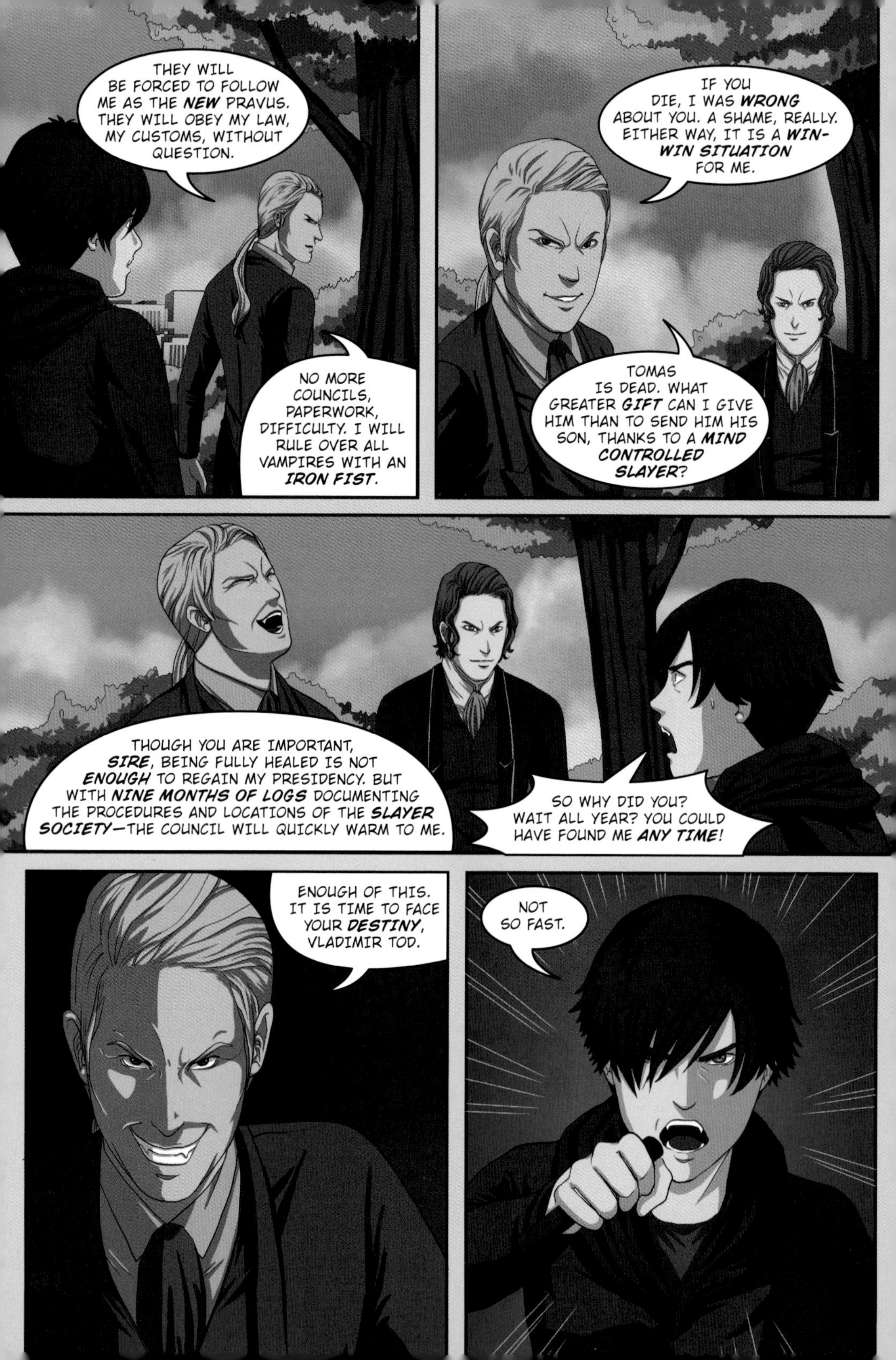
THEY WILL BE FORCED TO FOLLOW ME AS THE NEW PRAVUS. THEY WILL OBEY MY LAW, MY CUSTOMS, WITHOUT QUESTION.
NO MORE COUNCILS, PAPERWORK, DIFFICULTY. I WILL RULE OVER ALL VAMPIRES WITH AN IRON FIST.
IF YOU DIE, I WAS WRONG ABOUT YOU. A SHAME, REALLY. EITHER WAY, IT IS A WIN-WIN SITUATION FOR ME.
TOMAS IS DEAD. WHAT GREATER GIFT CAN I GIVE HIM THAN TO SEND HIM HIS SON, THANKS TO A MIND CONTROLLED SLAYER?
THOUGH YOU ARE IMPORTANT, SIRE, BEING FULLY HEALED IS NOT ENOUGH TO REGAIN MY PRESIDENCY. BUT WITH NINE MONTHS OF LOGS DOCUMENTING THE PROCEDURES AND LOCATIONS OF THE SLAYER SOCIETY—THE COUNCIL WILL QUICKLY WARM TO ME.
SO WHY DID YOU? WAIT ALL YEAR? YOU COULD HAVE FOUND ME ANY TIME!
ENOUGH OF THIS. IT IS TIME TO FACE YOUR DESTINY, VLADIMIR TOD.
NOT SO FAST.

COME ON— WHY DOESN'T IT WORK?

YOU SHOULD HAVE LISTENED TO YOUR UNCLE'S *WARNING* CONCERNING TAKING THE LUCIS WITH YOU EVERYWHERE, VLADIMIR.

SOME ROGUE VAMPIRE COULD EASILY *BREAK INTO YOUR ROOM* WHILE YOU WERE AT SCHOOL TODAY AND TAKE IT!

AND IF HE *WAS* CUNNING, HE MIGHT REPLACE THE REAL LUCIS WITH A *FAKE ONE*—

—SO AS NOT TO RAISE SUSPICIONS!

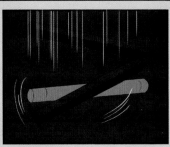

JOSS—SNAP OUT OF IT! DO YOU HAVE YOUR *CASE* WITH YOU?

ALL THIS TIME YOU PRETENDED TO BE MY FRIEND AND YOU WERE *ONE OF THEM*, VLAD?

I DON'T *WANT* TO DO THIS.

YOU HAVE NO IDEA HOW *DIFFICULT* YOUR DEATH WILL BE TO EXPLAIN TO HENRY.

THAT'S *TWO* OF THE THREE ITEMS WE REQUIRE. AND THE THIRD WE'LL COLLECT SOON ENOUGH.

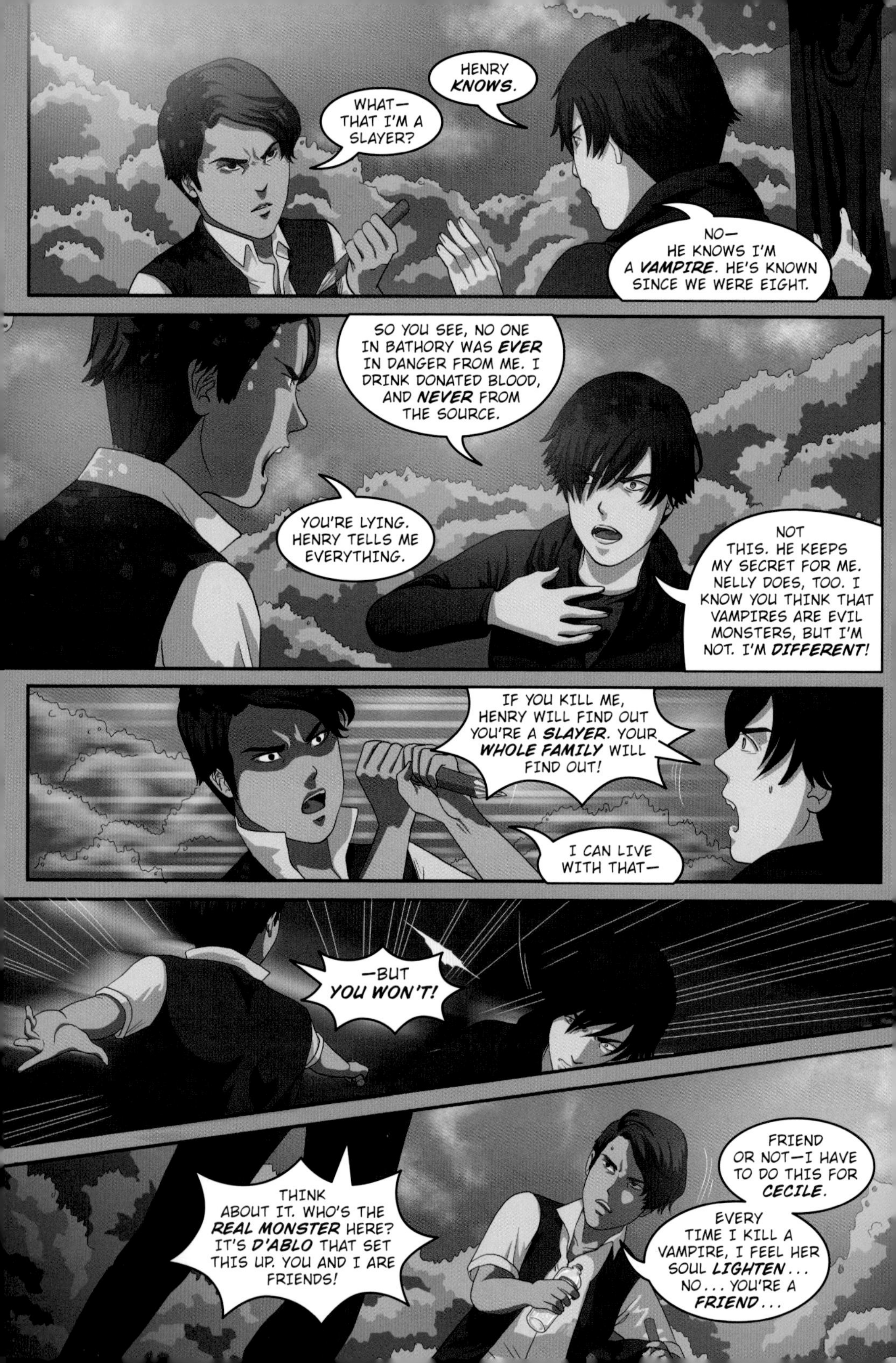
WHAT— THAT I'M A SLAYER?
HENRY KNOWS.
NO— HE KNOWS I'M A VAMPIRE. HE'S KNOWN SINCE WE WERE EIGHT.
SO YOU SEE, NO ONE IN BATHORY WAS EVER IN DANGER FROM ME. I DRINK DONATED BLOOD, AND NEVER FROM THE SOURCE.
YOU'RE LYING. HENRY TELLS ME EVERYTHING.
NOT THIS. HE KEEPS MY SECRET FOR ME. NELLY DOES, TOO. I KNOW YOU THINK THAT VAMPIRES ARE EVIL MONSTERS, BUT I'M NOT. I'M DIFFERENT!
IF YOU KILL ME, HENRY WILL FIND OUT YOU'RE A SLAYER. YOUR WHOLE FAMILY WILL FIND OUT!
I CAN LIVE WITH THAT—
—BUT YOU WON'T!
THINK ABOUT IT. WHO'S THE REAL MONSTER HERE? IT'S D'ABLO THAT SET THIS UP. YOU AND I ARE FRIENDS!
FRIEND OR NOT—I HAVE TO DO THIS FOR CECILE.
EVERY TIME I KILL A VAMPIRE, I FEEL HER SOUL LIGHTEN . . . NO . . . YOU'RE A FRIEND . . .

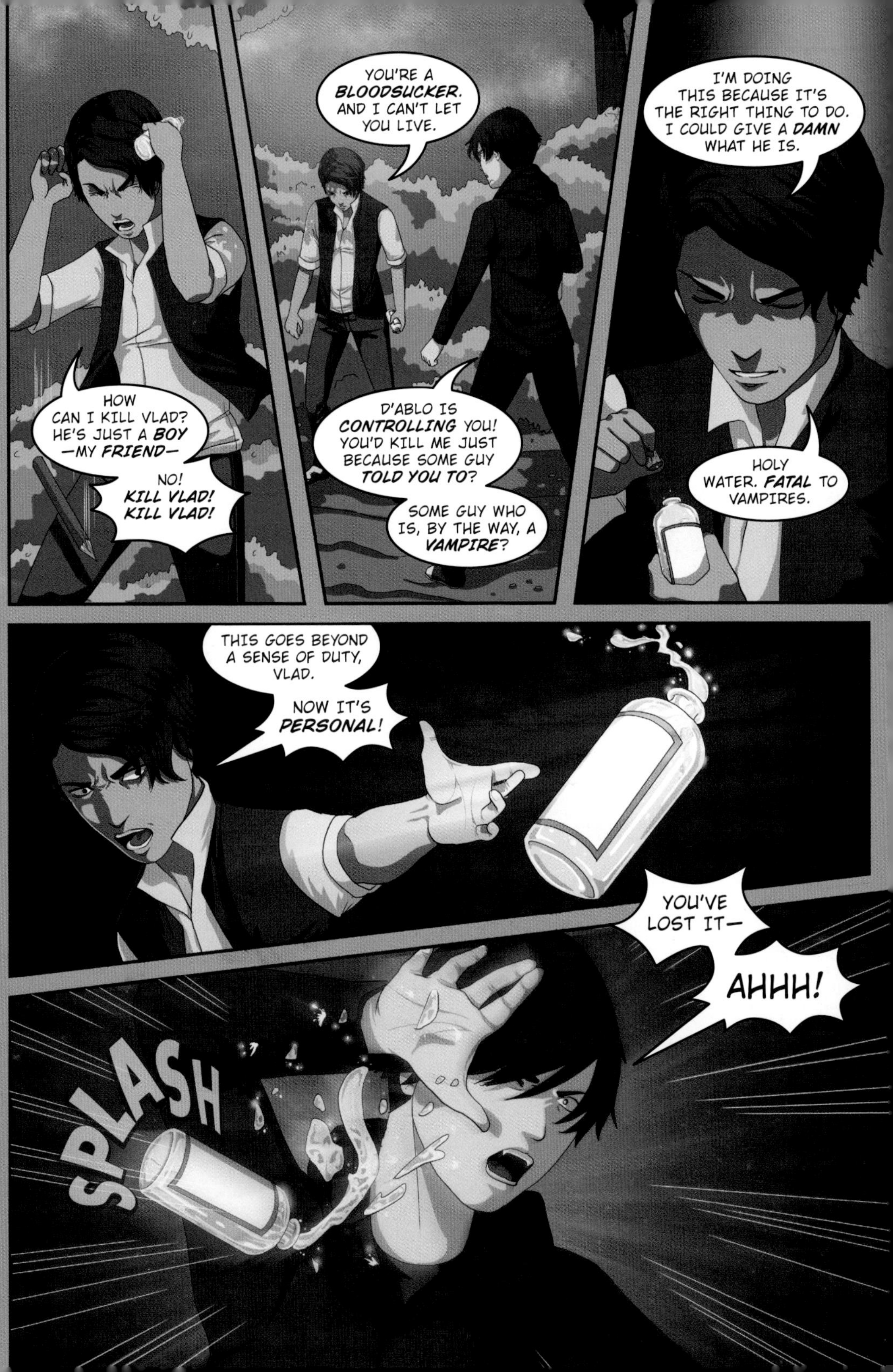
HOW CAN I KILL VLAD? HE'S JUST A BOY —MY FRIEND—
NO! KILL VLAD! KILL VLAD!
YOU'RE A BLOODSUCKER. AND I CAN'T LET YOU LIVE.
D'ABLO IS CONTROLLING YOU! YOU'D KILL ME JUST BECAUSE SOME GUY TOLD YOU TO?
SOME GUY WHO IS, BY THE WAY, A VAMPIRE?
I'M DOING THIS BECAUSE IT'S THE RIGHT THING TO DO. I COULD GIVE A DAMN WHAT HE IS.
HOLY WATER. FATAL TO VAMPIRES.
THIS GOES BEYOND A SENSE OF DUTY, VLAD.
NOW IT'S PERSONAL!
YOU'VE LOST IT—
AHHH!
SPLASH

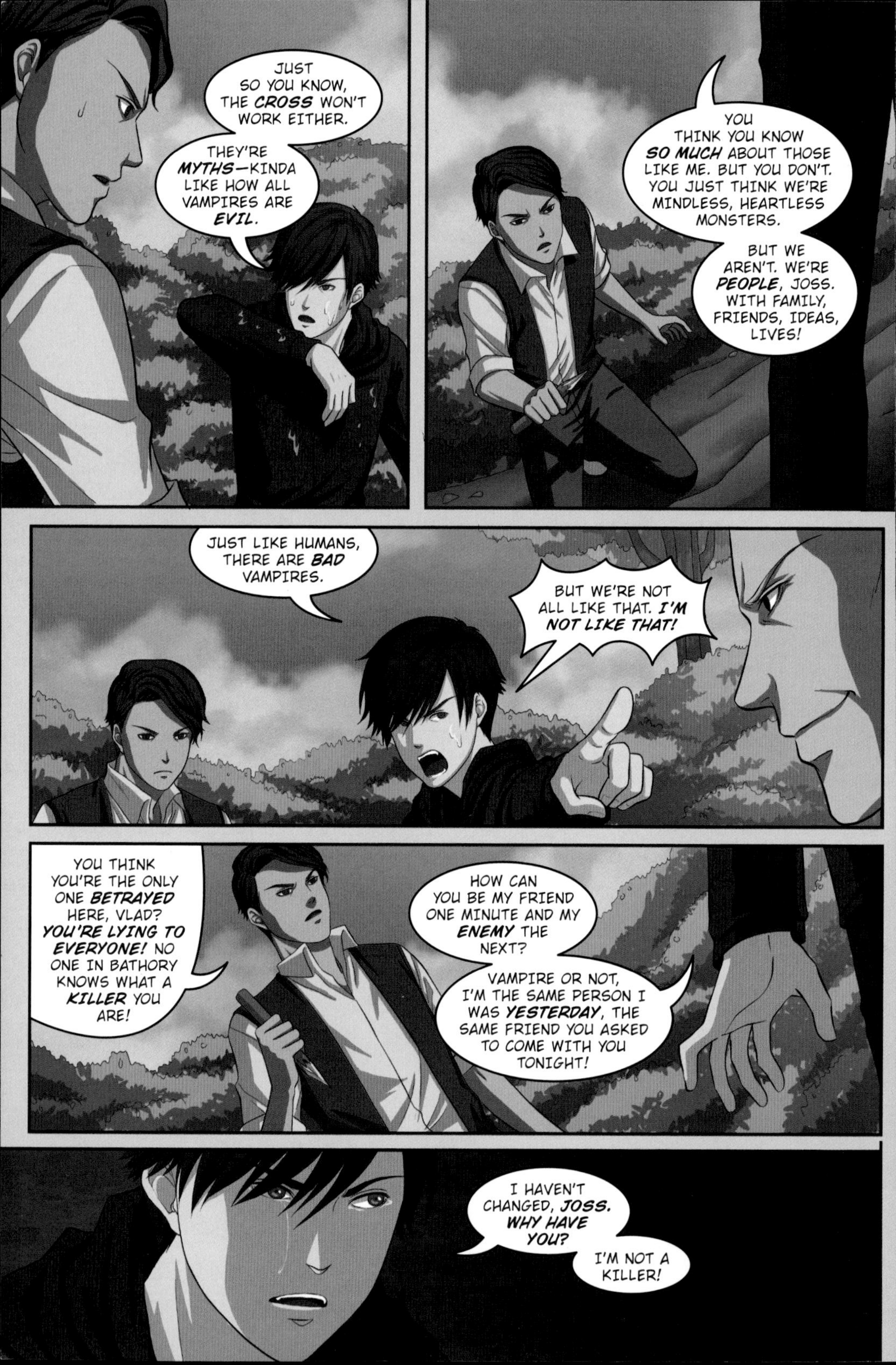
JUST SO YOU KNOW, THE CROSS WON'T WORK EITHER.
THEY'RE MYTHS—KINDA LIKE HOW ALL VAMPIRES ARE EVIL.
YOU THINK YOU KNOW SO MUCH ABOUT THOSE LIKE ME. BUT YOU DON'T. YOU JUST THINK WE'RE MINDLESS, HEARTLESS MONSTERS.
BUT WE AREN'T. WE'RE PEOPLE, JOSS. WITH FAMILY, FRIENDS, IDEAS, LIVES!
JUST LIKE HUMANS, THERE ARE BAD VAMPIRES.
BUT WE'RE NOT ALL LIKE THAT. I'M NOT LIKE THAT!
YOU THINK YOU'RE THE ONLY ONE BETRAYED HERE, VLAD? YOU'RE LYING TO EVERYONE! NO ONE IN BATHORY KNOWS WHAT A KILLER YOU ARE!
HOW CAN YOU BE MY FRIEND ONE MINUTE AND MY ENEMY THE NEXT?
VAMPIRE OR NOT, I'M THE SAME PERSON I WAS YESTERDAY, THE SAME FRIEND YOU ASKED TO COME WITH YOU TONIGHT!
I HAVEN'T CHANGED, JOSS. WHY HAVE YOU?
I'M NOT A KILLER!

YOU DON'T HAVE TO DO THIS. YOU WOULDN'T BE KILLING A MONSTER—YOU'D BE MURDERING A FRIEND.
AND WE ARE FRIENDS, JOSS—NO MATTER WHAT HE PUTS IN YOUR MIND.
I'VE NEVER SEEN PURPLE EYES BEFORE. NOT EVEN ON A VAMPIRE. WHAT KIND OF MONSTER ARE YOU?
VLAD... RUN. I'VE GOT THIS.
YES, RUN. THE MOMENT YOU LEAVE, WE'LL FEAST ON YOUR FRIEND SLOWLY—AND THEN COME AFTER YOU.
YOUR CHOICE, PRAVUS. YOUR FRIEND NEEDN'T SUFFER.
I CAN'T LET THAT HAPPEN. JOSS IS MY FRIEND. WHAT IF THEY DON'T STOP THERE? WHAT IF THEY FIND NELLY?
OTIS WILL AVENGE MY DEATH. YOU HAVE NO IDEA THE HURT THAT'S COMING FOR YOU IF I DIE.
I'M WILLING TO TAKE THAT CHANCE.
KILL HIM.

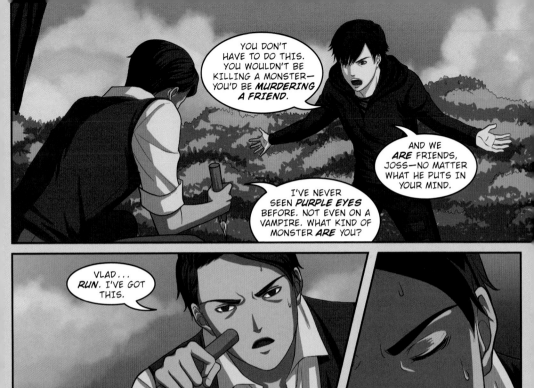

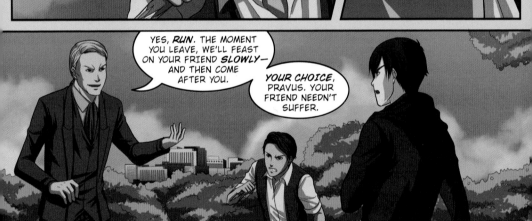

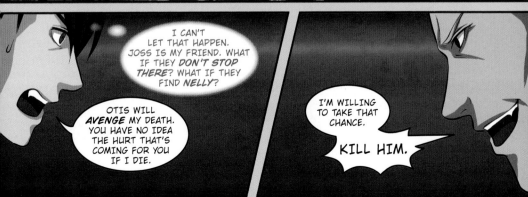

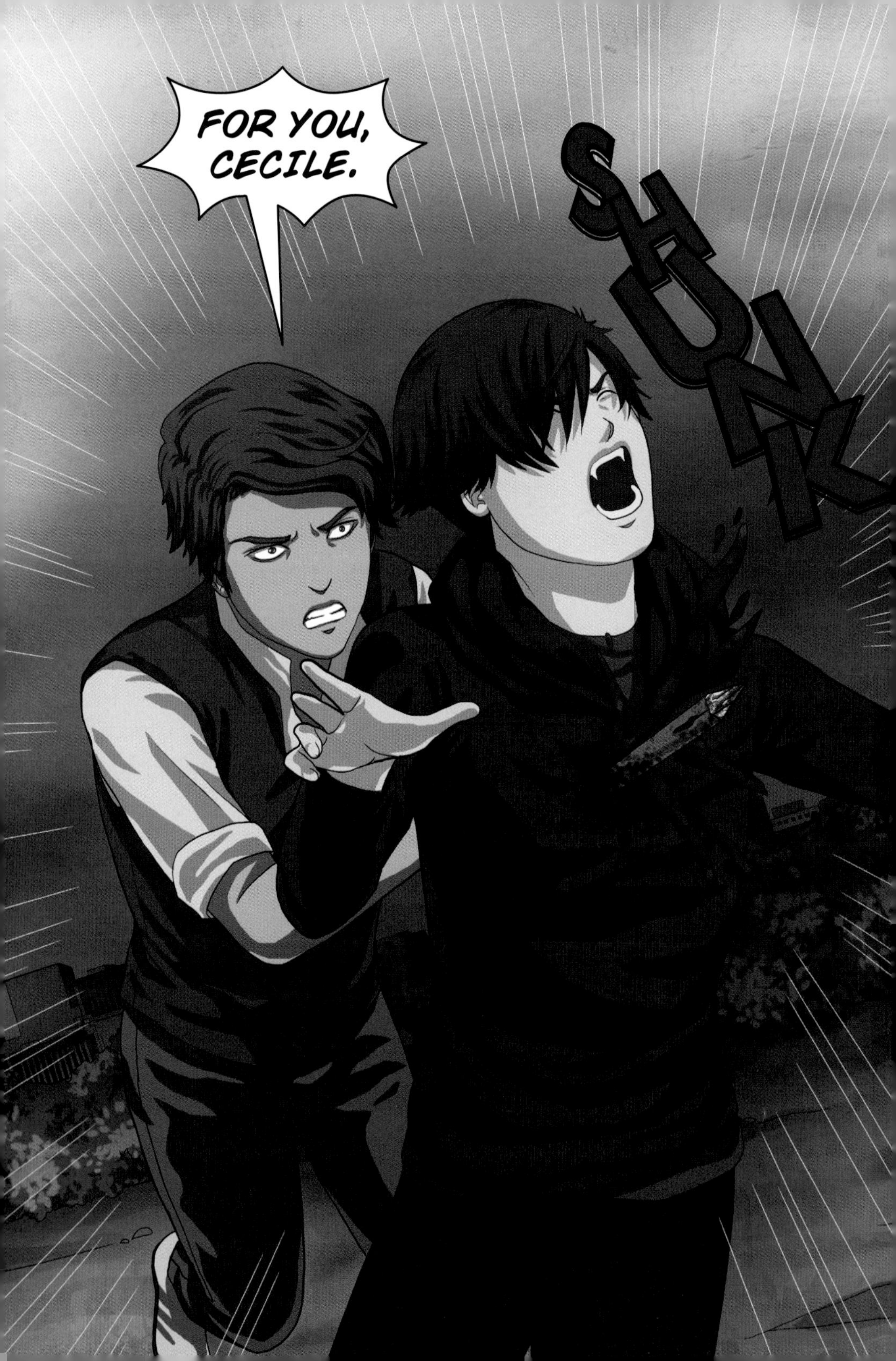
FOR YOU, CECILE.
SHUNK

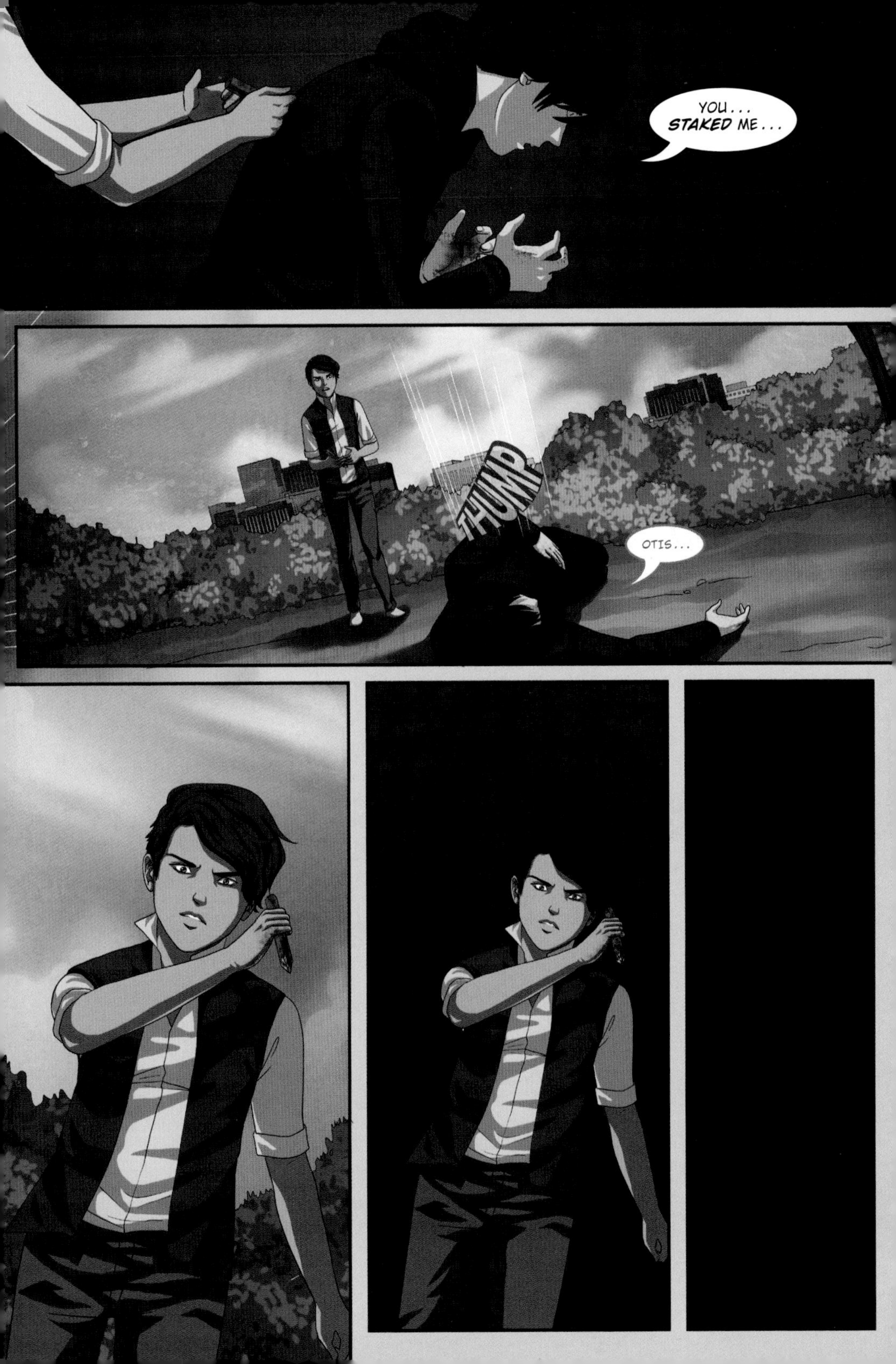
YOU...
STAKED ME...
THUMP
OTIS...

...OTIS?

BE STILL, *MAHLYENKI DYAVOL.*

...OTIS?

SLEEP, VLADIMIR. SLEEP.

I'M... ALIVE?

WHERE... WHERE AM I?

YOU'RE IN *STOKERTON GENERAL HOSPITAL.* ARE YOU THIRSTY? LET ME GET YOU A CUP OF WATER.

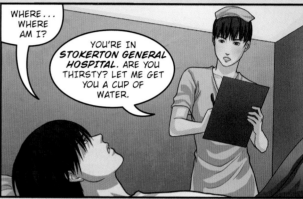

YOUR AUNT NELLY JUST STEPPED OUT FOR A MOMENT. I BELIEVE YOUR *UNCLE* IS IN THE WAITING ROOM. WOULD YOU LIKE ME TO GET HIM FOR YOU?

OTIS IS HERE?

GREAT. I HOPE A *MALE* NURSE UNDRESSED ME.

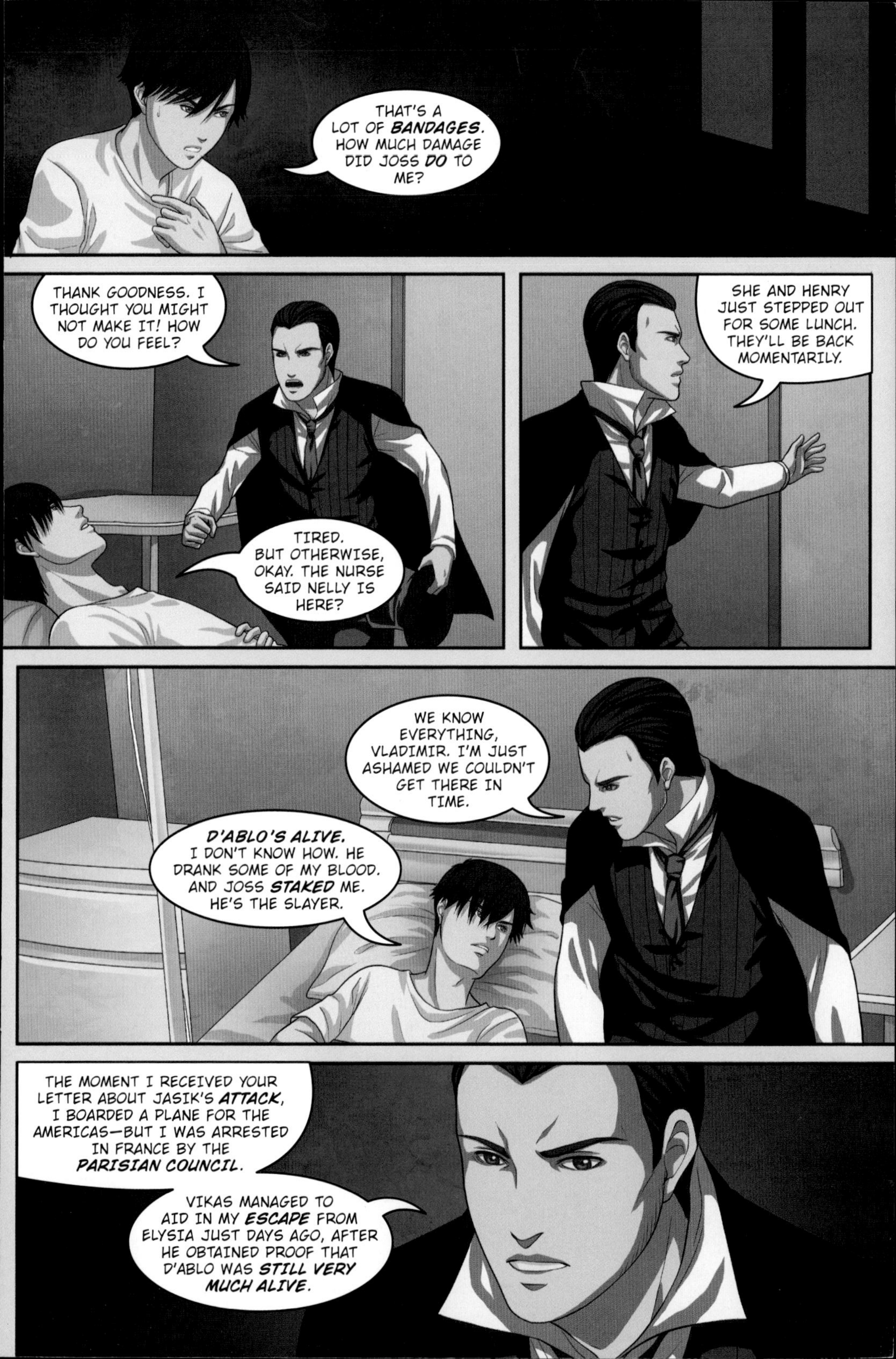
THAT'S A LOT OF BANDAGES. HOW MUCH DAMAGE DID JOSS DO TO ME?
THANK GOODNESS. I THOUGHT YOU MIGHT NOT MAKE IT! HOW DO YOU FEEL?
TIRED. BUT OTHERWISE, OKAY. THE NURSE SAID NELLY IS HERE?
SHE AND HENRY JUST STEPPED OUT FOR SOME LUNCH. THEY'LL BE BACK MOMENTARILY.
WE KNOW EVERYTHING, VLADIMIR. I'M JUST ASHAMED WE COULDN'T GET THERE IN TIME.
D'ABLO'S ALIVE. I DON'T KNOW HOW. HE DRANK SOME OF MY BLOOD. AND JOSS STAKED ME. HE'S THE SLAYER.
THE MOMENT I RECEIVED YOUR LETTER ABOUT JASIK'S ATTACK, I BOARDED A PLANE FOR THE AMERICAS—BUT I WAS ARRESTED IN FRANCE BY THE PARISIAN COUNCIL.
VIKAS MANAGED TO AID IN MY ESCAPE FROM ELYSIA JUST DAYS AGO, AFTER HE OBTAINED PROOF THAT D'ABLO WAS STILL VERY MUCH ALIVE.

WE WERE **MINUTES** FROM BATHORY WHEN I HEARD YOUR TELEPATHIC CRY FOR HELP.

D'ABLO MUST HAVE BEEN BLOCKING YOUR MIND AFTER THAT. I SUSPECT A **TEGO CHARM.**

WHEN I SAW YOU THERE, WITH THAT HUNK OF WOOD STICKING OUT OF YOUR BACK, AND ALL THAT **BLOOD** ...

. . .I JUST NEVER THOUGHT I'D GET THE CHANCE TO TEACH YOU, TO SHOW YOU...

...THERE'S SO MUCH I HAVE TO TELL YOU, SO MUCH TIME I WANT TO **SPEND** WITH YOU.

THE HOSPITAL IN STOKERTON IS **SPECIAL**—WE HAVE PEOPLE OF OUR KIND ON STAFF HERE. DOCTORS, NURSES, TOO. YOU'RE UNDER THEIR CARE RIGHT NOW, SO AS NOT TO RAISE SUSPICIONS.

I'VE NEVER BEEN TO THE HOSPITAL BEFORE. WON'T THEY KNOW I'M... **DIFFERENT?**

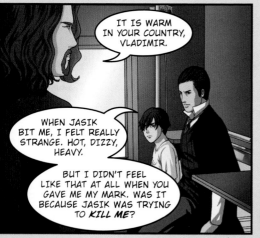

IT IS WARM IN YOUR COUNTRY, VLADIMIR.

WHEN JASIK BIT ME, I FELT REALLY STRANGE. HOT, DIZZY, HEAVY.

BUT I DIDN'T FEEL LIKE THAT AT ALL WHEN YOU GAVE ME MY MARK. WAS IT BECAUSE JASIK WAS TRYING TO **KILL ME?**

JASIK **WASN'T** TRYING TO KILL YOU— THAT'S AGAINST ELYSIAN LAW. HOWEVER, SOME VAMPIRES BELIEVE THAT THE BLOOD OF THE PRAVUS HAS **GREAT HEALING CAPABILITIES**—AND CAN STRENGTHEN AGAINST **SUNLIGHT.**

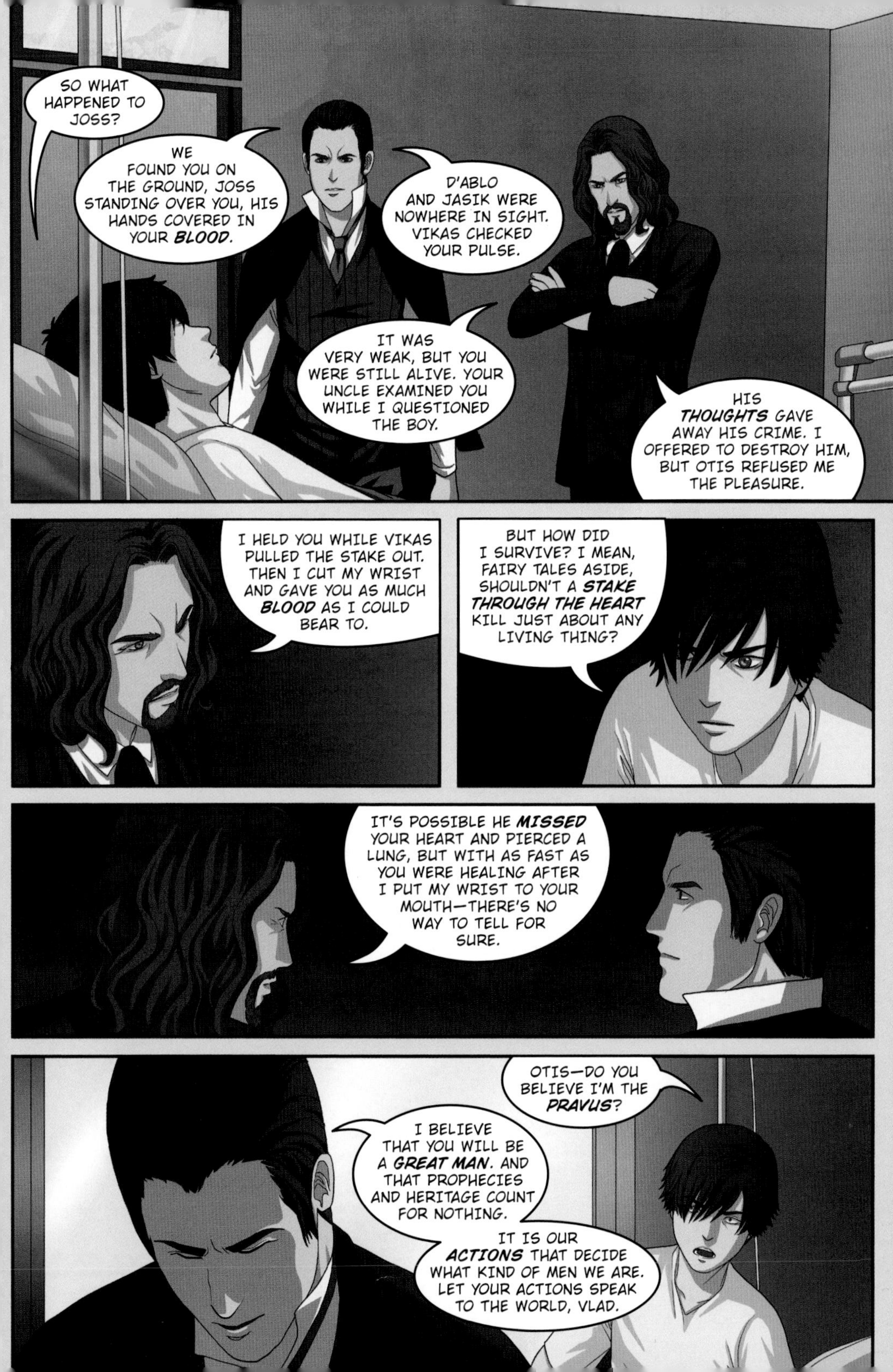
SO WHAT HAPPENED TO JOSS?
WE FOUND YOU ON THE GROUND, JOSS STANDING OVER YOU, HIS HANDS COVERED IN YOUR BLOOD.
D'ABLO AND JASIK WERE NOWHERE IN SIGHT. VIKAS CHECKED YOUR PULSE.
IT WAS VERY WEAK, BUT YOU WERE STILL ALIVE. YOUR UNCLE EXAMINED YOU WHILE I QUESTIONED THE BOY.
HIS THOUGHTS GAVE AWAY HIS CRIME. I OFFERED TO DESTROY HIM, BUT OTIS REFUSED ME THE PLEASURE.
I HELD YOU WHILE VIKAS PULLED THE STAKE OUT. THEN I CUT MY WRIST AND GAVE YOU AS MUCH BLOOD AS I COULD BEAR TO.
BUT HOW DID I SURVIVE? I MEAN, FAIRY TALES ASIDE, SHOULDN'T A STAKE THROUGH THE HEART KILL JUST ABOUT ANY LIVING THING?
IT'S POSSIBLE HE MISSED YOUR HEART AND PIERCED A LUNG, BUT WITH AS FAST AS YOU WERE HEALING AFTER I PUT MY WRIST TO YOUR MOUTH—THERE'S NO WAY TO TELL FOR SURE.
OTIS—DO YOU BELIEVE I'M THE PRAVUS?
I BELIEVE THAT YOU WILL BE A GREAT MAN. AND THAT PROPHECIES AND HERITAGE COUNT FOR NOTHING.
IT IS OUR ACTIONS THAT DECIDE WHAT KIND OF MEN WE ARE. LET YOUR ACTIONS SPEAK TO THE WORLD, VLAD.

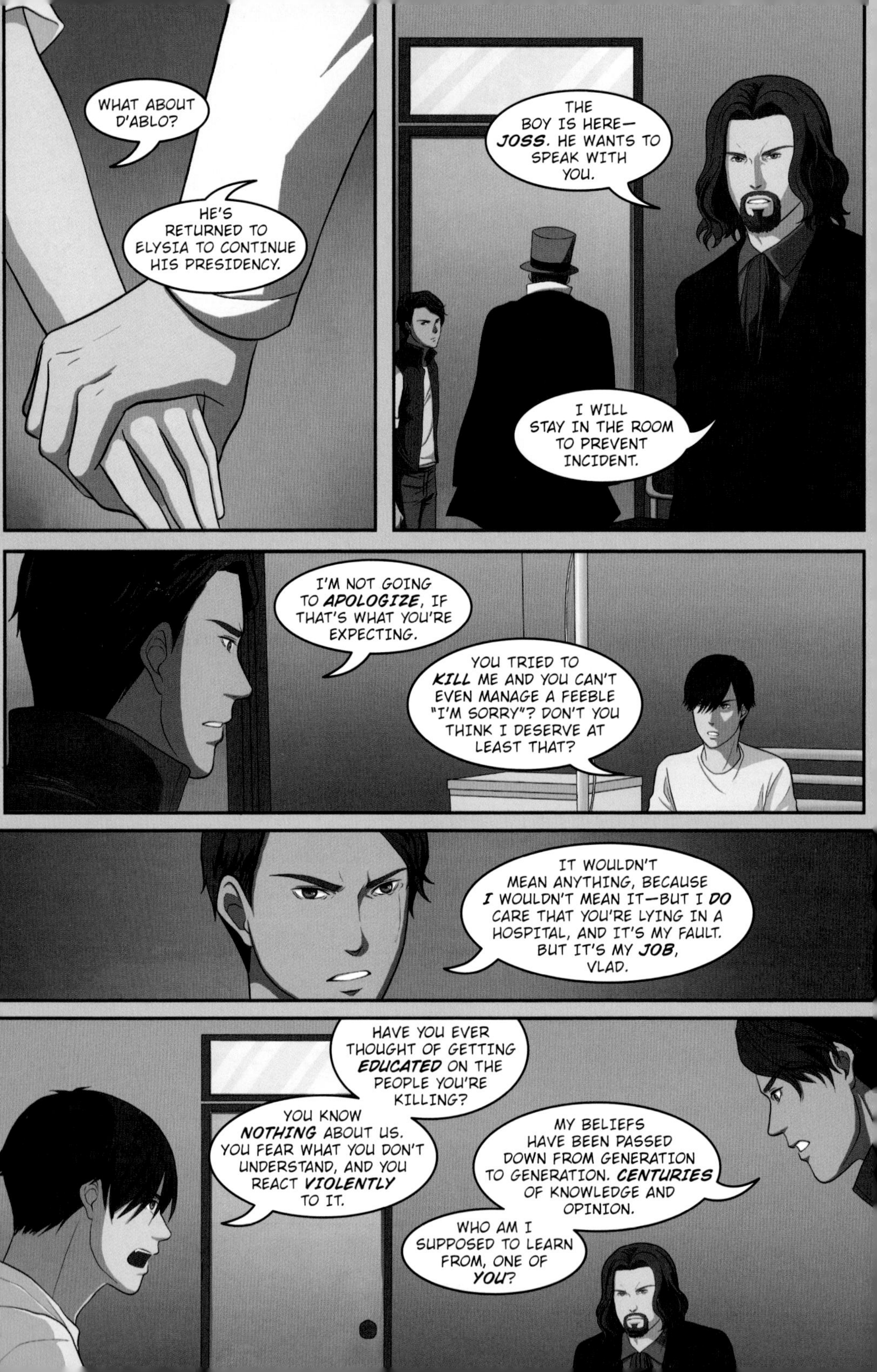
WHAT ABOUT D'ABLO?
HE'S RETURNED TO ELYSIA TO CONTINUE HIS PRESIDENCY.
THE BOY IS HERE—*JOSS*. HE WANTS TO SPEAK WITH YOU.
I WILL STAY IN THE ROOM TO PREVENT INCIDENT.
I'M NOT GOING TO *APOLOGIZE*, IF THAT'S WHAT YOU'RE EXPECTING.
YOU TRIED TO *KILL* ME AND YOU CAN'T EVEN MANAGE A FEEBLE "I'M SORRY"? DON'T YOU THINK I DESERVE AT LEAST THAT?
IT WOULDN'T MEAN ANYTHING, BECAUSE *I* WOULDN'T MEAN IT—BUT I *DO* CARE THAT YOU'RE LYING IN A HOSPITAL, AND IT'S MY FAULT. BUT IT'S MY *JOB*, VLAD.
HAVE YOU EVER THOUGHT OF GETTING *EDUCATED* ON THE PEOPLE YOU'RE KILLING?
YOU KNOW *NOTHING* ABOUT US. YOU FEAR WHAT YOU DON'T UNDERSTAND, AND YOU REACT *VIOLENTLY* TO IT.
MY BELIEFS HAVE BEEN PASSED DOWN FROM GENERATION TO GENERATION. *CENTURIES* OF KNOWLEDGE AND OPINION.
WHO AM I SUPPOSED TO LEARN FROM, ONE OF *YOU*?

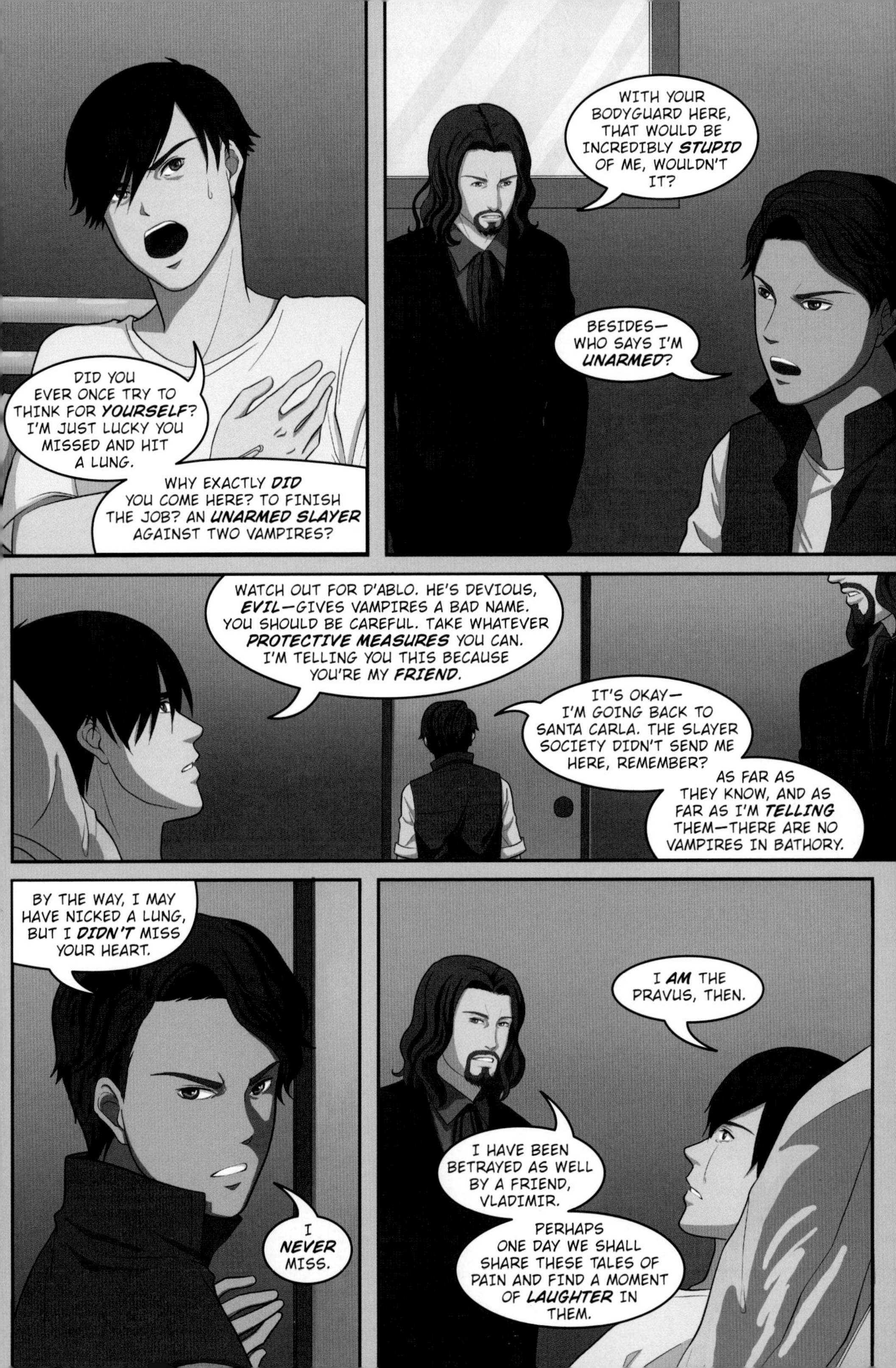
DID YOU EVER ONCE TRY TO THINK FOR YOURSELF? I'M JUST LUCKY YOU MISSED AND HIT A LUNG.
WHY EXACTLY DID YOU COME HERE? TO FINISH THE JOB? AN UNARMED SLAYER AGAINST TWO VAMPIRES?
WITH YOUR BODYGUARD HERE, THAT WOULD BE INCREDIBLY STUPID OF ME, WOULDN'T IT?
BESIDES— WHO SAYS I'M UNARMED?
WATCH OUT FOR D'ABLO. HE'S DEVIOUS, EVIL—GIVES VAMPIRES A BAD NAME. YOU SHOULD BE CAREFUL. TAKE WHATEVER PROTECTIVE MEASURES YOU CAN. I'M TELLING YOU THIS BECAUSE YOU'RE MY FRIEND.
IT'S OKAY— I'M GOING BACK TO SANTA CARLA. THE SLAYER SOCIETY DIDN'T SEND ME HERE, REMEMBER?
AS FAR AS THEY KNOW, AND AS FAR AS I'M TELLING THEM—THERE ARE NO VAMPIRES IN BATHORY.
BY THE WAY, I MAY HAVE NICKED A LUNG, BUT I DIDN'T MISS YOUR HEART.
I NEVER MISS.
I AM THE PRAVUS, THEN.
I HAVE BEEN BETRAYED AS WELL BY A FRIEND, VLADIMIR.
PERHAPS ONE DAY WE SHALL SHARE THESE TALES OF PAIN AND FIND A MOMENT OF LAUGHTER IN THEM.

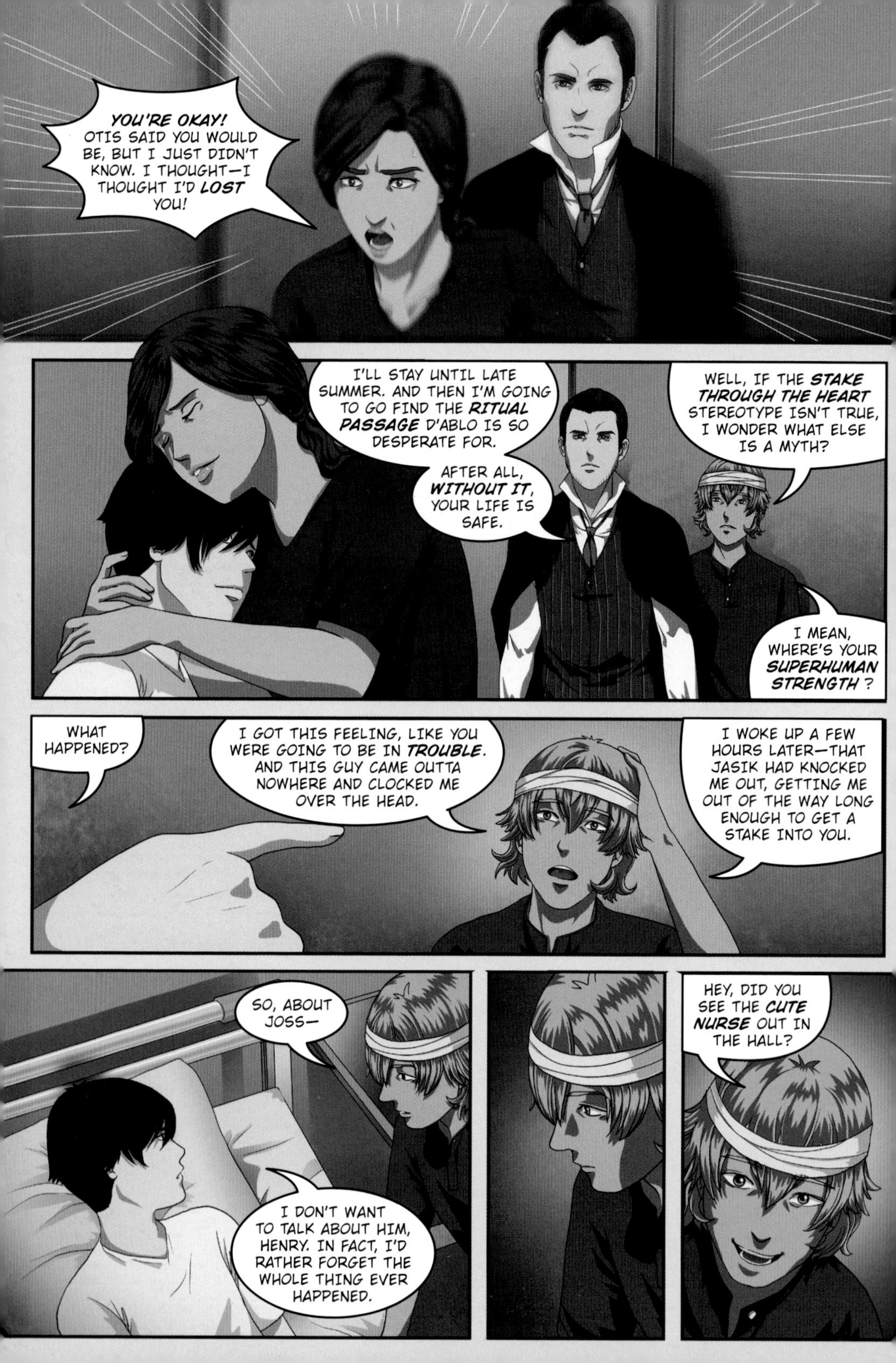
YOU'RE OKAY! OTIS SAID YOU WOULD BE, BUT I JUST DIDN'T KNOW. I THOUGHT—I THOUGHT I'D LOST YOU!
I'LL STAY UNTIL LATE SUMMER. AND THEN I'M GOING TO GO FIND THE RITUAL PASSAGE D'ABLO IS SO DESPERATE FOR.
AFTER ALL, WITHOUT IT, YOUR LIFE IS SAFE.
WELL, IF THE STAKE THROUGH THE HEART STEREOTYPE ISN'T TRUE, I WONDER WHAT ELSE IS A MYTH?
I MEAN, WHERE'S YOUR SUPERHUMAN STRENGTH ?
WHAT HAPPENED?
I GOT THIS FEELING, LIKE YOU WERE GOING TO BE IN TROUBLE. AND THIS GUY CAME OUTTA NOWHERE AND CLOCKED ME OVER THE HEAD.
I WOKE UP A FEW HOURS LATER—THAT JASIK HAD KNOCKED ME OUT, GETTING ME OUT OF THE WAY LONG ENOUGH TO GET A STAKE INTO YOU.
SO, ABOUT JOSS—
I DON'T WANT TO TALK ABOUT HIM, HENRY. IN FACT, I'D RATHER FORGET THE WHOLE THING EVER HAPPENED.
HEY, DID YOU SEE THE CUTE NURSE OUT IN THE HALL?

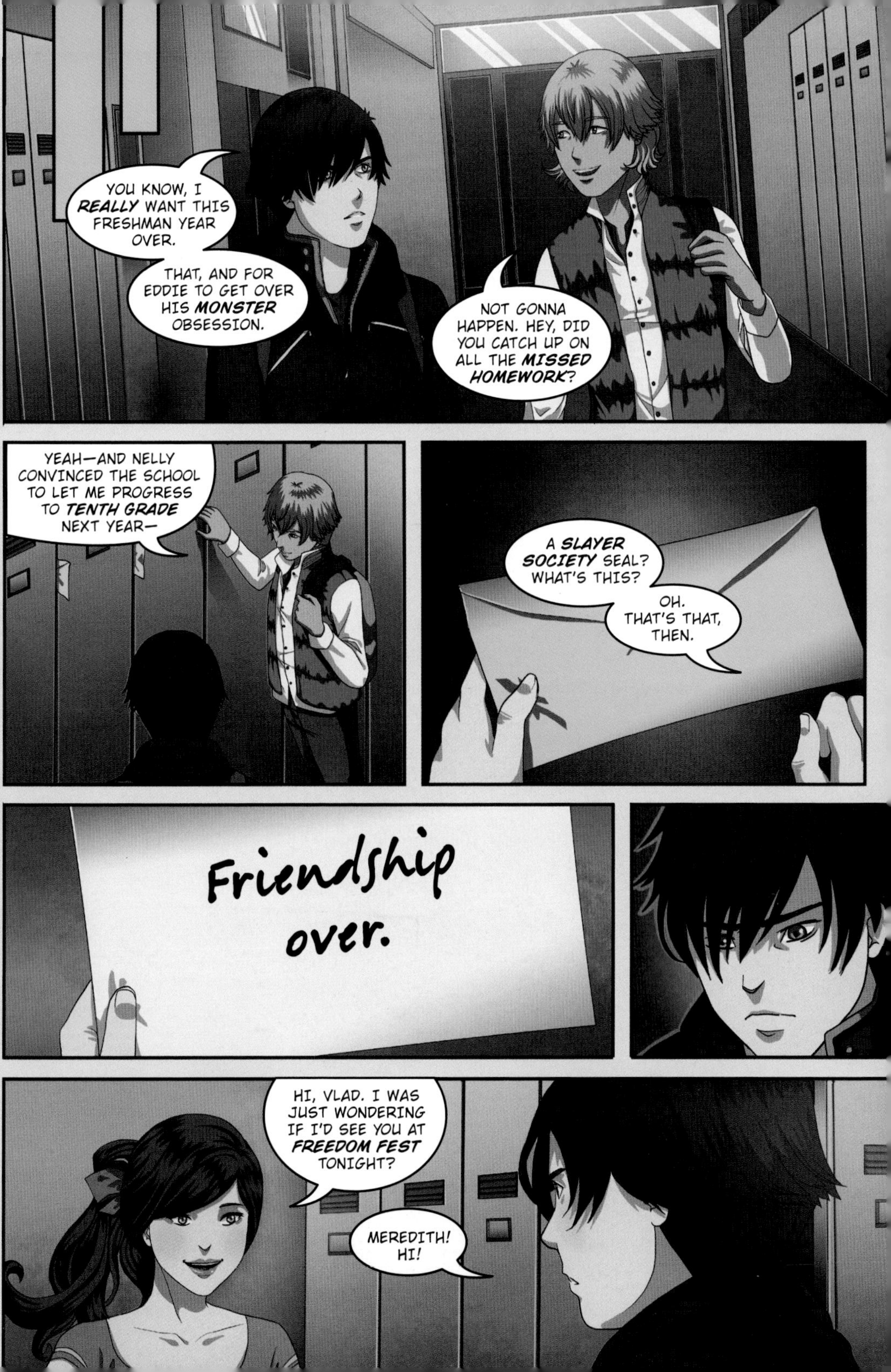

YOU KNOW, I REALLY WANT THIS FRESHMAN YEAR OVER.
THAT, AND FOR EDDIE TO GET OVER HIS MONSTER OBSESSION.
NOT GONNA HAPPEN. HEY, DID YOU CATCH UP ON ALL THE MISSED HOMEWORK?
YEAH—AND NELLY CONVINCED THE SCHOOL TO LET ME PROGRESS TO TENTH GRADE NEXT YEAR—
A SLAYER SOCIETY SEAL? WHAT'S THIS?
OH. THAT'S THAT, THEN.
Friendship over.
HI, VLAD. I WAS JUST WONDERING IF I'D SEE YOU AT FREEDOM FEST TONIGHT?
MEREDITH! HI!

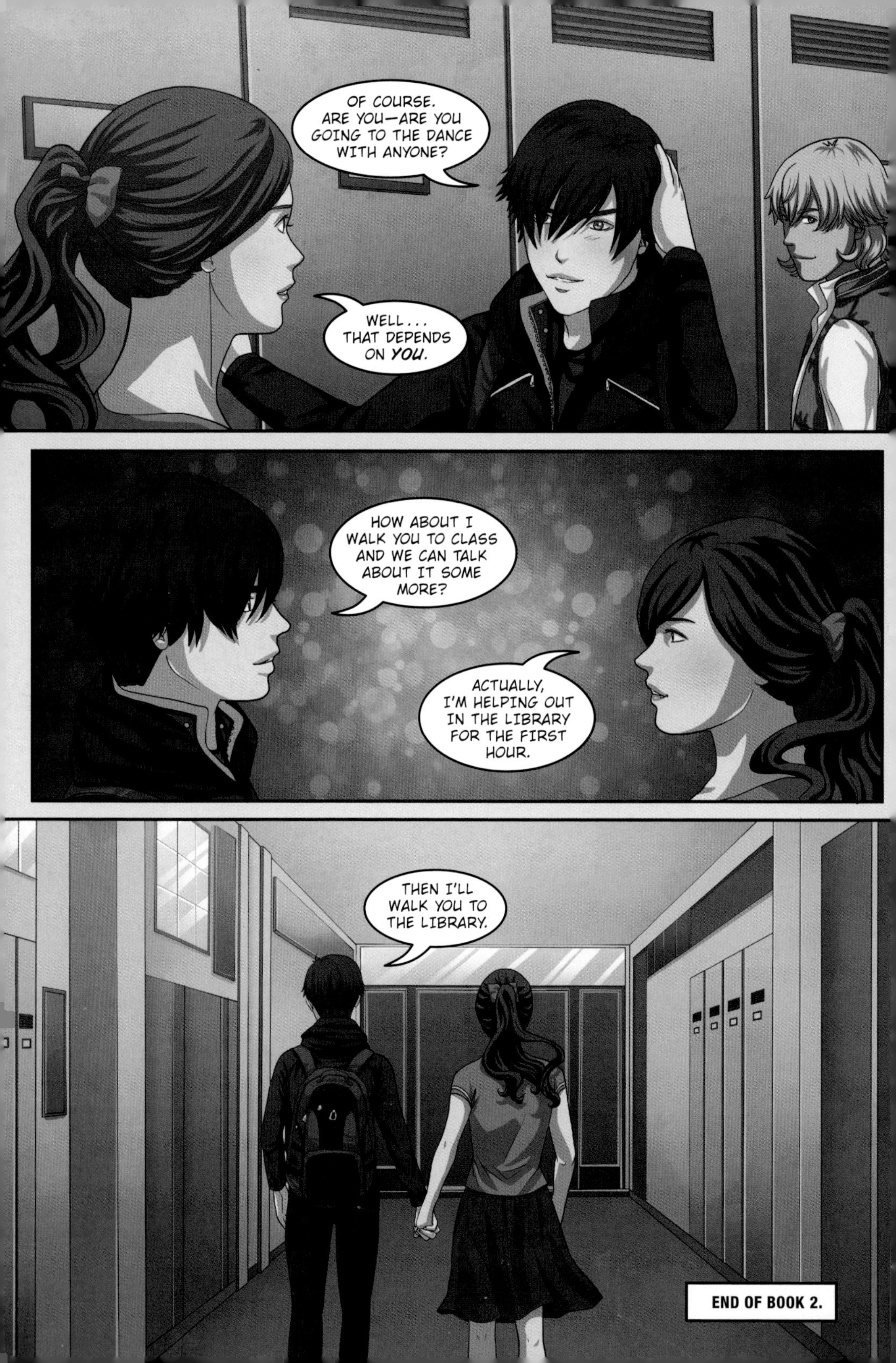
OF COURSE. ARE YOU—ARE YOU GOING TO THE DANCE WITH ANYONE?
WELL . . . THAT DEPENDS ON *YOU*.
HOW ABOUT I WALK YOU TO CLASS AND WE CAN TALK ABOUT IT SOME MORE?
ACTUALLY, I'M HELPING OUT IN THE LIBRARY FOR THE FIRST HOUR.
THEN I'LL WALK YOU TO THE LIBRARY.
END OF BOOK 2.